TERROR TALES OF THE SCOTTISH LOWLANDS

TERROR TALES OF THE SCOTTISH LOWLANDS

Edited by

PAUL FINCH

First published in 2021 by Telos Publishing,
139 Whitstable Road, Canterbury, Kent CT2 8EQ,
United Kingdom.

www.telos.co.uk

ISBN: 978-1-84583-194-3

Telos Publishing Ltd values feedback. Please e-mail any
comments you might have about this book to:
feedback@telos.co.uk

British Library Cataloguing in Publication Data.
A catalogue record for this book is available from the British
Library.

TABLE OF CONTENTS

COPYRIGHT INFORMATION

THE MOSS-TROOPER
M W Craven

The tavern was hot and smoky. The man ducked as he walked through the door, a legacy of an age when people were shorter. The ceiling was low too. It was washed with white paint; the exposed beams weathered and harder than marble.

The smoke made the man's eyes sting and, for a solitary moment, he considered waiting outside. But he needed a drink and this was the only place open. The tavern was last-orders-busy but there was a stool at the bar, in between the wall and a hulking brute who was scowling at a whisky. The man edged through the drinkers and the revellers. He dodged a staggering drunk. He ignored a woman with an L-plate pinned to her dress who claimed it was her hen night and he should buy her a drink.

When you lived in Gretna you got used to shit like this.

The man reached the bar and perched on the stool next to the scowling man. He caught the barman's eye and said, 'Whisky, no ice.'

The barman nodded, sent an empty mixer bottle crashing into the recycling bin and reached for the top shelf. He splashed two fingers of single malt into a tulip-shaped glass and placed it on the bar. He slid a small jug of spring water next to it.

'Smoky in here tonight,' the man said, reaching for the jug and opening up his whisky with a couple of drops of water.

'It's like the inside of a cigar,' the barman agreed. 'No idea why. I had a quick scout around earlier and no one's smoking.'

'Maybe they're burning the heather nearby?'

'Maybe,' the barman agreed. 'I've got the old cigarette smoke extractor fans on full belt, and they aren't shifting it,' he added before wandering off to serve another customer.

'It's not heather,' Scowling Man said.

His accent was English. Not the ludicrous accents of the Midlands, or the dopey accents of the south. This was a northern accent. Sharp and quick and a bit sing-songy. Newcastle or Northumberland, the man thought. Certainly no further south than Sunderland.

'It isn't?'

'Wrong time of year to burn heather.'

'I'll take your word for it; I work oot of an office.' He offered Scowling Man his hand. 'My name's Middlemass. David Middlemass.'

Scowling man grunted but shook it anyway. His hand was badly scarred, like a nail had ripped through it in an industrial accident. But not recently. It was white and knotty, not red and livid. Scowling Man looked old enough to have worked in the great shipyards that had decorated the mouth of the Tyne, so maybe that was where it had happened. His face looked like it had been hacked out of teak with a butter knife. He had fierce eyes, a blade of a nose and his skin was the texture of a pork scratching.

'I didnae catch your name,' Middlemass said.

'If you have to call me something, call me Storyteller,' he said through a mouth that, in the low light of the tavern, looked more like an old wound than a natural opening.

'Okaaaay,' Middlemass said. Despite Storyteller's full glass, he added, 'Can I get you a wee one?'

Storyteller shook his head. 'I'll not take a drink tonight.'

Middlemass turned his own glass in his hands before lifting it up to the light and swirling it. The whisky was the colour of straw. It smelled of peat and of oak barrels. He glanced at Storyteller. Perhaps he was a recovering alcoholic and the untouched whisky was a test of his willpower? Best to leave it alone.

'What brings you over the border, Storyteller?' he asked. 'I don't imagine you're looking for an anvil.'

Storyteller didn't respond.

'You know, because we're in Gretna,' Middlemass

explained. 'I know the whole married-over-an-anvil thing is a bit twee these days, but over five thousand couples a year still have their weddings here. Has the romantic allure from the old days, I guess.'

Storyteller studied his drink. 'You don't hear the name Middlemass that often,' he said after a few beats.

'I do. I hear it every day.'

Middlemass smiled; Storyteller didn't. Instead, he said, 'You'll be a Kirkcudbright Middlemass.'

'I've no idea.'

'Aye, you will be,' Storyteller said. 'Every Middlemass around here is from Kirkcudbright.'

'If you say so. I *do* have an aunt there, but it's fifty miles from Gretna and we don't get to see her too often.'

'Do you know your family's history?'

'I did one of those ancestry things a year or so ago. A Middlemass was killed during the Battle of Isandlwana during the Anglo-Zulu War. That's as far back as I went.'

'I don't mean recent history,' Storyteller growled. 'I mean *history* history. The time of Oliver Cromwell, of the Wars of the Three Kingdoms.'

'I've heard of Cromwell. I've no' heard o' the other thing.'

'The best known is the English Civil War,' Storyteller said, 'but there were an intertwined series of conflicts during that period. They were called the Wars of the Three Kingdoms.'

Middlemass shrugged. He hadn't come to the tavern for a history lesson. He had nipped in for a wee dram while he waited for his wife. She was visiting her sister and their inane tittle-tattle made his teeth itch. 'What's that got to do with my family name?' he asked out of politeness.

'Soon,' Storyteller said. 'But first I need you to understand that in the seventeenth century, where we are now was a dour and bleak part of the country. The near constant English-Scottish wars had turned the borderlands into a wild, lawless place. You only need to look how long the Reivers were active. Their clans were feuding and stealing for generations.'

'I've heard of the Reivers, obviously. I think Middlemass is an old clan name, as it happens.'

'It is, but it wasn't the Reivers that made this such a desperate place in the seventeenth century. They were largely finished by then.'

'Why bring them up then?'

'You need the context, laddie,' Storyteller growled.

'I *needed* a drink,' Middlemass said, put out. He threw back his whisky and made to get up. 'And now I've had it.'

'Sit!' Storyteller hissed.

Middlemass did. He didn't know why. It was if he didn't have a choice. Something was happening and for some reason he was right in the middle of it. He signalled for another whisky then said, 'Tell me aboot the Border Reivers then.'

'Although it was frontier law around here, ripe for the picking, the Reivers were little more than squabbling clans. The stories of raiding parties going back and forth over the border is a romanticised version of what it was really like. Nationality didn't matter and these clans were just as likely to steal from their neighbours as they were to cross the border. Disorganised rabble, and why, ultimately, they were easy to bring under control.'

'Didn't it take centuries?'

'Not true. They *raided* for centuries but that's because no one cared what was happening in the border area. But when the Crown *did* eventually take notice, it wasn't long before the Reivers had been brought under control.'

Middlemass asked, 'Are you a historian?'

'Of a kind,' Storyteller replied. 'Have you ever heard the term "moss-trooper", Middlemass?'

Middlemass shook his head. 'I havenae.'

'The moss-troopers filled the void left by the Reivers,' Storyteller said. 'And whereas the Reivers were mostly thugs and farmers, the moss-troopers were former cavalry from the Wars of the Three Kingdoms.'

'They were Scottish?' Middlemass asked.

'Most *were* Scottish moss-troopers, but today I want to talk about those who had served with Cromwell's New Model

Army, particularly the English Civil War cavalry veterans who took to outlawry as a viable form of employment. They wreaked far more havoc than the Reivers ever did, and for a while they turned the border area into hell on earth. And because they still had their weapons and horses, their cavalry tactics were more than a match for the small military forces sent to deal with them. Cromwell got so frustrated with the English moss-troopers he took the drastic step of refusing Christian burial rights to any taken into custody, and, as the New Model Army had been raised largely from soldiers who already held deeply Puritan religious beliefs, this was thought to be quite a punishment.'

'They were excommunicated?'

'That's a Catholic censure, but yes, it amounted to the same thing.'

'And that brought them to heel?' Middlemass asked, interested despite himself.

'A little, but, by and large the threat of the moss-troopers remained as potent as ever. So Old Ironsides – that was what soldiers called Cromwell – thought again. Came up with a solution that was attractive to both the Commonwealth *and* the English moss-troopers.'

'What was it?'

'This was when Cromwell was struggling to bring Scotland under the control of the Commonwealth,' Storyteller said. 'So, instead of diverting more and more troops to the border, he relinquished the threat of religious punishment in exchange for the moss-troopers' assistance in harassing Scottish interests.'

'What the piss does that mean?'

'It means that, as long as what they did was over the border, they could pretty much do what they wanted.' Storyteller paused and picked up his tumbler. He breathed in the fumes but, although it was close to his mouth, he didn't let any touch his thin, pink lips.

'Like the Sea Dogs that the Virgin Queen authorised to attack the Spanish in the sixteenth century,' Middlemass said, 'they carried Letters of Marque, which made their piracy legal.

Francis Drake and Walter Raleigh were both Sea Dogs.'

Middlemass had enjoyed history at school and he'd read extensively about the Elizabethan era. Which made his ignorance of the moss-troopers all the more confusing. The two periods weren't that far apart.

'Aye, like the Sea Dogs and the privateers and the slavers,' Storyteller agreed. 'Many terrible things happened when Cromwell let slip his dogs of war. Terrible, terrible things. The English moss-troopers were some of the vilest men ever to draw clean air and the worst of them was a man called Solomon Crozier. He was a giant of a man; rough-mannered and cruel. He and his brigands, all men of low character, lived in the ruins of the Housesteads Roman fort, and if I spoke of all they did, you would surely be driven insane.'

'That bad?'

'If there's a God, their souls are now rotting in the bowels of hell.'

'What's this got tae dae with my name, though?' Middlemass asked. It was getting late, and his wife wouldn't be long. But the rest of the tavern seemed to have blurred into nothingness as he was drawn deeper and deeper into what Storyteller was saying.

'The Middlemass clan, your ancestors, were Reivers back in the day, but by the seventeenth century they were semi-respectable. I'm not saying they didn't occasionally nip over the border to Cumberland to rustle sheep and cattle, but mostly they were God-fearing and honest workers. And because they worked hard, they had accrued a bit of land, a bit of money and some property. Solomon Crozier had mainly raided the south east of Scotland, but it wasn't long before he turned his cruel eyes towards the lands around Kirkcudbright. *Your* land.'

Storyteller's voice was so laden with doom that despite the heat and the smoke – and where *was* that smoke coming from? – Middlemass felt a sudden chill, like he was leaning against cold iron. He shivered.

'Crozier and his brigands arrived in the small hours,' Storyteller continued. 'They killed the geese your kin used as an early warning system, then rode in on their heavy, battle-hardened steeds, burning everything that would burn, smashing everything that would smash.' He stared hard at Middlemass and added, 'And killing everything that could be killed.'

Middlemass finished his drink. Held his glass up for another. The barman shook his head and tapped his watch – last orders had finished.

'Pour the drink, barkeep,' Storyteller said, his voice deathly quiet but all the more ominous for it.

The barman blinked. Then, as if he were sleepwalking, he grabbed the bottle of single malt and poured a generous measure into the empty glass. Middlemass put a twenty-pound note on the bar but the barman wasn't interested in his money.

What was *that* about?

Middlemass stared at the drink. He stared at Storyteller. He needed to know what had happened that night. 'Solomon Crozier killed my ancestors?'

'Slaughtered them like poxed cattle,' Storyteller said. 'He tied up all the men of fighting age and made them watch their babies being thrown on the fires that were now raging. His brigands raped the women, the girls, even the young men. The elders were dragged to the anvil and their ankles and knees and elbows were smashed with the smithy's hammer until they could only crawl like worms. The moss-troopers sported all night and the Middlemass men were forced to watch every minute of it. Any who shut their eyes had their eyelids sliced off; any who turned away had their head staked to the ground through their jaw. No turning away after that.'

'That's horrific,' Middlemass said, colour draining from his face, the whisky turning sour in the pit of his stomach.

'Aye, lad. It was. And just before first light, with the women and children dead and the elders dying, they dispatched the men. But not quickly. This was Solomon Crozier's favourite part, you see? He held competitions and gave gold to the brigand who came up with the cruellest, most novel way of killing. And without exception this brought out the most brutal, base urges of men who had forsaken their God many winters ago. They poured liquid iron down their victim's throats; they fed them to starving pigs. They let them be mounted by stallions until their insides were bloody and torn. A dozen more methods I won't say out loud. And when it was over, Solomon faded away, like mist in the sun.'

'Has any of this been verified?' Middlemass asked.

'It was verified, aye.'

'Because I didn't learn any of this in school.'

'Part of Solomon's cruelty was that he always left one person alive,' Storyteller said. 'Always a child. No one who could pose a threat, but someone who could tell the tale of what happened.'

'And he left one of the Middlemasses alive?'

'He did. Your twelfth great-grandmother. A young slip of a lass called Janet. She barely reached Solomon's knee but she was as fierce as a wolf and managed to stab him right through the hand with the dudgeon dagger she kept in her little boots. Solomon just laughed and told his men he'd chosen the right Middlemass to live.'

'Janet Middlemass kept the family name going?' He didn't think to ask how Storyteller knew this.

'She did, aye. Because there are two things you need to know about Janet. The first was that the young girl eventually became a young woman. A fine young woman of rare beauty. The bucks in the area all wanted to tup her, but she kept her legs closed. She used the money Solomon had overlooked when he raided and she rebuilt the family's property and their reputation. And when she was ready she turned her eyes to avenging her dead.'

'But she was just one woman?'

Storyteller stared into the distance, like he could see something no one else could.

'Aye, she was,' he said. 'But here's the second thing you need to know about Janet Middlemass. She was the granddaughter of *Margaret* Middlemass, and Margaret Middlemass was a witch.'

'A witch?' Middlemass scoffed. 'Away with yersel!'

'Of course, back then you didn't admit to being a witch,' Storyteller continued, unperturbed. 'Charges of witchcraft were becoming less frequent, but there was still the odd trial here and there. No, any woman who didn't want to be strangled at the stake and burnt to ash called herself a healer or a herbalist. But sneer all you like, laddie, Margaret Middlemass *was* a witch. And here's the thing, the power had skipped a generation. Janet's mother was no more a witch than you or I, but when that type of power *does* skip a generation, it sometimes returns with an unstoppable ferocity. If Margaret's powers were great, Janet's were greater. Now, power like this, raw and untamed, normally overwhelms whoever holds it. It's too much and they end up living in the gutter, gibbering like idiots.'

Middlemass checked his watch, anxious to hear the end of the story before his wife turned up, but it had stopped working. The smoke in the bar meant he couldn't see the clock nestled in amongst the gin selection either.

'Your wife won't get here until the story has been told,' Storyteller said patiently.

'How on earth can you know —'

'It's not chance that brought us together tonight, Middlemass.'

Middlemass gulped down his whisky, spilling some on his shirt. He didn't care. Storyteller rapped his knuckles on the bar and the barman, still glassy-eyed and trance-like, refilled Middlemass's glass.

'I think the power didn't send Janet mad like all the others because she had something to channel it through. Because of her burning desire for vengeance she was able to bring this power to a point. For the first time in centuries, a Middlemass was able to control it.'

'What did she do?' Middlemass asked.

'She summoned Solomon Crozier and all his brigands,' Storyteller replied. 'She sent out ravens and sparrows and magpies, and other birds of the field, and they whispered into the moss-troopers ears while they slept and, one at a time, they came. They came and they brought their families with them.

They didn't want to, but they had no choice. It was as if the devil himself was whipping their backs.'

What Middlemass was being told had happened. He knew that now, just as he knew that tonight was somehow time outside time. Knew the barman wouldn't remember anything, and that no matter how much whisky he drank tonight, he would remain lucid and clear-headed. He also knew that when Storyteller left, the smoke in the tavern would leave with him.

'What did she do to them?' he whispered.

'The moss-troopers slaughtered your ancestors, Middlemass. I suppose a better question might be what would *you* have done?'

'I'd have shown them no mercy,'' he said immediately, surprised how strongly he felt about it.

Storyteller eyed him shrewdly, and not a little sadly.

'I believe you, laddie,' he said after while. 'The Middlemass blood courses through your veins just as it coursed through Janet's.'

'Did *she* show them mercy?'

'Janet tied each moss-trooper to a stake,' Storyteller said as way of an explanation. 'They went willingly at first, only resisting when it was too late. I imagine the power of the hag had deceived their eyes and minds. And then she started. Whatever the moss-trooper had done to her family, she did to theirs, but far, far worse. If they had burnt a Middlemass child, their own child burst into flames. But not a natural flame, this was a flame from hell itself. It burned without killing. Their flesh spat and sizzled and dripped with fat but the sweet relief of death never came. She summoned the beasts of the night and of the sky and from under the earth and she bid them to gnaw on their bones. She skinned them alive. Everything that was done to her kin was done threefold to the moss-troopers and their kin. One-by-one the moss-troopers visited Kirkcudbright and one-by-one they suffered at the hands of the devil incarnate. She didn't flinch, she didn't smile. And she didn't stop. Not until she had finished.'

'Jesus,' Middlemass said.

'Finally, there was only one moss-trooper left. He had been summoned first and had watched it all, wondering what special horror was waiting for him.'

'Solomon …'

Storyteller nodded. 'Solomon Crozier watched his men and the families of his men suffer the witch's wrath and there was naught he could do to stop it. And all that time he was wondering what fate awaited him. He had no family so there was no one to suffer for him, and his fear was all the greater for it.'

'Whatever Janet did to him, he got off light.'

'Did he now?'

'For what he did to her family, to *my* family, there can be no punishment too severe.'

'When you hear it, you might not be so sure. You might think her just as much the monster as Solomon.'

'What did she do to him?'

'She let him live.'

Middlemass's shoulders sagged. Although it was just a horrible story, he somehow felt cheated. Even in the darkest Grimms' Fairy Tales, the bad guy or gal is supposed to get their comeuppance. Cinderella's stepsisters had their eyes pecked out by birds, Rumpelstiltskin tore himself in two and Hansel and Gretel pushed the witch into the oven.

'Why would she show him mercy?' he asked. 'I get the feeling Solomon wasn't the type of man to dwell on his own feelings for too long. Living with the knowledge you were a monster only works when the monster is remorseful. You say she saved the worst for him; *I* say he got off lightly.'

'I said she let him live,' Storyteller said. 'I didn't say anything about mercy.'

Storyteller turned to face him, and for the first time Middlemass saw his mouth properly. What had looked like an old wound in the half-light of the tavern, up close looked raw and weeping. Middlemass shuddered. He tried to turn away, but found he couldn't break eye contact.

'Janet Middlemass hexed Solomon Crozier,' Storyteller said

softly. 'And when a witch that powerful puts the hex on you, you stay hexed.'

Middlemass said nothing.

'She summoned the village blacksmith and, on the same anvil her kin had had their bones smashed, she had him forge a pair of iron shoes. Clogs, really. The man had been a friend of her father's and he did this willingly. The shoes he made were heavy and cruel and he took no care to smooth off the burrs and the bumps and the jaggy splinters. A more uncomfortable pair of shoes have never been made.'

'She made him wear them?'

Storyteller nodded. 'But first, she thrust them in the hottest part of the forge and left them there. When she took them out they glowed like the heart of the sun. The witch then leaned in and whispered some words over them. And only then did she ask Solomon to put them on.'

'And he did?'

'He had no choice. It was as if he no longer had free will,' Storyteller said. 'And they burned, laddie. How they burned. Solomon had laughed at the pain of others but he screamed at his own. Wept and begged for death. But the witch wasn't finished yet.'

'It got worse?'

'She had barely started, Middlemass,' Storyteller said. 'Because as soon as the shoes were on and his skin and flesh were bubbling, she told him what his *real* punishment was. "You'll wear these shoes forever, Solomon Crozier," she said. "You'll eat naught but salt, you'll take no whisky and you'll not feel the heat of a woman. Your shoes of iron will never grow cold and you'll never take them off. I command them to take you to every Middlemass alive now, and every Middlemass yet to be born. You'll tell them the tale of what you did to their kin and you'll tell it truthfully. *This* is your punishment."'

'"For how long?" Solomon asked the witch,' Storyteller said. 'And do you know how she answered him, Middlemass?'

Middlemass thought he did.

'Until he was forgiven,' he said.

'That's right,' Storyteller said. 'He is to walk the earth seeking out the witch's kin until he can find a Middlemass who forgives him.'

'Good luck with that,' Middlemass said. 'I know *I* wouldn't forgive him.'

Storyteller got to his feet.

'I'm leaving now,' he said. 'That wife of yours has just walked through the door and my part in your story is over. We will never meet again, although, I dare say I'll bump into your son in a few years.'

And with that, without a backwards glance, he limped out of the tavern. The smoke immediately cleared, like it had been sucked out of an aeroplane window.

'Who was that?' Middlemass's wife asked, taking the stool Storyteller had just vacated.

Middlemass stared at the scorched, still smouldering footprints on the tavern carpet. He looked at Storyteller's untouched whisky. He remembered his ruined mouth and the scar on his hand, a permanent reminder of the young witch who had run it through with her dudgeon dagger.

'That was Solomon Crozier,' he said.

BASTIONS OF DREAD

Often seen as a gentle, benign landscape compared to the bleak fastness of the Highlands, the Scottish Lowlands also boasts scenic hills, glens and lochs. There is much wilderness to be found here, though thanks to the presence of Scotland's two largest cities, Edinburgh and Glasgow, the Lowlands tends to be more populous and somewhat less geographically dramatic. However, in terms of history and mythology, this is a brutal, blood-soaked realm.

This was the land where most of Scotland's battles with England were fought, but also where civil strife took its bitter course, and where Reiver clans raided and feuded. As such, the ghosts that haunt the Lowlands are a veritable who's who of Scottish political notables, everyone from the Black Douglas (beheaded in 1463) to Lord Darnley, husband to Mary, Queen of Scots (strangled in 1567). Purely in physical terms, it is studded with castles, towers, gibbets and other relics of war and violence, though it is the castles that are perhaps the Lowlands' most outstanding historical feature.

Two in particular stand as proud and indomitable today as they ever did. But equally, they cast a timeless pall of fear, for both have long been renowned as bastions of dread, haunted not just by memories of the evil deeds that were done within their oppressive walls, but by a plethora of dark and dangerous entities.

***Hermitage Castle**, which sits in Liddesdale in the Borders region, only a few miles, in fact, from the frontier with England, has a fearsome reputation that is known to ghost-hunters the length and breadth of the British Isles.*

First built by the Scottish baron, Nicholas de Soulis, in 1240, at a time when, even though Scotland and England might technically have been at truce, there was plenty of skirmishing along the border, it was nicknamed the 'Guardhouse of the Bloodiest Valley in Britain'. An epicentre of strife, this was a place where both prisoners of war and plain ordinary prisoners frequently met their demise. However, it was during the occupancy of a descendent, William II de Soules, 'Evil Lord

Soules' as Walter Scott later referred to him, when Hermitage Castle became associated with truly despicable villainy. De Soules, who inherited the fortress around 1300, was notorious for changing sides several times during Scotland's Wars of Independence, (which won him few friends on either side of the border), but also because he reputedly dabbled in witchcraft and sorcery. When, in 1320, several village children went missing, allegedly kidnapped so that de Soules could sacrifice them to the Devil, local folk turned fully against him, approaching the royal court and begging for justice. King Robert I of Scotland, wearied by complaints against the lawless baron, is said to have responded: 'Boil him if you must, but let me hear no more about him.'

According to tradition, de Soules was subsequently ambushed by local men, and hauled to Ninestane Rig, a stone circle in the district, where he was immersed in a cauldron of molten lead. Whether this really happened is difficult to prove. That peasants could murder a baron in the 14th century and get away with it seems unlikely, but de Soules was widely hated, and historians who believe that in truth he was lured to Dumbarton Castle and beheaded on the orders of the king have not uncovered clear-cut evidence to support their version of events either.

Even then though, this is not the end of the atrocities associated with Hermitage Castle. In 1338, still a focal point in the border wars, the bastion was captured from the English by the heroic Scottish knight, Sir William Douglas, who then went on to taint his reputation by letting jealousy lead him to abduct a former comrade, another brave Scottish knight, Sir Alexander Ramsay, and seal him into an oubliette in the castle without light, food or water, where it allegedly took him 17 days to die.

Ramsay's emaciated apparition is only one of many now supposed to roam the lonesome ruin that is Hermitage Castle. In the care of Historic Scotland, the ancient site is well preserved, much remaining of the original medieval structure, but many visitors have reported inexplicable fear and disorientation while wandering around it. The cries and screams of children have been reported echoing up from unknown vaults, possibly the tortured souls of William de Soules' sacrificial victims, but most sinister of all is the alleged presence of Redcap Sly, a demonic spirit raised by de Soules during a Black Mass, who even now is willing to torment any visitor he takes a dislike to.

Further north, on the south shore of the Firth of Forth, stands the aptly named **Blackness Castle**. A gloomy coastal stronghold, this is now another key fixture on Scotland's paranormal map, and with good reason.

First built in the mid-1440s, it changed ownership regularly, playing its own key part in the turbulent years of Scottish history that would follow. Mostly used as a baronial residence and military fort during its 600-year history, it was also, for considerable periods of time, set aside as a prison, and not just for criminals, but for political and religious dissenters as well, most famously the Covenanters.

This radical Presbyterian movement had been hugely influential in Scottish affairs in the first half of the 17th century, but by the second half had become a persecuted minority and thus staged several armed revolts against the Crown, which led to the so-called 'Killing Time', a period between 1679 and 1688 that was earmarked by bloody retaliation against the group. This included the ransacking of property, hostage-taking and multiple extrajudicial executions, including an incident at Wigtown on the Galloway coast in 1685, when two Covenanter women were tied to stakes on the beach and left there until the sea had drowned them.

It is from this grim era that most of the darker stories concerning Blackness Castle come to us. While the Covenanter rebels were tortured and brutalised just about everywhere in southern Scotland, many were held captive at the castle, and numerous undocumented killings are said to have occurred in its courtyard. In addition, Blackness Castle boasted the Pit Prison, where, as it was located beneath the North Tower, the dungeons would be flooded to waist-depth twice a day by the rising tide, which made the occupants' experience of long-term incarceration utterly appalling.

Such tales might almost be expected of Blackness Castle, which, built into the living rock of the coastline, with its uneven floors, thick walls and hefty, rugged stonework, is as grim an object as one could ever see. And it's no surprise that all kinds of ghost stories are also connected to it.

As recently as the 1990s, a spectral knight in full plate-armour, roaring with incoherent wrath, is said to have chased a female tourist and her two sons clean out of the building. Since then – and this was a much written-about case – a ghost-watch vigil was continually disrupted when the society members were drawn from floor to floor, looking for the source of what sounded like furniture being thrown about and broken, but were never able to find anything. There have been numerous other reports of poltergeist activity, whispering voices and the like. However, most visitors to the site simply report a deeply oppressive and sorrowful atmosphere. One recent paranormal investigator wrote: 'I can't explain why. I neither saw nor heard anything strange. But the place simply terrified me. I couldn't wait to get out.'

As with Hermitage Castle, Blackness now stands in the care of Historic Scotland. Both are regarded as grand old monuments. They exude an air of peace, of violent times long past. They only resemble granite hearts of darkness. In reality, all evil has fled.

Really? Don't you believe it.

THE STRATHANTINE IMPS
Steve Duffy

'People always tell the truth around a campfire,' she said.

'Does this count, technically?' I said. She'd moved away from the bonfire, far back into the shadows, and I'd followed her there.

'Very good point,' she said, and smiled. So the things she told me, as the fire burned out and the noise of the festival faded away, and the short summer night wore into dawn – all those things I had to take on trust, and I pass them on to you with that caveat. Some of them can be looked up in the newspaper morgues; some you can Google. The rest, you'll either believe or you won't. To begin with the checkable things:

Amanda's father was the scion of one of the biggest and most prestigious publishing houses in the UK, heir to a large family fortune which he inherited when his parents died within a month of each other in 1969. Forbes, an only child, was then just twenty-eight. He'd been married to a fleetingly fashionable clothes designer who'd left him in between bereavements. She died too, a few years later, in a motorbike smash-up in Goa.

Forbes, left with sole uncontested custody of two children, Amanda (six) and her brother Euan (coming up three), lost no time in ceding day-to-day control of the firm to the board, engaging the first in a series of identikit nannies, and abandoning his Chelsea town house for the old family estate in Scotland. There he embarked on a chemically-assisted journey of inner exploration that derailed him entirely from the whole of the outside world.

There wasn't much room for passengers on board Forbes' voyage. Occasionally, guests would descend on the estate, visitors from London, hippy princelings and princesses, bearded troubadours and their gauzy gorgeous girlfriends, but for months on end the family were used to going without anybody's company but their own. Amanda's childhood played out like a summer holiday that lasted all year round, a storybook world of no school and deliciously safe adventures in the walled grounds of the lodge.

'Dad used to come out of the library once or twice every week,' she said, 'make a great thing of playing with us, banging drums and leading us around the house like some sort of crazy ringmaster. Or else he'd turn up at breakfast and get us to tell him our dreams, and he'd write them down in a journal. Most of the time it was just us and whichever Twinkle was around at the time,' 'Twinkle' being Forbes' generic name for the succession of child-minders that passed through Strathantine Lodge.

The high turnover in Twinkles may have owed something to the lodge's location, tucked away amongst ten thousand forested acres eight miles from the nearest village. The greater inaccessibility of its laird, holed up in the library with his £1000 stereo and his medicinal-grade trips, possibly also came into it. For whatever reason, none of the Twinkles stayed much longer than a season, and so there would always be a lingering sense of impermanence at the heart of Amanda and Euan's dreamlike childhood. Otherwise, they might have thought that nothing would ever change, or would ever have an end.

The lodge was so amazing (*said Amanda*). You've no idea. It was like a dream house that made itself up as it went along, a mad little castle in Bavarian gothic dropped on the Ayrshire coast. I'm not sure the family nuttiness began with Dad, you know. Anybody who'd build a place like that can't have been quite right upstairs, and it actually dates back to some stuffy old millionaire in the nineteenth century. All that dosh must have gone to his head, delusions of Glamis and Walter Scott and God alone knows.

There were terraces and gazebos, turrets and battlements

where the piper used to play, at least one folly in the grounds, and a boathouse where a miniature steamboat lay in its own wreckage. Inside, there was a great hall and a minstrels' gallery, it goes without saying, and on every floor rooms led on to rooms, rooms without end, each one different, each one more crazy than the last. We might have found Miss Havisham in one, and the brides of Dracula in the next, and Sleeping Beauty lying on a four-poster in the one after that. There was a big hydro pool in the basement, drained for decades, and unwashed stained glass windows like glimpses into long forgotten stories. Dad was cooped up in the library, happy enough so far as we could tell, and we were wandering around with Twinkle, or more often without her, left to our own devices. This was how we grew up, if you can call it growing up. As if Dad had been dropping the acid, but we were all of us having the trip. Those were lovely, lovely days, and we were so happy: up until the summer of 1976.

That was the heatwave summer, remember? The big drought, baking hot week after week, nothing but sunshine, not a cloud, not a sniff of rain. The lawns were dried to straw, and the whole forest felt combustible: everything smelled of dry pine and crackled like tinder. We were tanned little savages, running around half naked most of the time, and we only put our togs back on when Dad had some guests come to stay for a week or so, round about the middle of July.

His name – you'll love this – was Alge. I didn't know then if it was a given name or a nickname, or his surname, or something he'd just made up for himself. Twinkle and I called him 'Algae', because we both thought he was a bit scummy. The woman with him, Lettice, was kind and quiet, and I liked her a lot more. It was as if she existed wholly in Alge's shadow, though, and she hardly ever came out from it except with us kids. She befriended us straightaway, and we let her join the club. Not Alge, though.

There was something about him I found absolutely off-putting. If Dad had taught me anything it was to be accommodating of all different types of people, so it must have been something quite marked for me to react that way. It might have been nothing more than his looks. Alge was a podgy little man with a round piggy face and thick round specs, a long thin hank of receding hair on top and a straggly handlebar moustache. He wore the same loose cheesecloth shirt with a waistcoat over it every day of his visit, and he always smelled of sweat barely masked by patchouli. So yes, it might have been his appearance, but I don't think I was quite as shallow as all that.

There was his manner as well. Twinkle instantly marked him down as a perv, and that was spot on, I think: he would touch you, quite casually it would seem, but for just an instant too long, or in a way that didn't feel right. He would show a little too much interest if he found us on our own. He would tell us stories that were supposed to be funny, but somehow weren't. Kids have a radar, don't they? It's not always switched on – it wasn't ever on with Euan, he was everybody's friend – but when it is, it's very accurate. I made a point of never being alone with him, and particularly never letting him be alone with Euan.

Luckily, Alge stayed up in the library with Dad for the most part. He was doing research, he said, after a trip to Marrakech he and Lettice had just taken. He called it a 'pilgrimage', of course: none of Dad's lot ever just went on a holiday. He showed us slides he'd taken of Morocco, and it looked a wild place, the last place on earth, perhaps, but a beautiful place. But there was always a subtext at play, some ulterior motive. I remember even during the slide-shows, he would linger overlong on the naked street boys dancing on rooftops and beaches, draped across couches, sunlight and shadow.

Euan missed most of this, of course, so I took it on myself to keep us both out of Alge's reach. We'd pass the day playing cat's-cradle with Lettice, or folding paper fortune-tellers, or singing songs with her taking the difficult harmony parts. I showed her all around the estate, told her the stories we'd made up about things, and generally treated her like one of our Twinkles. I was keen to drag her out of the house for rambles, but she never seemed to want to be very far away from Alge. It was as if she needed always to know where he was, every hour of the day and night. At first I thought that was just soppiness or timidity on her part, or romantic obsession, which I found pathetic. Thinking back now, it's clear she had other reasons.

One day, I took Lettice up on the battlements to look out across the estate. The firth was absolutely placid, with hardly a ripple on the flat blue sea. The lawns and the terraces were uniformly brown, parched soil showing through in the places where we ran and played our games. Even the pines on the hillside were lifeless, like dried flowers in an arrangement. Twinkle had gone into town on her bicycle, a trip she made once or twice a week, usually with Euan on the handlebars. Alge, so far as I knew, was in the library with Dad. There wasn't even the cry of a gull to disturb the silence.

'It's paradise,' Lettice said, stretching back to sunbathe on the sloping leads. She sighed happily. 'Does all of this belong to you?'

'Well, not everything,' I said, trying not to sound too proud. 'All of the shore, and from the line of those trees over there to the folly on the far —'

I broke off. On the path that led up to the woods, two figures were heading for the treeline, walking briskly, hand in hand. One large, one small. Even at that distance I could see that it was Alge and Euan.

I glanced back at Lettice. She was looking where I was looking, and if I hadn't already been spooked, I would have been now. Under her peeling sunburn she'd gone white: absolutely blanched out with panic. It came to me that she'd been expecting something like this all along, that this was why she'd been so nervous. It hit like a gut punch: to realise that Lettice had been on her guard ever since she'd been here, that she'd been more worried about Alge than I'd been.

Seconds later we were both running downstairs. I knew Strathantine like the back of my hand, but that afternoon I ran from room to room, finding only locked doors, unopenable windows. The mazy layout of the lodge, the very architecture, seemed to be working against us. Finally, I dragged Lettice after me to the back morning room where the French windows opened with a stiff creak, and we ran out into the stillness of the afternoon. The hot blank void seemed to swallow up any noise we might have made, otherwise I would have screamed Euan's name.

Ignoring the path, I set off across the lawns. I knew the trail doglegged through the woods, so I reckoned this short-cut would head off Alge and Euan before they got any distance into the trees. Behind me Lettice was running full-tilt up the gravelled path – she was an ungainly sprinter, her elbows stuck out comically as she ran, but she was covering the ground fast enough.

I slipped between the trunks of the firs, and the close low branches scratched ruby-red tracks across my skin. I wiped the blood off, and I could smell it on my hand when I held it up to my nose. Just for a moment, I wondered if something else might be picking up its scent. It was the weirdest thing: I'd been running wild in these woods ever since I could remember, and I'd never known a minute's anxiety in them, nor anywhere on the estate, for that matter. But that afternoon on the path, I felt as if I was being watched, and by something that wished me no good. I couldn't see it, but it could see me; that was how it felt.

I shook myself like a dog shaking off water, trying to clear my head. There was no sign of anybody until Lettice, her chest heaving with exertion, came pounding along the path. Euan and Alge should have been somewhere in between us, but we'd lost them.

I suppose the panic I saw in her face must have been there to see in mine as well. I was about to say something when Lettice put a finger to her mouth. She lifted up her head and – of all the unlikely things – she snuffled at the air. At first I thought this was ridiculous: was she going to sniff them out like a lurcher? But then I realised what it was she was smelling. From in amongst the trees there came the rich, decadent scent of burning incense.

'Be quiet,' Lettice whispered to me, and gestured for me to

follow. We stepped off the path on to the drifts of fir needles beneath the trees, heading down towards the banks of the stream, following our noses.

The stream ran in a little gully through the wood, around the back of the house and down the terraces in little landscaped waterfalls into the firth. It had dried to a trickle in the heatwave: normally we'd have been able to hear it clearly from the path, but I remember there was no sound of water that day. But after a few more steps, we could hear Alge's voice. 'They're all around us, Euan,' he was saying.

Again Lettice put a finger to her lips, and I stopped. She raised a hand, made sure I was following her lead, and tiptoed forward. I followed behind her, so nervous I was actually trembling.

'You know, I think they've been in this place forever. It's been a special place, long before there were people. It belonged to them before we came and took it over. The air is thick with them, if you could only see. If you could only summon them. It's a knack, like any other. I can teach you how, Euan, would you like that?'

I couldn't make out what Euan said in response. He sounded as if he was out of breath from running. Alge spoke again, softly, crooning:

'They're always waiting to come to you – you just need to learn how to let them reveal themselves. All you have to do is be in the right space, stare into the fire, breathe in the smoke, and you have to *want* to see them, and they'll always be there. They wrap themselves in the flames, do you see? In the smoke and flame. Stop dancing now. Stop dancing and come to me, and look into the flames. *Azhar nafsak ya tifl allahab...*'

I could see them through the canopy of the trees, pinned in a bright shaft of sunlight. They were sitting on the bank of the stream with their backs to us. Alge had cleared a circle about six feet wide, scraped it clear of fir needles and old branches and piled the debris into a little cone in the middle of the circle. The smoke we'd smelled back on the path was coming from several joss sticks stuck into the soil, one either side of him. Alge's right hand was out of sight, but his left hand lay on Euan's shoulder.

'The djinn, Euan. Just as I told you. They'll writhe up out of the flames, naked and beautiful, and you'll see them. Once you see them, they'll always be with you. You'll learn to summon them – watch!' Alge took his hand from Euan's shoulder and reached down into his pocket. He produced a small glinting item: I couldn't make out what it was at first, but then I heard the scrape and grind of wheel on flint, and I realised it was a Zippo lighter. He touched it to the kindling, and I saw flames licking out.

The sight of fire broke the spell. I ran towards them, yelling – and I can still hear myself, how childishly outraged I sounded – 'You stupid idiot!' I pulled Euan away from him, and kicked the mess of kindling into the stream. 'You could have caused a forest fire! In the middle of a drought! How can you be so *stupid*?'

Alge just sat there, staring at me with a slack grin on his fat face. '*Aljaniu qadim*,' he was saying to himself, under his breath. '*Aljaniu qadim*.' I dragged Euan away, and stood with both arms protectively around him, glowering at Alge. Just as Lettice dodged between us and began to stamp on the smouldering remains with her wooden Dr Scholl's clogs, I saw one further thing, something I could scarcely begin to process. But it set me to running.

I ran all the way home, half dragging, half carrying Euan. There was no sound from behind us, and nobody followed us out of the woods. 'Are you all right?' I asked Euan, but he didn't say anything. He looked dazed, as if he'd barely woken from a long deep sleep. My mind was running in every direction, and I wondered what had been in that incense.

As we broke clear of the trees I heard the honk-honk of the horn on Twinkle's bike. She was turning the corner of the drive around the side of the lodge, and I waved to her with both arms. We met each other by the open French windows, where I tried to explain what had happened. Twinkle lifted Euan up, turned him from side to side and examined him. Calmly, he submitted to the manhandling, still saying nothing. I could see she was panicking, and I thought, had everybody except me realised the truth about Alge? Had everybody been waiting for this to happen?

Not everybody, it seemed. When Twinkle and I took Euan up to Dad and told him everything, he took it all in with a show of polite interest, as if he was listening to one of Alge's rambling tales of old Morocco. Once we'd run out of breath he nodded sagely and said, 'We've all got a lot to learn from Alge, you know.'

'*Dad!*' In all the years of his comparative failure as a father, I'd never been so angry with him. 'Dad, he had his flies unzipped!' There it was, the thing I'd hardly allowed myself to think about until I'd got Euan safe away.

He just looked at me with that bland incuriosity that was his unvarying response to the world and its events, the indifference that made me so mad. 'Did he? Well, it's a warm afternoon. Perhaps he was going to take a dip in the stream. Perhaps we all should.'

'Don't be *stupid*, Dad,' I pleaded, but he was smiling at me, as if by insulting him I'd somehow lost the argument, and that was that. Twinkle did something then that shocked me: I'd almost forgotten she was in the room with us, but she announced herself by tendering her resignation on the spot. She'd barely lifted her voice except in song for all the months she'd been with us, but now she let it all go. She told Dad exactly what she thought of him, of life at the lodge, and most particularly of Alge. I was so proud of her.

'You need to get your head out your arse and look after your children, and you need to kick those weirdo friends of yours into touch,' she concluded, and then Dad did something that I now think burned the last of the bridges between us. He simply turned away and ignored her, and he would not speak another word until we all left the room, defeated as always by the sheer inertia of his beatitude.

I spent the rest of that day in my bedroom with Euan. He was unusually quiet, and seemed happy to read or to just lie on his stomach on the bed, staring through the wide-open window as the warm honey light of the setting sun filtered through the room. Lettice came knocking at the door, but I wouldn't let her in. I said we didn't want to talk to anybody; I wasn't used to lying, and I'm sure she heard that in my voice.

Later that night, my stomach still knotted up from hunger and from fear, I heard the sound of car wheels on the gravel drive. Outside, Alge and Lettice's Bentley was pulling away from the house. Dad was standing in the drive, waving them off. After their tail lights had vanished round the corner he turned back towards the house, but I'd already pulled back from the window.

Twinkle stayed on at Strathantine for the best part of a month. I don't think she was working out her notice: I think it was more out of concern for us, and I'm not sure Dad even paid her for those last few weeks. One day, some friends of hers arrived in a mini-van, and she took her leave of us. There were tears on my side as well as on hers; she pressed a thin piece of card with a scribbled phone number into my hand, and hugged me so tightly it made my ribs creak. Euan submitted to her embrace without returning it, then politely waved goodbye, in that flat affectless way that had become the norm with him since the encounter in the woods.

Euan was a real worry by now, and Dad was no help whatsoever. It was as if they were both retreating into their own unreachable space. Of course Dad had begun that trip a long time ago, probably before we were born, but Euan went practically overnight from being a bright, lively child into a pale and passive ghost of himself. 'Dad, he's so withdrawn,' I pleaded, but all he'd say was: 'Euan is an old soul. He's finding his own centre. You should be prepared to let him travel on his own road. You can't make the journey for him.'

Old soul or not, I was horribly concerned for him, not least because I knew that dealing with this situation was more than could reasonably be expected of me. I was, I suspected, a pretty old soul myself, but I was still just a thirteen-year-old kid on her own. I tried my best to look after my brother, having no other option but to play the grown-up. Someone, I felt, had to care enough to guide him on that road, no matter what Dad said.

In a sense my job was all too easy. Euan ate the food I prepared; he came for walks with me, trotting by my side like a stolid little gundog; he required no great effort on my part by way of entertainment. He read his books, he watched the portable TV in his bedroom, and for hours on end he'd gaze out of the windows at the Scots pines behind the house. But he didn't chatter all day the way he used to: there wasn't the incessant string of babble at my elbow, the endless questions and endearing observations. He hardly spoke at all. This wasn't Euan travelling on his own road; it was Euan stuck down a dead end.

I desperately wanted to get him some help, but Dad was inflexible, not to say inert. He ignored everything I had to say whenever I tried to discuss it with him, leaving me with no other option but to carry on trying my best. To what end, though? I tormented myself with the possibility of running away. I think I might have done that, if the prospect of reality hadn't always been so distant from us. Never having seen it for myself, I hardly felt there could be anything real outside the walls of the estate. Where might we run to? On my mental map of the world there was only white space. It defeated me before I could even begin to think about it. I just couldn't do it; though it would have been better for all of us if I had.

One Friday at the end of August, the heatwave finally broke. I remember the black thunderheads massing out to sea, the incredible smell of the first raindrops on the parched Ayrshire countryside. The sound of the thunder was such a relief: it was as if a new dimension had appeared in the Flatland world of the drought. Even Euan seemed to rally for the first time in weeks, kneeling on the bedroom windowsill with the rain splashing in his face, watching as the lightning ripped and stabbed across the night sky. Then the next morning dawned grey and overcast, and he retreated into the new normal of unresponsiveness and passivity.

The first weeks of autumn were as damp and dull as the summer had been Mediterranean. Only into the second half of October did the sun come back, lower in the sky now, all but heatless, and accompanied by strong gusting westerlies. Dad stayed shut away in his library; I took him a meal up each day, which was left on its tray as often as it was eaten. I was allowed to phone the village shop and place an order for a food delivery each week. The van driver became our main contact with the outside world, and like the postman he came only as far as the gatehouse of the lodge. When I asked about a replacement for Twinkle, Dad said he was considering the matter. What was there to consider? It was just another of the unknowns I had to deal with.

I cleaned and dusted around the place as best I could, but in practice I concentrated on the areas we actually lived in. I found dustsheets, which I made good use of, and soon all the big rooms were shrouded and silent as we retreated to a handful of manageable spaces, like nervous squatters in someone else's house. Outside, after each autumn storm, the estate workers would come to tidy up the parkland, clearing away the fallen branches and stacking them into a resinous bonfire for the beginning of November.

Now and again, the phone would ring, and when I picked up, there was only silence on the line. It was sometimes the case that Dad was too far away – inside his head or outside the lodge – to answer the telephone, and often he unplugged his extension; actually, very few people rang us at Strathantine Lodge. Sometimes, Euan would pick up. Once, I found him sitting with the phone to his ear with a faraway look in his eyes, and when I took the receiver from him I heard, unmistakably, Alge's voice. Instinctively I let the phone fall with a clatter, then retrieved it only to bang it down hard on its cradle. When I'd recovered my breath I told Euan never to answer if it rang again. He looked at me with that same heartbreaking remoteness, and said nothing.

October was wearing on, and each day the dusk fell a little more quickly. All summer I'd relished the contrast between the dark coolness inside the lodge and the glaring blast-furnace of outside; now, I found myself leaving the electric bulbs on in the few rooms we used, or lighting fires in the grates. It felt as if the gloom and the chill were outward manifestations of what had become of our family, and I wanted to fight against them as best I could.

Early one evening, I was looking for Euan. I hadn't seen him since I'd made him lunch: I'd spent the afternoon doing housework, and now it was time for the evening meal.

'Euan?' I called, standing in the middle of the great hallway. The sun was down, and what light there was barely picked out the bones of the mullions in the high narrow windows, but I moved through the shadows with the confidence of familiarity. There was nothing to scare me in all that crazy old pile of a lodge; or there had never been anything.

I ran upstairs and checked the bedrooms, his and mine. No sign of him, apart from the crumby plate that had held his sandwich. I came back down the creaking oak staircase and turned left, heading for the kitchens.

As I passed the phone nook in the hallway, I noticed the receiver was off the hook, dangling from its cord. I was about to replace it when I heard voices coming from the earpiece. Or no, a voice, one only; quiet and furtive and only too familiar.

'Never call this house again!' I screamed at Alge, and slammed down the receiver hard enough (I hoped) to make his ears ring. But who had he been speaking to? Dad was a creature of his library; he just wouldn't have picked up the downstairs extension. There was only one other possibility. And listening now in the re-established silence, I thought I heard something from the kitchens.

The builders of the lodge had tucked away the staff and their various functions in a miniature wing all to themselves. To reach the kitchens you passed through a back parlour where the housekeeper used to hold court, in the days when there had been more staff than inhabitants. This back parlour was approached through a corridor with stone flagging, which opened on to a broad low-ceilinged space. An inglenook fireplace with the family shield in oak above it was flanked on either side by great high-backed settles made cosy by heaps of plump cushions. It was a favourite place of ours: to be sitting there with Euan and Twinkle when the fire was lit felt as snug and companionable as anywhere in the whole house.

But Twinkle was long gone now; and yet, as I paused at the end of the corridor, I could hear voices.

From where I stood I could see only the back of the nearest settle: the fireplace was recessed into the wall to my left, and the settles shielded it from view. The room was unlit, with only the flickering of the flames in the grate to set the shadows at play. The voices, like the firelight, were coming from the deep heart of the inglenook. Had I lit the fire down here? I was sure I hadn't, and it was not a thing that would have occurred to Euan, or so I thought. Dad, needless to say, would never think to do anything so practical.

Still I could hear the crackling of the fire, and mixed in with it, I could hear whispers. They were as soft as the flames that licked away at the logs, and in my heightened state of nervousness they seemed to me just as dangerous. They reminded me of the sound of Alge's voice on that summer afternoon, drifting through the trees, whispering words in some foreign language. But who were those words being whispered to?

The answer came when I heard Euan's laughter. He hadn't laughed much since Alge's visit, but I recognised his happy snigger immediately. How could I not? It had been at the centre of my world for so long. The voice seemed to respond, or perhaps it was only the rustling of the flames, and that's what made me break cover and dart around the side of the settle.

There was Euan, quite alone, silhouetted against the firelight as he knelt on the stone surround of the inglenook. He seemed not to hear me at first, and I called his name. He turned slowly, almost reluctantly, I thought.

'Euan, who was with you?' I asked him.

He just looked at me, and said after an uncomfortable pause, 'What do you mean, Mand? There's no-one here.'

'I thought I head voices…'

'Oh, I might have been talking,' he said, and turned back towards the fire.

And I felt at that moment that I was going entirely crazy, and I did not walk out of the parlour, I ran.

It's a terrible thing to be forced to consider, especially when you're only a child: the proposition that you might be going out of your mind. And I had nobody to help me through it. All I had was Dad, and I ran to him without the faintest expectation of help or even consolation. The library, ten times as large as the back pantry and three times as high, was likewise lit by nothing more than a log fire. Dad was sitting in his armchair with his feet up on a low table piled with books and papers. He opened his half-closed eyes as I burst in and said 'Well?' His voice was lethargic and somehow long-suffering, as if I was in the habit of disturbing his journeys in the higher void.

Now I was here, I didn't know what to say. In some sort of horrible fast-forward I imagined myself telling him my fears, pouring it all out as you might do to a parent who actually cared, and I supplied for myself the languid scorn with which he'd answer me. All I could manage in the end was to ask: 'Were you on the phone just now?'

'On the phone.' He gave it exaggerated consideration, as if to emphasise the banality of the question. 'No; no, I wasn't. Were you?'

'I picked it up,' I said, trying to talk around the lump in my throat. 'It was that friend of yours.'

'I have many friends,' he said serenely, and I thought, *lucky you*. 'Which friend in particular?'

'You know,' I said, and when he shook his head I said, 'Alge.'

'Alge?' He gave a little snigger, without any real mirth. 'Oh, I don't think so, Amanda.'

'I know his voice,' I insisted. 'It was him.'

'That surprises me.' Still his voice was low and even.

'It's not the first time – he's been ringing on and off since he was here with Lettice. He's been talking to Euan.'

'And he phoned just now?'

'Yes!' I was sure of that if of nothing else. 'I think he was talking to Euan again.'

He didn't answer me. Instead, he reached for the table, selected a newspaper from the pile, and handed it wordlessly to me.

It was a copy of the *Evening Standard* from the previous week, folded to a quarter-page article. Over a photo of a wrecked and burned-out car, the headline read CRASH COUPLE IDENTIFIED.

'Read it,' my father invited me. I got as far as the first paragraph, and then I had to stop, because I thought I was going mad again.

'"The driver of the Bentley that burst into flames on the Chelsea Embankment at the weekend has been identified as Algernon 'Alge' Venables, poet and contributor to various journals of the so-called counter-culture. Mr Venables was the driver of the car, and his passenger is said to have been Miss Lettice Barkley, his partner. The identities of the couple were established at post-mortem, the blaze having been so fierce as to render them unidentifiable by the usual means ..."'

I couldn't read any more. I was biting my lip so hard that I drew blood, or else I think I would have fainted. The taste of the blood filled my mouth as I let the paper drop to the floor.

'Poor Alge.' If there had been anger or bitterness in Dad's voice, that would have been understandable; likewise, grief. It would have been the natural response. Instead, he said, 'I don't think it was him on the phone just now, do you? No matter how badly he wanted to talk to Euan.'

I couldn't answer. I had to believe what I'd heard on that phone line, even if it meant I was crazy after all. But Dad was still speaking.

'Amanda, don't you think you're getting slightly obsessed with being a mother to your brother?' In that same tone, he continued: 'You know, if you really want a wee bairn of your own to play mummy with, you could always go down to the village dance on a Friday night. I'm sure there'd be plenty of the local lads who'd oblige.' He looked at me quizzically over the top of his granny glasses, and I had to run again. But where to? Only to another wing of the prison, a shuttered room where I could lock the door and cry behind it, and nobody would ever hear me.

The weeks after that were unbearable, and yet I didn't have a choice in the matter. I had to bear it; someone had to look after Euan. I feared for him in every possible way: I felt as if I was all that stood between him and something I couldn't even put a name to. All I could see was its shadow, that was all, its silhouette against the firelight.

Through it all Euan remained unreachable. Later that same evening, when I asked him if he'd been on the phone, he smiled distantly and said 'I picked it up, yes.' I asked who he'd been talking to, and he said, 'Oh, no-one.' So much for that.

Dad, though, showed signs of coming out of his shell a little as October came to an end. The high winds of autumn had brought down all the loose branches in the woods, and a few of the rotten older trees besides, and the bonfire on the old tennis courts was piled a good twelve feet high. The Strathantine bonfire was a local custom, probably the only one of which Dad approved. It was certainly one that he fostered: each Guy Fawkes' night all the local children were invited to the burning and encouraged to make masks, and sweeties and sparklers were laid on at the laird's expense. Dad would give a little lecture about ancestral fire ceremonies held at the waning of the year, and nobody would pay him the slightest bit of attention, and then the fire would be lit and everyone would have a grand time.

This year I was looking forward to the bonfire more than ever. For the first time since Twinkle left there would be outsiders around the place, if only for an evening, and it didn't really matter who they were, they would be other people, real living individuals. Dad constructed a poster that might have advertised a gig by Pink Floyd at the Roundhouse in '67, and I was sent on my bicycle to pin it up in the village shop. Even Euan bucked up, or seemed to: he spent hours with *papier-mache* and poster paints, designing masks for bonfire night and tossing them into the fire because they 'weren't right', apparently. When he finally came up with one he considered appropriate, I wasn't allowed to see it. I took this as an encouraging sign of individuation.

The night of the fourth was clear and cold: the moon was waxing gibbous, and there were only stray wisps of cloud. I was a long time getting to sleep that evening, and I ended up going down to the kitchen to get a glass of milk. As usual, I didn't bother with a light, and when I passed through the corridor into the back parlour I was surprised to see the low flicker of firelight in the hearth. Nobody had been in the back parlour all day, so far as I knew, but a small pile of kindling was alight in the fireplace. As I looked at the flames they smouldered out into wisps of acrid smoke, and the parlour was swallowed up again in darkness. Behind me in the corridor, I heard the patter of bare feet on flagged stone floors, and what might have been the stifled sound of laughter.

Guy Fawkes' day came in bright and cold, a thin nagging wind that tore the last of the clouds from the sky. I spent the day making chocolate crispies and toffee apples for the evening's celebrations, and Dad went out and played the part of a responsible adult with the gardeners as they made the last structural adjustments to the bonfire. Euan was with him, and I took all this to be a good sign.

By half past four the sun was dipping into the sea: I watched it go down, like a great beacon out on Ailsa Craig. For once, Dad actually came and ate with us in the back parlour. It was the last time we were together as a family, and I can hardly bear to think of it now. At six, we went to open the gates and lit the braziers to guide our guests, and by seven there were fifty or so villagers and their children gathered happily around the pyre, the adults in their scarves and gloves, the children in their home-made masks.

A polite cheer greeted the appearance of Dad, on the once-yearly occasion of his wearing of the kilt. He looked, as usual, both embarrassed and amused. I glanced around for Euan, but I couldn't spot him among the masked children clustered around the eats. 'Welcome, feasters,' Dad announced, his quiet voice straining to be heard above the ambient chatter. 'Welcome to the closing of the year gone by. Welcome, imps,' and the kids obligingly whooped and squealed, 'welcome to the fires of Samhain.'

He held aloft the resinous torch, and then touched it to the nearest brazier. The fire bit into it eagerly, and he lifted it again, before thrusting it into the heart of the pyre.

In no time at all the bonfire was alight, and the people around it oohed and aahed and began to clap. Dad imposed a steady beat on the applause with his rhythmic clapping and stamping, and began to sing in a high piping voice:

> *Circle of light, circle of sound,*
> *Circle of ancestors, gather around,*
> *Come to the fire, come to the light,*
> *Come to the dance on a Samhain night!*
> *Summer is out, winter is in*
> *Samhain night and the veil is thin*
> *Come to the imps as they dance the old round*
> *Come to the bonfire, come out of the ground!*

Some of the children took up the chanting, and soon they were weaving in a laughing, skipping conga line around the bonfire while the adults waved their sparklers and clapped gloved hands. Tigers, lions and monkeys, dogs and cats and hares, their masks brought to life in the dancing of the firelight. Dad beamed at them like a priest well pleased with his congregation.

Usually I would have been in amongst them, circling the fire. At this moment, though, I was starting to worry about Euan. The imps had danced past me three or four times, yet there was still no sign of him. Was he with the adults? I decided to climb the side of the hill till I could look down from above and see everybody all at once.

The hillside ramped sharply by the side of the tennis court, and soon I could see everything; but I still couldn't see Euan. The emotional fatigue of the last few months had left me constantly on the edge of panic, and I could feel that formless fear rising again in the pit of my stomach as I squinted through the mounting shower of sparks. Behind the bonfire, away from the circle of light, lay the dark bulk of the lodge.

Not entirely dark.

Up on the battlement where Lettice and I had once basked in the summer heatwave, there was a gleam in the darkness; a lit torch, being swung in circles. I couldn't see from that distance who was swinging it, but I knew it had to be Euan.

For a second time and space seemed to become inverted, and I was simultaneously staring down from on high at Euan, running towards the woods in the glare of the hammering sun, and squinting up through the bonfire blaze in the here and now. The same panic that had overtaken me on that July afternoon came back, redoubled, and I ran once more towards the danger. Dad saw me, and he called out, 'Amanda!' but I was already halfway to the lodge.

Inside was dark, and I fumbled for the lights. Nothing. I snapped the switch up and down, but the power was off. As I've said before, I didn't need light to find my way around the house, and I was off running again, dodging the furniture in its dustsheet shrouds, those dull and hulking ghosts who shared the lodge with us.

As I clattered around the echoing wooden gallery, making for the staircase that gave access to the battlements, I thought I could smell smoke, and I tried to remember which rooms I'd lit a fire in that day. None on this floor, I was certain. There was dad's library, but as always he'd have locked the door behind him on leaving. The question was far back in my mind, though, because all I could think of was Euan.

At the top of the spiral stairs, the door to the roof was open wide. It wasn't just the exertion that choked off my cry of 'Euan! Euan, are you there?' Panic takes you by the throat and by the pit of the stomach and most crucially by the brain; it pummels your body while it stops your mind from putting two and two together. A case in point: there was nowhere to hide on the battlements, and very soon I realised that Euan wasn't up there. Far below the bonfire imps sang and laughed and shouted, and for precious seconds I was totally incapable of working out what to do next. Into the stunned silence came a whisper. *He came back down before you could make it up here,* said the Sensible Amanda who'd been pushed out of my consciousness. *You need to go back down and look from room to room.*

And, more insistently, *find out what's that burning smell.*

At the foot of the spiral staircase there was no doubt about it: the smoke was thick enough to catch at my throat. I think if there had been any light I must have seen it. Light was coming from the minstrels' gallery, though: the big tapestry that took up one whole wall was on fire. The flames had taken hold of the old thick material, the stag and the hounds being eaten up along with the hunters and the trees. *Oh Euan,* I thought, *no …*

Fire at my right. I swivelled round to see a figure with a torch, a small figure, racing along the corridor and darting into one of the bedrooms. Again my mind seized up. I didn't know whether to run outside and sound the alarm or chase down Euan and rescue him. The speed at which the tapestry was burning left me only one option: I had to make sure Euan was safe.

When I burst through the bedroom door the four-poster bed was already ablaze. Keeping my distance, moving around the walls, I checked out the whole of the room. No Euan. How could it be? I hadn't seen him come out again. The answer was in the small connecting door, which I discovered by falling backwards through it.

The door led to a bathroom, tile and porcelain, non-combustible. A further door opened to the next bedroom, which was already on fire. I managed to skirt around the flames and reach the door to the hallway. Back in the direction of the gallery, that small shape with the torch was silhouetted against the orange glow of the burning tapestry, and I thought I could hear laughter down the corridor. 'That's not Euan,' I thought, even as I raced towards it. 'That's not his voice.' But I thought I knew the voice from somewhere; and again I got a flash of that afternoon, back in the woods, standing next to Lettice while strange murmurs drifted through the pines.

Long before I could reach it, the figure was gone. I came up with a hard thump against the banister of the gallery, and what little breath I had was knocked out of me. Across the gallery, on the farther side, the figure was moving. It paused and turned to face me, as if we were playing a dreadful game. Instead of Euan's face, I saw the frozen features of a mask.

The *papier-mache* was painted red, with blue and yellow swirls running up and down it. It had huge white eyes with round staring holes to see through, and it must have been a trick of the firelight, because for a second I thought that behind those eyeholes there was real fire.

'*Euan!*' I couldn't help it. The scream was dragged out of me.

And for a moment I thought there was a reply, from somewhere back in the corridor I'd just come from; I thought it was my brother's voice, crying out my name.

The figure on the far side of the gallery laughed again. I could hear it even from a distance. 'Amanda!' it called, and I couldn't tell if it was the voice of Alge, dead in a blazing car on the Embankment, or the voice of Euan, who I loved so much, or the voice of something that has no voice in the rational world except the crackle of hungry flames in dry tinder.

I looked back down the corridor, but the fire was already out of the bedrooms and surging along the walls and ceiling towards me. Euan's voice came again, or so I thought; this time it was from below, somewhere in the great hallway, and I pelted down one set of stairs while the masked figure danced along the parallel flight on the other side, touching its torch to the draperies and paintings as it went. Everything was burning.

I ran from room to room calling for Euan, but I couldn't hear him any more. The sound of the fire was loud now, the roaring of a beast set free and feeding on the dry dust of centuries. Outside I could see people, come down the hill from the bonfire and clustering at the windows to see what was going on. I screamed to them to look for Euan, and ran on. Some of those faces looked like the mask of the creature upstairs, and then when I looked again it would be just another of the village children, close up to the glass, watching me as I ran and screamed.

As on that day back in the summer, the very bricks and mortar of the rooms seemed to be working against me now. Several times I ran head-on into a closed door I'd thought was open, or a wall where I thought there was a door. I picked myself up out of sheer desperation and stumbled on, trying to keep my mind clear, covering my face with one arm to keep from breathing in the smoke.

Back in the hall, I heard voices from upstairs again. Without stopping to look I ran for the stairway, but when I was halfway up a whoosh of flame at my feet sent me staggering backwards, arms flailing for balance, feet unable to find the steps. I must have landed on my head, if I ever landed at all and I'm not still falling, because that's my last memory of childhood and of home; the sensation of falling, and there being nothing to stop me.

The next I knew I was lying on the lawns, high up on the terraces, barely conscious, pressing myself flat against the damp chilly grass as if I might fall off the surface of the earth into the void above. The lodge was fully ablaze, flames streaming from the windows, black smoke blotting out the moon and stars. Dad was by my side, not holding my hand or stroking my head, just staring at the conflagration with all the concern of a curious passer-by. 'Amanda,' he said, when he saw I'd come to. 'You're all right – just a bump on the head.'

'Where's Euan?' It came out as a scream, and Dad flinched as he always did from conflict.

'They're doing their best,' he said, turning back to the fire. 'You see, they can't go in there. The firemen. It's past that now.'

And gravity came unstuck, and I fell off the earth's inert

surface.

My memories start up again in a patchy sort of way the morning after, when I woke on a sofa in the gatehouse of the lodge. Again, Dad was with me; again, he told me that they hadn't found Euan. All the memories of the night before hit me at once with the force of a boxer's punch; I started sobbing and I didn't stop. Dad didn't leave my side through it all, but there was no reassurance in his presence. He told me I was lucky they'd found me and brought me out, but for my part I wished they'd left me inside, with my brother, where I belonged.

We stayed on at the gatehouse for a week while the fire crews searched the rubble of Strathantine Lodge and the police took statements out of nothing more than habit, it seemed to me. They were unable to determine the source of the fire, which had taken hold with unnatural rapidity. They were unable to say if an accelerant had been used, or who might have had a motive to do such a thing. Worst of all, they were unable to find any trace of Euan, or of anybody else that might have been in there. The fire had taken every clue.

In the end, there was no active requirement for us to stay on the scene; nothing except the sucking, aching absence of my brother, the hopeless draw of the smoking ruins. Dad had been in touch with the family firm, who wired us money to buy a change of clothes and a second-hand car. We set out for Dad's old pad in Chelsea, and all through that long journey I don't think we spoke about anything that mattered. The space between us was unbridgeable.

The flat had been kept in good order by cleaners who came once a month. Dad unlocked the front door and let himself in, as if only that morning he'd stepped out for a stroll down the Kings Road to Alge's place, perhaps, for one of their adventures. 'Are you coming?' he asked, when I didn't follow him.

'I thought I'd get us something for dinner,' I said, and he smiled vaguely. 'Aren't you the sensible one,' he said, and turned away, for the last time as it happens.

I didn't bother with dinner. Instead, I found a phone box and used up the last of my change calling the number I'd kept safe in my pocket all this time, written down on the inside of an old Rizla packet. Then I waited in Sloane Square like one of London's dead-eyed street waifs, until Twinkle emerged from the underground and carried me away.

I spent the next decade roaming round the country with Twinkle and her traveller friends, living in caravans and draughty farmhouses and sometimes old buses with the seats ripped out, learning the way the world worked, making friends with other outcasts just like me. It wasn't easy; I kept having spells in which everything became too much for me, and once or twice I almost fell backwards down that staircase for good, but the travellers helped me through as best they could, and here I am, more or less reconciled, the best Amanda I can be given what I had to work with.

Dad never came looking for me. After I phoned and told him who I was with, but not where I was, he set up a bank account and fed monthly payments into it, and in this way he washed his hands of the last of his encumbrances. I didn't miss him much, but I did miss Euan, I missed him horribly. I miss him still.

And on nights like tonight (*she said, staring at the embers of the bonfire*), you know, I still look for him in the flames. I always, always look for him. I never see him, but sometimes there's that other face, the face of *papier-mache*, the one I wish I'd never seen. If only I could have looked behind the mask that evening, just to be sure, you know? Just to be sure.

SPIRITS OF PALACE AND TOMB

Edinburgh is one of the world's great cities. Not just the seat of royalty and home to the Scottish Government, but a beacon of culture and learning, famous for the elegance of its streets, shops and parks and the magnificence of its unmistakeable skyline.

But this wasn't always so. At least, this wasn't always the whole story.

Not for nothing was Edinburgh described by 19th century philosopher, William Hazlitt, as a 'city of palaces and tombs'.

Like most great metropolises, Scotland's capital has suffered over time from war, civil strife and horrendous injustice. Originally a volcanic rock dating from the dawn of prehistory, it was first fortified in the Bronze Age by the Votadini tribe in their efforts to resist the northward advance of the Roman legions. There was further bloody conflict in and around the growing city throughout the Dark Ages and Middle Ages as various other foreign powers sought to possess the stronghold. When there were no invaders to be repelled, Edinburgh was the centre of civil warfare during the Scottish Reformation and the Wars of the Covenant (which in 1666 saw an entire army of captured Covenanters, all of them fellow Scots, marched into the city and hanged ten at a time on the Mercat Cross in Parliament Square). Even after the Union of the Crowns in 1603, there was the War of the Three Kingdoms (or the English Civil War), with all the incredible violence that entailed, and then the Jacobite Risings.

Whenever Edinburgh wasn't itself at the heart of these bitter battles, there was regular rioting and dissent in its streets, and numerous executions (some legal, some little better than lynchings) of so-called traitors and spies. On top of all this, from Scotland's passing of the Witchcraft Act in 1553 to its abolition in 1736, dozens of women were publicly strangled or burned (or both) in Edinburgh, on the most spurious charges.

If this wasn't enough, the capital saw untold suffering in purely social terms. Even in the days prior to industrialisation, the city had a reputation for being a den of misery: a warren of noisome passages winding between teetering slum-tenements, filth and sewage running everywhere. The Nor Loch, a manmade waterway north of the city centre, originally created for defence but mainly used to drown witches, was so polluted with household refuse and unwanted corpses, that it became a major threat to public health. The majority of the city's population were impoverished: beggars and vagrants thronged the streets, while those who actually had somewhere to live were often forced to endure damp, cramped, rat-infested squalor, the everyday sorrow caused by this made even worse in 1645 when the plague visited, killing over a third of the population.

Little wonder that uncountable numbers of ghosts are still said to wander Edinburgh, both above and below ground.

The Castle itself is a hive of supernatural activity. The phantom piper who walks the battlements is one of the most famous and time-honoured visitants, but there is also a headless drummer who apparently roams the corridors, beating out a steady tattoo, while disembodied voices have been heard on all levels, some of them speaking with French or American accents, suggesting they are the spirits of prisoners of war who died there long ago.

Equally famous for its ghosts is Greyfriars Kirkyard, the great Gothic cemetery in the middle of the city, where the manifestations range from the harmless and benign to the dark and dangerous. At the lighter end of this spectrum sits Greyfriars Bobby, the friendly spirit of a loyal hound who sat by his deceased master's grave, fed and watered by the citizens, until he died of old age, at which point he was interred in the same plot. At the other end, is the violent soul of George McKenzie, better known as 'Bluidy McKenzie' for a terrible incident after the Battle of Bothwell Bridge in 1679 when, as a Minister of the Crown, he imprisoned 1,200 captured Covenanter rebels in an enclosed field next to the Kirkyard, turning it into a makeshift concentration camp, where they were kept with no shelter and minimum food and drink for months on end. Many perished, the survivors then facing either execution or transportation to a life of slavery in the West Indian plantations. McKenzie himself is buried in the Kirkyard in a very ostentatious tomb, which his tortured spirit is said to guard with extreme violence; more than one visitor has been assaulted for getting too close.

If the streets of Edinburgh supposedly echo with the horrors of the past, the underground regions are all that and more.

In the mid-18th century, population growth in Edinburgh saw many respectable businesses, cobblers, tanners and the like, relocate into the city's subterranean Vaults, turning them into actual shopping streets. However, in 1795, extensive flooding forced many of these shops to close, leaving the Vaults vacant, so that a literal underclass was able to move in. In no time it was a fetid warren, a windowless labyrinth often interconnecting with sewers and plague pits, crammed with ruffians, thieves and drunkards, but also debtors, urchins and penniless immigrants from Ireland or rural Scotland. Recreation was provided by illegal taverns, brothels, gambling dens and fighting and ratting pits. Edinburgh's Hellfire Club, a much-feared coven of Satanists, rapists and drug-abusers would convene there, specifically in the dungeon-like rooms under South Bridge. How many murders were never even detected in that half-hidden netherworld, let alone solved, can only be guessed at.

Perhaps unsurprisingly, visitors to the Vaults now run a gauntlet of ghosts.

'Mr Boots' is by reputation the most terrifying: a brutal male spirit, notable for his thigh-length boots, who has supposedly chased and assailed visitors physically, sometimes kicking them, or hitting them with heavy stones. The crying and laughing of children has also been heard, along with a menacing, incoherent whispering and a distant, angry shouting, while one chamber resides in permanent darkness as no light can ever successfully be struck there and electric bulbs supposedly shatter.

In modern times, ghost tours are regularly held in the Vaults (as they are throughout much of Edinburgh above ground), while ghost-hunting television specials have also been hosted there, sometimes live, and sometimes claiming spectacular results, including one episode of Living TV's Most Haunted, in which a member of the crew appeared to be gruesomely clawed by an invisible entity while live on air.

GIE ME SOMETHIN' TA EAT AFORE I DEE
John Alfred Taylor

'Guid as a MacDonald's?' asked the counterman.

Alex Latimer had wondered if there was a good meal to be found anywhere in Scotland. 'Much better. A real American hamburger.'

Alex meant it too, though he'd have said so even if the hamburger had been a disappointment – always tell people what they want to hear. But it was good to have something that tasted like home after the things he'd eaten since his flight from London.

'I was worried, 'cause I had a twasome of the Big Macs when I was up to Glasgow, and liked them fine.'

'Oh, Big Macs are all right,' Alex grinned. 'Shouldn't say anything against them since I'm a MacDonald myself, at least on my mother's side. Though likely no relation to the fast food MacDonalds.'

'And now you're here to track down your ancestors?'

'One of them.' After another bite: 'This the right way to Kilmarnock?'

'Aye. Just keep going down the A77. There's one place to beware of,' he warned. 'Don't get off on the B7061 just before Fenwick. There's little chance of doing such, it's so clearly marked – but I've heard of people doing that. Just a word to the wise, sir.'

Alex had known he was on the right road already, but he'd asked because locals liked to show off their local knowledge, whether in Scotland or Carnegie, Pa. That made them easier to con.

The counterman wished him 'guid luck' when he left. Alex hoped the wish came true, because he *was* looking for an ancestor, Malcolm MacDonald. Or more accurately, looking for what Malcolm was supposed to have been carrying.

Malcolm's wife and son died in a raid led by the Campbell Earl of Argyle, so when Malcolm MacDonald joined Montrose and his Irishmen, he bore the only wealth left to him wrapped in rags under his buff coat, a great circular Highland brooch all gold and jewels. So Alex's mother had said.

The later part of her tale had been even stranger. Though wounded in the debacle at Philiphaugh, Malcolm escaped on his horse as Graham of Montrose sailed into exile. Luckier than the murdered camp followers or the Irish soldiers lined up and shot, Malcolm MacDonald rode west toward Kilmarnock, where his cousin and his cousin's wife would give him shelter for a night or two.

MacDonald was near starving by the time he reached Drumtrodden Castle. 'Gie me somethin' ta eat afore I dee.' His cousin's wife gave him a stoup of wine to stay him till she brought bread and beef, but never brought the beef.

The wine was laced with laudanum.

Because she was an ardent Covenanter, and her less ardent husband wanted no involvement with a dangerous fugitive, she persuaded him to help drag Malcolm MacDonald to the entrance of the castle's pit prison – the Scottish equivalent of an oubliette – as soon as Malcolm was unconscious.

They dropped him in, lowered the stone flag that closed it, and attempted to forget he'd ever been, never knowing whether he died of his wounds or hunger or thirst, since the pit prison's ventilating shaft went all the way to the roof. And except for the woman's deathbed confession years after her husband's burial, no one would have known a thing concerning Malcolm's fate.

But according to Alex's mother, neither the cousin nor the wife had known of the great golden brooch concealed under MacDonald's buff coat. Which meant the brooch might still be with his remains in the pit prison.

'I ken no castle of that name,' said Mrs Ramsey, the widow who ran the bed and breakfast. 'But Hugh Gifford, one of the dominies of the Middle School, kens all about auld times. I could ring him up and see if he'll be free to talk after dinner.'

He was, and eager to talk, too, after Alex spun him a yarn about wanting to write a family history for the MacDonalds of Canada and the United States. Not only was the schoolmaster knowledgeable, but it was a relief for Alex not to have to translate from deep Scots – though there was still a burr in Gifford's pronunciation, he used few dialect words. 'What happened to your ancestor is a sad story, but those were bloody times. The great Montrose himself danced on air when he came back from the Continent a few years later.'

'There was a man,' Alex agreed, 'whether right or wrong. Graham dressed for his hanging like it was his wedding.'

'Aye. *Noblesse oblige* and all that. But back to your quest. Though a word to the wise – I'd certainly wait till morning before trying to find the place – it's hilly and overgrown with gorse. No pleasure to walk through at twilight. Besides that, the locals say the place is cursed.' The schoolmaster laughed. 'Perhaps another reason to wait till morning. Let me draw you a map.'

Next morning, Alex was glad he'd taken Hugh Gifford's advice to wait. The ruins of Drumtrodden were hard to find, even with Gifford's map, and tangles of gorse were everywhere. At least the gorse was in bloom, yellow flowers spangling the green thorns. On the way up he scouted a few paths that might make things easier once it was dark.

Judging from what remained, like so many sixteenth century Scottish buildings called castles, Drumtrodden must have been a tower house, a z-plan with towers placed at diagonally opposite corners of the central block so each could cover two sides with their defensive fire.

It took Alex an hour to be sure he'd found the slab over the pit prison. The iron staple that had been used to lift it was rusted away, but he had crowbars in the boot of his rental car, and one corner of the stone was broken away by frost and would give him a place to start. Though he'd need some lengths of lumber to brace it while he levered the slab up step by step. Lumber he'd better buy somewhere else than Kilmarnock, if he wanted to cover his tracks.

Alex got on all fours and peered into the dark crevice, but couldn't make out a thing. 'See you tonight, Malcolm,' he chuckled, 'though maybe you're lucky you didn't get your meal. Scottish cooking can kill you.'

Alex would swear to that. One component of the breakfast served at his hotel in Glasgow had been a circular slab looking like cranberry jelly made from powdered coal. The waiter explained it was black pudding. One taste and he'd decided black pudding wasn't for him – almost as characterless as tofu, though with a flavour of sorts, if salt and used motor oil was a flavour. His breakfast next day had featured black pudding again. And this morning Mrs Ramsey had put black pudding before him with a loving smile.

Though the worst had been the chicken supremes stuffed with haggis in a Glasgow restaurant whose décor and seating came from a razed church. He'd heard of haggis, and ordered it out of curiosity, automatically assuming haggis meant a bomb-shaped pudding in a sheep's stomach. (Bobbie Burns had a lot to answer for.) But haggis also meant organ meats, Alex discovered, and the chicken supremes were delicious, though terribly greasy. Greasy enough to loosen his bowels to the point where he had to remain in Glasgow an extra day. Bombs didn't have to be bomb-shaped.

From his experience the amazing thing about Scottish cooking was how your stomach could be bloated and griping with hunger at the same time. Probably some secret culinary revenge aimed at the Sassenach.

Just before Alex stood up, he thought he heard a faint sound from below. Only an echo.

Once out of the gorse the path down to the car was easy. But a hundred yards away Alex noticed he was no longer alone: two road workers were filling a hole near the car. The one with iron-coloured hair lifted his head as Alex descended, then beckoned. Alex cursed under his breath, then realised being noticed didn't matter now, because he'd already drawn attention to himself locally.

The old guy pushed his cap back and gave Alex a long look before speaking. His eyes were pale blue and bleak, as if the sky was looking through the weathered pink mask of his face, with one eye disconcertingly unfocused, staring up and to the left. 'You the Yank?'

'I'm American, yes.'

'Been up to the castle? To Drumtrodden?'

'To what's left of it. Why?'

'It's no a canny place. Specially after sundown.'

Alex used a joke to override his alarm at being questioned, pointing back over his shoulder at the gorse and asking, 'Do you think I'd try to go through that tangle at night? Even if I'm American, I'm not a total fool.'

The old road worker cackled and touched his cap. 'You're no fool, sir. Even if you're a Yank. Just a word to the wise, sir though you dinna seem to need it.'

Did every one of these sheep-loving yokels want to give a word to the wise?

That morning Alex had told Mrs Ramsey he'd be driving up to Edinburgh to do research in the University library, and wouldn't be back till next afternoon.

'No breakfast? Then I'll take some shillings off your bill.'

'Not at all. Just knowing I can come back to such a hospitable place is worth more than you charge.'

Though if he found the brooch tonight he'd never be back, and Mrs Ramsey could 'whistle o'er the lave o' it'. And he'd never have to swallow her murderous scones again.

He spent the day in Glasgow like a proper tourist, looking at the Burrell Collection, and then checking out the Necropolis to get himself in the mood for the night's work.

Alex ate a late dinner. The Black Angus steak was overdone – perhaps Scottish cooks could be trusted with oatmeal if nothing else – but two shots of The Famous Grouse made up for it. He didn't turn back down the A77 till it was fully dark, then drove fast, passing and being passed by hurtling lorries.

It was eleven when Alex pulled the rental car off the narrow road under the remains of Drumtrodden and drove the vehicle up into the gorse to hide it. Rather than use his flashlight, he let his eyes get used to the dark and opened the trunk by the hint of sky glow from Kilmarnock, putting the bundle of crowbars and lumber over one shoulder and the pack with his climbing equipment over the other.

He was glad he'd scouted the paths by daylight, though he still ended up caught by the gorse more than once, and even had to backtrack to find the right path. But finally he was inside what was left of the walls, and felt he could risk the flashlight, keeping the beam low, and turning it on only a few seconds at a time till he found his way to the slab.

Alex laid the flashlight down, one lonely horizontal beam against the darkness, and glanced around a second before setting to work. The walls around reared up in shadow, lidded with the dark clouds rushing overhead. It was like being at the bottom of a well, except he wasn't at the bottom of a well. But Malcolm MacDonald was. All Alex had to do was take the lid off the place.

'Here I come, Malcolm,' he whispered into the cleft at the corner, unable to resist the impulse. 'Hope you don't have any black pudding down there.'

Alex listened for a second. No echo this time.

He cut the tape on his bundle, and got the long crowbar under the weathered corner of the stone, levering it up as far as possible and straining to slide a length of lumber under on a diagonal. He rested a moment, and slipped another crowbar in at the side once he was breathing normally.

Ten minutes' work with the crowbars and the timber braces, and the slab thudded upside down beside the pit it had covered for three and a half centuries.

Alex had saved a miniature of The Famous Grouse for this moment.

The whisky finished, he opened his pack and put on his climbing harness. Tape slings went around two different blocks of masonry, and he clipped the tapes together at the other end with a carabiner, threaded the rope through, and hooked the ends into his descender.

Ready to go now, except for the flashlight – he didn't want to lose that on the way down, so he tied a cord around just behind the flare at the head, then another loop near the back, and attached it to the waist-band of his harness.

Alex took a quick look into the pit before he descended: the bleached light showed nothing but the rough sides of the shaft and the almost featureless floor beyond. His ancestor must have survived long enough to crawl away from where he fell.

'Hope you have a present for me, Malcolm,' Alex giggled, and then lowered himself backward over the edge, bending his knees and tucking his neck into his chest so he wouldn't hit his head on the far wall of the shaft while he walked himself down.

After a second he realised the length and width of the shaft allowed him to chimney. Still he'd need the rope. No other way to come up once the cell opened out below. It was dark with the dangling flash pointed down, but reflected light allowed him to see enough to continue.

Alex's boots scraped off the bottom of the shaft, and he let his legs dangle, hanging and resting on the end of the rope before he descended farther. He gasped for breath as he turned there, realising how out of shape he was.

He thought he heard a scraping below, tried to hold his

breath to listen. Then he felt a faint current of air on his trouser leg, definitely heard a soft thudding afterward. That was no illusion.

Had some burrowing animal found a way into the cell through a gap opened by a tree root?

There was the scraping again; a second later a grip like a mantrap snipped onto his right ankle. A great weight dragged him down.

The flashlight pendulumed and strobed, but the middle of each swing showed him all he needed to see: long yellow teeth and sunken eyes in a tangle of red hair and red beard. What was left of the buff coat gave off the stink of mildewed leather.

Then the other bony hand clamped on his knee, and Malcolm MacDonald, starved more than three hundred years, ripped a bite from Alex's calf.

Alex screamed in agony, jerking and setting the two of them swinging wildly.

The grip on his ankle loosened, but a moment later he felt Malcolm clawing at his waist, fastening on the belt of his climbing harness. Alex could only whimper as the ancestor whose body he had planned to loot climbed him like a ladder.

All the time MacDonald had been chewing his first bite. He swallowed with a gulp as he hugged Alex's shoulders.

Alex saw his face come nearer in a terrible parody of a lover seeking a kiss. Leather over bone, with teeth in the middle and hair blooming everywhere. The revenant's breath was horrible: dry, hot, and putrid.

Alex fainted when the yellow teeth met in his cheek, but was unfortunate enough to regain consciousness more than once before it was over.

GLASGOW'S DANCING CORPSE

The year 1818 was a vintage one for those interested in mankind's attempts to conquer mortality. There were two signal events that year that would go on, firstly, to cause widespread and intensely heated debate, and secondly, to implant the idea for the first time ever that science might one day challenge God's hegemony over life and death.

The first of these incidents occurred in London in the January of the year, when a relatively young woman, only 20 years old, published her first novel, the outrageous tale of an ambitious medical student's successful attempt to restore life to deceased flesh by stitching together a patchwork body, the constituent parts having been harvested from the corpses of executed murderers, and subjecting it to repeated electrical shocks.

That author, of course, was Mary Shelley, who in an age when Jane Austen was considered racy enough for most young ladies, had penned what would go on to become the most famous and frightening horror novel of all time: Frankenstein.

For the second incident, we move forward by nine months and travel 400 miles north to Glasgow, where a truly dramatic and macabre event was unfolding.

The city's first public hanging in a decade was a major occurrence because it was a double-event. It seems incredible to modern eyes, but hangings were a huge draw in olden times, crowds flocking from far and wide to watch the brutal demise of the latest felons to terrorise society (so many anticipated on this occasion that soldiers had been posted on the bridge over the Clyde to prevent spectators lining the parapets there and causing the entire structure to collapse).

In this case, only one of the two damned souls was a murderer, Matthew Clydesdale, condemned for drunkenly beating an old man to death. The other man on the gallows was Simon Ross, who faced death for theft, and who, harsh as that might seem, got the worst of it even *then, for when the trapdoor opened and the pair fell side-by-side, it was Ross who lingered longest at the end of the rope. However, if Clydesdale was thought to have been lucky in this regard, his luck was about to run out – at least, in the eyes of the huge crowd gathered outside Glasgow's High Court. Because, while Ross was taken away and given a Christian burial, Clydesdale's corpse was now transported to the Old College quarter of Glasgow University, where two esteemed clinicians, Dr Andrew Ure and Professor James Jeffray, were to conduct several gruesome experiments on him, the primary one being the exposure of his corpse to electrical currents conducted through metal rods from a primitive battery.*

The actual results of this ground-breaking study have been clouded by the sensational stories that spread like wildfire through the city when word first got out about what happened next. And to understand that we need to understand the age.

Though Edinburgh mass murderers Burke and Hare would not give body-snatching a really bad name for another ten years, the 'resurrection men' were hated and feared by ordinary folk in that era. Petty criminals could earn good money by disinterring freshly buried corpses and delivering them secretly to eager anatomists, who, while they were allowed by law to dissect the remains of executed criminals, reckoned they needed up to 500 cadavers per year, which even the most hard-working hangman could never have provided. Because the outcome of this was often well-publicised medical advance, the authorities were inclined to turn a blind eye to these night-time outrages, but common people were appalled by the mere notion. Add to this the 'unnatural acts' described in Frankenstein, *and it was easy for the entire process to become shrouded in horror.*

According to one version of events, Clydesdale's corpse actually came back to life and began struggling with the leather straps holding it to the dissection table. Heaven only knew what the murderer would have done to his captors had someone not thought to promptly stab him to death with a scalpel!

Another tale circulated to the effect that Clydesdale was suspended in ropes when the electrical rods were applied, and that he immediately began dancing, astounding the scientists gathered by performing a frenzied and demonic jig, which only ceased when the rods were removed.

In a third, even more lurid version, the dead convict shrieked and wailed and waved his hands about, clearly not seeing the room around him but lamenting that he was among the damned and suffering the torments of Hell.

The true results were only actually established in the 1980s, when the notes of the medical team who carried out the experiment were finally published.

And in some ways, they are no less horrible.

To start with, quite remarkably, the doctors themselves admitted that this was a genuine attempt to restore a dead man to life. And at first they thought they might have succeeded. Apparently, as soon as the inert figure was charged with electricity, 'Laborious breathing instantly commenced. The chest heaved and fell; the belly was protruded and again collapsed with the retiring and collapsing diaphragm.'

Some of the scientists attending the procedure were so shaken at this point that they apparently fled the chamber. But worse was to come.

When the electrodes were applied to the dead man's skull, 'Every muscle in his countenance was simultaneously thrown into fearful action. Rage, horror, despair, anguish, and ghastly smiles united their hideous expressions in the murderer's face.'

It's little wonder that one of the learned men observing is recorded as having fainted.

None of this would upset us today. We know all about the stimulus of nerve structures via electricity, and defibrillation is a commonly used medical procedure in which electrical currents are applied to a faltering heart.

Back in 1818, however, in the midst of the Frankenstein *scandal, it's hardly a surprise that it caused terror and panic throughout Glasgow. Or that Professor Jeffray's house would later be attacked, stoned and burned by the sort of torch-wielding mob that, during the next century, both Universal and Hammer Horror movies would dine out on.*

LAND OF THE FOREIGNER
Tracy Fahey

Thirteen days. I've been on the island for thirteen days when I see it. Thirteen days at sea, trying to calibrate my position on this strange new map of the Solway Firth. Thirteen days of staring at my new sketchbook with its stiff, blank pages. Thirteen days of waiting for the front door to close so I can surrender to sharp, noiseless jags of crying. Thirteen days of aimless, circular walks; salt tears drying cold on my face in the wind. Thirteen days of thinking *I can't do this.*

At first it seems a tangle of rocks and sharp lines, but as I squint into the fierce morning light, the jumbled shapes resolve themselves into dark skeletons. I frown. It's a ship, or what remains of one. From my vantage point on the jetty, I watch foamy white waves crest against the wreck. Spars of blackened wood jut out; strange, alien. I raise my phone and snap a series of photos; white skies, grey water, black bones. Flicking through the images, I frown; enhancing, cropping, saving. Out of pure habit I open my WhatsApp and upload them to the thread before I bite my lip. *I can't do this.* There's no signal here on the island. More importantly, I promised you I wouldn't.

My breath is a thick flurry in my throat. *I can't do this.* I close down the app and jam my hands in the pockets of my gilet. The ship bones glare back at me, silhouetted hard against the sky. I stand on the soft sand. A wreck at the wreck.

And for the first time in thirteen days, I feel the almost-stirring of a desire to draw.

There's the familiar heart-sink as I push the cottage door open.

'Hey.' Maybe if I act normal, we'll go back to normal.

'I'm in the kitchen.'

'OK!' I kick off my boots. Sand spatters the stone flags. I'll try to remember to clean it up before you see it. We're walking across so many land mines now. The kitchen is dark; as usual you haven't switched the light on. You're at the sink, shoulders hunched. With a guilty stab I realise you're washing the breakfast dishes I left carelessly scattered on the table.

'Hey.' I try to sound upbeat. 'I found the most amazing wreck on the rocks. Not far from the jetty.' I point at the kitchen window, with its view of the boats.

You keep your back turned, scrubbing the cereal bowl in short, determined jerks. 'Oh yeah?'

I stand on one stockinged foot. 'Mmhmm. Think I might try drawing it.'

'That's good, I guess. Good for you to start again Lorna.' *Lawna.* Those flat New England vowels that once made my heart beat faster.

'I might talk to the fishermen about them. About their history. I'd like to know what happened.' I watch the dark curls tangle over your collar. Your hair's getting longer now. I like it.

You let the water out of the sink and wipe your hands on the tea towel. 'Just be careful. You never know what you're asking about. Some things have long histories.' The old pipes gurgle as you hang up the dishcloth. 'I mean, you're Irish. You should know that.'

With a flick of pain, I hear those missing endearments. *Honey*, you'd add. *Darling. Baby.* Now your sentences are sparse. Empty.

'Sure thing,' I say lightly and open the drawer to sort through my pencils. 'Do you want to …?'

You clear your throat. 'I gotta get back to the sanctuary. Marina needs me to check the figures.'

I think of Marina, those hard grey eyes that look past me to you. She disturbs me, and I've lost the right to tell you.

'OK, then, see you later.'

But the front door is already shutting behind you.

I stir into wakefulness. The sheets are cold on my skin. The bed smells unfamiliar. I stretch out a hand, but of course you're already gone. I close my eyes and picture you at the sanctuary with Marina; your clever dark eyes intent on the cliffs, white specks of hovering birds. Rolling over, I bury my face in your pillow; that warm, deep scent of you, skin and hair and that soap you like. With my eyes closed I can almost pretend everything is fine.

I try and draw from photographs, but the sketches feel clumsy, second-hand. My pencil is awkward on the page. I blow away a flurry of eraser crumbs and check my phone out of habit. No signal. There's just the landline here; the ugly plastic phone on the wall. I can't think about everything I miss. I can't. *I can't do this.*

So instead I throw my sketchbook in a bag, pull on the jacket that hangs beside the door, and take the long, meandering walk to the north jetty. It's warmer today; almost hot. The island is starting to flower. Gaudy May bushes cluster in the hedges, their yellow flowers baking in the midday sun, scents of coconut and childhood. This place disconcerts me; so similar and so different to home.

The sea breeze is almost a relief; blowing in cool gusts among the fishing boats. Beyond them, the wreck is still there, still covered by the tidal flow. Out a little are two fisherman, their bodies half-swallowed by water. They're out with the haaf nets now, carrying the rectangular wooden frames and dipping them like pockets into the cold water.

I shiver and remember the time I went swimming in the Atlantic. He and I. Both of us screaming in shock and excitement as the waves beat us back on the shore. His wet-suit on the peg. The salt taste on my tongue. The maritime series I did. The little one of the breakers that hung in his studio. How the light fell on it that last evening. Watching his long-fingered hands patting and twisting clay maquettes into life. How he looked up and caught me; saw those memories in my eyes.

And now I'm here. Banished like an anchorite; walled in by the sea on all sides.

Your face, cold and still with shock. The storm of your words. The silence afterwards, thick and hostile. I waited for you to map us out of it, tell us what to do next. *We tried it your way, Lorna. Now it's my time.* There was nothing I could say. And here we are now, nowhere I recognise.

Taking a deep breath, I sit cross-legged on the jetty. I get my pencil out and start to draw. The sound of the graphite hissing on paper calms me; the deep slashes of black capturing the dramatic contrast of wreck and sky.

'What you drawing there?'

I jump slightly. An old man stands behind me.

'Sorry, you gave me a fright. I'm just drawing that.' I point over at the wreck.

He peers at my page. 'Ah, one of the haunted ships.'

'Tell me about them.' I remember your caution. 'That is, if you don't mind.'

'Nae bother.' His faded blue eyes scan me carefully. 'You're the new lass, aren't you? With the American lad?'

I nod.

'You're not American yourself?'

'No, Irish.'

'Good on you.' I'm used to the reaction; Irishness is a passport around the world, especially in Scotland.

'Thanks,' I say, and feel idiotic. 'It's so beautiful here. So remote. It's very like the Irish countryside where I'm from.'

'Aye.' He sticks his hands in his pockets. 'Must be a bit of a change, though.'

I think of the Scots Gaelic signs, different in spelling, similar when you sound them out in your head. It's been a long voyage; trying to navigate to this island, on this island. You and I in the car, radio swallowing the need for words.

I change the subject. 'The ship?'

'Oh aye. Well, it's a Spanish ship there. Pirates, you ken.

Whole fleet of them came sailing here to loot the island, but the wind blew them off course and they hit the rocks. There's wrecks like this all over the Firth.'

I'm entranced. 'A real pirate ship? I'm surprised it's not a tourist spot.'

He shakes his head. 'We steer clear of it here. Some nights, folk have seen lights on it, or shapes moving where no one should be. They're not to be gone near.' There a pause, then, looking out to sea, he spits on the sand. 'Cursed be the axe that hewed ye.'

'Why do you say that?' I'm fascinated.

He smiles then, his face a red-brown fissure of wrinkles. 'Ach, it's something my mother always said. No luck attached to those ships.'

'I'd like to go out and explore them when the tide is out.'

He's silent for a moment. 'Well, mind how you go. Those Spanish pirates were looking for bonny lassies like you.' He nods and picks up a coil of rough rope.

I watch him walk down the jetty. He doesn't look back.

Sometime that night, in the darkness of the bed, I turn to you. You're lying on your back. Definitely not asleep, I can tell from your breathing; too shallow, too quiet.

'I'm going to go to the mainland tomorrow.'

You sigh. 'Right.'

'I want to go to the library. Do you need anything?'

'No.' You turn away with a cross shrug, a sign for me to stop talking. I do. We lie like that, two effigies in our mattressed tomb, until I sleep, strange dreams of ship timbers, jagged against the waves. When pale dawn streaks the sky, you slide out of bed and make your careful way down the stairs. I listen to the stranger downstairs, clattering the saucepans and wonder how long this silence can last for.

It tastes feels like freedom, that clear, salt wind that tangles my hair. The sounds are hypnotic; screams of gulls, the susurration of the waves, and the sharp crack as they break against the wooden side of the boat; *shurrrr-ACK, shurrrr-ACK, shurrrr-ACK*. I see Kirkcudbright draw nearer, the giant castle dominating the horizon, rows of crooked houses and shops like teeth below it. My boots clack on the wooden gangway and I'm there. Back in civilisation. I catch sight of my reflection in a window; tousled hair, unmade-up face, tatty anorak. For a moment I close my eyes and picture myself back in Dublin, in the gallery, with him … No. I can't think about that.

The library, oddly, is in a converted church. The cool of the interior calms me. War memorials bracket the shelves; a stained glass window floods the floor with intricate coloured shapes. I wander round the aisles, through popular fiction, non-fiction, young adult literature, the brightly coloured books of the children's corner, before giving up.

'Is there a local history section here?'

The girl behind the desk is absorbed in her phone.

'Yeah.' She barely looks up, a flicker of resentment in her face.

I'm patient. 'Where exactly?'

The girl jabs a thumb at an old filing cabinet to the right of the desk. 'There's your best bet.'

'Thanks,' I say, but she's already thumbing through her phone. I see red hearts flash up on her Instagram page.

She's right. The cabinet is full of clippings, graded by a random system I can't quite guess at – alphabetical? By era? But search as I may, I can't locate anything about the Spanish wrecks the old man told me about. I'm as surely at sea as I was on the boat. Dusty and a little cross, I give up and resign myself to an afternoon of rambling around the shops until the boat comes in.

I've missed it; those aimless rambles around urban spaces. Not that Kirkcudbright is a metropolis, but there's a strange illicit joy in staring at displays of shoes (too pretty and impractical for the island), buying a mango drink with basil seeds from the halal shop, stuffing a swathe of colourful fashion magazines in my bag to read later in the cold grey light of home. And there's so many artists – granted most of them are hawking tourist wares of ceramic cottages or paintings of waves and rocks – but seeing their little studios, their prints, their willow work, their photographs and paintings, all stir within me a deep, grinding envy. Even the town sign is a palette dotted with paint.

Finally I sit down, an overpriced latte in my hand and do what's been on my mind all along. I check my phone. The signal has come up; my screen is dotted with notifications. Facebook. Twitter. Instagram. Pinterest. Email. WhatsApp. It's been two weeks surviving with just a landline. I'm almost overwhelmed. I flip in and out of the apps on my screen; so many notifications, so little news. And then I see it on Whatsapp. Three new messages. My heart blunders in my ears.

Him. Xaquin.

My hands are shaking. I press the icon of his face; dark and brooding.

'Where are you?'

'I miss you.'

'Come back.'

I read them. Three stupid, tiny messages. But I look at them, on and off for the rest of the afternoon. I only delete them when I'm on the boat back. As they disappear from the screen, I lean over the side and let the spray lash my face like a flagellation. *I can't do this.*

I'm standing on the bones of the wreck. The sea is quiet today, lacing the rocks with a white, mild froth. But I'm not deceived. I've seen how quickly it can rise, whip, crash. I wobble. It's hard to balance. The old wood is rotted and slippery, washed with seaweed, polished with pebbles. I stroke the blackened spars, imagining the ships in full sail off the coast, tossed in a storm, men shouting, straining hard against the pull of the sea, the tumble and roar of the waves.

Here on the Firth I float between two worlds. Home and the

island. England and Scotland. You and him. There's a fragment of figurehead under my fingertips; a sliver of an impassive face, cracked and worn. I think of her, breasting the fierce sea, and shiver, in spite of the steady warmth of the sun. I focus my camera and start snapping; mesmerised by the textures of the dark timbers, the fragment of figurehead. I think of him then. How much he'd love this. How he'd touch the wood with those clever hands, gauging the best way to capture their volume, their essence. There's a crevasse in my chest; a vacuum of air.

I try to remember how much he hurt me. I try to remember how much I hated him. But even as those feelings rise they drown in the memories of that last night. Your face. Your dear, numb face.

A wave flips up, licking me with a careless flourish. It splashes; jumping I stumble, slip, ankle caught between rock and wood. I thrust out a hand to steady myself on the rocks. A piece of metal digs sharp into my palm.

'Ow!' I clench my fist over the cold shard, and then open it. It's a coin of some sort. It's pitted and black and strangely oily to the touch, but I put it in my pocket. The sea is starting to rise now, in that sly treacherous way it does, so I slide carefully off the old timbers and hop-skip over the rocks to the shore. The old fisherman is sitting on the jetty, on a rickety wooden chair, face tilted to the sun.

'Hello,' I call. He turns his head and sees me, sees the camera in my hand, the wreck behind. An expression flits over his face – wry disappointment, resignation – I can't tell.

'Look!' I show him the coin. 'See what I found.'

He looks me full in the face. 'You took that from the ship?'

'Yes, I think it might be an old Spanish dollar. Pieces of eight, just like in *Treasure Island.*'

He makes a sound that is halfway between a snort and a laugh. 'Be careful, Irish lassie. Always be careful what you take.'

His blank brown gaze is disconcerting. 'Right,' I say, pocketing the coin again. 'Good luck with the work.'

I walk home the long way, buying time. The house is in darkness when I get there. I sit in the thick silence and download the photos onto my computer. The impassive, one-eyed figurehead; her broken nose, her splinter of mouth. The grain of the wood. The white curl of waves against the wreck. A shadow falls over the window. I sigh and get up to flick the kettle on, pushing back my hair, preparing my welcoming smile.

But when I go to the door there's no-one there. I wait up for a few hours as the gloom greys to charcoal, before I give up and go to bed. Somewhere in my dreams I hear the door creak open, but I don't even open my eyes as your weight presses down your side of the bed.

I'm the first to wake. I slip out of bed, your body a grenade I don't want to touch. All I can think of are the photographs on my computer. I print them off, touching the glossy surfaces possessively. The wreck. My wreck. By the time you come down for breakfast I'm surrounded by sheets of paper, smudged with black.

'Lorna.' You're shocked into speaking. It's been weeks, months since you've seen me like this, completely absorbed. Your presence is disconcerting; it brings me out of my trance. 'What are these?'

'It's the old wreck. Remember I told you about it?'

You look at the sketches, flipping them over. 'I like them,' you say. It's a tiny thing, but it's a chink in our deadened silence. 'So did you find out anything about it?'

'Yeah. The old fisherman at the harbour. It's part of an old fleet. A proper pirate ship.'

'Wow. Good detective work.' You stand close to me. The closest you've been in a while. The heat of your arm is palpable against mine. I'm breathing a little harder.

'He said they were Spanish pirates.'

Your face closes up. I've said the S-word. He hangs between us; a dark spectre. 'Right,' you say, your voice carefully neutral. 'Guess I'll head back out now. Marina'll be waiting at the sanctuary.'

I breathe in. Behind me, the door closes with a polite click. I grab my jacket and throw it across the room in a hot spurt of frustration. The old coin rolls out and spins on the stone floor with a chittering *cling*. I pick it up. It's slick and slightly warm to the touch.

I draw all that afternoon, and the next morning. I'm finally in that zone, you know; that miracle place that I always crave. That place where there's nothing but the marks on the page; where the world melts back into hushed irrelevance. The old clock ticks. Birds flit by the window sill. I forget about where we are; this island, floating in the sea. I forget about my untethered self. I draw and draw.

'Lorna?'

I start, and realise the room is purpled in twilight. The light has deepened into velvety shade, the furniture casts indigo shadows.

'Alex.' I rub my eyes with dirty, charcoaled hands. 'Sorry, I was miles away.'

You look at me then. No love, just coldness. 'Who was that outside?'

'Outside?' I blink, confused.

'I'm not stupid, Lorna. I saw someone outside.' You articulate the words slowly and carefully. 'At. The. Door. Just now.'

'There's been no-one here. Are you sure you saw someone? I didn't hear a knock.'

'Don't play me. I know what I saw. If someone's been here …'

'Someone?' I realise what you mean, the knowledge tilts me; makes me dizzy. I place my palms flat on the table. 'Oh for God's sake! You can't think—?'

But you do think it, you do. Improbably, you think he's here. I see it written harsh on your face.

'Don't push me too far.' You say it *fah*. I used to laugh teasingly when you did, loving the accent. Now it's just one more thing we don't do.

You pick up the old coin from the table and examine it, before setting it down on the window sill. 'Well, I guess I'll leave you to your drawing.' The contemptuous flick on the word 'drawing' makes my eyes sting with tears. 'I'm going back out. Don't wait up for me. I'm going to Marina's for dinner.'

It's only after you've gone that I give in. Tears shiver down my cold cheeks, puddle on the charcoal sketch.

All the long next day, I draw. My right wrist aches from the effort of holding the pencil, so I switch to a brush, pooling dark inlets of ink on the sketches beneath. You come back at lunchtime; a surprise. I wash my inky hands and make sandwiches, thick doorsteps of bread; slabs of cheese with the French grain mustard you like. You eat without comment but your eyes flick over my work.

'They're good,' you say grudgingly, finally.

'Don't sound so surprised.' I try and smile, but it's not returned. You continue to chew.

'You're hungry. Didn't Marina feed you properly last night?'

'Mmm.' You refuse to be drawn. I used to like your self-control, now I yearn for you to lose your temper. Shout at me. Anything but this horrid, polite silence.

There's a sharp knock at the door. We both jump. 'Who is it?'

You look at me strangely. 'Well, I don't know. Answer it.'

I know it's not him. How could it be him? But my heart knocks hard in my chest anyhow. I open the old door.

'Oh.' It's the old fisherman from the jetty.

'Morning, lassie.' He has a plastic bag in his hand. 'Morning to you, too.' He nods to include Alex.

'Hello,' I say stupidly. 'How are you?'

'The haaf netting went well today. Thought you might like fish for dinner.' He holds up what I think is a sea trout.

'Oh thank you.' I'm already wondering how you bone fresh-caught fish.

'Yes, thank you. You're so kind.' You're all charm now, shaking his hand. 'I'm Alex. I work for Marina in the sanctuary.'

The old man chuckles. 'I'm Tom. And sure I knew who you were. There aren't many folk on this island.'

'True enough.'

I go and put the fish carefully on a plate. Voices overlap in a buzz of conversation; fish, birds, the island. I stow the plate in the fridge, leaning for a moment into its cool hum. The door closes.

'Nice old guy.' You stand beside me, inspecting the fish. 'I'll gut it later if you like.' There it is; that kindness that once melted me. Just a flash, but it's enough for now.

The weather's changed. Sheets of drizzle sweep over the island. I shiver when I go for my morning walk, face cold and wet in the rain. The waves below whip up into a cold froth of salt, covering the wreck. I sniff in the damp air. It feels charged with electricity. You're at home today, working on the computer. The handles of the plastic bag bite my fingers; the milk carton hangs heavy as I walk. Nearly there. The rain comes down harder now. I see you outside and wave, but you don't wave back. I wipe a wet hand over my forehead and look again, but you're gone.

'I'll make the tea now, I got the milk from McTaggart's,' I call as I take my boots off. My blonde hair is plastered to my head, dark and sopping.

'Great.' I open the kitchen door. The table is still a drift of my drawings. Twenty-three at the last count. You look up.

I cock my head. 'You're not wet!'

He looks up, startled. 'Why, should I be?'

'I just saw you outside.'

He raises his eyebrows. 'Not me.'

'Oh.' I'm disconcerted. 'Maybe I just imagined it.' I flick the kettle switch on, and get the mugs out. 'Just going to the bathroom.'

When I come out, you're standing by the coat-rack. Your face is startled. My phone is in your hand.

'I thought it was ringing.'

Liar, I think as you drop it back in the coat pocket. I know what you were looking for. And then a wave of shame; relief too, that I deleted those texts. If you'd found them … I turn away and put teabags into the mugs.

Rain patters on the window pane. I bring out the tea, and put a mug by your elbow. Light catches the old coin on the sill. I pick it up. My thumb traces the metal grooves as it heats in my hand. There's a wave of weariness. How much longer can we keep doing this? How much longer before you break? Or before I do?

I drop the coin in my pocket. It sits there, warm against my thigh.

Twenty-five drawings now. I'm a fever of work. Outside the rain still rages. The ink flows, sure and straight, in bold lines. I'm lost in the motion. Cups of tea cool beside me, undrunk. From time to time I glance up, thinking I see Alex outside, but it's just the gulls, flying low in the rain.

I'm upstairs that evening, trying to scrub the stains off my hands when the knocking starts. Damn it. I wipe my grey hands hastily on the old towel and run downstairs.

'Hello?' The door swings away from me, catching in a wet gust of wind.

No-one. I look in every direction, squinting in the gloom. *Surely I'd see whoever it was.* I replay the knocking; an unmistakeable sound of knuckles on wood.

When you come back, face shiny with rain, I tell you. Or I try to. Your face tells me you don't believe me.

'Honestly. It scared me. I can't think who would have done it.'

'Probably some kids.' You're inspecting the fridge. It doesn't take long, I forgot to go shopping.

'Maybe we could go back to the mainland once the storm dies down?'

He says nothing, but his face darkens. I persevere. 'Just for a night. Or back to Ireland? Take a break?'

'I don't know what you want me to say, Lorna.' Your voice is cool. 'It's your fault we had to leave Dublin. We agreed this was my time, my chance to take up a job I wanted. A fresh start. And now, what a surprise, you want to leave.'

I open my mouth, but there's nothing to say. The anger is plain and stark on your face. It swallows me whole.

'We're not going back to Dublin. And that's that.'

'Right.' I breathe in and rub the coin in my pocket like a talisman. Outside, boats bob up and down on the jetty, stirred by a fierce sea.

It's the third day of storms.

Twenty-seven drawings now.

I'm scratchy after a night of bad dreams; a night of swimming awake in the dim room, your body an angry hunch beside me. I think you're asleep and reach one tentative finger across, craving to touch that creamy skin I know as well as my own.

'Go to sleep, Lorna.' Your voice cuts sharp through the darkness.

It's no use. I'm wide awake. I go downstairs and study the last drawing. It's bigger than the others, more ambitious. The subject is the same; the wreck again, but this time lashed by waves. The dark spars thrust through the water, jagged bones. I stand back and study it. It's good. I know it's good. But there's still something missing.

The sky has lightened to a pearl grey when I find it; the perfect addition. A dark figure on the rocks. The face is obscured by dark slashes of hair. I can almost feel it, soaked and whipping; an angry flag. My ink flowers black and bold on the page.

'Oh, you're up.' You're on the stairs, sleepy, barefoot, hair a wild tangle. I want to stroke it, but last night's argument still hangs heavy in the air. When the phone rings and Marina calls you into work it's a relief.

After you leave I can't settle down to any more inking. That last piece has exorcised whatever it was about the wreck that galvanised me. I'm tired and spent and, oddly, craving a cigarette; a pang I haven't felt in years. I toy with the notion of going to McTaggart's shop, cracking the cellophane of the pack, taking that deep, acrid inhale. But the rain pelts down, harder and harder, so I pull the old coin out of my jeans and turn it over and over in my fingers; a worry bead.

That night, the sea is wild. We hear it over the din of the rain on the roof; a crashing, omnipresent roar. I'm cleaning the kitchen. An unusual step, but what's the option? Sitting stiffly beside you on the sofa? Trying to avoid seeing how you flinch when our arms brush together?

Somewhere over the water, there's an opening in the gallery. The big glass window steamed up with condensation; blurred figures massing around the bar. I dunk the mop in the bleach-scented water and twist it savagely in the plastic colander. There'll be sparkling wine and catalogues; fresh flowers in the vases. He'll be there, of course, lapping up praise, a smile for every pretty girl in the room.

'You want some popcorn?' You inch your way gingerly over to the microwave, stockinged feet curled up to minimise contact with the wet floor.

'No,' I say shortly, and slop some water out on the stone flags, harder than intended.

'Please yourself. Oh yeah, you always do.' The microwave whirrs, you tap your fingers, waiting. The air is filled with crackling and the warm scent of butter.

My shoulders tense. *I can't do this.* I want a fight. I need a fight. Those words within need to spill out before they corrode us to the bone. 'What's wrong with you?'

'Do you really need to ask?' Your voice is cold. The popcorn snaps; one final smothered pop, and it stops.

I let the mop drop out of my hands. The plastic handle stutters and lies still. 'Yes. Yes I do.' I need this fight. I look at you, your dishevelled hair, your narrow, clever face and my heart turns over in anger and longing. It was just a *kiss.* He kissed *me.*

And as we face each other, the silence shatters. A pounding at the door.

'Jesus!' You jump. 'Who the hell is that?'

I'm livid. 'How should I know? Marina? Tom the fisherman? McTaggart from the fucking *shop*?'

The pounding comes again.

'Maybe there's been an accident?' You cross the floor, jostling against me in an almost-push.

'Don't shove me!'

'Shhh.' You pause with one hand on the door, panic-stricken at the thought of someone witnessing our fight. 'For God's sake, calm down.'

The hammering starts again. And then a deep voice calls.

'LORNA!'

Now it's my turn to jump.

'LORNA, COME OUT.' Oh God. I look at you.

'DIOS MIO! COME OUT!'

Him? I'm panic-stricken with guilt. Those messages he sent. He's come. I grab the door handle.

'Lorna.' Your voice is a whip crack. 'Do *not* open that door.'

The thumping intensifies. I imagine I see the wood bend inwards. 'But what if it's an emergency?'

You're pale with rage. 'As God is my witness, if you open that door, it's over.'

For a moment I consider doing it anyway, throwing it recklessly open to the rain and roar of the waves, open to him. But even in this red rage I don't want to.

'GO AWAY,' I shout, and just for a second, your face relaxes.

'Lorna, he's crazy. Don't let him in!' You've picked up the landline. 'I'm calling the police.' But even across the room I can hear it, the *dee-dee-dee* of the disconnected line.

Your eyes meet mine. 'What the hell do we do?'

'LORNA.'

'Oh God, I don't *know*.' I'm crying now. In the crack under the door I can see the dark outline of feet.

You drag the heavy old dresser out from the wall. 'Come on, help me.' Together we pull it over to the door, lean its solid old weight against the frame.

He's still out there, shouting my name. Still hammering at the door. And just then, as the wind howls, the lights go out. This is a horror film. We grab each other. *Could we make a break for it? Could we reach the next house?* But the storm is whipping up outside, louder and louder. The roof tiles creak; the whole house seems to sway.

'Did you tell him you were here?'

'No!' It's the truth. You can see it in my face.

'He's lost his mind!'

'Yes.' I cry harder. 'I'm scared of him, Alex.'

And somehow, in the welter of noise, the rage of the storm, the shouts, the banging, it's all you want to hear.

'I'll protect you. I won't let him in.' Somewhere overhead there's an almighty crash. Intense light flashes. Our faces revealed; pale and raw and stunned.

'LORNA. COME OUT.'

I close my fingers around the old coin in my pocket. I throw it hard at the door. It spins and rolls under the crack between the wood and the stone flags.

And then everything stops.

He's gone.

The wind spirals back down, the rattling dies away.

We sit with our backs to the dresser. Somehow your hand finds mine. I grab it and press it, tight, tight, our fingers together knotted and rigid. We watch the window as the orange dawn streaks the sky.

'Is it safe?'

You inhale sharply. 'I think so. Let me go see.' You lean over the sill, trying to see outside the door. 'I see something ...'

You slide behind the dresser.

'Be careful!' My voice is strained.

'Sure.' There's the sound of the latch being lifted. A creak. Then silence.

'Jesus H Christ. Lorna!'

'What?' I'm already squeezing behind the dresser. The door is open. You're standing there, stunned.

'Look.'

It's *me*. My heart jolts in my chest. 'Oh God!'

'It's OK, baby. It's just a ... a thing.'

And as I look closer, it's not me. Just a ship's figurehead, carved to look like me, propped up against the side of the door. There's my blonde hair, my hazel eyes, the uneven teeth. The face I see every day when I'm brushing my teeth in the spotted bathroom mirror. *If that's his, it's the best work he's ever done.*

I touch it. It feels dry, flushed with an unpleasant heat. I shiver, withdrawing my hand. Our eyes meet.

'What will we do with it?'

Your face is grim. 'I know exactly what we're going to do with it.'

We burn it.

You get the petrol we keep in the shed for the mower and slosh it over the awful effigy. I watch, trembling, and hand you the matches. I just want it gone.

And as the sky lightens to pale orange, the smoke drifts upwards. The figurehead crackles and sparks. We stand there like soldiers, watching it burn, right down to a smouldering heap.

'It's over,' I say and breathe deep in the smoky air. The ashes are sour on my tongue.

'It's over, honey.' You pull me to you. A great sob chokes in my chest. Your arms are light and warm, but you hold me tight, just like I remember. We're finally here; we've found our way back. I map the dear, familiar contours of your face under my fingertips, and we kiss.

We kiss warm and deep.

We kiss as the ashes drift around us, circling slowly upwards, rising, twirling over the waves, floating above the wreck and into the Firth beyond.

THE BLOODIEST OF ENDS

The Reformation was one of the most dramatic events in world history. Commencing with Martin Luther's demands for reform in 1517, it gradually evolved into a full-on challenge to papal authority all across Western Europe. But despite the idealism with which these new movements were promoted, this was still the chaotic Middle Ages, and a new series of bitter struggles commenced, religious wars and persecutions erupting all over Christendom, leading to some astonishing atrocities over the next two centuries.

Scotland was no exception, many Scottish martyrs dying terrible deaths.

Prominent Protestants like James Ravelson and Helen Stark ('along with her sucking infant'!) were respectively burned at the stake and drowned in a sack at Perth in 1544, while Father John Ogilvie, a Catholic, was hanged and disembowelled in Glasgow in 1615. And even when neither politics nor religion were to the fore, the laying of violent hands on churchmen now became much more common. After all, the apparent supernatural status of God's Anointed had been called out. Clerics were mere mortals like the rest of us.

Two amazingly grim examples of this can be found in the Scottish annals.

Gilbert Kennedy, 4th Earl of Cassillis, was described as a profane and rapacious man. In that regard he is probably not much different from other landowners of the 16th century, but in the year 1570 he was especially enraged to be denied lands that he'd expected to inherit from Crossraguel Abbey in South Ayrshire. The beneficiary of the ruling was the Commendator of Crossraguel, one Allan Stewart, a man whose claim to be the new abbot was also hotly contested by Kennedy.

In due course, having exhausted various legal means by which to take ownership of the lands, Kennedy sent 16 ruffians to abduct Stewart and bring him by force to his coastal stronghold of Dunure Castle. Stewart continued to refuse to sign over the estates in question, so Kennedy had him dragged down to the so-called Black Vault, where he was stripped naked, rubbed all over with goose fat and then (with the aid of Kennedy's enthusiastic kitchen staff) tied to a spit and roasted over an open fire. How long this abominable torture lasted is unclear, but it was done at least twice, and on both occasions Stewart continued to be poured with fat so that he would cook rather than burn.

Incredibly, the abbot survived the ordeal, primarily because he was rescued by his own supporters, though not before he had signed over the disputed lands to Kennedy. He was even able to denounce Kennedy himself at the Cross of Ayr in front of the Scottish Privy Council, though he was described in court records as being horribly burned and crippled, and indeed he never walked again. To complete the astonishing story, Gilbert Kennedy, who had treated a holy man in a manner that would have been unthinkable a few decades earlier, was only fined.

The second case relates to the murder of Cardinal David Beaton in 1546.

Beaton was the last Scottish cardinal prior to the Reformation, but a vain and ambitious man, who made himself one of the regents of the infant Mary, Queen of Scots by forging a document from her late-father, James V. He was also an eager hunter of Protestants, some of whom he imprisoned in a nightmarish bottle-shaped dungeon, which can still be seen underneath St Andrews Castle, others whom he consigned to the flames, including the learned George Wishart, part of whose conviction was secured on the grounds that he was a married priest. Wishart was executed by being hanged in a fire at St Andrews in 1546, a grim spectacle that Beaton watched without guilt, even though in two days' time he would be a guest at the wedding of his own illegitimate daughter.

Beaton's demise came two months later, partly in revenge for the death of Wishart, but also because his main enemies, the aristocratic Leslie family, whose political interests in their native Fife had been nullified by Beaton's own rise to power, saw it as their big chance. John and Norman Leslie were among a group of armed men who seized St Andrew's Castle in May that year. They protractedly and savagely beat Cardinal Beaton, finally stabbing him to death and hanging his mutilated corpse by an arm and leg from one of the parapets, so that it would mockingly form a St Andrew's Cross. In later years, a children's rhyme – 'for stickit is your cardinal, salted like a sow' – referred to the murderers' treatment of the body, which they afterwards pickled for preservation so they could keep it in the dung pits under the castle and continue to abuse it at their leisure.

This latter slaying is particularly interesting, as theories held (and still do), that Henry VIII of England, who found Cardinal Beaton's confirmed Catholicism a nuisance, might actually have been behind it (and indeed, it cleared the way for Protestantism to take root in Scotland). A sure indication that the end was coming for churchmen who thought they could command princes.

PROUD LADY IN A CAGE
Fred Urquhart

'Here, hen, are ye sleepin'?'

The voice came from among the women skirling and shouting obscenities around the cage, laughing lewdly and gloating over the prisoner's humiliation. It came from a small wizened-faced witch who had joukit past the English guards and was rattling the iron bars. The prisoner stood erect and looked disdainfully over the harridan's head. But she could not ignore her. The leering face grew larger and larger, blotting out the other women; the rattling got louder and the voice shriller, drowning the screams and the jeers.

'I cannie stand here all day till you come out o' yer daydreams, hen. I asked a civil question, and I want a civil answer.'

Bella Logan came back through the whirling currents of centuries until her eyes focussed on the woman's face. She shook her head to clear away the nightmare. She was aware again of the intense cold, and her teeth chattered.

'Are ye all right, hen?' the little woman said, peering inquisitively with bird-bright eyes through the glass and thin gilt bars encircling the enquiry desk. Bella recognised her as Mrs Cessford, who lived in a vennel on the banks of the Tweed with her grandson, Zander, a tall skeleton-thin lad with long carroty hair who did odd jobs in the supermarket.

'Ye look as if ye'd seen a ghost, hen.'

'I'm okay,' Bella whispered. 'I think.'

She closed her eyes for a moment and saw again the crowd of harpies and the great iron bars of the cage. Her neck was still raw from the rope that had been around it.

'Is it yer monthly, hen?' Mrs Cessford leered sympathetically.

'Oh, I ken what it is!'

Bella nodded. It was a lie. But better to pretend to this old bitch than have her blazoning the truth abroad. Not that anyone would believe what had been happening to her. The cold terror of it drooped over her like a frozen shroud.

'I was wantin' the shredded wheat, hen,' Mrs Cessford said. 'I've been huntin' everywhere but I cannie find it. Where have they put it? Or are ye no' sellin' such simple things as shredded wheat in this braw new place? I cannie see why ye needed to move. The auld store in the Wool Market was guid enough for me and folk like me. I don't think I'll ever get used to this great barn o' a place.'

Bella held her throat with one hand as she directed Mrs Cessford to Aisle Seven where the cereals and their assorted companions were shelved. 'Ta, hen!' Mrs Cessford leered and set off, her shopping bag and the supermarket's wire basket slapping against her spindly shanks on either side. 'You watch that period now, and I'll dance at yer weddin'.'

Bella shivered. The enquiry desk that stood on a raised dais in the middle of the new supermarket had felt like a refrigerator ever since she set foot in it this morning, just before the store opened for the first time. She was in the cash desk of the old store, and while this new building near the railway station was going up, Mr Stott, the manager, had offered her promotion, asking her to take charge of the enquiry desk the owners thought necessary in the new supermarket's vastness. 'Our public is sure to get lost and need a helping hand, Miss Logan,' Mr Stott had simpered. Bella experienced a pleasant glow of satisfaction, thinking of the rise in salary, when she entered it for the first time. But the glow had been dispelled by the sudden unearthly chill that had crept through her limbs. And then *that* had happened.

Despite the darts of icy cold that still pierced every part of her, her neck burned. It was a great red-hot itch. She closed her eyes and massaged it with her fingertips. Then she felt herself being drawn back into the nightmare. Once again the rope was almost choking her. Once again, she could see the great backside of the horse she'd been dragged behind, her hands tied at her back. The soldier on the horse had turned round every now and then, laughing and jeering at her as he jerked the rope to make her stumble. And the watching crowd laughed with him, shouting: 'Come 'n' see the prood leddy bein' draggit through the mire! Come 'n' see braw Bella o' Buchan drinkin' in the reek frae the horse's dock!'

They had come to an iron cage suspended by chains from the castle's battlements. The cage was about six feet high and three feet in diameter. It swung a yard and a half above the ground. The rope was taken from her neck, her hands were untied; then two soldiers lifted her and flung her so violently through the door of the cage that she fell, banging her forehead against the bars. She was raising herself on her knees when the door clanged. A herald started a proclamation, but she could hear nothing until he came to the words: '… be incarcerated here in this burgh of Berwick-on-Tweed during His Majesty's pleasure. And may God have mercy on her and cause her to repent and plead for the mercy of His Majesty.'

'Never!' she cried, standing straight in the narrow cage and looking disdainfully over the heads of the crowd.

It was then that the harpies had surged forward, surrounding the cage and cackling obscenely.

Bella lifted her handbag from the floor beside her feet and took out a small mirror. Looking to make sure nobody was watching, she held the mirror to her neck. There was a broad red weal around it.

She shivered with cold and dread. Had she fallen asleep and was it a nightmare? But she knew she hadn't slept. And the livid weal was not out of a dream.

Bella Logan was totally lacking in imagination. She knew nothing of history or tradition; she was prosaic and unromantic. She never read a book. Every week she bought two or three women's magazines but never read anything in them except the knitting patterns. She knitted constantly. In the cash desk in the old store she had always had a partly knitted jumper or pullover, scarf or socks on her knee, knitting needles clicking quickly between customers. A part-finished magenta cardigan was in the pink-and-fawn striped knitting bag lying at her feet this morning, but she hadn't managed to take it out yet. She never made mistakes with her additions on the cash-register, never dropped a stitch or made miscalculations with her knitting. In The Kelpie, the pub seven miles from Berwick that she visited on Saturday nights with Rod Wishart, she chalked the scores of the darts team on the blackboard, and never once had anybody found her making a mistake. She did the mental arithmetic easily, automatically, and was usually talking to somebody while doing it.

Bella was twenty-two. She was an only child, lived with her parents and was dominated by her mother. Mrs Logan, in her turn, was dominated by her mother, Mrs Dickie, a formidable eighty-three-year-old. Mrs Dickie's name was Isabella, though she'd always been called Bella. She had christened her daughter Isabella too, but Isa Logan had insisted on being called Isa since she was four years old; she would never, on any account, answer to 'Bella'. Yet when she christened her own daughter Isabella, she decreed that the child was to be called 'Bella' from the start. 'After your granny, dear. You love your granny, don't you? So what could be better than being called after her? We can't have two Isas in the house. It would be a fine how-d'ye-do and cause no end of trouble. So Bella you're going to be, my girl. And like it.'

Bella Logan never protested. She accepted the name as phlegmatically as she accepted everything else. When rude boys at school used to shout, 'Let me rub your belly, Bella!' she had always tossed her head and sniffed. Once, after he had been to Sicily for ten days' holiday, Rod Whishart had said: 'Bella! It means beautiful in Italian. Bella bellissima!'

'So what?' Bella said.

She had been walking out with Rod Wishart for three years. They had never had sexual relations, though often Rod's need had been urgent when they were walking over the golf links in the dark or when they'd been coming home in his firm's car after drinking at The Kelpie. But Bella would never do anything to ease him. 'I'm not going to do it till we're married,' she said. 'I respect myself if you don't, Rod Wishart. My mother would have fifty fits if she knew what you keep trying to do.'

'Well, let's get married then,' he always replied. 'What're we waiting for?'

'I'm not going to get married till I'm twenty-five. I don't see why I should tie myself down.'

'What about me?' he said. 'I can't go on like this. I want us to get settled down and … and, well, I suppose we should have some bairns …'

'I don't want to be a mother just yet,' she said primly. 'Besides, you keep saying your firm might shift you to another territory. We'd better wait till that gets settled.'

Rod was the representative for a company that sold agricultural foods and seeds to farmers. He spent most of his life in the open, standing in farmyards talking about the price of cattle cake, grain and fertilizers. At the weekend, he played full-back for a Berwickshire rugby team. He was twenty-nine, a big dark young man with a ruddy complexion and blue eyes. He went out with the boys several nights a week. Bella's father, owner of a good-going small builder's business, kept saying: 'It's high time you stopped playin' rugger, Rod, and did some tackling in your own back yard.'

Rod always said he'd retire from rugger when he was thirty. 'And then it'll be up to Bella.'

This year he was going to Jugoslavia for a holiday with some of his team-mates. 'It'll be my last fling with the boys, Mr Logan.'

Last year Bella had gone abroad for the first time. She and Rod went to Majorca, but what between Rod's amorousness, brought on by the strong sunshine and the Spanish atmosphere, and the food not agreeing with her finicky stomach, she had not enjoyed herself. This year she was going to be a devil, though, and give abroad another chance: she and

Peggy Allardyce, her best friend, were going to Venice for a fortnight in September.

Peggy Allardyce, who ran one of the cash-desks, had taken over the enquiry desk while Bella was at lunch. 'My, you've got a fine cosy wee corner here, dear,' she said when her friend returned. 'It's real groovy, and I love it. You're a right lucky-bag, Bell.'

Bella made a face, but she said nothing. She started to shrug out of her cardigan while watching Peggy click-clack on high heels towards the exit. But she had scarcely sat down at the desk before she quickly pulled the cardigan back on. It was chillier here than outside. She picked up her bag of knitting. There were few customers in the supermarket at this hour, and it was hardly likely anybody would stop to ask her anything. As she was counting her stitches somebody placed a dead-cold finger on her forehead and pressed it into her skull. The pain and the cold were excruciating. Then the finger moved backwards over her skull and down her spine. As it moved, icy waves swept over the rest of her body. She gasped for breath and huddled her cardigan tighter around her.

The rain was coming down in torrents. She clung to the bars of the cage with hands so frozen she was sure the skin would come off if she let go of the iron. Her palms burned. Her saturated gown clung to her body, encasing her like armour. The cage had been pulled up higher; it hung now about ten feet from the ground. The downpour had driven away most of the crowd who came to gloat, but many women had taken refuge from the deluge in doorways and windows, from whence their gimlet-brimstone eyes probed into her humiliation and their frog-gawped mouths opened to shout insults. Among them were the old witch with the dirty white hair who came every day and the red-headed youth who was always with her. The English sentries still stood around the cage. They were almost as soaked as she was, but every now and then they took turns to escape into an embrasure in the castle walls and sheltered there for a while.

She had been in the cage for seven days and seven nights. She was fed and watered like an animal, but the cage was never mucked out. She thought of what they had done to William Wallace at Smithfield last year. Fine handsome Sir William who had endured such degradation and agony before death mercifully came. She remembered Sir William, after the battle of Stirling Bridge, coming to Methven Castle to discuss his campaign against the English with her father, the old Earl of Fife. She had been but a child in that year 1297 but she had fallen in love a little with the handsome knight. She closed her eyes. A quarter of his tortured, dismembered body had been displayed here in Berwick last year. She wondered if her own head might not grace a spike on Berwick's walls, unless Edward, the so-called Hammer of the Scots, God rot him, considered it important enough to flaunt on London Bridge.

She clasped her hands around her neck and shuddered.

'The braw leddy's pee-ed hersel'!' the white-haired witch shrilled. 'See ye! The grand leddy's water is juist like yours and mine.'

After a time the rain slackened. It turned into a drizzle. She wanted to shake her shoulders to ease away the dress clinging to her back, but she would not do this before the rabble. She was gazing upwards, intent on ignoring all taunts, when there was a creaking of the chains by which the cage was suspended. It began to come down. Its descent was so uneven that she was forced to grip the bars to steady herself. It was about shoulder-high from the ground when a scullion ran from the castle gate carrying a plate of food. He thrust the plate through the bars and emptied its mess of boiled oatmeal and pieces of half-raw meat on to the floor.

'Eat hearty, my lady!' he jeered before running back to the gate.

A big brosy-faced soldier standing in the embrasure laughed. He fumbled with his crotch and shouted: 'Wouldst like a taste of this meat, lady? Put thy hand through the bars and grasp it.'

She turned her back on him, but this made her face the doorway in which the old witch and the red-headed youth were sheltering. The youth put his hand between his legs and imitated the soldier, shouting lewd remarks.

She had such a convulsion of disgust that her entrails seemed to rush in icy globules up to her throat. A great wave of terror coursed through her. Bella did not know whether she screamed or not. She came back to the present, clutching her throat. Someone was making spine-shuddering scratching noises on the glass of the enquiry desk.

A tall thin gangling youth with greasy carroty hair hanging well below his narrow shoulders was leering at her. 'How ye doin', Miss Logan?' he mouthed. The wisps of his straggly moustache and beard could not hide the blackened stumps between his yellowed teeth. 'Gettin' on all right then?'

'I'm managing quaite well, thankew, Zander,' Bella said, giving him a cold nod.

'Well, ye know where to apply if ye want anythin',' he leered. 'If ye get into any trouble, Miss Logan – er, Bella, d'ye mind? – juist you give me a wee shout and I'll be here at the toot.'

'I don't think I am likely to have any trouble, thankew, Zander,' she said through pursed lips. 'I am quaite capable of looking after myself, if I may say so.'

Zander gave her a mock salute and, sidling and squirming, said: 'Well, duty calls! I'd better get crackin', Bella, or I'll have auld Stott on my top. See ya, Bella!' He gave a high screeching giggle and wavered away.

Though Bella fought against them, trying not to think of them, the nightmares or hallucinations continued. Every day, at different times, sometimes once, sometimes twice, she would be dragged back by a gigantic ice-cold hand into that iron cage with its smell of excrement, and see again those gloating, pitiless faces revelling in her humiliation. And then, wondering if she could endure another minute of the agony, she would be dragged back as suddenly into the present, and with frozen hands and feet and a cold dread at her heart she would tell herself that probably she was sickening for influenza.

Bella told nobody about these experiences for fear of being laughed at. She felt she should tell her mother, but she was afraid Mrs Logan would whisk her off to the doctor. As it was, Mrs Logan said one lunchtime after the uncanny happenings had been going on for about a week: 'You're off your food, dear. I'm wondering if your new job agrees with you. You're looking kind of peakit.'

Bella assured her mother she was all right, and she forced herself to eat what was put in front of her. Ten days after the supermarket opened, she did something she had never done in her life. On her half-day she went to the Public Library. She was there for three hours, looking at books an assistant librarian kept bringing to her. 'What does little Miss Prim want?' asked another assistant, an auburn-haired girl who had been at school with Bella, though they never acknowledged each other when they met.

'She wants something about the history of Berwick.'

The auburn-haired girl sniffed. 'Can she read? It's the first I've ever heard tell of it.'

At last, after looking through a great many volumes, Bella discovered that Berwick's ancient castle stood once where the railway station was built. Many atrocities had taken place in the castle. One was the hanging from its walls in July 1306 of a cage imprisoning Isabella, the beautiful young Countess of Buchan. This punishment had been ordered by King Edward I of England because the Countess, acting as the representative of her brother, the Earl of Fife, who was Edward's prisoner at the time, had crowned Robert the Bruce as King of Scotland at Scone. The Countess had been kept in this cage for four years, then she had been removed to another prison, and her end was not known.

On her way to meet Peggy Allardyce, Bella tried to imagine what the Countess of Buchan must have felt like after four years of being battered by the elements and the even more merciless crowd, but even with what she had experienced in her own supernatural flights, if indeed they were supernatural, she could not picture what state Isabella of Buchan must have been in by the time she was taken to another prison. Before she reached the café in the Scotsgate where Peggy was waiting, Bella had turned her mind to the dress she would wear at the rugger club dance the following Saturday night.

That evening she considered confiding in her mother, but after a lot of deliberation she decided against it. She knew her mother would either laugh and tell her she was daft, or she would insist on taking her to the doctor. One thing Bella was aware of, however. Every time she experienced the terrors of the cage she had noticed that either old Mrs Cessford or her gangling grandson was in contact with her before or after the happening.

Next morning, fighting against the chill creeping up her legs, she saw with a sense of fatality Mrs Cessford approaching the enquiry desk.

'Can I have a word with ye, hen?' The witch stretched her gap-toothed mouth into an ingratiating smirk.

Bella stopped knitting and said: 'I suppose so. It's what I'm here for, isn't it?'

'Ye'll have heard about my misfortune, hen?' Mrs Cessford said. 'I swear to you, it wasnie my fault. It was a mistake. I had the money in ma purse. It was juist absentmindedness that made me put the stockings in ma bag instead o' into the wire-basket wi the other things I was buyin'.'

'I'm sorry,' Bella said. 'I don't know what you're talking about.'

'But ye've seen the paper surely, hen? It was front page news in the *Berwick Advertiser*: "Elderly Widow Accused of Shoplifting in Woolworths." Ye must have seen it.'

'I never read the papers,' Bella said.

'Well, I tell ye it was a mistake. As sure as I put up ma hand to the livin' God. I would never dream o' doin' sic a low-down dirty trick. I tellt the magistrates that, but they wouldnie listen. They just said: "Fined ten pounds. Next case." Oh, it was sic an affront! I'll never be able to hold up ma head in our neighbourhood again. So that's why I've come to you. I was wonderin', hen, if yer faither – him that's so big with the Toon Cooncil – could maybe help a puir auld widow-body. I ken I'm Labour and he's a Scottish Nationalist, but surely he wouldnie let politics stand between him and helpin' a puir body to get a cooncil hoose.'

'But my father has nothing to do with the Town Council,' Bella said. 'He only does contract work for them occasionally.'

'Oh, but he's got their ears all right. And a word in the right direction is all I want. You speir him for me, will ye, hen?' Mrs Cessford whined.

'I'm sorry,' Bella said. 'I know my father couldn't do it, and I'm not going to ask him.'

'Oh, but ye're a prideful wee madam!' Mrs Cessford's small black eyes blazed. 'Ye wouldnie lift a finger to help a puir auld widdy. It's a pity I asked ye. I should ha'e kent better after the way ye've treated my grandson, him that thinks the world o' ye. I've tellt him often enough that ye're a stinkin' wee hoor and that he should look elsewhere for a guid decent lassie.'

'Your grandson is of no interest to me whatever. Now, will you please go or I'll call the manager?'

'You'll regret this, my braw leddy. You'll live to rue the day ye crossed Mercy Cessford. I've seen ye canoodlin' in the back o' his car wi' yon big fitba' player. Ye may think ye're lucky to be on the pill, but it'll no' aye work. It's nae mair to be trusted than the French letters we had when I was young. I juist hope yet get caught, ye wee bitch.'

Bella rose and stepped out of the desk. Mrs Cessford skirled with spleen and flounced away, shouting: 'Ye'll regret it! Just mark my words. Ye'll regret it!'

Mouth primmed with disapproval, Bella was settling herself in her chair again when she felt the icy blast sweeping up from the floor. She stood and held on to the sides of the desk, fighting against it …

That night the nightmares followed her home. She went to bed about midnight, after watching television with her parents, and fell asleep almost at once.

When she opened her eyes it was pitch-dark. A fiendish gale from the North Sea was howling around her. The cage was swinging so violently that she had to cling to the bars to steady herself. Sleet and snow enveloped her. Her tattered filthy clothes were clamped to her soaking body. Her wet hair was plastered over her face. She gave great sobbing breaths and pressed against the bars. High above her were wild screams. A flock of seagulls was circling the cage, drawn to it by the stench of excrement and the remains of rotten food.

Then, above the screaming of the seagulls, she heard other unearthly wails. Three figures in snow-encrusted cloaks that caused them to stand out in ghostly manner in the darkness were hovering around the cage. The sentries had taken shelter in the embrasures of the castle walls, knowing nobody would try to rescue her on such a wild night.

'Are ye there, Leddy Bella? Are ye there? Ye're no' sleepin', are ye?'

Mercy Cessford, the witch, pressed her ghastly wizened face against the bars. Her features had a luminous gleam: the long nose and the high cheekbones stood out, shining grotesquely, and a wide black gap showed instead of her nearly toothless mouth.

'We ha'e brocht ye a visitor, hinny,' she cackled. 'A braw visitor for a braw leddy that's no sae braw now as she aince was.'

Isabella shuddered and closed her eyes, trying to blot out the three awesome faces. On one side of the witch was her grandson, the red-haired warlock. On Mistress Cessford's other side was another warlock, a tall man wearing a tall black hat. Amber eyes with a reddish glow burned into her under the frown of his thick black brows.

''Tis the Master himself come to visit ye, prood leddy,' the witch said. 'He has come with an offer of freedom.'

'Silence, Mercy,' the warlock cried. 'Let me deal direct with the lady. I do not require your offices of mediation.'

'Isabella of Buchan,' he said. 'I can set you free. Only I, Lucifer, can set you free. But in return I wish your allegiance. Will ye swear to give me that in return for my unlocking this door and taking you speedily from hence? Whither wouldst like to go, madam? To your castle at Methven mayhap, to wallow again in silks and fine raiment, to eat once more fine cooked meats and dainty sweetmeats?'

Isabella unclasped her hands from the bars and put them over her ears, trying to deaden the sibilant voice. A violent gust of wind shook the cage and sent her tumbling to the floor. She lay there with her arms over her head.

'All I need, lady, is your word,' the devil whispered. 'Your promise to be my handmaiden sometimes when I need thy help. I will not be a hard taskmaster. Mayhap I might never seek thy services. All I require if your oath of allegiance.'

'No, no!' Isabella cried, but her words were whisked away by the wind.

The Master laughed and whispered. ''Tis a small price to pay for thy freedom, lady.'

'Will ye no' join our coven, Leddy Bella?' cackled the crone.

'Hold your tongue, Mercy,' the devil ordered. Then wheedlingly he whispered: 'A silken dress again, a hot perfumed bath, meat served on a silver platter ... What dost say, Lady Buchan?'

'Go away! Go away!' she screamed. 'Leave me in peace, you foul fiends!'

The devil laughed, then he and his minions began to fly around the cage, flapping their arms and making their cloaks fly out so that they looked like gigantic bats. Bella screamed and screamed ...

She awoke in her mother's arms. 'There, there, my wee pet,'

Mrs Logan soothed. 'It was just a bad dream.'

'Mammy, Mammy,' Bella sobbed. 'I can't take it any longer.'

And it all poured out. Mrs Logan slept with her for the rest of the night. She would not allow her to go to work. And she accompanied her to the doctor at half-past ten, saying: 'Your granny is of the opinion that it must be your nerves. Maybe the doctor'll prescribe Sanatogen or Wincarnis or something like that.'

Dr Nesbitt gave Bella a thorough examination. At her mother's prompting she told him about having nightmares but did not mention their nature. She admitted that her legs and arms and shoulders ached and that she had unnatural spells of icy coldness. 'There's nothing wrong with your heart and lungs,' Dr Nesbitt said. 'You're as healthy a young woman as I've ever come across. A lassie like you should take more exercise. All that's wrong with you is that your muscles are getting cramped with aye sitting in that confined space. Go for long walks on the golf course or along the banks of the Tweed. Go down to the sands and get the sea breezes into your lungs.'

He gave her a prescription for a tonic and told her to take a week off work.

In that week she had no hallucinations during the days, but every night she had visitations from the demon and his witches. She managed not to waken up screaming, and she contrived to hide it from her mother. Mrs Logan noticed, though, that Bella remained pale and nervous, so she had a word with her husband, who, in turn, had a word with Rod Wishart. 'I suggest,' Mr Logan said, 'that you ask your firm for the new territory they keep promising you, then I think you and our Bella had better put up the banns. The quicker she's away from the climate of Berwick, the happier her mother and me'll be – even if we are going to miss her.'

As soon as Bella returned to the enquiry desk the happenings started again in daylight. She learned, however, to control them a little, making them fainter and farther off, by rising and opening the door of the desk, and she would cling to this while the emanations from the Middle Ages lasted.

One day she was not quick enough. Her mind was so occupied in counting the stitches of a yellow pullover she had started to knit for Rod that the icy waves of terror had swept up from her ankles to her waist before she started to rise. She was forced to sink back into her seat. She clutched her throat and succumbed to the full blast of the chilling, cruel medieval dread ...

The cage swung high above the crowd, but for once the harpies in the crowd were not looking and jeering at her. Most of them had their backs turned. They were watching two great piles of brushwood and logs. In the centre of each pile was a stake. Sagging in her own filth and wretchedness, beaten by the weather, her clothes hanging in sodden tatters, her hair matted and her skin corroded by wind, rain and dirt, Isabella of Buchan saw the old witch, Mercy Cessford, and her grandson being dragged through the crowd by hefty English soldiers. They were tied to the stakes. The old witch screamed imprecations all the time, but the young warlock was able only to gibber. For once, the crowd was silent. There were no jeers and taunts like those usually directed against the Countess. Some women were weeping. Many must have been thinking: 'There but for the grace of God ...'

A herald proclaimed: 'Hear ye! Hear ye, citizens of Berwick. Whereas the perfidious witch, Mistress Mercy Cessford and her demoralised grandson, the warlock Zander Cessford, have perpetrated divers cantrips and incantations against the person of His Majesty, King Edward the First of England, Scotland and Wales and the territories beyond, his Majesty has decreed that the said witch and the said warlock shall meet their deaths by burning. And may God have mercy on their souls!'

A sigh of despair rose from the crowd, and there were some half muffled shouts of protest when fiery torches were thrust into the pyres. Isabella leant her forehead against a cold iron bar and sighed with the crowd. As the first thin smoke came through the brushwood, the old witch looked up at the cage and keened: ''Tis thy fault, prood Bella, for not doin' what the Master askit. And 'tis thy fault for crownin' the Bruce and bringin' the wrath of King Edward upon us. Ye will regret thy work for centuries to come. My dyin' curse on ye, prood leddy.'

And then the old woman started to scream again. Isabella closed her eyes. The woman's screams turned into throat-strangling retches. The warlock shrieked every few seconds. But gradually the screams became fainter, and finally, ceased. When Isabella opened her eyes she could see nothing but the flames and, above them, great clouds of dark grey and black smoke. Swirls of wind blew the smoke into the cage. Her eyes were stung, her nostrils filled, her throat seared by the salt of strong iron tongues being thrust into them. Isabella started to cough. She clutched her throat and struggled against the billows of smoke ...

Bella coughed and coughed, her throat scalded by the sour-sweet clutch of wood smoke, until she slumped in a heap on the enquiry desk. She recovered consciousness lying on the floor with her head on a folded rug that had been taken from a pram. The infant in the pram was yelling with temper. Its mother, her back turned to it, was leaning against the pram shoogling it, her mouth half-open, looking at Bella and Mr Stott and the spectators who had gathered.

'I want my mother,' Bella gasped. 'I want —'

'Now now, Miss Logan, take it easy,' Mr Stott murmured in agitation, on his hunkers beside her. 'We'll get you sent home presently. You seem to have had a wee turn, but you'll soon be all right. I would take you home myself, but I can't leave the market. I'll get somebody else to take you in their car in a minute.'

That evening Peggy Allardyce came to see Bella in bed. 'Isn't it awful,' she said when she had finished commiserating with her friend, 'there's been a terrible fire in Percy's Vennel and two folk were burned to death. Auld Mrs Cessford and her grandson Zander. You know him, Bell, don't you? Yon nice laddie with the ginger hair that does odd jobs like filling the shelves and sweeping the floor. Poor soul! What a dreadful death!'

'Yes, isn't it?' Bella said, handing Peggy a knitting pattern.

'D'you like this, Peg? I think it would be smashing in powder-blue and white.'

'What's this I hear?' Rod said when Mrs Logan showed him into Bella's bedroom later on. 'I hear you fainted in the street and the Fire Brigade had to be called out. And fancy being brought home in a police car!'

'Funny, aren't you?' Bella said.

'Never mind, dear,' he said. 'Your fainting days are over. I heard this morning that the firm are putting me in charge of their Perth territory, so we'd better get spliced. Okay by you?'

Bella gave a little nod and said: 'I suppose so.'

She made no objection next morning when her mother would not allow her to return to work. She wrote a short note to Mr Stott, giving in her notice.

In the next few weeks, getting ready for her wedding, she did not have time to think about her other-worldly experiences, except one evening when she was approaching the supermarket to meet Peggy and she had a faint emanation of once again standing in the cage with the wind and the witch and the warlocks whirling around her.

But she was aware of much more than a faint emanation on the evening that Rod announced that his firm had got them a house near Perth. 'It's at Methven, about ten miles from Perth,' he said. 'A very nice house I hear, with four bedrooms, a lounge, a kitchen, bathroom and two lavatories, and all the usual. It's built where the ruins of Methven Castle used to stand.'

Bella heard no more. The ice-cold terror swept over her again, and she found herself on the back of a prancing horse while the clash of battle raged all around her. She was watching a tall man in armour on a black horse. He had a circlet of gold on his helmet, and the June sunlight sent sparks from it as he galloped full tilt against some English knights. Beyond the battlefield she could see her father's castle of Methven, and she was still gazing towards its towers when the English soldiers surrounded her and took her prisoner.

THE GHOST ROAD

Can a road be haunted?

Regular travellers on the A75, which runs from Stranraer, on Scotland's southwest coast, to Gretna Green, which sits inland on the M6 motorway, will tell you that it most certainly can. And is. And that one particular section of it, the so-called Kinmount Straight, which links Carrutherstown and Annan, is so severely haunted that it actually poses a threat to life.

At first glance, the A75 is none too dramatic a route, passing through some areas of conurbation but mostly through open, flattish countryside. It's also a well-used road, traversing towns like Eastriggs, Dumfries and Castle Douglas, ultimately connecting the M6, one of the busiest motorways in Britain, with the ferry terminals at Cairnryan.

The route has supposedly suffered more than its fair share of road crashes over the years, though this allegation is difficult to prove, and it probably seems safe to say that, if this was the case, Transport Scotland, part of whose remit is the safe operation of the Scottish Trunk Road Network (which involves meeting national casualty reduction targets), would have made some kind of safety-related survey by now, checking on road surfaces, speed limits, blind bends and the like. However, what is undeniable is that there have been many reports of curious and frightening incidents along this stretch of road, and they go back a long time. So much so that some motorists will not even travel along the A75, especially not after dark.

It all seems to have started, or at least the problem first came to public awareness, in the mid-1950s, when lorry drivers began to spread the word that they were seeing unusual things along the route, particularly in the vicinity of Carrutherstown. Some reported spectral, semi-translucent figures attempting to flag them down and sometimes standing in the road itself, while even scarier stories circulated about drivers who'd been sleeping in lay-bys being woken at the dead of night by knocks, bangs and scrapings along the sides of their parked vehicles, subsequent searches revealing that they were entirely alone.

Several times, early morning drivers would call at snack vans or roadside shops to buy refreshments, and describe eerie and mysterious processions of people whom they'd sighted stumbling along the verge during the night: ragged folk, like wartime refugees, many carrying backpacks or babies, or pushing carts. Inevitably, any drivers who'd stopped to offer assistance, had found that there was nobody there. On a couple of occasions, these phantom roadside stragglers were said to have been clad in what looked like medieval-era clothing.

But the supernatural side of the A75 really hit the headlines in 1962, when two brothers, Derek and Norman Ferguson, regaled the local press with a terrifying experience they'd had on the Kinmount Straight.

It was the early hours of the morning and they were driving through misty darkness, when they had to swerve sharply to avoid a large bird, which seemingly appeared from nowhere and swooped at their windscreen. They were shaken up, but continued their journey, only for a human figure to suddenly appear in front of them. They braked hard, but the figure – up close, an old woman minus eyes, waving her arms wildly and screeching – vanished just before they struck it. Badly alarmed, the brothers drove on, only for a succession of bizarre creatures, including over-large cats and ferocious dogs, to come leaping at them out of the mist. When they finally stopped, too traumatised to go any further, their car began to violently rock as though dozens of pairs of hands were pushing it from side to side. The brothers jumped out and found a roadway bare of life. At which point they heard the laughter of multiple raucous voices from close by.

They leapt back into their car, but it now wouldn't start. As they struggled to get the engine going, a pair of headlights emerged from the murk in front of them. A horn began blaring, but there was nothing the two brothers could do. They didn't even have enough time to get out of their vehicle again, as what looked like a huge wagon bore down on them, travelling at full speed.

And vanished into nothingness at the last second.

Weird occurrences on the A75 have continued into modern times.

Figures in Victorian garb have allegedly crossed the road apparently unaware of approaching traffic, causing drivers to brake or skid. Similarly clad individuals have been spotted along the verge. One *especially disturbing phantom is said to resemble a man with long hair, who dashes at cars screaming. He is credited with causing several minor accidents and near-misses. In the last decade, a female motorist was so convinced that she had knocked down a man in a red top who came out of nowhere and stood directly in her path, that she called the police, who thoroughly searched the area, but found no trace of a body or blood, or any sign that an actual collision had occurred.*

Phenomena have even been reported in buildings adjoining the route, staff in the Blacksmith's Shop in Gretna claiming to have witnessed poltergeist activity and the appearance of dark, featureless forms.

No explanation has ever really been offered, though it was noted that a number of incidents have occurred in the Kelstead Plantation, a part of the route that passes through dense woodland, which is close to Kinmount House, a 19th century mansion that is very Gothic in appearance and occupies part of what was once an extensive 13th century estate. However, despite having been used as a hospital during the two world wars, Kinmount House itself has no history of haunting or disturbance.

The mystery of the A75 goes on. And at present, drivers who use it, particularly at night-time, do so entirely at their own risk.

DRUMGLASS CHAPEL
Reggie Oliver

Recently, in the *Guardian*, I saw Nick Levkas mentioned as a possible future director of the National Theatre. I was not surprised, but it saddened me a little that we had lost touch. In the late Seventies and early Eighties when we were starting out in the profession, we had been close. Our careers had run on parallel lines for a while and then diverged; his, as a director, enjoying a markedly upward trajectory, mine, as an actor, not so much.

I had not seen Nick for at least a decade, though I had been to quite a few of his acclaimed productions. Several times I asked my agent to put me up for a show he was mounting, and once or twice I had even been bold enough to drop him a personal note, but there had been no response, not even so much as the offer of an interview. I took this to be the natural tendency of very successful people to sever connections with their less than successful past, so I decided to waste no time on resentment. Besides, though I remain 'on the books' as an actor, I had begun to achieve in other spheres.

Then, just over a week ago, I went to see a friend in a new play at Colchester, not far from where I live. It was a matinee, and I arrived at the theatre early to have a snack lunch before seeing the show. There were not many people in the theatre bar as I entered, but a tall, thin, grey haired man sat at a table by the window with a coffee and a croissant. He was consulting a mobile phone, dressed entirely in black with a collarless silk shirt and a velvet jacket. Draped around his neck, a black silk scarf decorated with white polka dots offered some relief from this sepulchral uniform. It was a costume of calculated distinction.

Half a minute passed before a vague sense of familiarity turned into positive recognition. I decided it would be rude not to make myself known, so I walked over to his table. He had still not taken his eyes off the mobile when I spoke to him.

'Hello, Nick.'

When he first looked up, he seemed, for a moment, enraged by the interruption. Then his face underwent a transformation; one dictated, I suspect, more by politeness than pleasure.

'Good grief, it's Alan isn't it? Long time no see! What on earth are you doing here?'

I explained my presence. He nodded perfunctorily when I mentioned my friend in the cast. In turn, I asked him why he was there.

'Oh, some people are interested in a London production and may want me to direct it.' His manner was so off-hand and condescending that it angered me. I thought of apologising with a hint of sarcasm for disturbing him, but that would have been to exhibit weakness. I wanted to show him that I was out of his power and no longer needed him to give me a job. Unbidden, I sat down opposite him.

I said: 'I understand this play is all about nuns in Africa.'

'Yes. Rather a hot topic at the moment.'

'What? Nuns or Africa?'

'Both, I believe.' We laughed. The tension was eased: Nick seemed reconciled to my presence.

'So, Alan,' he said, leaning back in his chair, and surveying me with a critical eye like a headmaster with a former pupil, 'what have *you* been up to?' There was again, I thought, that slight note of condescension, the implication being that I would naturally know all about *his* activities, while mine were too obscure to have come to his attention. Perhaps I was being over-sensitive. I gave him a brief sketch of my recent life, and we went on to discuss the theatre in general. He spoke about the present scene with brisk authority, as if in command of everything there was to know about the subject, a characteristic of his with which I was familiar. It had been one of the keys to his success as a director that he always appeared to know exactly what he was talking about. Views other than his own were to be listened to politely, then dismissed.

Wishing to stem his rather didactic flow of information and opinion, I diverted the conversation to recollections of past times when we had worked together in an outfit called the Ruffian Theatre Company. He laughed when I first mentioned it, but nervously, I thought.

'Oh, my God! The old RTC!' The acronym began to be used late in the company's history when it became more established, and the novelty of its name had worn off. It was the RTC which had first made Nick Levkas a force to be reckoned with in the theatre; in spite of which he did not seem altogether happy that the subject had been raised. I kept my reminiscences light and amusing, but he was unwilling to join in the fun. He kept saying that he could barely remember anything about 'those days'. I felt frustrated, even a little hurt.

'But you must remember the time we went to Edinburgh for the Festival with *Last Man In*,' I said, 'and those two weeks at the Drumglass Chapel?'

I saw shock on Nick's face, covered almost immediately by a blank look. Then he said, in his usual, decisive way: 'No. No. That's all a complete blur, I'm afraid. So much has happened since then, hasn't it?' The three-minute bell rang. 'Well, we must be off to take our seats.' He stood up. 'Good to see you again, Alan.' He shook my hand formally and darted off to buy a program.

I did not see him in the interval, nor after the show. When I went round to visit my friend in the production, I told her that Nick Levkas had been in.

She said: 'So, it's true! I did hear a rumour he was in the audience. Someone told me he'd actually left in rather a hurry, just before the end. What was all that about?'

Some days later, an envelope containing a picture postcard was forwarded to me by my theatrical agent. The image was a striking black and white photograph of Lon Chaney as the mad, vengeful clown in the silent film of *He Who Gets Slapped*. On the reverse was written:

'Good to see you, looking so well, mate, after all these years. You mentioned Edinburgh and *Last Man In*. Well done for bringing up the subject! I suppose I can understand why you did, but don't try to be in touch again. No offence, but let's call it a day, eh? Best. Nick.'

I was shocked. There was something decidedly unbalanced about his rejection of our former friendship. That use of the word 'mate' was uncharacteristic. He had, it is true, come from quite a poor background, but, when I first knew him, he had done his best to eradicate all traces of his origins. It was as if, once more, he had forged for himself a fresh personality and was trying to burn newer boats. But why had he bothered to write at all? And there remained the mystery of why my mention of Edinburgh had triggered such a violent reaction.

I tend to feel very ashamed of things which, at the time, I barely notice I have done or said. It is my moral blindness that most upsets me. Therefore I felt guilty, even though I could not quite work out what my offence had been.

I had not mentioned Edinburgh out of malice, but simply because it had come into my head as one of the most memorable events of my association with Nick. Perhaps, at the back of my mind, there was a certain curiosity to see how he would react to something in our past which I still remember vividly. When he said he had completely forgotten it, I had taken his words literally, but this was clearly not the case. Something at Drumglass Chapel had affected him even more deeply than it had me.

Nick and I had been at drama school together and when we came out and were struggling to find work, we decided to start our own theatre company to make a name for ourselves. That is to say, Nick decided and I was his first recruit. The name, Ruffian Theatre Company, was of course Nick's idea and derived, I think, from the fact that our first major production was Joe Orton's *The Ruffian on the Stair*. We were both very ambitious, but Nick was the more dynamic character. I, having inherited some money, was able to finance the venture to some extent, especially in its earliest phase. In those days, there were plenty of fringe venues around London where we could perform our work; the difficulty always was to get the public to come and see us, but we began to acquire a certain reputation. Nick was generally the director and I one of the main actors and there was a floating population of performers whom we recruited mainly from drama school friends.

Then, in the summer of 1979, Nick wrote a play which he believed was going to transform our fortunes. It was called *Last Man In*. We rehearsed it and put it on for two or three nights at a couple of fringe venues. It went well, but Nick believed it could go much further. It was early July when Nick proposed that we should take it to the Edinburgh Fringe for the Festival in August. I said that it was far too late to find a decent venue for the show, but Nick was determined. Within three days he had rung me up to say he had found a theatre for the first two weeks of the Festival. I saluted his enterprise and asked how he had managed it.

'It's a new venue,' he said. 'Just opened for the Festival. Called the Drumglass Chapel Theatre. It's a disused church of some kind, owned by the Council and leased out to this live wire called Kirsty Wang.'

'Is she Chinese?'

'No, she is not Chinese. Don't interrupt. Not as far as I know. I've only spoken to her on the phone. She has a Morningside accent and talks like Miss Jean Brodie, but she's very keen on really cutting edge, radical young theatre. That's why I was able to persuade her to take us on. That, and the fact that she's got a late evening slot free. We will be one of four shows in the theatre every day during the Festival.'

Further questions from me were dismissed or answered perfunctorily. It would not be quite true to say that I was swept away by his enthusiasm and dynamism. I had many reservations, but I recognised Nick as an irresistible force, and even agreed to stump up some cash to pay a deposit on our 'slot'. I learned a little more about our future venue as we prepared for the journey North.

The day's performances at the Drumglass Chapel were to start in the afternoon with *Gas-Oven Gertie!* – a musical about the Holocaust. The title and subject matter were intended to provoke outrage, and did so, together with a good deal of useful publicity. However, those who went to it in search of a healthy dose of moral indignation, or challenging ambiguity were disappointed. It was mostly worthy and a little sentimental, with a few cautiously signalled jokes. The music was pleasant enough, though.

The evening's program began with *The Means and the Ends*, one of Bertolt Brecht's lesser-known and, it must be admitted, duller plays. As such, it was billed, naturally enough, as 'Brecht's neglected masterpiece'. In addition, very late at night, a well-known actress was doing a one woman show about Rosa Luxemburg, but that was to be expected. In those days of early Thatcherism and radical dissent, an Edinburgh Festival rarely went by without someone performing a one-woman show about Rosa Luxemburg. We were given use of the stage from half past nine to eleven-thirty, between Brecht and Rosa Luxemburg, perhaps in a misguided bid to inject some light relief into the program.

Our play, or rather Nick's, *Last Man In,* was set in a cricket pavilion in the Home Counties. Two young drifters, Deena and Finchy, the former an addict and part-time prostitute, the latter a drug dealer, are camping in it out of the cricket season. Into this milieu comes Charles (played by me), the young upper-class secretary of the cricket club, on a routine inspection of his club's pavilion. Deena and Finchy appear at first to be intimidated by him as he threatens to call the police and have them evicted, but the tables are turned and they begin to menace him. The end of the play sees Charles trussed and blindfolded, in nothing but his underpants, a gibbering wreck, and possibly about to be killed.

It was a play about class, power, sexual ambivalence and menace, not uninfluenced by Harold Pinter but, as Nick always insisted, 'more raw.' The humour, of which there was, happily, a decent amount, was certainly Pinteresque.

Though I enjoyed playing such a substantial role I had realised that, as in life, it is always more emotionally exhausting to play the victim than the aggressor. That was one of the reasons why I rather dreaded a two-week run of the play in Edinburgh.

The company had been lent a small flat for the run by some acquaintance of Nick. This involved sleeping on floors and sofas for the rest of us while Nick laid claim to the one bedroom. But we were young.

Having arrived in the morning by the overnight train from London, we, that is Nick, myself, with Carol and Tim, the two other actors in the show, dropped our bags at the flat and went straight to the theatre. There were two days before the festival began and our opening performance.

Drumglass Chapel was situated not too far from the centre of things just across the Leith from the castle and hard by Dean Cemetery. My first sight of it rather lowered my spirits, as do most Scottish ecclesiastical buildings. It was a substantial but somewhat squat edifice of gothic pretentions built entirely of red sandstone and granite, the colour of dried blood. The central perpendicular style doorway had recently been given a coat of bright scarlet gloss paint. No doubt this had been designed to cheer it up, but it looked to me like a mouth of Hell.

The door was unlocked, so we entered. The entrance hall was built of the same dried blood sandstone. A screen of dark polished oak separated the hall from the main body of the chapel beyond. It had been sunny outside but the interior was only dimly lit by the gothic windows with leaded panes of thick greenish glass. On one wall a wooden panel was inscribed with a list of 'Ministers' of the chapel, and the beginning and end dates of their periods of office. The last name, 'Jabez McCreel' had '1939-' written after him, but no termination date for his ministry. A large, framed sepia photograph of a man with a chin beard but no moustache hung beside the wooden panel. A label on the frame proclaimed the sitter to be the same Jabez McCreel. It was a severe ecclesiastical face with a long thin mouth and fierce little eyes. (I have always associated moustacheless beards with religious fanaticism, maybe because they seem to me to represent such a wilful abnegation of aesthetic allure.) The picture gave the impression of dating from rather earlier than 1939, perhaps the turn of the century, but I was the only one of my company who paid the least attention to such mysteries.

I think we had arrived in the expectation of being greeted, and were rather disconcerted by finding no-one about. Nick, as always the first to act, sighed with exasperation and pushed open the double doors which gave access to the main body of the building.

Above us was a gallery with benches running round three sides of the chapel. In the main body of the hall chairs were stacked up around the sides, but there were no pews. At one end was a raised wooden stage on which had stood a pulpit, now removed. In the middle of the stage was a long table of polished oak with bulbous legs. I guessed that this was a relic of the chapel's religious past, a 'Lord's Table' on which communion was celebrated: the low church apology for an altar. At the back and to one side, behind a low wooden screen, was a harmonium. In the gallery a lighting console had been set up, while, from metal gantries across the ceiling, there hung a substantial array of lights.

'Wow!' said Nick. 'Great space!' The rest of us agreed that it was indeed a 'great space' because that was what one was meant to say in those days about any environment in which one was privileged to act. I had my reservations. There was no way of knowing the nature of the services conducted here in the past, but to me the place still reeked of religious oppression. The fierce eyes of Jabez McCreel had made an impression on me.

'Glad you like it!' said a voice. We turned and saw a large, square-shouldered woman in her early thirties, with long lustrous black hair and a fair amount of copper-coloured jewellery. 'Hi, I'm Kirsty Wang.' It was, as Nick had observed, a clear-cut Morningside accent.

Her skin was pale, her eyes as dark as her hair, suggesting

partly Asian origins; but what I was most aware of was the strength of her personality. Though well-built she was far from fat and by no means unattractive, even if I felt personally immune. Nick came forward and shook hands with her. I sensed an affinity between them. People with a mutual interest in power often enjoy an instant rapport: how long that lasts will depend on circumstances. I noticed that Kirsty, while paying little attention to Tim and myself, gave Carol a brief but hard and suspicious look which was cautiously returned with similar intent. I knew that Carol suffered from a deep, almost slavish admiration for Nick, but had no idea if it had been taken any further.

Kirsty began to show us round the chapel, addressing all her remarks to Nick. I was impressed by her enthusiasm for 'the space' as it was insistently referred to, but did not altogether share it. The hall was spacious, and, having been built for sermons, hymns and liturgies, did not have the best acoustic for naturalistic speech. There was a reverberant echo which varied considerably, depending on where you stood on the stage. When I mentioned this, Kirsty said that the problem could be rectified by the use of screens. Nick frowned at me as if to imply that my objections did not show the right spirit.

Other misgivings I did not share, because I knew they would be dismissed out of hand. In the dark polished wood and ensanguined stone, in the vagrant echoes, in the absence of any decoration, even in the form of carved texts or stained glass, I detected a note of puritan rigidity, almost of menace. It was fanciful I knew, even as I sensed it, but I felt it nonetheless and it would not leave me. On an impulse, Carol sat herself at the Harmonium at the back of the stage and tried out a few chords. The sounds that emerged were like tormented groans.

'Please don't touch that!' said Kirsty, and Nick gave her a warning frown.

We passed from the hall into a passage leading to the dressing rooms, once a vestry. This was lit by only a few small, opaquely glazed gothic windows. It was as if everywhere in the building, contact with the outside world was to be kept at a minimum. On one of the walls of the passage was a framed photograph, identical in size and arrangement, to the one of Jabez McCreel in the entrance hall. This time it was of a woman and bore the legend:

Mizpah McCreel
'And she shall prophesy the Day of His Wrath.'

The face carried a certain resemblance to Jabez, but more because it reflected a similar cast of thought than any particular feature. There was a stony rigidity about the set of the mouth and the jawline, but in the eyes there was the far look of the visionary.

I asked Kirsty whether she was Jabez's wife.

'Sister, I believe,' she said, and seemed surprised, even rather offended by the question. At that moment I thought I could detect in Kirsty a look of Mizpah: the dogmatic, the enthusiast. It prompted me to enquire further about the Chapel and its history. When Kirsty spoke, it was almost as if the words came out of her involuntarily in a fluent monotone, like a well-practiced but rather bored tour guide.

'It was a Protestant millenarian sect, an offshoot of the Seventh Day Adventists, or some such. Apparently Jabez and his sister had worked out that the world was going to end in 1939. Something to do with numerology and the *Book of Daniel*, and *Revelations*, of course.

'The usual thing. Then 1939 came and the Great Disappointment, as it was called, when the world didn't end. A lot of followers drifted away. Well, Jabez and Mizpah did their calculations again and came up with the idea that 1939 was actually not the end of the world but the beginning of the reign of the Antichrist, Hitler being the Antichrist naturally. Or it may have been Stalin. I forget. So far so good, but then they prophesied that the Reign of the Antichrist would last for forty years until he was finally defeated in a great battle and then the Last Things would happen. Well, the Antichrist, whichever it was, went under rather sooner than expected, and there was another Great Disappointment. Some people clung on, but Jabez and Mizpah died and the place was sold. The new owners neglected it in the hope that it could be destroyed and an office block put in its place. But the council wouldn't have it, and eventually took it over. Then this year I managed to get a lease with a grant. So here we are.'

'You seem to know all about it.'

'Yes. Actually, my mother was a Jabezite, as they were called.'

'Really? So, did you — ?'

'Right. Dressing rooms. You want to see those, I expect.'

Her interruption was so abrupt that I did not need a warning look from Nick to halt my questioning. But I could not help recollecting that it was 1979, the end, according to the McCreels, of the reign of the Antichrist, but also the true beginning of the end.

We saw the dressing rooms which were adequate; we met Dave who would do our lighting, and supervise the stage management. Kirsty took us briefly into her office where we were introduced to a girl called Imogen who handled bookings and publicity. She was a pale blonde, dressed in black jeans and a T shirt which accentuated her spectral thinness. As we came out of the office, Tim murmured to me:

'That's *Anorexia Nervosa.*'

'You seem to know everyone,' I said. Carol giggled. Kirsty, who was walking ahead of us with Nick must have heard. She turned round and gave us a reproving look.

Thereafter, in private, the three of us would refer to Imogen as 'Ann'. Childish, I know, but it made for a bond between us. Nick did not share in the joke, and this, I now see, was the first of the rifts in our relationship.

Nick seemed exhilarated by his choice of theatre. Tim and Carol expressed enthusiasm, as did I when called upon to do so, but an inner and seemingly irrational uncertainty would not be appeased. Kirsty told us that that night, there was to be a party in the Chapel to mark its opening as a theatre and we were all invited. There would be some refreshment, but the bringing of a bottle was advised.

While Tim, Carol and I returned to the flat, Nick remained behind to talk to Kirsty. After fixing a scratch lunch for myself and the others, I wandered around Edinburgh. The art gallery for some reason was shut so I climbed the steep, narrow streets that led up to the castle. It was a bright day, but windy. Already eager actors were out everywhere, publicising their forthcoming attractions. In the course of my wanderings, I was accosted by several people dressed as clowns with fixed greasepaint grins smeared onto their faces. One of them was on stilts and seemed almost as tall and menacing as the dark tenements that flanked my way to the Castle Mount. As he stood over me in the narrow street, I was returned to a childhood when shadowy relatives and well-meaning friends of my parents would loom above me and ask how I was enjoying school. The clown stooped to hand me a leaflet. It was for *Gas-Oven Gertie! The Outrageous Holocaust Musical at the Drumglass Chapel!* I began to feel there was no escape.

Later that day we ran through the play in the flat with Nick, then, rather later than we had planned, set out to attend the celebrations at the chapel. I carried with me a bottle of Spanish Merlot – that was what it said on the bottle – the only reasonable looking wine I could find at the off licence and tobacconists where we made our purchases.

It was dark when we arrived at Drumglass Chapel. The scarlet doors were open and from within came the thump of amplified music. The chapel was illuminated by green floodlights which gave the red sandstone façade a sickly indefinable colour, like putrefying flesh. The shadows cast by its gothic ornamentations were pitch black; dark green lights glittered in the leaded panes of the windows.

Inside, all was noise. Two vast speakers stood like black monoliths on either side of the stage where a band of sorts was playing. It was the age of punk, and the band's name, Groin Strain, was emblazoned in blood-red gothic letters on its members' black T-shirts. There were about a hundred people in all. We mingled. I saw Nick talking to Kirsty in a dark red sparkly outfit by the makeshift bar where I had deposited my bottle of Merlot. It was almost immediately taken away and emptied into a vast cauldron of 'punch' on whose foaming surface floated slices of orange and lemon, but not before I had used it to pour myself a glass of unadulterated wine. I began to talk to a girl with hair dyed a shiny bright blue. She was in the Brecht company and told me that she was 'really into theatre.'

Out of the corner of my eye I caught sight of Imogen from the theatre office. Her skeletal limbs were encased in a bright green lurex jumpsuit, which made her look like a giant tropical insect. She was dancing on her own, close to the band, a look of rapt concentration on her white face. A shifting kaleidoscope of coloured lights illuminated the stage where, beside the band and its paraphernalia, rather incongruously, the Chapel's 'Lord's Table' stood, an isolated relic of the building's religious past. I wondered why it had been placed in such a prominent position.

The playing of Groin Strain gave way to a kind of impromptu cabaret. Someone told jokes, another did a magic act; several people attempted to sing with the band. The only act which I remember distinctly was the last one in which Imogen performed a dance on the table to the rhythmical backing of Groin Strain. Her moves were supple and sinuous: eroticism was suggested but somehow negated by the stony-faced impersonality with which she performed. She was watched in an attentive but bemused silence. No-one whistled, or called out, or applauded while her shiny green limbs wrapped themselves round the bulbous table legs and she worked her meagre body up and down them, until she ended by performing the splits on the table top.

This finale was greeted with a storm of applause, and some cheers, more I think from relief that her unnerving performance was now over than anything else.

Immediately following this, Kirsty walked briskly onto the stage carrying a microphone and what looked like two large dusty sheets of cardboard. These she placed on the table and proceeded to make a speech of welcome which was punctuated by whoops of enthusiasm from the audience. She told us how the Drumglass Chapel had just acquired 'a new and vibrant identity' and how we were all a part of it. (Loud cheers.) She added that the Chapel's oppressive and destructive past was ended and consigned to 'the flames of history'. It was an odd phrase, but I guessed it signified something because, immediately following it, she made a beckoning gesture. Onto the stage, to more loud cheers, came Dave, her stage manager and electrician. He was wearing a leopard skin patterned robe, making him look like one of those lamp-stands in the shape of Nubian attendants that were once so fashionable among the rich and tasteless. He was carrying a large stainless-steel dish of the kind used to pass round sandwiches at municipal functions.

He placed it on the table while Kirsty held up the two pieces of cardboard, so that I could now see what they were. She had removed the sepia photographs of Jabez and Mizpah McCreel from their frames. She placed them on the steel dish, still holding them upright so we could see their faces while Dave set light to them with a small blowtorch. A great roar of approval went up from the crowd. Within seconds the McCreels were engulfed in flames. Kirsty let go of the pictures, raising her hands above her head as she did so in a hieratic gesture; Dave followed suit.

Someone set up a chant of 'Burn in Hell! Burn in Hell!' It was taken up by others and accentuated by a heavy percussive beat from Groin Strain's drummer. This was too much for me so I left the hall. Outside on the steps of Drumglass Chapel the Edinburgh night was pleasantly cool. I drained the glass of Merlot which I still had with me. I was not quite sure why I had been so violently impelled to leave: some atavistic sense of propriety, I suppose. I sat down on the steps and was joined after a few minutes by Nick.

'Anything the matter?' he asked. He sounded more indignant than concerned.

'Just the heat – and the noise,' I said, almost immediately ashamed of my dishonesty.

'Your exit was a bit conspicuous. Quite a lot of people

noticed.'

'I don't believe in Hell.'

'What's that got to do with it?'

I shook my head. Nick sat down on the steps with me.

'Well, you haven't missed much,' he said. 'Almost as soon as you'd left, something went wrong with the sound system. There was the most godawful noise and then the amps just packed up. Groin Strain is furious. It's their equipment, you see, and they alone are permitted to destroy it.'

The following night – the day before the Festival officially began – was to be our technical dress rehearsal, the first time we were able to perform in the theatre. Unfortunately, because on the eve of the Festival rehearsal time in the theatre was at a premium, we were booked in with Dave the lighting man to do our 'tech run' between two and four on the morning of the day we opened.

The only person who did not appear to be unhappy with this arrangement was Dave. Like many theatre technicians, Dave was very competent and amenable, but appeared quite uninterested in the theatrical product itself. His easy confidence and indifference were assisted by a regular consumption of weed, and a mild herbal aroma accompanied him wherever he meant.

Our play had few lighting cues but adjustments had to be made to the positioning of some of the lamps. Nick, as in all things theatrical, had a very precise conception of what he wanted. This involved shifting a large scaffolding tower on wheels around while Dave on top of it adjusted the lamps that hung from the gantries across the ceiling. Nick sat in the gallery at the lighting console, directing proceedings, while Tim, Carol and I moved the tower. We began to be very tired of Nick's meticulous instructions. It was past three in the morning, and we simply wanted to rehearse the show and go to bed.

Nick himself was becoming impatient, but more with the technical inadequacies of the theatre, and its inability to give him the effects he wanted. As we were moving the tower yet again, we heard him mutter: 'Come on! This stupid place! This stupid, sodding chapel!'

A strange sound, like a groan was heard, not human but somehow in imitation of a living human. It seemed to come from the harmonium, but wherever it came from it distracted us, so that, in the act of turning the scaffolding tower we moved it too quickly for the wheels at its base to adjust.

I remember vividly that long, slow moment when we realised that the back wheels of the scaffolding tower were off the ground and we had lost control of it. It remains an image in my dreams to this day. The tower began to tilt, gradually at first, then with increasing speed. Tim, Carol and I let go of the falling structure and scattered, calling up to Dave as we did so. We saw him take in the situation with preternatural calm, then, just before the tower crashed to the ground, he jumped clear of the platform on which he stood and rolled away. The scaffolding hit the floor with a clanging sound which seemed to echo round the hall for an age after the fall.

'What the hell do you think you're doing?' Nick shouted from the gallery, more irritated than concerned.

Dave, who was the first to recover his composure, called up to him: 'It's cool, bro. No bones broken.' That night considerably revised my views on cannabis.

I cannot remember exactly when we got away from the theatre in the morning but I know that a green and yellow dawn was well into the sky when we emerged. The streets were still empty, apart from a milk float which we stopped to purchase a couple of pints. None of us wanted to talk about what had happened. I knew that if I so much as mentioned that my dread of the theatre had been greatly magnified by the incident, Nick would have been scornful. I sensed, though, that he had not been unaffected.

It is often said in the theatre, though usually without much truth, that a difficult dress rehearsal makes for a good first night. In this instance, however, it turned out to be true. The shock and exhaustion produced by those traumatic early hours in Drumglass Chapel had perhaps forced on us that fierce, monomaniacal concentration needed to bring off a successful first performance. For once the intense, oppressive atmosphere of the chapel worked in our favour. At the end of the show Nick came to the dressing room, accompanied by Kirsty who brought with her a bottle of Australian sparkling wine. She appeared to be more exultant than Nick and watched him closely as he handed out carefully qualified praise to the cast, announcing that he would be giving notes the following morning in the theatre. Kirsty informed us that a critic from *The Scotsman* had been in that night, rather as if this had been secured through her particular expertise. I seem to remember us going off to a pub, or a club or an Indian restaurant, that Kirsty and Nick joined us for a while, then left together.

The following morning there was a review in *The Scotsman,* and it was enthusiastic. I have a vague recollection of the words 'stark', 'vibrant', 'searing' and 'disturbing' being used, and they were all good ones to find in a review in 1979. My own feelings were mixed, as they always have been towards criticisms of any description, especially when they are couched in such modish terms. Were the reviewers sincere in their appreciation, or were they merely bending to the fashion of the day? I tried to put such thoughts from me and rejoice in our success, because, as each day passed, the review – whose encouraging adjectives were now pasted across our posters – and word of mouth were steadily building the audiences.

Whenever I entered that blood-red mausoleum of a theatre in the days following, I still experienced a lowering of the spirits, and there were some objective reasons for this. There were tensions between the companies. Though our own tiny ensemble was comparatively immune, we were conscious of a certain resentment from the others because our show was the only one to have received unequivocally good notices.

The companies of *Gas-Oven Gertie!* and *The Means and the Ends* were perpetually at war. Both were comprised of a dozen or so performers, and, as they shared (with us) the same smallish dressing rooms, there were disputes between them over allocation of space for costume racks, make-up, wigs, personal props and the like. There were even mutual charges of theft. *Gas-Oven Gertie!* was accused by *The Means and the Ends* of not vacating the dressing room quickly enough after the end of their show, while *The Means and the Ends* – according to *Gas-Oven Gertie!* – was guilty of barging in on them before they had had a chance to change. The Rosa Luxemburg actress was not cantankerous, merely depressed. Her audiences were scant, and *The Scotsman* had suggested that her one-woman Rosa Luxemburg was not nearly as 'challenging' as the previous year's Rosa. A general air of fractious discontent pervaded the theatre.

Other factors, rather less understandable, played their part in the atmosphere of malaise. There was, for example, the question of the harmonium. A number of complaints had been made that it emitted sounds at odd moments. This was thought to be impossible because someone needed to know how to operate the 'patent mouse-proof pedals' to produce any sound at all. The casts of *Gas-Oven Gertie!* and *The Means and the Ends* nearly came to blows when the one accused the other of sabotaging them by sounding the organ during their performance. It was eventually established that none of *The Means and the Ends* company was in the theatre at the time, but suspicions remained.

I myself heard it once at the end of one of our shows, a long base note, almost like a growl of a beast, but not one of flesh and blood: something with rusty iron and rotting wood for lungs. I was the only one who heard, so I said nothing about it. The noise had, however, aroused my curiosity.

It was early one morning, a few days after I had heard the sound. I needed something from the dressing room and Imogen from the theatre office had let me in. She always appeared to be there, though what she did in the office all day was anyone's guess. I thought, though, that I detected a look of slight relief on her thin face that I was disturbing her solitude.

'I won't be a minute,' I said.

'Fine. I'll be in the office if you want me.'

I went to the dressing room and fetched the book I had accidentally left behind the night before. When I came out, the chapel was silent. No sounds penetrated from the street outside. Imogen's office door was shut, but I could hear no typing or telephoning from within. It was then that it occurred to me that I should take a closer look at the harmonium.

At the end of the chapel, between the stage and the back wall there was a semi-circular way, like an ambulatory in a medieval church. It was only from this passage that one could gain proper access to the harmonium which was guarded from the stage by a low wooden screen. One went up a little staircase on the left of the harmonium to arrive at the bench and the console. I mounted the steps, sat down on the bench and studied the instrument. It was in a terrible state. The 'patent mouse-proof' foot pedals were flat on the floor and could not have generated any air; many of the ivory covered keys were cracked and some had lost their skin altogether. The wooden frame was worm-eaten, and crumbling away. I pressed one of the keys by way of experiment: a faint asthmatic cough was the response. It reverberated through the chapel for rather longer than it should have done.

I rose from the bench, intending to leave the sinister enclave, but as I did so, I noticed that there was another set of wooden steps to the left of the harmonium. They were identical to the ones by which I had ascended to get access to the console, but they led nowhere. They appeared to have been created merely for the sake of a symmetry invisible to all except the harmonium player. On the lowest step, enclosed by the high wooden back of the instrument an inscription in Roman capitals had been carved into the polished wood.

VIA MORTIS

It meant 'the way of death', or perhaps 'the road of death'. What was that about? I decided that my exploration must end.

Coming down into the dried blood passage and making my way to the entrance, I felt no better. The feeling of oppression, enhanced by the inscription on the step that went nowhere – and why in Latin? – had not left me.

Something glinted as I passed by on the way to the front entrance. I stopped and saw that the frame that had held the photograph of Mizpah McCreel had been put up again. There it was restored to the wall with its glass and its rough wooden backing, but no picture in it. I wondered at this as I scrutinised myself, darkly mirrored in the glass. It reminded me of Dr Dee's polished obsidian 'scrying stone' in the British Museum.

I was so absorbed by this vision of my anxious face that I started violently when I saw a reflection of something pale flitting past my shoulder. I turned and was confronted by Imogen who had come up behind me so silently that I thought for a moment she was a ghost.

'Sorry,' she said. I looked at her carefully for the first time. Despite her paleness and awful thinness, there was something likeable about her. She seemed to have no guile, and none of the urge to power that I had detected in Kirsty. No doubt there was a wound behind her anorexia, but it did not seem to be a fatal one; perhaps it was even a source of strength.

I asked what the frame was doing there.

'Kirsty put it up. I think she wants to put something in it.'

'Not another picture of Mizpah McCreel?'

A hint of a smile twitched her lips. 'Oh, no! Maybe a poster or something. She hasn't decided yet.'

'I see.' I wished her a nice morning and went on my way, faintly conscious that Imogen was staring after me. Or perhaps I was vain enough to believe she was. I forget.

By the end of the first week our audiences had increased but those for Rosa Luxemburg had dwindled to such an extent that the actress concerned decided to leave, thus forfeiting the deposit she had made on her second week. Nick announced this to us on the Monday evening, so we had no opportunity to sympathise with Rosa, or bid her farewell, because she had already gone. Kirsty was standing beside him as he told us. I got the impression that she was there to intimidate us, to prevent us asking questions or even making comments. In any case, Kirsty and Nick left before any discussion could take place. The rest of us, I think, felt relieved that the actress's agony was over, and perhaps too that we were no longer under pressure to vacate the dressing room quickly after the performance. I was ambivalent. I had been vaguely comforted by the fact that our company was not the last to leave the theatre at night, and I guessed that my fellow actors may have felt the same. During that week we usually contrived to leave the theatre together after the show. The subject was not discussed, but it became an unspoken rule. There was one night, though, when that did not happen.

Nick had become more detached from us as the run progressed. This was to be expected. He was establishing contacts, drinking with producers in the Festival Club at night, talking to media people and theatre critics. I noticed that he was confiding less in me than he had been, and was occasionally away from the flat where we were staying at night. Though I did not see him often with Kirsty I sensed that they were an item because whenever I saw him in the theatre it was always with her.

On the Tuesday of the second week Kirsty came to our dressing room to tell us that she would be away for two days and would be leaving the office in the hands of Imogen. She was looking harassed, having spent the afternoon, I gathered, resolving yet another acrimonious dispute between *Gas-Oven Gertie!* and *The Means and the Ends*. Nick, who was standing beside her as she made this announcement, added: 'So, try to keep out of trouble while she's away, guys.'

I noticed again that tone of condescension mingled with matey familiarity which was increasingly becoming a feature of his personality. I became aware that Nick might possibly be some sort of participant in Kirsty's absence. A glance at Carol told me that she too suspected, but we did not discuss it.

As we were leaving the theatre after the performance, I glanced at the empty picture frame in the passage. The glass barely reflected us but I thought I saw some kind of subtle movement in its dark interior. Was that a face? A face with firm set ascetic features, and a glittering fanatical stare? No. It was an illusion, so we passed on and left the theatre. Imogen followed behind turning off the lights as she did so and locking the gothic double doors of Drumglass Chapel.

I was not as careful of my health then as I am today, and would eat anything without much thought for its nutrient value. Tim, Carol and I had begun our fortnight in Edinburgh by cooking most of our meals in the flat. By the second week, a certain lassitude had set in and we had resorted to take-away meals or eating in cheap restaurants and cafés. This, in addition to the quantities of alcohol we consumed at the Festival Club, was bound to take its toll. It did so for me after an Indian takeaway, the remains of which I unwisely finished off for breakfast on the Thursday morning.

The consequences, which had been festering for most of the day, only became acute towards the end of our performance of *Last Man In*. I felt that I was suffering some sort of retribution for the careless lifestyle I had been leading. Guilt has always come naturally to me, but I could not help feeling that my quasi-ecclesiastical surroundings had enhanced this natural predisposition. The result was that, when the performance was over, I found myself confined to the lavatory while my fellow actors reluctantly (or perhaps not so reluctantly) took their leave of me.

At some point I must have blacked out, because the next thing I knew I was still in the back stage lavatory, and in darkness. Tim and Carol had presumably left the theatre without warning Imogen of my continued presence, and she had left the building after throwing the mains switch.

At first, I was strangely calm. The ache in my stomach had left me; I felt drained and empty with a dry mouth and a slight headache, but no sensation of nausea. The blackness was complete, but my other senses were alert. I groped for a light switch but it did not work, as I had expected. The silence was all-enveloping. I felt my way into the dressing room and to a chair.

Because I was completely deprived of sight, the possibility that I had gone blind did occur to me, but it did not seem likely. I felt my eyes. Nothing hurt, but I had no other proof. I even entertained the wild idea that I was dead.

It seems very odd to me now that such a possibility had taken hold over my mind, despite its absurdity. I was inside my body, my sense of touch functioned, I heard myself cough, so hearing was unimpaired. No, I was not dead. The afterlife could not be as banal as this: merely a lightless replica of the real world. I almost smiled at my own thoughts.

I sat for some time in the dressing room in the complete dark, afraid to move beyond it. It was possible that some entrance to the theatre was unlocked, though how I could find it was going to be a problem. At every moment inertia seemed the most desirable option, while at the same time I knew I must move. Eventually I felt my way to the door and opened it.

It seemed at first as dark in the passage outside, but I began to see patches of less impenetrable blackness. Death was still in my mind, and it somehow gave rise to the bizarre thought – one which seemed to come out of nowhere – that I was undergoing a kind of rehearsal for death. Perhaps it was not so strange, my being an actor, and considering the play I was in, but I wondered at it. It surprised me as much as the images that well up from my subconscious in dreams. It was like coming into your own house and finding a stranger sitting on your sofa.

I crept forward, trying not to jolt my brain into any more harrowing thoughts. But they kept coming. *Via Mortis*. The Way of Death. That was why I was possessed by these tormenting notions. No. Stop! I must find the front door and see if I could get out.

I doubted, even if I found a door, that it would open. Imogen was too conscientious for that. Perhaps this was what death was. You were still conscious, but you were shut in somewhere in the dark, deprived of nearly all sensation, knowing nothing except that hell was empty, and empty miles of dark air lay before and behind for all eternity.

But then, what would be the point of rehearsing for this? It would only increase your fear, not your preparedness. Fear is the most primitive of emotions; it had evolved to save you from death by heightening your senses, not to fill you with despair.

The noise at first came almost as a relief. At least it distracted me from these thoughts. To begin with, I could not identify it. It sounded like muttering or scuffling, from within the building, but at a distance. It was so faint and indistinct that I wondered whether it was just another trick my mind was playing on me. It seemed to vary. There were bouts of silence, then something like laughter, then a faint chant of some kind – was it two voices or one? – then a conversation which became more animated. I could hear no words, but it could have been an argument. It gathered intensity and venom: a high-pitched cry, thin and strangulated, and finally silence again. But there was no silence for me because I could hear my heart banging against my chest. I must find a door.

I found none. I blundered against cold granite walls but could feel no wood. I had no idea where I was. Darkness filled the space around me, vast as a starless night sky, confining as a coffin. Occasionally the blackness was disturbed by vagrant shreds of greyer matter, no sooner seen than evaporated into gloom. Then a great roar. It was the harmonium and I must have been very close to it. Someone or something had played a chord on it, the most vicious, least harmonious I had ever heard. All the works of Berg and Schoenberg were infantile, sentimental pipings compared with this one lost chord.

The noise rang in my ears for what seemed like minutes after it had been sounded, shattering all thought and meaning. It was while I was beginning to recover my senses that I saw them.

I knew them from the photographs which had been ceremoniously burnt at the theatre's opening. Like their photographs, Mizpah and Jabez McCreel appeared to me in monochrome, their features faintly outlined in silvery grey. Their long thin mouths were agape, their eyes open, but both eyes and mouth appeared to be veiled by a thin skein of grey gauze, like a cobweb. Their arms waved, as if to threaten, but the gestures were so feeble and futile that they excited only pity. It was purely the strangeness which created terror, but this was bad enough. Then they began slowly, arthritically, to dance.

I watched transfixed until something within shut down all

consciousness, and saved me from anything more.

Imogen found me the next morning just before ten, lying on the entrance mat just inside the front door of the chapel. She stirred me gently into wakefulness with her foot. I looked up at her and she stared down at me, unreproachful but curious. She seemed to me in that moment refreshingly normal.

'And what happened to you, laddie?' she said in her crisp Scottish voice. I explained my history as far as the blackout on the lavatory, but no further.

'You haven't seen Kirsty, have you?' she asked. 'She was supposed to meet me here this morning.'

I shook my head.

'Are you all right? Can I get you something?'

'Oddly enough, I don't feel too bad, but I am incredibly hungry. Is there somewhere near here where one can get breakfast?'

Imogen took me round the corner to one of those cafés that used to be called (with some reason) a 'greasy spoon'. I ordered a fried breakfast, as unhealthy as only a Scottish greasy spoon could make it; Imogen declined food and settled for a cup of milkless tea.

I apologised for what had happened, but she had decided to shoulder the blame. 'I should have checked more thoroughly before locking up,' she said.

I said, rather fatuously: 'No harm done.' But it had been, for once, the right thing to say. Any tension there had been between us was gone.

I asked her how she came to be working at the Drumglass Chapel Theatre. She told me that she had known Kirsty as a girl when both had been taken regularly to the Chapel, because Kirsty's parents and Imogen's grandmother had been Jabezites. I pressed her for further details about the Chapel and its doctrines, but Imogen was unwilling to oblige. She only said: 'My Gran got out in the end, but she didn't hate them. At the end they were pathetic. Pathetic, but still dangerous. You can't kill the dead.'

The cryptic finality with which she said this seemed to

forestall further discussion, so I offered her a piece of buttered toast instead. It was the least harmful element of my meal. She took a tentative nibble.

'Thank you,' I said involuntarily. She almost smiled.

'Ah, there you are!' said a voice from the doorway of the café. It was Nick. As usual, he gave the impression that we had somehow kept him waiting. He looked pale and tense, and was carrying a copy of *The Scotsman*. I thought at first he was the bearer of bad news. So apparently did Imogen.

'Have you seen Kirsty?'

'No. No. Why do you ask?' He seemed on edge. 'No. Look!' He threw *The Scotsman* on the table. 'We've won a Fringe First.'

That, in those days was, and for all I know still is, a considerable accolade. So, we finished our Edinburgh run with glory and good audiences, but, even so, I was glad to leave Drumglass Chapel.

Kirsty did not reappear, and I heard later from Imogen that the Police had made enquiries. She became a missing person, but, having no close relatives and few concerned friends, the case was soon dropped.

Following the Edinburgh success, our company performed *Last Man In* in London, once more to some acclaim. On the back of it I got a small part in a rather dull television series about a bank, and Nick was offered an assistant directorship at the Royal Court. We barely saw each other after that, and very soon not at all, until Colchester.

It was only yesterday that I received Nick's postcard through the post. His strange message and the image of Lon Chaney, the sinister clown in *He Who Gets Slapped* – bringing to mind those ubiquitous clowns in the Edinburgh Festival streets – are now inextricably linked in my mind. Then this afternoon I had a call from Carol. We were always on good terms and had kept in touch with each other after Edinburgh. She had married and moved to Devon. We exchanged Christmas cards; I had even become godfather to one of her children, but it is still something of a coincidence that she should call me today.

'Hello, Alan. How are things? Have you had a visit from the police?'

'What!?'

'I just have.'

'But why?'

'Well, you know they've found Kirsty Wang's body?'

'Good God! No! After all these years! When did this happen?'

'A couple of weeks ago. Oh, Alan, don't you ever read the papers or watch the news? You are *so* out of touch.'

'I live in Suffolk.'

'That's no excuse.'

She told me that Drumglass Chapel was at last being pulled down to make way for a block of luxury apartments. The foundations, when exposed, revealed a labyrinthine network of underground passages and chambers, in one of which a corpse had been found lying on a table. Though almost forty years had elapsed, the dry atmosphere in the chamber had preserved the body in a mummified condition. It was quite rapidly identified as the body of Kirsty Wang, missing since the 17th of August 1979. A violent and possibly homicidal end was suspected, as the hyoid bone in her neck was found to be fractured in two places. One newspaper, Carol told me, had included the curious detail that the underground passages had been accessed by a carefully concealed entrance beneath the harmonium in the Chapel. It was known only to a very few select devotees of the millenarian sect known as the Jabezites. According to the report, the passages had been used for a kind of ritual initiation known as 'The Second Death', said to be modelled on the rites of Eleusis in Classical Greece. This, given the Jabezites' origins in nonconformist Christianity, seemed to me unlikely, but I let it pass.

'So what did the police ask you about when they came?'

'Just general things about the plays at the Chapel and when she disappeared. And, of course, I had to tell them about Kirsty and Nick.'

'What do you mean?'

'Well, that they had a thing going. Surely you knew that?'

'I suspected. But you're positive about that?'

'Oh, yes. I actually saw them together. You know. At it. On what you insisted on calling "The Lord's Table" as a matter of fact. It was all rather horrible because you know I fancied him like mad at the time.'

'I rather gathered that.'

'Well, of course, afterwards he would barely speak to me. And no chance of him ever giving me a job again.'

'Par for the course. So they'll be talking to Nick?'

'Bound to.'

'And me.'

'Almost certainly. What are *you* going to say?'

'What *can* I say? I have nothing to say really.'

That was not quite true. It is rather that I have no idea what I am *going* to say, if I am interrogated. I can predict nothing, not even that Nick will become Director of the National Theatre, though his appointment has now been announced. I have begun to feel sorry for him.

THE DEVIL IN THE DARK CITY

Edinburgh, that great seat of learning for so many hundreds of years, was once known somewhat irreverently as 'Auld Reekie'. Apparently, this was an affectionate nickname, which was traced by author Robert Chambers back as far as the mid-17th century, before the Industrial Revolution, but a time when, thanks to the town's vast clutter of tall, close-packed chimneys, a huge pall of dirty, smelly smog permanently engulfed it.

'Auld Reekie' might seem like an amusing term now, an idle but fond reference to a distant time when things were not quite as they should be, but in truth there was little to get dewy-eyed about. We have already discussed in this book how in such conditions of darkness and smog, squalor and crime flourished. By the mid-18th century, when thanks to its debating societies, gentleman's clubs and teaching hospitals, Edinburgh was at the forefront of the Age of Enlightenment, many of its lower streets and underpasses still existed in a state of permanent night. And the city would certainly go on to boast some infamous villains who made use of this: Burke and Hare, Deacon Brodie, though perhaps the most frightening of them all was Major Weir.

The Major Weir story, which reached its culmination with a ghastly spectacle in 1670, sits at the heart of Auld Reekie legend, combining many aspects of the bad old Scotland of religious zealotry, superstition, ruthless politics and weird criminality, shrouding it all not just in smog, but in a genuinely impenetrable mystery.

Thomas Weir was long a renowned figure in Edinburgh. A career soldier who had performed good service during both the Irish Rebellion of 1641 and the English Civil War, he was later appointed commander of the Edinburgh City Guard. In this capacity, he became known for his strict Presbyterian beliefs and for being a dour, humourless man who would utter loud prayers in public. For these reasons, he wasn't especially well-liked, but at least he was respected. He was unmarried but said to live cleanly and frugally with his sister, Jean (also known as 'Grizel'), in an unremarkable house in the West Bow quarter of the city.

At this stage there were no obvious flaws in his character, though other military veterans were unimpressed by his brutal mistreatment of the Marquess of Montrose, a distinguished warrior in the Royalist cause, who was held in Weir's custody on the eve of his execution in 1650. However, this aside, there was nothing bad anyone could really say about Weir.

Which makes the events of 1670, when he was 69, all the more bewildering.

That year, even though there was no suspicion about him whatsoever, Weir volunteered a confession to the Lord Provost of Edinburgh that he was in league with Lucifer, in whose name he had committed secret murders and at whose instigation he had performed bestial sexual acts with his sister, Grizel.

So unexpected was this that, even at a time when it didn't take much more than an accusation of witchcraft to lead someone to the gallows or stake, the authorities hesitated to act. Noting that Weir had recently emerged from a long illness, they assumed that he was delusional and attempted to dismiss the case. But Weir insisted that he was guilty, that he was responsible for countless vile acts and that he was a warlock who had been consorting with demonic beings. Grizel made no denials either, though she was less coherent and was even described by one onlooker as having 'lost her wits'. However, the magistrates were impressed by her story (to which others also attested) that one night in 1650 her brother had been driven away by a stranger in a burning coach and had later returned with knowledge that the Royalists would lose all at the battle of Worcester, which they duly did in 1651.

Weir was examined by doctors, who declared him perfectly sane, and now other witnesses were coming forward to tell equally scurrilous stories. Unearthly music and eerie singing had been heard from the Weir house late at night. The 10-foot-tall spectre of a deformed woman had been seen on a nearby lane. Weir's walking stick, a hefty piece of timber, the handle of which, rather oddly, was carved into the image of a human head, had been seen moving on its own and even beating a path for him along the crowded thoroughfares. It was even recollected that Weir's mother, Lady Jean Somerville, had been a noted clairvoyant.

In the end a trial was inevitable, as was the guilty verdict, though it didn't help that, when questioned in court, Major Weir made comments like: 'I have lived like a beast and should die like one'. His wish was granted later that year, when he was garrotted and burned along with his walking-stick at the Gallowlee just outside the city (his stick supposedly performing 'rare turnings' in the flames), while Grizel met the same fate in the Grassmarket. In both cases, the watching crowd stood in awe-stricken silence.

The story doesn't entirely end there. The gigantic woman was allegedly sighted again, along with Grizel's blackened ghost, while riotous night-time sounds still allegedly emitted from the now-empty house in the West Bow. It was finally bought in 1780 by one William Patullo, who fled on the first night with his wife, claiming they had been woken by the spectre of a calf entering their bedroom and rearing up onto their bed.

The house was demolished in 1830, with no trace of it left in modern times. Today, no one even knows where it once stood. The case remains a singular, perplexing mystery.

TWO SHAKES OF A DEAD LAMB'S TAIL
Anna Taborska

Remember the urban legend about the dealer who got put away, and then all the hoods and heads from the neighbourhood hightailed it over to his place to look for his fridge full of acid from the Sixties? Well, I knew that dealer. No, seriously, I really did know him.

I was fifteen when I met him. A girl from school had invited me to a party, along with some of her out-of-school mates. Apart from the usual teenagers getting drunk and smoking weed, there was a smartly dressed man with long grey hair tied back in a ponytail. He introduced himself to me (a new kid he hadn't seen around before) in a soft, reassuring voice. He disappeared briefly from view, returning a while later with cups and a large teapot. A hush fell on the room and people gathered round, holding out teacups as he poured. He noticed my hesitation.

'You can have as much or as little as you want,' he soothed in tones as velvet as the light cast over the room by the tie-dye scarf-covered lamps.

The mushroom tea was vile. I settled back in my chair and waited. A little time passed. Then the room started to breathe. It transformed into an organic entity. The walls moved gently in and out. An art student's sketch of a marble horse's head snorted and tossed about on the wall. And everything turned a shade of purple I'd never seen before, or since.

How the man got my number, I don't know. Perhaps he'd asked and I'd given it to him – I don't remember. But he leant me a copy of *Amazing Dope Tales* (it's probably still lying around somewhere in my mother's house), and he phoned me a few times, suggesting that I drop out of school and move in with him to help him 'raise his daughter' (who was older than I was).

I didn't drop out of school. Eventually I'd go on to do my A-levels and go to university, where I'd learn how spiders spun different webs under the influence of different drugs. But at the time, the next thing I knew was that the man was in prison and everyone was heading for his place to look for The Fridge.

Was there really a refrigerator filled with uber-potent LSD in a North London flat somewhere? I don't know. But this isn't a story about an acid chemist being busted on his way to Ireland in a decommissioned ambulance full of prohibited substances and drug-making apparatus. This is a story about sheep.

'Wake up!' my husband Dan was hissing at me from his prime position in the window seat. 'We're nearly there.'

I hadn't meant to fall asleep. Towards the end of the journey the train from Euston to Carlisle passed through some spectacular countryside, and I'd been hoping to soak it all in, but as usual the train's rocking motion proved too soporific for me to resist. I fought the urge to go right back to sleep; well, a sharp shake from Dan helped, and we were soon throwing on our jackets and pulling our bags off the luggage rack. My in-laws were waiting for us outside the station.

I don't know why my husband always insisted we go on holiday with his parents. No, that's not strictly true. I do know. His parents were generous and my husband loved 'cash savings'. Despite bringing in a six-figure salary as a hedge fund manager, he always insisted that I pay my way and half the household bills. Not easy when I never averaged more than two novels a year, and never more than a 4K advance on either of them. Why was I still married to him, you ask? Well, he was nice-looking, fairly intelligent, and occasionally a good laugh. Not really my type; not the usual long-haired, black-leather-jacket-wearing laidback stoner that I'd tended to go for since my teens, but you know what they say … every girl's crazy 'bout a sharp-dressed man, and perhaps Dan's clean-cut look, immaculately tailored wardrobe and go-getter confidence are what turned my head in the first place. And Dan's parents, although generally disapproving and occasionally mocking of me, and despite their modest pensions, were generous when it came to family vacations, so that neither Dan nor I ever had to put a hand in our pockets when we were with them. And now we were in my in-laws' car, being driven by Dan's father at the start of another family holiday.

Dumfries and Galloway. Not a part of the world that had ever come on my radar. Well, perhaps a wee dram to your man Burns now and again, but that was about it. And more's the pity, I thought, as we drove past miles of rolling fields, the odd patch of snow still sparkling here and there. Scattered about the gentle landscape were the pale specks of sheep, which would soon glow a curiously pretty shade of peach-pink in the sunset.

After about quarter of an hour's drive, the M6 morphed into the A75 – some say, Scotland's most haunted road, known as the Ghost Road. Over the years, phantom stagecoaches, roadside spectres, ghostly beasts and shrieking apparitions have been reported by disturbed motorists, and apparently some long-distance lorry drivers avoid the road at all costs. We drove along in blissful ignorance, past Gretna Green, the famous haven for young couples escaping England since the latter half of the eighteenth century to take advantage of Scotland's relaxed matrimonial laws and marry without their parents' consent.

Another fifteen minutes and we left the Ghost Road, turning right at Carrutherstown onto the B725, in the direction, as the crow flies, of the small town of Lockerbie, where the doomed Pan Am Flight 103 came down on 21 December 1988, killing all two hundred and fifty-nine onboard and eleven people on the ground.

Thirty-two years later and the United States is still trying to extradite the suspected bombmaker from Libya. To this day, the Lockerbie bombing remains the deadliest single terrorist attack in the history of the United Kingdom, and the second deadliest terrorist attack in American history after 9/11. But we weren't going as far as Lockerbie.

A minute after our turn onto the B725, as we were crossing Dalton Burn, I saw it. Dusk fell early at the beginning of April, but there was still enough light, and I know I saw it in the ditch: the overturned, rusting skeleton of what must have once been an ambulance – dirty, decomposing, overtaken by nature; the scraggly dark contours of sheep feeding on the grass that grew around it and inside it. No peachy lambkins these. Although I had but a brief glimpse, something about those murky unkempt shapes voraciously devouring the outgrowth from that rotting vehicle unnerved me and made me feel slightly sick. A reaction, you'll agree, entirely out of proportion to the situation, but it stayed with me for the next couple of minutes, and then it was dark and we were turning into the driveway of the impressive one-storey U-shaped converted farmhouse that was our destination.

Dan and I grabbed our things from the car boot and hurried after my in-laws across the frosty, gravelled courtyard and into the house. The grey-slate-roofed, whitewashed farmhouse had been gutted inside and turned into a contemporary holiday home. A fitted kitchen with a large breakfast bar opened onto a vast open-plan space with a dining table and a living area. Two big black leather corner-sofas faced each other across a large square oak coffee table, there was a handmade pebble fireplace with a glass-fronted wood-burning stove, and enormous glass patio doors running the length of the main section of the house opened onto the darkness of the garden and whatever lay beyond.

Dan's parents had driven up from Manchester a couple of days earlier and had already made themselves at home. There was a partially completed jigsaw puzzle on the coffee table. The lid of the cardboard box lying on one of the sofas intimated that the configured thousand pieces would reveal a picture-postcard verdant landscape, dotted with … you guessed it … sheep. A quick flashback of munching, grinding jaws; protruding incisors ripping up fetid, polluted vegetation, and two banks of molars churning, pulverising. Boggly ovine eyes staring blankly into space.

'What are you doing?' Dan's impatient snarl brought me out of my reverie and I quickly followed my husband into our allocated twin room, unpacking some toiletries and anything that would benefit from being hung up in the wardrobe. Half an hour later, we were back in our warmest jackets and headed for The Butchered Lamb: as unpleasantly named a pub as ever I'd patronised. The road to the pub was almost pitch black. Luckily Dan's parents, ever prepared, had a torch, which they shone at the road ahead of us.

There was no pavement to speak of; only a narrow road with tight hedges on either side, and I wondered how on earth a car would see us in time to stop before it flattened us. But there were no cars – either on the way there or on the way back. Only scuffling noises in the hedges, which no one apart from me seemed to hear, as the others walked slightly ahead of me, talking and laughing loudly.

I'd never known Dan or his parents to leave a pub before closing time, and tonight was no exception. It was midnight by the time we got back to the farmhouse. The three of them called it a night, but it was way too early for me to retire. I've never been much of a morning person or one to go to bed before two or three a.m. Night-time was just too precious; it was the only time I really had to myself – no demands, no phone calls, no pressure. I promised Dan I wouldn't disturb everyone by having the TV on, and I settled down to a horror novel, a debut by an author whose short stories frequently appeared in the same anthologies as mine.

It wasn't long before I had the distinct feeling that I was not alone in the vast living space. I looked around for Dan or one of his parents, but nobody had come in from any of the bedrooms. The silence in the house was unnerving; not even the fridge was buzzing. I sat very still for a while, surveying the empty room and listening. Eventually I returned to reading my book. Then it came again, that feeling that something had moved across the room without my seeing it. From my position on one of the sofas I could see the kitchen to my left and the large dark expanse of patio doors on the right. I sat motionless, watching, listening. The sensation of movement came again. Careful not to make a sound, I scoured the room again, and then I saw it creep forward: a tiny mouse. It hadn't noticed me. I watched as the little creature inspected the kitchen floor. Finding nothing of interest, it sat back on its haunches and proceeded to clean its face with its paws. It must have caught sight of me then, as suddenly it bolted past the patio doors and disappeared into a little gap somewhere between the wall and the floor.

I made a mental note not to blurt out anything about the night-time visit to Dan or his parents, lest they harboured latent muricidal tendencies that might prove fatal for my furry little companion. It must have been about three a.m. by the time I was sleepy enough to go to bed.

I woke up to the *Mary Celeste*. No sight or sound of my husband or my in-laws. And for once their enthusiastic bickering hadn't woken me up at some godforsaken time of the morning. I hadn't even heard Dan get out of bed.

'Dan?' But there was no sign of any of them anywhere. My gratitude at having been allowed a lie-in soon turned to a tinge of annoyance at having been left behind without so much as a note, and even a slight sense of abandonment. I looked out through the patio doors. Still no sign of anyone, but the sight that greeted me went some way to lifting my spirits. The profound blackness of the previous night had been replaced by a stunning vista of grassy fields stretching away as far as the eye could see, and sheep: not the gloomy monstrosities of the previous night, but placidly grazing ewes surrounded by little lambs – sweet as anything and whiter than the patches of snow that were already melting in the late morning sun. As I watched, I saw a lamb tense up on its four little legs and spring into the air (once, twice, three times) in what looked like an expression of sheer boundless uncontained joy. I was mesmerised. I watched the bouncing lambs for a while and then I decided: screw Dan and my in-laws; I'd have breakfast and then I'd go for a walk on my own and take photos of sheep.

My mother-in-law had left out half a loaf of sliced bread for me on the breakfast counter. I found some jam and butter in the fridge, and made myself a round of toast. I put on the kettle and started to look for the teabags – where the hell were they? Some folk can't face the day without a cup of coffee; with me it was tea. I decided to brave the kitchen cupboards. There was more stuff in there than I'd expected: a cornucopia of perfectly edible and potable products left behind by previous guests. There were half-full packets of pasta, opened boxes of cereal, hardly touched bags of sugar and flour, abandoned coffee jars, a container of drinking chocolate powder and ... a pretty metal tin with faded paisley patterns containing what could only be loose-leaf tea. Success! Well, partial success at least. A nice English Breakfast teabag it wasn't, but it was tea and it would do.

Half an hour later I was headed across the back garden, past what the holiday-home brochure described as a 'rotating summerhouse' (a large shed which could be swivelled round to face the sun at different times of day), and down a path leading along the neighbouring fields and past the sheep. I took some photos, but decided not to get too close so as not to disturb them. Besides, I didn't like the way they were starting to look at me. Beady eyes staring right at me, following my every move. *Just because you're paranoid, doesn't mean sheep aren't out to get you*, I thought (only half-jokingly) and hastened my pace. A chill, stale, southerly wind started to blow, and I wondered vainly whether it was blowing from Sellafield, the notorious nuclear site forty-four miles away, which so vexed environmental activists and had been polluting the Cumbrian coast and the Irish Sea since 1950. Then the path I was following inclined upwards a bit, curved a little, and I came face to face with something that stopped me dead in my tracks. *Dead* being the operative word.

Lying in front of me, just off the path, was the stinking, rotting, maggot-infested corpse of a sheep. Or most of it. One of its legs was missing; or rather, I thought it was missing, until I saw it lying a couple of metres away. Likewise, its bottom jaw lay some distance away, stripped clean of flesh, skin and hair, but otherwise complete. Most of the top jaw and the rest of the head were still attached to the body, but the animal's toothless dental pad was missing, snapped or perhaps mauled off – posthumously, I hoped. Two small, slightly curved horns and the gaping hole of what I guessed might have been the top of the animal's windpipe pointed up at the cold heavens. Patches of black fur protruded from under the head, and the dirty white wool on the body still bore the pink of a farmer's mark.

I moved off quickly, but it wasn't long before I encountered another corpse, this one without much of a head, and with the wool on its chest ripped open, ribs exposed to scavengers and the elements. I hurried on, hardly looking at this unfortunate beast, determined not to let a couple of dead sheep ruin my walk. Alas, as I rounded another bend in the path, I came to a small ditch, from which a bramble-obscured stream seemed to emerge and flow back in the direction of the holiday home. Just above the ditch, and upstream from the little brook, lay a third ovine carcass – perhaps the most disturbing one of the three. It wasn't as disgusting as the other two; it didn't stink as much, there were no maggots in evidence and it was pretty much intact, albeit skeletal. The wool on its top half had largely come away and now formed a soggy pale-coloured mush underneath the body, while the bottom half was still covered in black and white fur. What rendered this sheep truly horrific was the position it had assumed in death. The body lay stretched out on its back, ribs spread like a grotesque fan, hind legs splayed wide in awkward, painful, distressingly anthropomorphic vulnerability. Apart from those morbidly spread legs, the dead animal rested like a person might lie on a bed or a bier, back and neck straight, head facing skywards. 'Topping' the entire macabre effect (if you pardon the pun) was a patch of fuzzy black fur covering the top of the skull, almost like curly human hair. The effect was utterly chilling: a skeletal homunculus gazing up at an indifferent sky, the juices of its decomposition having long since permeated into the stream beneath.

I finally managed to tear my eyes away from the melancholy

humanlike carcass, and looked half-heartedly towards where the rest of my walk would have taken me. About ten metres away lay another dead sheep – this one large, fleshy, woolly and much fresher than the others. *That's it, I give up*, I thought, suddenly feeling tired, depressed and not a little nauseous. I turned to go back, and that's when I heard something behind me. A creaking, scuffling noise, and then an eerie, growling, almost human sound – like the death rattle deep from a dying person's throat combined with the low, rasping, rumbling bleat of a sheep. Instantly every tiny hair on the back of my neck stood up, and I honestly thought I was going to have a heart attack. I spun round to where the fresh carcass had been lying, but it was no longer there; it was up on all four cloven-hoofed legs, getting its bearings and gaining speed as it advanced towards me. Its bloodshot sheepy eyes dead, yet demented; jaws grating and clacking as it rapidly closed the distance between it and me.

Crazed with fear, I turned and ran, almost tripping over the skeletal carcass which had somehow rolled onto its front and was scrabbling in the mud at the top of the ditch, trying to haul itself up, empty eye sockets fixated on me as I narrowly avoided falling into the ditch and ran on back down the path towards the holiday home, back to where the other sheep carcasses were stirring in some kind of unnatural, twisted animation and coming for me, jaws snapping, teeth grinding. Now, I wasn't the fittest person, but luckily I had a head start: the reanimated monstrosities started off slow before they got going, almost as though chilled bones and stiff muscles had to readjust from death back to a perverse semblance of life. I dodged past the headless, rib-exposed carcass – at least this one didn't have anything to bite me with, but somehow it sensed me none-the-less and redoubled its repulsive efforts to writhe in my direction.

By the time my path was blocked by the three-legged carcass, my heart felt like it was beating somewhere in my throat and my lungs were on fire. I knew I couldn't stop; the other three dead sheep were right behind me, and as I glanced back, I saw at least three more coming up behind them. If I stopped, they'd be on me. Exactly what that would entail, I had no idea and even less desire to find out. Screaming, I ran straight at Tripod, and the three-legged stinker hobbled right back at me in what from a distance probably resembled a zombie sheep game of chicken from hell. At the last moment, I threw my camera at the thing's head and veered off the path, hardly believing my luck when Tripod swerved too late to get me, the jagged protrusion of its remaining top jaw missing my leg by an inch. Heart thumping, head pounding, I ran; the ovine zombie apocalypse close on my heels.

With the last of my strength, I tumbled over the low wire fence separating the farmers' fields from the back garden of the holiday home, and crawled on hands and knees through the grass, mud and last of the melted snow to the summerhouse. I pulled myself in and collapsed on the wooden floor, coughing and panting. At least I'd quit smoking a couple of years earlier; if I hadn't, I'd probably be dead by now. The sun-shed had no door; I had to get to the house and lock myself in, but I was too exhausted to move. I wondered how on earth I'd make the final few metres to the entrance door, and that's when I heard the gurgling, rasping *baas* – a few metres away, I reckoned, and coming closer. They'd briefly lost sight of me, but if the Headless Wonder had managed to come after me, with no eyes and no nose, then doubtless they could sense me in some unspeakable, unthinkable way of their own. I had to get to the house.

I can't say I'd caught my breath, but at least I no longer felt like I was dying. I lifted myself from the floor of the sun-shed and raised my head slowly, planning to peer out before making a run for it, but I was greeted by the horrific sight, sound and smell of one of the recently deceased. It had evidently tracked me to the summerhouse and now bleat-howled in triumph, its stinking maw of a rotting, maggot-spewing mouth just inches from mine. As it lunged forward, I dodged sideways, thrust a foot out of the sun-shed and pushed off from the ground, causing the wooden structure to rotate and the entrance to turn away from the monster, bringing the shed to a halt when it was facing the house. Most of the sheep were still behind the summerhouse, although now rapidly heading around it, in my direction. I raced to the door, pulling the keys out of my pocket as I ran. My fetid ovine entourage threw itself after me. I felt one of the bastards nip at the leg of my jeans, and just as I made it to the door it went for me again. I kicked at it, and my leg went right through rotted flesh into the stinking innards beneath. I gagged in shock and disgust, but managed to pull my foot back out. The beast paused for only the briefest moment, but by then I was turning the key, and I was in the house, locking the door and falling against it, while the monsters outside pummelled the door with their heads or haunches or whatever other horrid body parts they still had left. Shaking like the proverbial leaf, I crawled to the bedside table where I'd forgotten my phone, and picked out my husband's number.

'Are you on drugs?' Three-quarters of an hour had passed since my gibbering phone call, and Dan was standing over me, livid.

'They had these evil bulging eyes,' I tried to explain, 'and they had to be dead because their ribs were sticking out all over the place, and one had no head, but their jaws were clanking, and there were maggots everywhere, but they were coming to get me ...'

Dan leaned in really close and peered into my eyes.

'You are, aren't you? You're on drugs. And you stink. What the fuck have you been doing?'

'The sheep,' I stuttered. 'They might come back!'

'What the fuck have you taken?'

'Nothing!'

'Don't lie to me!'

Had I been in a fit state to notice, I would have seen that my husband's face was turning a worrying shade of red. He grabbed my arm and dragged me over to the sofa, sitting me down roughly. 'Your pupils are as big as saucers. What the hell have you taken?'

'Nothing.' I whined defensively.

Dan wasn't buying any of it.

'Talk me through everything you ate, drank and otherwise put in your mouth since you got up this morning. Or should I say: afternoon.'

'I got up at 11.40,' I said indignantly.

'Whatever. Just tell me what you had to eat.'

'All I had was toast,' I sighed. Dan continued to glare at me. 'I had two slices of bread, which I toasted, then I put butter and jam on them, and then I had some tea.'

'Tea?' Dan's grip on my arm tightened. 'There isn't any tea.'

'Yes, there is.'

'No, there isn't. My parents forgot to bring the tea.'

My husband pulled me up and marched me over to the kitchen counter. He started going through the cupboards, taking out all the boxes, jars and packets. He pulled out the tin with the loose-leaf tea I'd helped myself to, opened it and held it up to the light. 'Is this what you had?' he asked.

I nodded.

'You idiot! Can't you see it has mould in it?'

Dan thrust the tin in front of my face and shook it. He was right there did indeed seem to be some mould in it, which I hadn't noticed earlier. I clapped my hand over my mouth.

'God, that's gross,' I said.

'You really are a moron,' my husband concluded. I was beginning to agree with him. 'And where are Mum and Dad? They said they'd be right behind me; they were just going to finish their drinks.'

'Maybe the sheep got them,' I ventured hesitantly. Dan cast me a filthy look. I was starting to think that perhaps he was right, perhaps it had all been a bad trip. Maybe I'd visit my mother when we got back and try to find my copy (the dealer's copy) of *Amazing Dope Tales*. If I'd read it all those years ago, I certainly couldn't remember any of it.

I glanced at my husband. He was pacing up and down the room, something he only did when he was really pissed off with me.

'You're unbelievable,' he was saying. 'Not only do you sleep all day, you fuck yourself up with dodgy tea, and you drag me all the way back here. I still had half a pint …'

I let my husband's voice fade out, and I watched him walking up and down. Despite the slightly thinning hair on top of his head, the waving arms and angry red tinge to his cheeks, he still looked pretty good. He paced up and down the whole length of the patio doors. He strode, head up, back straight – a confident, angry man. *He walks like he still has a future* – I thought to myself. He must have realised I wasn't listening because he stopped abruptly and glared at me. Just as he opened his mouth again to renew his chastisement of his stupid wife, there was a tremendous crashing sound, shards flew everywhere, and an undead sheep came flying through the plate-glass, its jaws clamping onto my husband's neck. It flicked its head sideways, taking my husband's throat with it as it landed hard on the wooden flooring. Blood gushed everywhere. The vile beast's molars ground up my husband's flesh as it stared at me with its dead red eyes. Then it sprang. The last thing I heard was a vile, gurgling, resounding:

'*Baaaaaaaaa!*'

I'LL BE IN SCOTLAND BEFORE YOU

Pearlin' Jean, O Pearlin' Jean,
She haunts the house, she haunts the green
And glowers on us a' wi' her wullcat e'en

For all the silver in English bank,
Nor yet for all the gold,
Would I pass through the hall of Allanbank
When the midnight bell has toll'd ...

Berwickshire folk song, circa 1800

Many a ghost story in the western world has sprung from tales of nuns who strayed into the arms of lustful men. There are numerous country houses all over Britain and Europe where the mournful shades of women in monastic robes are said to emerge nightly from the solid brickwork behind which they were once immured for this heinous transgression.

The case of Pearlin Jean, probably one of Scotland's most famous ghosts, does not involve immurement, but it does centre around a nun who fell in love with a layman and found her life forfeit when he inevitably abandoned her.

It all began in the early 1690s, when Sir Robert Stuart, first Baronet of Allanbank, was in France, Paris in fact, to complete his education. It was here where he first met a beautiful French woman whose name is lost to history but who with the advantage of foreknowledge, we can refer to as Jean. The accounts vary as to whether Jean was a private citizen or a nun drawn from the Sisters of Charity, though most seem to favour the latter. Either way, the twosome were instantly attracted and commenced a sexual

148

relationship, though it was only a matter of time before this ended in tears.

To Stuart, Jean was no more than a distraction, an enjoyable diversion while he was away from home. When he was due to return, he ended the affair abruptly, which mortified his lover, not just because her beau was abandoning her, but because she had broken her all-important vow of chastity for nothing. Stuart was unconcerned by this, telling her that he was already engaged to be married and would be reuniting with his wife-to-be as soon as he returned to Scotland.

The next day, he left his Paris lodgings in a horse-drawn carriage, only for Jean to step out in front of him, weeping and begging him to stay. Irritated, Stuart urged the driver to continue. The nun refused to step aside and was subsequently run down, a wheel of the carriage passing over her head, inflicting a fatal injury. Again, the stories differ at this point, some alleging that Stuart simply drove on, not the least embarrassed, another claiming that, in a brief fit of remorse, he stopped, climbed out and knelt beside the poor woman as she died, her last words to him: 'I'll be in Scotland before you.'

Folklorists are mostly unconvinced by this supposed snippet of dialogue, regarding it as a fanciful addition to the tale, and pointing out the same phrase in the popular song 'Loch Lomond', which originated as a Jacobite ballad featuring a brave rebel who returns to Scotland before those of lesser courage as he'd been despatched there by the English hangman. Whatever the truth, whether those were indeed the nun's last words or not, she did return before him. Because when Stuart was approaching Allanbank House, his ancestral home near Allanton in Berwickshire, he was stunned to see a ragged, bloodstained figure sitting on top of the arch over the entrance gate.

It was Jean, but this was only her first manifestation. From here on, a progressively more terrifying haunting commenced. The tapping of high-heeled French boots parading around the house could often be heard, doors would open and close and ornaments were flung from wall to wall. Eeriest of all, whenever the ghost was seen, which was regularly, she was covered head-to-foot in bloodstained lace, but at the same time appeared to be decaying in tandem with her actual corpse, which presumably still lay in its grave in France. In due course, the spectre was no more than a skeleton clad in bloody lace, the appearance of which almost drove Stuart out of his mind.

Attempted exorcisms and clearances failed, at one point seven local ministers from the Church of the Reformed Faith joining forces there to pray, though even this sterling effort was defeated. Somehow or other, Stuart commissioned a portrait of the nun, presumably from memory, and hung it between paintings of himself and his wife. Reportedly, this allayed things a little, though his wife eventually became indignant and had the picture moved, after which the haunting returned to its former violence.

The name 'Pearlin Jean' was eventually derived from the phantom's Pearlin lace shroud, and if it sounds as if there is something almost affectionate about this, that could be because after the laird's premature death, which followed within a handful of years, the grotesque figure continued to be sighted, but staff at Allanbank House now felt much less threatened by it. However, in a footnote to the main story, there was one very frightening incident in the 1700s, when a certain Thomas Blackadder, who was a guest at Allanbank for a grand ball, encountered a mysterious and alluring woman there, whom he agreed to meet in the moonlit orchard afterwards. But when he went out, he beheld a form so terrifying that it drove him to flight. For ever after, he refused to divulge the details of the assignation, though those in the know concluded that his 'date' had been Pearlin Jean.

Allanbank House was demolished in the early 1800s, though so intense had the haunting reputedly been that as late as the 1920s, the landowners could find no tenants who would occupy the new buildings there.

THE RINGLET STONES
Charlotte Bond

'Breathe in, Meg. Can you taste it? That's fresh air, that is. *So* much better than that city smog we're used to.'

Meg thought of their apartment in Glasgow, the way the back gate opened onto a common leading down to the river. Sure, there was litter and the odd abandoned bike, but there were also daffodils in spring, and daisies and family picnics in summer. Sometimes a mist hung around the river, but no smog.

She thought of the tiny, shitty terrace she'd grown up in and how that *did* stink – of cat pee and stale beer. Erika, with her private education, her parents' five-bedroomed house with its separate music room, had probably never smelt anything worse in her life than a particularly pungent air freshener.

But standing just outside the Glentrool Visitor Centre, Erika was animated and radiant in a way Meg hadn't seen recently. So, she said, 'Yeah. Nice and clean.'

Because that's what you do when you love somebody: help keep them happy.

'This is gonna be great,' Erika said, throwing her arm around Meg's shoulders. 'So much better than a dumb party at Darren's. You'll love it out here. This'll be a weekend to remember.'

The ease of her embrace and Erika's joyful tone gave Meg hope that maybe she'd been wrong: maybe this weekend would be good for them, and not just another nail in the coffin of their relationship.

They approached the visitor centre and looked at the board detailing the various trails through the forest. Once again, Meg was shocked to realise just how big Galloway Forest was; the closest she'd been to such an expanse of nature was the park behind her nan's where she'd holidayed as a kid.

'The forest can be *our* thing,' Erika had said. 'Somewhere neither of us has been before. That'll make it special.'

Together, they picked a trail, and Meg smiled brightly, even though her legs ached just at the thought of walking so many miles.

The place was busy but not crowded, but Meg felt hemmed in by the trees towering over the path.

You're just being ridiculous, she told herself. *No one else looks like they're losing it due to a bunch of trees.*

So, she didn't freak out when the midges got tangled in her eyelashes; she made appreciative remarks when they passed the various natural art installations on the trail; and when Erika said, 'Look! An unmarked path. Let's explore,' Meg didn't object, even though the idea of departing from the marked trails made her stomach flip.

Despite her agreement earning her a light kiss on the lips from Erika, Meg soon began to regret her decision not to speak up. After less than a quarter of a mile, the rocky but obvious path turned into little more than bare patches of flattened grass. The trees drew closer to them so that she was constantly pushing branches out of her face.

A deep unease crept through her; it was so quiet among the trees.

On the main trail, there had been the chatter of families, the clack of cycle chains, the barking of dogs. A city girl through and through, Meg would be the first to admit she knew virtually nothing about nature, but she felt sure there should be some noise beyond their own breathing and footsteps. Birdsong, at least. Maybe the bellow of some deer. Mice or squirrels or rabbits in the undergrowth. Even a solitary bee. But there was nothing. Meg looked down at the ground, uncertain if they were even following a path now, or whether the grass ahead of her had merely been flattened by Erika.

Breathless and panicky, Meg stopped and looked around. *There has to be some life here,* she told herself. She thought of all those leaflets they'd pored over in the B&B that morning.

There'd been pictures of red squirrels, roe deer, and even wild goats – where were those animal now? Yet despite the silence, she had the distinct feeling that they were being watched.

Up ahead, Erika turned and glared at Meg. 'What's the matter? You can't be out of breath already?' she asked, panting heavily herself.

'It's … so quiet. I just think –'

'You just think *what*?' Erika demanded. Her cheeks were flushed and strands of her red, curly hair were plastered to her head with sweat.

Meg swept her own long, sweat-slicked fringe out of her eyes. 'Don't you think it's quiet?'

'Of course it's quiet. It's Galloway Forest not a Glasgow estate. What were you expecting?'

Meg, feeling her own anger rising, shrugged and said, 'Robins, squirrels, deer, blackbirds – like the leaflets said.'

'You never try anything new and then you complain if it's not *exactly* how you imagined it.'

'That makes no sense. How can I complain about something new if I never try anything? You're just contradicting yourself.'

'Don't spoil this, Meg,' Erika snapped.

Meg drew breath to respond with: 'Well, don't criticise me then,' but she swallowed her anger. That's what you did with someone you loved: sometimes you let them have the last word, even when that word was against you.

Erika's shoulders sagged, the anger draining away. 'Look, I … just want this weekend to be perfect. Something for you and I.' She glanced over her shoulder. 'I'm sure there's some fabulous view just over the next rise, something only you and I will see. We've got our phones. We won't get lost. Just a bit farther, yeah?'

Before she could stop herself, Meg asked the question that had been coating her tongue like a bitter taste. '*Why* does this weekend have to be so perfect?'

Turning away, Erika said over her shoulder, 'We've just been working too hard. We need a break, some relaxation. So just a bit farther, yeah?'

There was no spectacular view over the next rise, but there was one over the rise after that. The trees suddenly ended and scrubland led down to an azure loch with a pebbled shore. Meg was so relieved she forgave Erika her smugness.

They walked down to the loch's edge and splashed cold water on their faces. 'Which loch do you think this is?' Meg asked, unfolding the map. 'There are a couple of unmarked ones near Loch Dee – maybe it's one of them?'

'It's *our* loch. Come on, let's explore.'

'Wait a minute.' Meg took a spare hair bobble from her pocket and looped it several times around a branch near where they'd come out of the forest. 'So we can tell the spot we came in at.'

'We'll make an explorer out of you yet,' Erika said with a dazzling smile.

It was pleasant, strolling along the lochside, so much cooler than slogging through the tightly-packed trees. Their talk became lighter too; it was almost like the early days, when they'd chattered and laughed together so much.

The loch seemed to be shaped like a U, curving around then back. Meg tried to keep track of which direction they were heading based on the sun, but it was all guesswork, a scattering of survival facts gleaned from her general reading.

By her reckoning, they must have been about three-quarters of the way around the loch's circumference when they came upon a tumbledown cottage. What remained of the walls barely reached higher than their heads. The roof was gone and the door had long since rotted away.

'It's a crofter's hut,' Erika said, peering into the roofless ruin. She pulled back suddenly, a scowl on her face. 'Think it's being used by a squatter, look.' Inside lay an abandoned sleeping bag; the floor was littered with food packaging.

'Wow, look at these,' Erika said, pointing at the stones around the doorway. Meg saw that runes had been carved into the stones and then molten iron poured into the indents. A quick glance at the holes where the windows should be and the remains of the fireplace revealed more of the same. She looked over her shoulder and shuddered; *she* might be a city girl, but her grandmother had grown up on a remote farmstead. The stories she'd told on dark nights had contained stones such as these.

'Let's go,' Meg said, backing away from the hut, even out of its shadow. 'This place is creepy. Let's find somewhere nice to eat lunch.' Erika sighed but followed without question.

They walked, wordlessly, for another fifteen minutes before they selected a pair of flat stones, warmed by the sun, to be their lunchtime seats. Erika instantly tore into her pre-packed sandwich but Meg merely opened a packet of crisps, nibbling on a few before putting the bag away again.

'Come on, give it up,' Erika said as she finished her sandwich. 'You've been quiet and weird since that hut. Tell me what those carvings are all about and why they freak you out so much.'

Meg took a swig of water, washing the salt from her mouth. The silence of the forest extended to the loch; she felt as if the trees stood as listeners, waiting for her words as much as Erika. 'They're called ringlet stones. My nan told me about them. Runes are carved into the stones and then iron is poured into them before they're used around doors and windows. Fairies hate runes and they hate iron, so it's double protection.'

Erika snorted. 'Fairies? You got all weirded out by fairies?'

'No – well, not really. Didn't you think that place felt sinister? I mean, normally people nail up horseshoes or leave out milk and that's enough. But if you've got ringlet stones, it means you need the house protecting from a curse or a monster or something truly horrible.'

'Well, it would take more than a monster Tinkerbell to freak me out,' Erika replied.

'Just because you haven't got any imagination,' Meg snapped. It was an accusation she'd thrown out before, but never with such venom. Erika had no right to mock things she had no experience of, but she always thought her way was the best way, her knowledge the superior information. But the jibe had felt petty, even as Meg said it, and she dropped her gaze.

Erika stood up. 'Alright then grumpy-guts. Let's see if we can find our way back to the trail.' Her voice was full of forced brightness, but as she strode off, Meg heard her mutter, 'Heaven forbid we should have any fun or adventure.'

They couldn't find the hair bobble that Meg had tied to the tree. 'You must have made it too loose,' Erika said as they scanned the edge of the forest. Meg knew she hadn't but she said nothing; instead, she just kept searching the ground, looking to see if it had fallen down.

Eventually, with her cheeks flushed and glittering with perspiration, Erika said, 'Why don't we just start making our way through the trees? I mean, this bit looks familiar, doesn't it? Even if it's not exactly the right spot, it's better than just walking backwards and forwards.'

'I don't know,' Meg said uncertainly.

Erika rolled her eyes. 'No, of course you don't, so I say let's try it.' She strode forward into the forest, and Meg followed, mute and sullen.

Why didn't we bring a compass or something?

Because we were supposed to stick to the trails.

This is so like Erika: always doing what she thinks is best, no matter what anyone else says. Why on earth do I put up with her?

Meg pulled out her phone and checked it; fifty percent battery, zero signal. She shoved it back in her pocket.

The land angled up and then down until eventually they came out at another loch. 'Well, that's something,' said Erika. They pulled out the map and pored over it, but were none the wiser.

'We didn't come across a loch on the way here,' Meg said carefully. A dreadful anxiety, built on an impossible idea, was growing in her head.

'That's because we haven't gone back the way we came, have we? There's bound to be a sign or something nearby. Which way shall we try?'

'This way,' Meg said without hesitation.

It won't be there. It can't possibly be there.

'Fine.'

The crofter's hut *was* there.

'Must be another one, just like it,' Erika said, not meeting Meg's eye.

'With the same scummy sleeping bag in it?' Meg said, gesturing inside.

They tried again, choosing a path through the forest just opposite the ruined hut. They walked up; they walked down; they came to the hut again.

'What is this, the fucking *X Files*?' Erika said, a touch of hysteria in her voice.

Meg stared at the iron runes in the stone; she knew exactly what this was. This place was a curse, and they were caught in it now. Even though she knew, deep down, that they'd never find a way out of the forest, she followed Erika on another three useless, scrabbling journeys through the trees, always arriving back at the same spot.

'*Fuuuuck!*' Erika screamed at the sky before sinking to the ground, trembling and breathing hard.

Meg sat down too, choosing a spot a little higher up the shore so that she was sitting in sunlight. The shadows chilled her too much, even though the day was still stiflingly hot. Her watch said it was four o'clock; the sun was already touching the top of the tall pines. Soon, everything would be in shadow.

We're stuck. We're fucking stuck. We can't leave. We're stuck. The words went round and round in her head until she realised that she'd fallen into a daze and the shadows of the trees were almost touching her toes. Erika was motionless, already swallowed up by the gloom and staring at the ground in her own funk. Meg was gathering her strength to go over there when a sharp noise echoed over the loch.

clackclackclack

Icy fingers of fear squeezed Meg's heart. Erika's head snapped up.

clackclack clackclack

Erika scrambled over to where Meg sat. 'What was that?' she whispered. 'Maybe a deer? Like, the antlers or something.'

'Too … metallic,' Meg said, her mouth dry. She had

imagined that sound hundreds of times in her childhood, never really believing that it existed somewhere out there in the world.

I hear her at the ither door,
Speirin' after Tam.

Meg stood up sharply, as if she could leave her fear on the ground behind her. 'Let's get into the hut.'

'What, that thing? What good would that do?' Erika said.

Meg, who was already marching towards the hut, turned and snapped, 'Look, this place is cursed – how else do you explain how we walked out of here and back four times? That hut has ringlet stones on it, and they were put there for a reason. I don't know if they still work, but it's sure as hell worth a go, isn't it?'

That awful noise echoed around them again, and Erika hurried after her.

As Meg stepped over the threshold, a shudder ran through her body, like when you're walking along a road and a car speeds past you too close. Erika pushed past her, slung her bag on the floor, then sat down and glowered. 'What do we do now? Just wait around until that thing goes away?'

'I don't think it'll go away before morning,' Meg said, her nerves tight.

'Why? What is it?'

Meg didn't answer but instead pulled out her phone; still no signal. 'Yours?' she asked, as she shoved her phone back in her pocket. Erika produced hers with the same result.

'Well, if we're going to be staying here for a bit, I'll go and get some wood to start a fire,' Erika said, adding scornfully, 'if you think I'll be safe from monsters, that is.'

'This isn't a joke,' Meg snapped. 'I really think there's something out there. I don't think either of us should go anywhere.'

Erika rolled her eyes. 'For God's sake, Meg, why are you always—' Erika stopped, took a deep breath and said in a calmer voice, 'Look, I'm not going to argue with you that there's something nasty out there. I mean, those noises were weird. But what I can tell you for sure is that we'll freeze our butts off tonight if we don't get some wood. Can't you feel how cold it is already? And the sun hasn't even gone down.'

Meg realised that Erika was right; it was cold, more so that it should be after the heat of the day. *It's just because we're in the shadows, surely. It can't be more than that – can it?*

'Fine,' she said reluctantly. 'We'll both go. But keep your eyes open.'

As Meg wandered the loch shore, looking for twigs and dry wood, she thought, *I must be mad. It can't be Jenny, it can't. I mean … she's not real, is she? Just some story Nan made up to make me go to sleep.*

But then, we are in a forest that turns you around and spits you back out exactly where you started. Maybe this is a place of impossible things.

As she snatched up every stick she could find, Meg kept glancing up: across the water, into the trees, along the loch shore, ready to bolt at the slightest hint of movement. She was relieved to see Erika, a few yards away, keeping up the same level of alertness.

When both of them had an armful, they returned to the hut and dumped their gathering by a scorch mark on the ground that indicated a previous fire had burnt there. Their argument over the best way to stack the wood was arrested by the sound of something crashing its way through the woods towards them. They both stood up, unconsciously drawing closer together, but the wall at the back was too high for them to see over.

Whatever was heading towards them was large. An image rose up in Meg's mind, one she'd seen in a picture book: a wizened woman with sparse, lanky hair, grey skin, and a grin that showed a mouth full of metal teeth. But what tumbled over the threshold was not a hungry hag but a young man, about their age, who stared at them wide-eyed, clutching a bundle of firewood to his chest. For a moment, stunned silence connected all three of them, then the man said, 'Who the hell — ?'

clackclack clackclackclack

He backed away from the door and pressed himself against the wall. Meg and Erika exchanged a glance before Erika reached out and gently took the firewood. 'Here. I'll put that with our pile. Sit down.' The man let go of the wood and didn't so much sit as slide down the wall until he ended up crouched on the floor.

'Are those yours?' Meg asked, nodding towards the sleeping bag. The man's eyes were fixed on the doorway and he gave no indication he'd heard her.

'She means the sleeping bag,' Erika put in, and the man gave a slight nod. Meg was stung that he'd answered Erika but not her, so she turned her back on him and set about arranging the branches for the fire again.

After a few moments, the man said, 'You're doing it wrong. Here. Let me.' Shuffling over to her, he took apart her structure and started building it anew.

He and Erika will get on great, she thought bitterly.

Within a few minutes, the man took a lighter out of his pocket and set alight a bundle of dry bracken he'd stuffed in the centre of the fire; it quickly began to blaze.

That done, he settled back, looking if not at ease then certainly less terrified that he had done. After glancing at each of them, he asked, 'How did you get here?'

'We were walking off-route,' Erika said, 'following a path or something, but then we found this place and,' she pushed some hair out of her face, a gesture of awkwardness, 'well, you'll laugh at this, but we couldn't leave. Every time we tried to walk away, we ended up back here.'

'I won't laugh,' the man said. 'I've been stuck here for three days.' Erika and Meg looked at each other. 'I'm a park ranger. I was walking the Water of Trool Trail and I found smears of blood on the leaves. We've had a few incidents of poaching recently, so I decided to follow it. I found myself here and here I still am.'

Meg frowned. 'But wouldn't we have heard about it if a

ranger had gone missing?'

The man snorted. 'Not likely. Bad for PR. I'm Sean, by the way.'

'Erika. Meg,' Erika replied, pointing to each of them.

clackclackclackclack

'And that,' said Sean softly, 'is Jenny.'

Meg felt her insides turn to ice. 'Really?' she asked, her voice husky with fear, just as Erika said, 'Who?'

'Jenny with the iron teeth,' Sean said. When Erika continued to look blank, he cleared his throat and recited *Jenny Wi' the Airn Teeth*, the Alexander Anderson poem that Meg's nan had told her countless times in her childhood. It had made her afraid in those days, hiding under the bed covers, but out here, with the sunset turning the sky a hue of bloody colours, it was terrifying. Sean's recitation held no inflections, no emotion.

> *What a plague is this o'mine,*
> *Winna steek his e'e,*
> *Though I hap him ow'r the head*
> *As cosie as can be.*
> *Sleep! an'let me to my wark,*
> *A'thae claes to airn;*
> *Jenny wi' the airn teeth,*
> *Come an' tak' the bairn.*
>
> *Tak' him to your ain den,*
> *Where the bowgie bides,*
> *But first put baith your big teeth*
> *In his wee plump sides;*
> *Gie your auld grey pow a shake,*
> *Rive him frae my grup –*
> *Tak' him where nae kiss is gaun*
> *When he waukens up.*

It was like he was delivering a business lecture rather than a poem about a terrifying childhood creature who came in the night to snatch children who hadn't gone to sleep yet, her arrival announced by the thump of her feet and the *clacking* of her teeth. Yet even so, just hearing those words spoken in this isolated place sent shivers down Meg's spine.

Whatna noise is that I hear
Comin' doon the street?
Weel I ken the dump-dump
O'her beetle feet.
Mercy me, she's at the door,
Hear her lift the sneck;
Whisht! an'cuddle mammy noo
Closer roun' the neck.

'So, a bogeyman,' Erika said disdainfully when he'd finished. 'You expect me to believe that there's —'
clackclack
The noise had come from just the other side of the wall that Meg was leaning against. The back of her neck pricked, as if Jenny's cold breath was gusting over it already.

Very slowly, Sean reached into his sleeping bag and pulled out a tatty old scarf. He bundled it up and then threw it through the doorway.

'Watch,' he whispered.

A heavy stillness descended on them, muffling even the crackling of the fire. The doorway looked out onto the pebbled shore, about fifty yards from the loch. The scarf lay in a small, crumpled heap, an unnatural shape in a natural setting.

There was a blur of movement as something shot past the entrance, seizing Sean's scarf as it went. Meg was left with impressions rather than a definite image: grey skin, tattered rags fluttering around lanky limbs, and the flash of firelight on metal teeth. The *clacking* sound echoed around the lochshore, gradually growing more distant.

'What … the fuck …?' Erika's breath was coming hard and fast.

'Best to believe it,' Sean said, standing up and going over to his sleeping bag. 'On the first night, I saw a deer drinking from the loch. I thought it was beautiful. Then Jenny appeared, and by morning, there was nothing left of it but a few bloodied bones.' He climbed into his sleeping bag. 'My mam said she'd go away if you went to sleep, that Jenny only wanted those kids who were awake.'

'Well, that's simple then,' Erika said with a relieved laugh. 'We'll just go to sleep and then wake up and all this will be over.'

clackclackclackclackclackclack

'Yeah, good luck with that,' Sean said, bunching his jacket into a pillow. 'See just how well you sleep with a monster prowling around outside.'

Meg lay back and looked at the stars. A horrible chill ran through her as the lack of roof dawned on her. Just how effective were runes around the doorway, windows and chimney if the roof was gone and all Jenny had to do was climb over the walls?

She hasn't so far. If she had, Sean wouldn't be here.

Maybe it'll be alright.

It has to be alright.

Although Meg tried to sleep, exhausted by a day of hiking and an evening of constant, prickling fear, sleep eluded her. Neither she nor Erika had a sleeping bag with them, and Meg felt too vulnerable lying in the open air with nothing covering her.

No way to bury your head and hide from the monster, she thought as she stared out of the doorway into the dark night. The loch was illuminated by the half-moon above, the ripples like dancing silver. Even on those rare occasions when she began to drift off, the clacking would startle her – all of them – awake.

After over an hour of them trying to get to sleep, Erika rolled over and whispered, 'Why don't we just make a break for freedom?'

'With Jenny out there?' Meg whispered back. 'No way.'

Erika glanced at Sean. 'You really believe his bogeyman story?'

'It's not *his* story. I heard it too when I was a kid. It scared the shit of me then, and it does so even more now that I'm alone in the dark with her.'

'You can't really believe—' Erika's words died abruptly as something ran through a patch of moonlight about ten feet away from the hut entrance. The shape had been indistinct and crouched over, but it had definitely been human rather than a deer or a fox.

Erika licked her lips nervously. 'Maybe Sean's lying and it's just one of his mates ...' Meg gave her a look; Sean's fear when they'd first met him had been real enough, and there'd been a frenzied look to his eyes that spoke of someone who genuinely hadn't eaten for days.

Before Erika could argue further, Meg said, 'Look. I don't know if what is out there is Jenny—'

clackclackclack

'—or something else, but do you want to sleep outside with that thing prowling around?' Meg pointed at the door and hearth. 'Those are runestones. They keep away all kinds of bad stuff, and they seem to be working, don't they? After all, whatever that thing outside is, it hasn't come in yet, has it? And remember how the forest changed? Do you want to try and get through it right now in the dark?'

Erika frowned, clearly considering.

Please don't go, Meg muttered to herself. *If you go, I'll have to go with you.*

'Fine. We'll stay here, for tonight at least. Happy?'

'Happ*ier*,' said Meg lying back down.

clackclack clack clackclack

Meg squeezed her eyes shut. *Please, just let us get to sleep. The poem says she goes away if you go to sleep.*

clack clack

Gran says she goes away if you go to sleep.

clackclackclackclack

How the hell are we going to sleep?

In the darkest hours of the night, Erika said, 'I've got a splitting headache, Meg. Can I grab a couple of painkillers?'

'Sure.' Meg dug her medicine packet out of her bag. She practically carried half a pharmacy with her at all times, never knowing when one of her multiple, fleeting illnesses might strike: steroid cream for her eczema; haemorrhoid cream for her backside; anti-fungal cream for thrush; paracetamol; ibuprofen; co-codamol; and a host of other pills that she'd taken one or two of and never disposed of. Her hand hovered over an old, forgotten strip, one she'd purchased when the panic attacks had stopped her sleeping. She frowned. What if —

'The *good* painkillers,' Erika specified.

Her thoughts disturbed, Meg dug out the co-codamol. 'When do I ever give you anything but the best?' she asked, tossing the tablets over to Erika. Her pride smarted when Erika didn't meet her gaze.

Sean crawled forward as Erika dug out a water bottle. 'Got any food?' he asked, his eyes gleaming in the firelight, and Meg felt a stab of pity as she remembered he'd been here three days.

They piled all the food in front of them and, although it looked a lot, Meg knew it wouldn't last them more a day when split three ways. 'Lucky we stopped at that bakery,' Erika said, splitting two sausage rolls and an oat cookie between them. After that banquet, they all tried to settle back down and sleep.

Listening to the gentle slosh of the loch water, Meg thought of the pills she'd seen. *There are only two left so we'd have to split them like the sausage rolls. Would two-thirds each be enough to break the curse and get us out of here?*

The distant squeal of a rabbit jolted her out of her thoughts and then its dying screams made all of them cover their ears. Cold, hungry, and feeling wretched, Meg tried to empty her mind and get some sleep.

All the stories say she won't get you if you go to sleep. Sleepin' weans are no for you – that's what the poem says. Please, please just let us sleep and this all be over.

'Glad it didn't rain last night,' Sean said as they sat in the dawn light, munching on another cookie split three ways. 'That happened my first night and it was pretty miserable.'

'Look, I think we should spend the day trying to find a way out,' Erika said, her eyes fever-bright. 'I mean, there must *be* a way.'

'Sleep,' Sean said distractedly, licking his fingers. 'I told you, the only way to escape Jenny is to go to sleep. All of us.'

'I mean there must be a *proper* way out,' Erika snapped, 'not a stupid one that you're just guessing.' Sean merely shrugged.

As soon as it was bright enough to see, the three of them set out. They did one circuit of the loch, going slowly, and carefully examining the trees for any sign of Meg's hair bobble. When they reached the hut again without finding it, Erika suggested just picking a direction and walking.

Like we did yesterday, Meg thought wearily. *Four times. With the same result.*

But she didn't say anything, because that's what you do when you love someone: you don't deny them hope.

They chose a direction and all three of them walked until they reached their starting point again.

'At least it wasn't a wasted trip,' Sean said, indicating the blackberries he'd gathered and carried in a fold of his t-shirt. Of all of them, he seemed the most chipper; Meg reasoned that after three days alone with a monster, even two moody women must be better than no company at all.

'Okay, well how about—' Erika began but Meg cut her off.

'I can't walk any more, I'm sorry. I just … need to rest.' She sat on the ground, letting her head hang forward so the sun beat down on the back of her neck.

'Yeah, you've got no choice but to sleep in the daytime,' Sean agreed. 'I tried not to, but you need the rest.'

'But if we keep going, keep ourselves active,' Erika pressed, 'then maybe we can sleep through tonight and *break the curse*.' She made air quotes with the last three words.

'After what we saw and heard last night,' Meg asked, 'how can you still not believe?' She wanted to be angry, but she was too exhausted.

Erika pointed angrily at Sean. 'What if it was one of his

mates? What if this is some stupid prank?' Her voice had a sharp edge to it, the sound of someone keeping wild panic under control.

'Oh, yeah,' Sean retorted, stepping closer. 'And how did we prank you to end up back here no matter which direction you go?'

Meg let the two of them rage at each other. She was too tired to intervene. Even her teeth ached. But listening to Erika's angry voice eventually got under her skin; it always did.

Standing up, she shouted, 'Alright, fine! I'll go with you.'

The other two stared at her, shocked; Erika recovered quickest. With a smug smile, she said, 'Perfect. Let's go.'

Meg felt as if she was pulling lead weights behind her. She slouched as she walked, the ground tugging her down with its sweet promises of rest. Lost in the effort of placing one foot in front of the other, Meg walked straight into Erika's back when they were no more than twenty paces into the forest. Looking up, Meg's surroundings shocked her wide awake. Small white intestines were strung through the tree branches like garlands. A tiny heart hung from a leaf like a gory trinket. The leaves were splattered with blood, still bright red, and fur, still soft. Meg thought of the animal squeals she'd heard last night and the undefined shape that they'd glimpsed briefly running through the moonlight.

'Let's go back,' Erika whispered. Wordlessly, they turned and hurried back the way they'd come.

When they arrived back at the hut, they found Sean already curled up asleep. Erika lay down and closed her eyes, squeezing out the tears that had been clinging to her lashes and not bothering to wipe them away.

Meg felt sure she couldn't sleep now. The horror of such a sight had driven away all tiredness, leaving a light-headed vacuum in its place. But as the shock faded like a bad dream, the weariness crept back in and she, too, lay down. Her dreams were filled with gnarled hands reaching for her in the dark *clackclack clackclack*

and teeth gnashing, ready to devour her, teeth going *crunch crunch rustle crunch.*

A scream sent her scrambling to her feet, instantly awake.

Erika, red-faced. Finger pointing. Hands pounding Sean.

Sean, white-faced. Shying away. Crisps falling from fingers and mouth.

It took a second for all of these jumbled images to make sense to Meg, at which point her thoughts mirrored Erika's shrieks. 'You bastard! You ate the lot! You fucking bastard! You fucking, fucking bastard!'

Sean caught her wrists, halting the blows that had been raining down on him.

'Three days! *Three days* I've been here, and I'm starving. I only wanted a little but I was so hungry. Look, I'm sorry, I'll put some back and ...'

Meg walked away, in a daze, to the loch. She hunkered down, tiredness and dull panic making her dizzy.

We're going to die here. Either through not eating or being eaten. We're going to die.

The sun was setting, her surroundings growing dark. From somewhere within the trees came that terrible sound that announced the drawing in of the night, the time when all good children should be in their beds, asleep.

clackclack clackclackclack

'Here, have my bit. I'm not that hungry,' Meg said, offering her sandwich to Erika. It was a lie; she was ravenous. But that's what you do when you love somebody: you go without so they can have more.

'Thanks,' Erika said, taking it and nibbling at it. Neither of them looked at Sean who was sitting on the other side of the fire, his gaze on the dancing flames. 'Isn't it weird how quiet it is?' Erika went on.

Oh yeah. I mean, it's not like I commented on that very fact yesterday or anything, Meg thought, with a touch of bitterness.

'There're no crickets or mosquitos, no fish, nothing like squirrels or rabbits in the forest.'

Then where did that rabbit from come last night before it was pulled apart and strung up through the trees?

It must have wandered in and got lost, just like us, poor bastard.

Meg thought she detected the distant bark of a fox, but it was so faint, she might have imagined it.

clack clack clack

'We should try and get some sleep,' Sean said, going over to his little corner.

'All right for those of us with sleeping bags and a full belly,' Erika muttered. Sean stiffened and paused, then continued climbing into bed.

clackclack

Erika buried her face in her hands. 'God, why didn't we just go to Darren's party? We could be drinking now and chatting and safe and —'

'So why didn't we?' Meg snapped, her patience suddenly at an end. She was tired of Erika stealing her ideas, of Erika's inability to believe what was really happening. Most of all, she was pissed off that this was, if you thought about it, all Erika's fault. '*I* wanted to go to the party. It was *you* who insisted we come on holiday, *you* who took us off the normal paths and —'

'I just wanted us to have a good time!' Erika shouted, her fists clenched. 'One good time and then ...' Her face paled as her anger drained away, replaced by guilt.

Meg felt as if her insides had been liquified. 'Go on,' she said, her voice cold and hard. 'Say it. Say why it was so important to you that we had a good time.'

Erika's shoulders slumped. 'One good time before we went our separate ways.' She stared at the floor.

'One good time before you left me, you mean.' Meg felt almost dizzy with the relief of it being finally out in the open; now, she could deal with it, rather than just worrying about it.

Erika drew breath to speak, but Meg said, 'As much as I hate to agree with the pig, I think we should try to sleep. It's not like we've had any luck with your plan of walking out of here, is it?'

Erika poked the fire with a thick twig. Meg lay down, her back to them all. After a while, she heard Erika lay down as well, not too far away.

clackclackclack

There'd been a time when Erika would have curled up behind Meg, wrapping her arms around her lover's waist, lying so close that Meg could breathe in the scent of her lemon shampoo. Now, the scrap of cold ground between them felt like an insurmountable chasm.

Around them, the trees rustled in the night-time breezes and water lapped gently over pebbles.

clackclack clack

Erika gave an irritable huff of breath and rolled over, kneeing Meg in the shin; her eyes closed, Meg pretended not to notice. The sound of iron teeth had been coming from different directions yet always moving closer, circling them.

clackclackclackclack

With a frustrated scream, Erika sat up, digging her fingers into her hair as if she might rip it all from her scalp. 'I can't fucking sleep with that noise going on.'

Reflexively, Meg put a hand on Erika's back, but Erika twitched away and stood up, pacing in frustration. 'Sleep, they say – yeah, sure, sleep when there's a monster out there that's just sharpening her teeth, ready to rip us to shreds. But no, we have to fall asleep and –'

'For God's sake!' yelled Sean, kicking off his sleeping bag. '*No one* will get any sleep if you don't shut the hell up!'

Erika turned on him, eyes blazing. 'Well, maybe I could sleep if I wasn't so hungry, if some bastard hadn't –'

Sean was on his feet now too, face to face with Erika. 'Maybe when you've been here three days, you'll understand how starving *you* feel.' He poked a finger in her chest so hard that she took a step backwards.

Erika's rage was incandescent. 'We might not last three days thanks to some pig who ate all our food.'

She shoved Sean back, using both her hands.

'Mind the fire!' Meg shouted, but neither of them so much as glanced at her.

'I didn't eat all of the food, only some of it, you ignorant *bitch*.' He shoved Erika hard enough that she stumbled back two steps, her boot plunging into the fire. She screamed and backed away, flapping her foot to get rid of the flames that devoured the grass caught up in her laces, not realising she was backing out the doorway into the night.

The flames on her shoes went out. Erika gave a shaky laugh and looked up.

Jenny barrelled into her from the side, the weight of her scrawny body sending them both sprawling. The two of them crashed to the ground just beyond the light of the fire so that only Erika's legs were visible. The air was filled with screaming, the sound of the tearing flesh. Erika's legs kicked out and scuffed the earth. The screams turned into gargling cries then raspy breaths, quiet enough for the sound of intestines slithering into the dust to be heard.

Erika's legs kept twitching for several minutes after the gurgles ceased, when the only noise in the still night was the sound of meaty mastication.

Meg stared at her lover's legs, numb.

I should have helped. I should have got up. Or reached out. Or moved.

But it was so fast. I couldn't ... She didn't... It was so fast and now she's —

No, Erika can't be gone. She's Erika! She lights up every room. You can hear her laugh from the other end of our flat. She can't ... be ... gone.

The legs slid across the ground as Jenny dragged her prize away. Meg bolted to her feet and would have raced out into the darkness if Sean hadn't pinned her down. 'Don't,' he breathed into her ear. 'It's no good. She's ... If you go out there, you'll be dead too.' Still Meg fought until Erika's feet vanished from sight, then all the energy leaked out of her and she went limp.

Meg sank to her knees then slumped onto her back, breathing hard. Above her, stars sparkled in a midnight sky.

If Erika was here, we could have looked at the stars together, side by side. It would have been the perfect moment she was searching for all that time. The perfect moment before we went different ways. But there's just me now.

She left me, just like she said she would.

Hysterical laughter exploded from her, then transmuted into sobs. Turning her back on the stars, Meg buried her face in the cold, uncaring earth.

Meg drifted in and out of sleep, bolting upright at the slightest noise. When dawn finally arrived, she sat up but ate and drank nothing. She was aware of Sean leaving the hut, coming back sporadically, encouraging her to drink. But Meg kept her eyes fixed on the loch water, the only thing that moved on this still, summer day. In her head, moments from her life with Erika played over and over in a disjointed fashion. A vague fear filled her that if she didn't think about such precious moments, they'd slip from her mind, as lost as Erika was.

The shadows lengthened and Sean came back. Her throat dry, Meg accepted some water, but nothing else. She thought the darkness would help but the stillness made her ears buzz and the *clacking* of Jenny made her shudder. That sound brought up images of soft, beautiful flesh made bloody by iron teeth.

When the moon crested the trees, she could take it no longer. *I just want to sleep and forget*, she thought, her eyes gritty as she dug through her medicine bag.

Briefly, she considered taking both sleeping tablets herself, but they were pretty strong and she didn't want to overdose. Besides, would the curse lift if only she was asleep? It wasn't worth this risk. This was a one-shot deal.

She shook Sean's shoulder then pressed a pill into his hand. 'Sleeping tablets. I don't know if they'll work but worth a try.'

Sean sat bolt upright. 'You had these all the time?'

She met his gaze squarely. 'I only had two. That's not a problem any more, of course, after you pushed my girlfriend out of the protection of the stones.'

He stared at her, ashen-faced. 'I ... I—'

'Or we put it down to bad fucking luck and just try to get the hell out of here.'

He opened his mouth to reply then merely nodded.

They took one each. Sean undid his sleeping bag, draping it over both of them like a blanket. Meg stared at the sky, trying to make her mind as empty as that void, but the memory of Erika's smile lingered.

After a while, she heard Sean snoring. Above, the stars were starting to blur slightly. On the other side of the wall came the sound of fingers scrabbling at stone.

clack clack scrabble clack

Meg could feel the drug making her limbs heavy, filling her mind with static. Before she closed her eyes, the sky above was blotted out by a thin figure. As sleep dragged Meg down, she felt a cold breath gush over her face.

clackclackclack

Oh shit, she thought, *Jenny's realised no roof means no runes. Why didn't we...?* And then the darkness claimed her.

Meg woke up whole and uneaten.

The two of them set off on their morning routine to check the perimeter of the forest. They found Meg's hair bobble.

Of course. There it is, she thought dully. *We played by the rules and now we've been let go. Some of us, anyway.*

Sean was too excited to bother going back for his stuff, worried that the path might vanish if they didn't follow it now.

They climbed and scrambled, squeezed through narrow gaps in the trees and tore themselves bloody on brambles. The path widened and became stonier before disgorging them back onto one of the main trails.

Of course it did.

Sean sank to his knees, laughing and sobbing so hard that strings of drool clogged his mouth. Meg stood by, silent, empty, until he stood up, wiping his face.

'We're back, thank God, Meg, we're back.'

'Two of us are.' The flat voice didn't sound like her own.

Sean put a hand on her shoulder; she could feel that he was trembling slightly. 'About that —'

'An accident. I don't want to talk about it,' Meg replied, stepping out of his reach. His hand fell away and he nodded.

'What are you doing to do now?'

'Go home. Tell the police we went hiking, got lost, Erika walked out one night then didn't come back. A terrible, awful accident.'

'You don't think anyone will believe the truth?'

Of course they won't.

'Would you? If you hadn't been there?'

Sean ran a hand through his hair. 'I guess not. I'm sorry about Erika.'

Hearing her name spoken aloud caused such a wealth of emotions to surge through Meg that she was unable to stop the tears from falling or to speak for some moments. 'I'll mourn her,' she said eventually. 'I'll remember her. After all, that's what you do when you love someone and they leave you: you move on and live the best life you can.'

Of course I won't.

'Well, I'm here if you ever want to ...' The words dried up on his lips, his expression showing that he knew just how empty the offer was.

'Sure. Thanks.' Meg forced a smile onto her face that was equally empty.

Meg walked with Sean as far as the car park. 'I'll phone the police,' he said, heading towards the closed visitor centre. Meg lingered at the edge of the forest. Watching him go inside, she thought of the life that lay ahead of her, the one without Erika, the one where she could never tell the truth to anyone or mourn her girlfriend properly.

She was going to leave me, she told herself. *She did leave me.*

But that doesn't mean I have to leave her.

She turned and walked back along the path, hoping that it wouldn't be beyond a city girl to find that path again, to lose herself in the forest so that she could come to that hut and Erika and Jenny.

Because that's what you do when you love somebody.

THE REAL MR HYDE

In 1886, a novella that would go on to thrill readers of dark fiction for centuries to come, The Strange Case of Dr Jekyll and Mr Hyde, *received its first publication.*

It was the work of Edinburgh poet and novelist, Robert Louis Stevenson. Classified initially as one of the penny dreadfuls (lurid tales of crime and murder, published cheaply for the entertainment of the masses) it was ignored by the literati until a glowing review appeared in The Times *newspaper, at which point it became an instant best-seller and would never again be out of print.*

Though in essence a mystery thriller, it tells the now well-known story of Dr Henry Jekyll, an outwardly respectable medical practitioner who develops a serum that brings out his inner darkness, transforming him into a completely different person, Edward Hyde, who gives full vent to his many vices. In due course, Jekyll loses control over Hyde, and chaos and tragedy result.

Regarded not just as an intelligent, imaginative and frightening horror story, but as a learned analysis of the duality of human nature, the balance between good and evil, lust and restraint, violence and charity, the book became a huge success for its author, and was read so widely even during his lifetime that the term 'Jekyll and Hyde' would pass into common parlance as the go-to phrase for any person suffering from split-personality disorders.

It was also the culmination of an obsessive interest Robert Louis Stevenson had harboured all his adult life about the potential for vicious behaviour that most humans keep buried deep within themselves. This was partly inspired by his association with an Edinburgh-based French teacher, Eugene Chantrelle, who in 1878, very unexpectedly, was convicted of poisoning his wife with opium. Having liked and admired the man, Stevenson was stunned, especially when he heard that Chantrelle, who was hanged that same year, was also suspected of having poisoned others in France, mostly for the pleasure it gave him.

More than anyone else though, the blueprint for Edward Hyde came from a much more infamous Edinburgh criminal, Deacon William Brodie, who, during the 1770s and 1780s, led two completely different lives.

Deacon Brodie, whom Stevenson unsuccessfully attempted to immortalise in a stage-play of the same name while he was still a teenager, was to all intents and purposes an esteemed pillar of his community. A popular figure in Edinburgh high society, he was a cabinet-maker and locksmith by trade, head (or 'deacon') of the Wrights' Guild, a member of the town council, and so well-regarded generally that he counted among his friends Robert Burns the author and Henry Raeburn the painter.

At least, this was the William Brodie that most people knew, the William Brodie who walked abroad by daylight. The William Brodie who came out at night was a much more sinister figure. To begin with, he frequented brothels and 'low taverns', had an excessive gambling habit, and kept several mistresses, none of whom knew about each other even though at least two of them had children by him. But that wasn't by any means the worst of it.

Because Brodie was also a violent housebreaker.

Yes, bizarre as it may seem, this well-to-do gentleman who could mingle comfortably with the highest echelons was also an habitual burglar, who used his skills and connections to gain easy access to the houses of the wealthy. But not only that. He and a gang of like-minded felons were also known for committing street-robberies (ie thefts with violence). No crime it seemed, was too heinous for Deacon Brodie when he was out after dark. He always went armed, and whoever you were, man, woman or child, you could expect to be misused by him. Though there is no written record of Brodie standing accused of murder, several unsolved murders in Edinburgh, clearly the work of some footpad or other, were put down to him.

In later years, questions would be asked as to just how savage a thug Brodie was, and whether or not his reign of terror had been exaggerated. The point was raised that he never made huge amounts of money from his crimewave. Though a counter argument, allegedly put forth by those who knew him, held that he was never really in it for the money as much as for the kicks (which of course would tie in, in Robert Louis Stevenson's mind, with the motivations of Mr Hyde).

There is no doubt that the manner of Brodie's death also did its bit to sensationalise his life. On October 1 1788, he walked to the gallows at the Edinburgh Tollbooth in flamboyant fashion. Not just wearing his finest clothes, but visibly unrepentant as he smiled and waved to the 40,000-strong crowd that had gathered to watch, and even apparently singing verses from The Beggars' Opera. *So happy did he seem to be that unfounded rumours later spread that he had pre-planned an escape and survived his execution by the ingenious use of a concealed steel collar.*

In normal circumstances, this would more than explain how he came to take his own unique place in Edinburgh's urban mythology. But bogeymen don't become bogeymen for nothing. The notorious villain was a real individual and his crimes were equally real. Robert Louis Stevenson's fascination with those among us who are able to vent our darker side at will, usually when night falls, is easily understandable when he grew up in a city that had been genuinely terrorised by the mysterious and menacing dual-personality that was Deacon William Brodie.

COULTER'S CANDY
Johnny Mains

Coulter rises through the nicht
Gie's his wife an awfu' fricht
He burns the caunle half the nicht
Making Coulter's Candy

Coulter's Candy (1845)
Robert Colthart

'It's Mad Rabbie! Gie us a dance if ye can move yon thunderous belly o' yours!'

Robert Colthart raised his head warily as the despised nickname was thrown his way.

'Ah'll come ower and molocate ye, ye stinking wee shites!' he roared across the street.

'Ye cud nivir catch us!' the children yelled at him. 'We micht aw be stick thin, but yiv let yerself go! How diz a man git tae the state ye hiv in these times?'

'Yir mithir's wud be aye chillt tae the bone if they kent ye chatted suchlike tae yir elders! Should cowpit a kettle o' boilin' watter ower yiz!'

Robert shouted once more, but then a shattering stab lit up his brain and he had to close his eyes as the sudden flash of light made him feel faint. His balance started to go; he buckled, weaving to and fro like thread in a loom. He fell, and fell hard.

Robert came to on the thick, wooden kitchen table at his house on Overhaugh Street in Galashiels. He turned his head weakly and threw up onto the stone floor. His wife hushed him back gently down as he tried to sit up.

'Just wait, Robert. Doctor's oan hiz way.'

'How did ah git back here?

'Shuggie and Rab foond ye oan the street, thocht ye wir drunk tae begin with, then they goat really worried when ye wouldnae answer them.'

'How lang hiv ah been oot fir?'

'A guid oor. Doctor's on hiz way, mind that he hiz tae see a few ithers in the toon first.'

'This came on affy sudden, huv nivir felt anything like it afore. Ahm scairt hen, real scairt.'

'I keep oan banging at ye tae lose that fat. An yir still insisting on wearin' that daft outfit tae aw the fairs; the amount o' extra cloath ah've hud tae buy frae the haberdashers; it's a guid thing *ah've* been bringing in the pennies.' His wife was blunt in her manner, making Robert smile weakly.

Robert tried to sit up again, but heaved and threw up over his suit of colourful ribbons and strips of cloth and tweed.

'Ahm dyin' Mary,' he moaned weakly, unable to even prop himself up to wipe the spit that made a new home on his chin. 'Di ye think it's because o' hir? But ah finished hir, ah—'

'Enough!' his wife barked. 'Ye ken wi dinnae mention yer wee trip unner this roof! I dinnae believe in that nonsense, and ye sure as hell didnae dae ony of the stuff ye sed ye did.'

Robert closed his eyes as someone banged on the door. He tried to think, to search through his fractured, dying memories until …

April 1880, Monday

Selkirk courthouse was packed with the curious, alleged offenders and more children than Bailie Thirlsemere had ever seen in open session in his entire career. He had tried, without success, to clear the court of anyone under the age of fourteen, but his requests were ignored. Such was the way of these backwards county affairs. He travelled from Edinburgh once a month, one of three bailies who rotated and spent the week travelling to the various courts, bringing the law to the land of farm and textile.

'We now come to Robert Colthart, is he here?' Thirlsemere enquired, peering down at the packed congregation.

'He's aye late, ahm sure he'll turn up soon,' one helpful onlooker piped up.

'Well, he had better get here or he'll be spending a week in Jedburgh, and he won't be late for that appointment!' the bailie retorted, causing much mirth.

A few minutes later there was a ruckus outside the room and the children started to cheer and shout, 'Ally Bally, Ally Bally Bee!'

It was the bailie's first time dealing with the famous 'candy man' although he had been forewarned of the spectacle he was about to witness by one of the other bailies who had dealt with the 'grotesque fool' on more than one occasion.

The door to the courtroom was flung open and in walked Robert, dressed in a gaudy suit of strips of ribbon and cloth, all dyed vibrant colours. He wore a large felt hat; around the brim were freshly-picked asters, Queen Anne's lace, Batchelor buttons, coreopsis, chicory and cardinal flowers. He smelt of burnt sugar and aniseed. The children, as one, yelled in delight but were soon disappointed to discover than on this occasion Robert had brought none of his famous sweeties with him. Once the hubbub had died down, the bailie opened up the proceedings.

'Robert Colthart, it is charged that on the fifteenth of April you were at Galashiels train station—'

'Aye, selling ma Coulter's candy fir a wee bawbee!' Robert sang to his audience and they fell about laughing.

The bailie brought his gavel down on his plinth twice. The sharp cracks cut through the room. Everyone fell silent.

'One more outburst and it's seven days for contempt,' he said coldly.

Colthart nodded meekly.

'As I was saying,' the bailie continued, 'you were standing at

Galashiels station on that morning when your character received a respectable salute from a number of those present, as is the nature of your localised fame. You were very jovial, but not of drink, at that moment when the excursion train drew up from Hawick. You were recognised and shouted at by a number of characters, which you did seem to take umbrage with. One Mr Mackenzie Cornet from Hawick handed his whisky bottle to you so you could take a drink from it; however this happened at a rather critical time, for the guard's whistle was heard in clear sharp tones. You took the bottle, drank deeply from it then smashed it amid the wheels of the train and handed back the neck of the bottle back to the aggrieved Mr Cornet. Is this correct?'

'Yes, yir honour,' said Robert, a faint smirk playing on his lips.

'It was then the guard came and remonstrated with you for breaking a glass bottle on railway property, punishable by a fine, so you hit him with your stick, which I see you have not brought along with you today, and you had to be forcibly removed from the station. Do I have the facts correct, Mr Colthart?'

'Aye, ye do, yir honour.'

'And that would have been the end of it, were it not for the fact that you then verbally assaulted an elderly gentleman who was paying you no foul and then proceeded to hit Mrs Elspeth Menzies on her posterior, also with your stick.'

'Posterior? No, yir honour. Ah skelped hir airse,' Robert said, in all seriousness.

The courtroom cracked up. Thirlsemere had to bang his gavel more than twice this time to get the crowd under control.

'I've had enough of you and your charade, Mr Colthart. I find you no more than a common pedlar and an uncouth ruffian who does not deserve clemency at this juncture. However, I am a fair man, so I will let you get your affairs in order and you must present yourself at Jedburgh Jail by the end of this week. Sentence is three months. I hope that this sentence will dissuade you from making a mockery out of me or this court if we should ever meet again. That is all.'

The bailie cracked his gavel one final time as the courtroom erupted in outcry. Several of the children started to cry, others sang 'ally bally bee' in support.

Robert stood there, stunned, oblivious to everything around him.

'Well, yir just goanna huv tae sell like crazy afore ye git tae gaol,' his wife said, hands on her hips, giving Robert the look of death. 'Why did ye hiv tae gie the bailie a moothfu'?'

'He hud it in for us richt frae the stairt, hen,' Robert tried to plead. Mary was having none of it.

'Take yer sweeties an' git tae Newtoon. The mart is oan the morrow, ye'll make a guid whack when the farmers bring their cattle in oan the trains. If ye stairt oot now, ye'll be able tae shelter at wan o' the mills the nicht.'

'I dinna git ye.'

'Yir walkin' tae Newtoon, we dinnae huv the money tae git ye oan the train. Load up yir bag and jacket and get oan yir way.'

"Tis an eight-mile walk!'

'Ah dinnae care. Git yir stuff an' git oot. Git back bi Thursday an ah'll give ye the fare tae git tae Jedhart on Friday morn.'

Tuesday

Robert stopped for rest in Melrose. The town was in deep slumber, the odd tied-up horse eyeing him as he stalked past, his heavy stick making its usual tap, tap on the cobblestones. He walked to the ruins of the Abbey and found himself a decent spot and hunkered down, wrapping his thick coat around him. He closed his eyes and tried to sleep, but the prospect of gaol pervaded his every thought. He was scared. He had never experienced prison before; he genuinely thought that his exploits were never enough to see him sent to gaol. That dirty

Bailie bastard. Finally, Colthart fell into an uneasy sleep.

He was up before the village rose, nipping out of town to make his way to Bogle Burn and up that hellish, punishing hill before it took him in a meandering manner to Newtown; his destination. The mist hung low, coming from the Eildon Hills that loomed majestically above him. He would get there before the first train arrived and be able to take a good income for the day. And damned what the wife would say to it, he'd take the train back to Galashiels.

He saw the tree ahead, an old gnarled and weather-punished oak, said to be eight-hundred years old by the locals and storytellers. It would take seven men, all linking hands to make a circle around its circumference, its trunk was that magnificent and regal. Robert had spent many an hour on his travels shading himself from the sun. Legend surrounded the oak, and myths were seeped into roots that were said to go down into the soil a league deep or more. But ask what those legends were and faces would become blank, puzzled as if no-one really knew what magic the tree held. It was a place that had always brought an uncanny peace to Robert's soul during troubled times and he wondered if the tree would be able to provide its familiar sense of comfort. He dropped his heavy stick and large hessian sack by the tree, took off his hat which he placed on top of it. Then he found the gap between the two biggest roots before they were swallowed by the earth and made himself comfy and closed his eyes.

'Ye want tae kill him, divvint ye?' a voice, gentle, waif-like, whispered in his right ear, the voice coming from behind him, almost as if it was coming from the tree itself.

Robert's eyes snapped open and he got up and spun around, crouching. There was no-one there. He laughed and sat back down, chiding himself for allowing his deepest thoughts to spill out of him. Of *course* he wanted the bailie dead, but not at a price detrimental to his wellbeing. He could hardly travel up to Edinburgh and creep around the streets looking for him. And what was he going to do if he found him? Give him a sweetie and hope that he would choke to death on it?

Two hands came out of the trunk of the oak; if Robert had noticed he would have seen where they joined the bark; the soft, smooth skin was indistinguishable from the tree itself.

They grabbed Colthart's face and pulled him back; he screamed sharply as he tipped up, arse over heel, and passed through the trunk and fell down into a molasses black space. He landed with a crash, bones jarring in his body.

He lay there in the darkness, trying to steady his breathing, but the air felt heavy, unreal. The surface he was lying on was hard and crunchy and crackled like spun sugar as he tried to get up. He managed to sit and held his hands out, trying to find the place where he'd fallen through. His heart was as fast as the tapping of a woodpecker.

'Help!' he tried to yell out but his voice felt deadened, reduced to a whisper.

He heard noise, a slow, wet, slithering thing coming from his right. His body tensed up and he thought that at any moment now his heart might burst in his chest and end him. The slithering stopped and that voice, the one he'd heard when he was on the other side whispered, 'Div ye want him deid? Ah can take ye back tae that day afore he send ye tae jail.'

'Who are ye?' he cried, tears spilling down his cheeks.

The inside of the tree was flooded with light. In front of him stood a woman, wearing a dress of tattered leaves and twigs. She was *beautiful*.

'Yiv spent mony a moment by ma tree,' she continued, 'an' ah've niver felt such sadness an' fear come aff ye afore. Ah wish tae help.'

It was at that moment a memory burst forth, a flash of a small leather-bound book, of local myths and legends being read to him by his mother in the glow of candle light, her words soft and soothing and comforting.

'No!' he gasped as he realised who he was speaking to and shrank back in fear. 'Yir a witch! Ye'll no do tae me whit ye did tae Thomas of Erceldoune!'

The Fairy Queen threw her head back and laughed. Robert tried not to notice her small, sharp teeth.

'Ah, Thomas the Rhymer.' Her face softened as she cast her mind back to her lover that she had imprisoned in the roots of the tree for seven years. 'Dinna be afeart, Robert, that wiz over five hunnert years ago. Whit ah do tae pass ma time huz changed. And ony road, ye hiv a family, no?'

Robert nodded.

'Ah would nivir steal a man frae hiz family. But that bailie haz pissed oan ma tree wance or twice during his tenure, an' ah'd like tae be able tae gie him his just desserts.'

'An whit's the catch? Whit di ye want in return?'

'All ye'll need tae dae is find a tree near this wan an' carve a smaw wooden cross oot o' it whin yiv finished wi' the bailie. And wan o' yir boilt sweeties.'

'Why?' asked Robert, genuinely curious.

'The forest needs tae mark the deid. Thir are many such trees. dinnae kid yerself thinkin' yir the first ah've helped wi summat like this.'

'An' the sweetie?'

'Although ahm no' – *strictly* like ye, ahm still o' this earth. Ah can indulge.'

Robert put a hand in his pocket and plucked out one of his famous red and white candies. He passed it to the Fairy Queen who closed her hand over it. Once she opened it again, it had gone.

'Right, ahm going tae take ye up noo. Ye'll be back tae the stairt o' Monday morn, an' it just so happens that the bailie wull be comin' frae Mosshouses Farm tae git tae Gala. He's got a sair bunce oan him frae all the fine whisky he wiz supping wi' the heid o' the fairm, Angus Dalgliesh. He'll be takin' hiz time. It'll take aw the time in the wurld tae git a guid spot tae jump him.'

Robert calculated the quickest way to get to him would be going over Gattonside.

'Ah can dae it, ah'll be loaded doon wi' ma bag, but ah can dae it.'

'Leave yir bag here, because as soon as yiv done the deed, yi need tae make yir way back tae the tree and sit doon where yi were afore an' ah'll come and take ye back tae today. An ye micht need this—' The Fairy Queen held out her hand and on it was a small knife with a rough wooden handle.

'Ahm sure ye'll use yir stick tae git him aff hiz horse, but wance ye do, slip this intae hiz throat an' move it fast awa' frae ye, that'll get him aff this Earth awffy quick, and nae blud on ye,' she smiled.

Robert nodded and took the knife. In that instant he felt his body being pulled backwards. This time there was more pain, a terrible pain, as he left the tree and was back above earth.

Monday

Robert looked at his sack that contained the candies and his coloured jacket, then down at the knife that was in his hand. The thought of turning up at the court and dealing with the bailie in a polite manner and getting off with a fine didn't even occur to him. He picked up his stick and made off back towards Melrose, instantly swallowed by the thick mist.

Bailie Thirlsemere shook hands with his host and got on his horse.

'Mind and be careful now, ye dinnae want tae be comin' aff yer steed in this weather,' Angus laughed, stroking the horse's luxurious mane.

'I'll certainly mind my way,' Thirlsmere remarked as last night's whisky made him wince.

He bade Angus a good morning and set off, the day beginning to lift. He rode past Mosshouses Cottages and down the meandering track that split off and would take you down to Langshaw if you had business in that direction. Thirlsmere did not, and hoped to make it to Galashiels in slightly over the hour. It was a hard track and his rump was feeling it, the unyielding saddle doing its best no doubt to give him sores by the time he arrived at his lodgings where he would spend the next couple of days.

Just past the turn to Langshaw he spotted a man on the ground, his face covered in blood. Thirlsmere didn't have time to waste, but wanted to make sure than man wasn't dead at the very least.

'You, sir,' he remarked from on top of his horse. 'There's a farmhouse only ten minutes from here on foot if you need assistance.'

The man got up, groaning and squatted on his haunches.

'Whit day is it?' he asked groggily.

'Ah, drunk all weekend were we? I hope you haven't got into any trouble or I am in no doubt that I'll be seeing you in the next few days!' Thirlsmere chuckled.

'Whit day is it?' the man insisted.

'It's Monday, you debauched fool. Now, out of my horse's way or it'll have no choice but to leave imprints on that coat of yours.'

'And yiv no sentenced Robert Colthart yet?'

'What? No, that's today. How –'

Before the bailie could finish, the bloody-faced man swung his heavy stick and smacked him in the ribs. Thirlsmere cried out and crashed to the ground. The horse galloped off.

Another crashing blow, this time to Thirlsmere's head. He tried to shout out for help, but his breath was cut short as the knife was punched brutally into his throat.

Once the deed was done, Robert wiped the knife on the long grass next to the track and fled across the fields, back to the tree as quickly as he could. The Fairy Queen was right, the only blood of the bailie's was on his hands, not a spot landed on his clothes.

Before he went to the tree he washed his hands and face in the Bogle Burn, the ice cold water making him gasp. The small cut on his palm that he used to smear blood over his face stung. He washed his stick off, and as he had been instructed, found a tree and carved a cross into it. Bits of bark fell onto the ground and were trodden underfoot when he finished and climbed up the embankment and saw that his bag was still there. He smiled and threw his stick down by it and sat down between the two big roots and closed his eyes. Again the hands appeared from the trunk and quickly drew him in. He lay on the ground, trying to gather himself

'Yir tasks are dun?' the Fairy Queen asked.

'Aye, they've been dun. Here's yir knife back.' He passed it over. She clasped the hilt and jabbed the blade into the ground. Small fibrous roots climbed up the knife and pulled it under until it was no more.

Robert noticed the sweetie he had given the Fairy Queen was on the ground; it had acquired a bit of dirt, but not too much. He grabbed it, and not adverse to the odd sleight of hand trick himself, deposited it quickly in his pocket. If she wasn't going to eat it, well, that was just a waste of expensive sugar, he thought to himself.

'Weil, it's time fir ye tae git back,' the Fairy Queen said, smiling. Those sharp teeth again. She knelt down and stroked Robert's unruly hair back off his face with a pressure that he thought was strange, but didn't say anything.

'Yir no gonna try an' slouster me or onything funny like —'

But before he knew it he was sitting against the tree.

Tuesday

Robert reached out with his cut hand to put on his hat and saw that it was no longer fresh, but a cut that had had a full day to heal. Trying not too hard to think about the otherworldly magic he'd experienced, he picked up his sack and decided that as he was so near he should go into Newtown and see how much money was to be made there.

He had a great day's trade, both at the market and at the train stop and sold all of his stock in record time. Once on the train back home he folded up his colourful jacket and put on his old one, sat on the bench and rooted through his pockets and found the sweetie the Fairy Queen had dropped. He dusted it off and popped it into his mouth and gave it a good 'sook'.

By the time he got back to his house he was ravenous. His wife asked what had happened at court and Robert simply shrugged and said that the bailie hadn't turned up and he supposed he would just have to wait to be called to the court again. He ate well and spent the evening making a large batch of candies, not turning to bed until the early hours.

His dreams, when he finally slept, were horrific. He saw the bailie in them and he was unable to tell where his skin ended and the molten sugar that was dripping from it, began. The Fairy Queen was there too, laughing away, her small teeth larger now and she pulled the bailie's neck back and bit into the hole that had been made by the knife.

Robert screamed himself awake.

Wednesday

She's cursed me, he thought to himself as he washed and peeled the sugar beets. He then cut the beets into small chunks and threw them into his massive pot and brought them up to boil, stirring continuously. That was the only action that calmed him down and stopped him from tipping the pot up and wrecking his 'factory.' It was just a ramshackle shed, built much to the dismay of the landlord, but the extra money that he got went a long way to soothe the pain he felt.

After the beets were tender, he used two strips of hessian sack to grab the handle of the massive beet pot and pour the water from it into a large leather bucket. He collected all the beet pulp and dressed it in cheesecloth, hung it over the bucket and let the water run freely from it. Once done he slapped the cheese cloth onto the table and opened it up. He then picked up a handful of the still-hot mashed beet and crammed it into his mouth. He forced handful after handful in. He was so hungry, so ravenous. This muck wasn't what he was wanting to eat but Robert ate so much of that he started to vomit on the table. He slopped up his stringy discharge and gulped it back down until he slumped into the corner of the shed and fell into a deep food coma.

Night after night, the routine was the same when he was making his sweeties. He'd eat himself into a stupor on pulped beet and then the next day would go out and sell his 'Coulter's Candy' to the children and others curious to meet the famous candy man. But a curious and awful thing started to happen; the children, and it was mostly the children who fell prey to it, started to get sick. Once they went home and had supper they would begin to be violently ill and it wasn't long before the local doctor was swamped with case upon baffling case. Then the children started to die; infirm adults also turned up their toes. Robert couldn't really remember at what point he started to get the blame, but it was published in the local rag that it was *his* sweeties that were spreading a strange sickness. His business, his fame, his legendary Coulter's Candies were no more. Snuffed out in an instant. Worse was to come; even though Robert wasn't selling his sweeties any more people were still dying at an incredible rate and through it all Robert piled on pound after pound. He'd make vats of his sweeties and dump them. All he was interested in was gorging on the pulp. His frame was a small one so the sugar went to the place it could freely explore its expanding surrounds: his belly. He looked like his wife had when she was expecting the twins. He wondered if they would have died from eating his sweeties if they hadn't died a few moments after being born.

Robert woke up from his nightly food coma. He was smiling. He got up steadily, went to one of the cupboards and grabbed his tinderbox, a box of Kelso matches, and a candle then left the house.

Robert was breathing heavily; his lungs felt they were going to collapse in on him. The stick was aiding him a little, giving him respite when he needed to rest, but not much. His jacket he had taken off and hidden in a nook along one of the dykes the other side of Melrose.

Finally, he came to the tree and smiled as he walked past it. He nipped into the woods and picked up deadfall branches and placed them around the foot of the tree. Hours and hours he spent, building a pyre, the largest deadfall just tickling the bottom of the lowest hanging branches. He stuffed dried leaves and moss in between the branches then bent down, lit the candle, and placed it in a small space that looked like a church shrine. The flame licked, the wax spat and he blew on it ever so gently, like a lovers kiss, and the moss burnt, then the smaller sticks caught and crackled and the fire danced and then the larger dead branches make large cracking noises as the flames took hold. Before long, Robert was standing back as the heat was too strong, and the tree – that infernal, horrible tree – was a raging pyre and if anyone was awake to see such a thing, they would marvel at how red the sky had become.

Through the noise of the tree crackling, Robert fathomed that he could hear the screams far below him in that damned kingdom. He imagined the Fairy Queen ablaze, her skin blistering and dripping as the heat consumed her.

'Curse me, wud ye?' Robert said, sitting down now, the smoke getting to him.

He watched as charred and blackened things crawled out of the trunk and fell into the raging fire. Some managed to miss the fire and hit the scorched earth. Every time that happened, Robert would get up, slowly, waddle across to them and bash their brains in with a swift heft of his stick. He threw them into the pyre. The smell was horrendous, but still Robert did not leave his vigil.

The morning brought the full destruction of the tree. Robert grinned when the wind picked up, lifting the ash and taking it into the air, like snow. All that was left of it was the base of the trunk.

He kicked away smoking embers and peered down into the remains. The Fairy Queen launched herself at him, her charcoal fingers clawing and breaking on his face, but he easily threw her off him and she crashed into the ground.

Robert approached her with his club. She feebly raised her arm.

'Yir a trickster, ah knew ah shoudna huv trusted ye,' he hissed.

'Ah can remove the curse, just leave me be,' she wailed, her voice croaking.

'Do it then.'

She closed her eyes. He felt something leave, something resolved. She opened them again, her eyes were bleeding.

'It's done,' she whispered. She dropped her arm by her side.

Robert brought the heavy stick down and split her head in two. Brain matter splashed onto his breeks. He picked her up and dropped her down the tree hole then walked away, back to Galashiels. He had thought about carving mention of the dead on the trees, like the Queen had told him to do on the death of Thirlsmere, but he had enough of the forest now. He smiled as he left behind the carnage and even managed to whistle his little song that he sang for the bairns when he was selling his candy.

He nearly gave himself a heart attack walking back up the Bogle Brae, and when he finally got to Melrose, he was starving, but it was a *different* kind of hunger, not the kind that would see him only to feast on pulped beet. He stopped in at Burts Hotel and drank a frothy beer and ate a liver sausage with mashed potato. He was feeling better than he had done in a long time. Why, even on the way out of Melrose, a group of children pointed at him and ran towards him asking him if he had any of his candies. They were sad when he didn't, but were utterly delighted when he started to sing 'Coulter's Candy' and they all joined in.

Things slowly started to get back to normal and the unexplained deaths dropped off as quickly as they had started. But try as he might Robert could not shift the weight he had put on, and the locals, with quick-to-forget memories began to tease him, to say that he was getting 'awffy fat aff yir ane vat!'

His trips out were becoming fewer and fewer, and he would send Mary out to sell on his behalf. Sometimes she wore bright colours, but more than often she would just hold out her tray of sweets with the slogan, *The famous Coulter's Candy* lovingly painted on a wooden board. Robert's behaviour changed; he became a mean drunk, getting in and out of scrapes, and although he was never sent to gaol, he was heavily fined each time.

The headaches began, and they were sure brain-splitters, but during these times he would leave the house and try to kill the pain with ale; he'd be found slumped in the corner of the Harrow Inn, not caring if he was stared at by the coach drivers who came in for bed and board. Sometimes he was dressed as the candyman, garnering the odd remark, sometimes not.

On this morning, the one of his collapse, he woke up feeling bright, the last punisher a distant memory. When Mary asked him if he wanted breakfast, Robert said he would pass, that he was going to skip breakfasts from now on and try to get down to his fighting best.

He took the train to Melrose, leaving the station and walking the mile or so to the Eildon Tree. What he could see of the Eildon Hills looked beautiful and braw in the dappled sunlight. Finally he reached his destination and sat down by the blackened and ruined stump, smiling benignly as he thought of all the panic in the surrounding area that had been created by its destruction. Who in their right mind would destroy the magic tree and what kind of supernatural retribution would be wrought by the underworld on the locals? The local newspaper had been full of the story and who the most likely perpetrators would be. Luckily his name had never been mentioned. He opened up his small bag and brought out a pie and an apple and ate heartily. The world all around him was eerily still. He didn't care to look into the tree trunk, but he did piss on it before he left to get the train back to Galashiels.

'It's Mad Rabbie! Gie us a dance if ye can move yon thunderous belly o' yours!'

  'Ah'll come ower and molocate ye, ye stinking wee shites!'

  'Ye could nivir catch us!'

And now he lay on the table, his breathing laboured, a long crackling rattle deep in his chest every time he struggled to take in air.

The Doctor shook his head sadly.

'I'm afraid he's oan hiz way oot,' he told a sobbing Mary. 'Let's git him moved tae the bedroom and let him die in peace.'

Word soon began to spread through Galashiels that Robert Colthart was dying. The children, the ones who had survived the blight, gathered outside his house on Overhaugh Street and started to sing. Before he slipped into that deep, final sleep, Robert was paralysed with complete and total terror as he heard a familiar voice sing:

Ally, bally, ally bally bee,
Dinnae cross the Queen Fairy
If ye dare you'll soon see
Yir death frae Coulter's Candy

'He's a heiffer,' the men gasped as they struggled through with Robert's body, and it took several more men to get him up onto the slab.

'That'll dae,' remarked Doctor Woodhead curtly and he paid the helpers for their efforts.

Once they had gone his assistant undressed the deceased and the Doctor was taken aback by how large Robert's stomach actually was. He had seen large men in his time, but because Robert's frame was so thin, it looked impossible for one man to carry his own weight like that.

As eager as he was to open the stomach up, as per Virchow's

Post-Mortem Examination, it was advised that he start with the brain. He grabbed his saw and after ten minutes of brutal sawing, removed the top of the skull. That marvel, the brain, was before him. It looked abnormally large, and Woodhead removed it, although it did give some resistance, but with a slurping noise it was freed. Once under the light of the lamp it was obvious to see how he had died; the tumour was pronounced on the frontal lobe, a horribly darkened red mass. He took his scalpel and cut into it but the scalpel wouldn't go any further.

'Funny,' he remarked to his assistant who looked at him with one eyebrow raised. 'I'm meeting a strange resistance. Can ye pass us a bigger blade?'

Using the heftier implement, he pushed into the brain tissue deeper and cut around what was obstructing his way. He lifted it out, and rubbed away the flecks of greyish-pink matter off it. He held the offending object in his hand and brought it again to the lamplight. Woodhead looked at his assistant with confusion and dawning horror. The assistant, who had seen and indulged in many of what Woodhead was holding, threw up on the spot.

It was a famous red and white Coulter's Candy, half-sooked.

At the Eildon tree, new growth slowly twisted its way out of the burnt earth, as it always does.

DISHES SERVED COLD

On November 28 1440, an astonishing act of violence occurred in Edinburgh Castle, which would have horrific repercussions for many years to come.

It all began when William, the 6th Earl of Douglas, who was 15 years old, and his brother, David, who was 12, were invited to dinner with King James II, who, at only nine, was younger than both of them. The young James was delighted to see his two cousins, and to share a cheerful repast with them, but had no idea that he would shortly be presiding over a scene of carnage to match that of (and provide a partial inspiration for) the blood-soaked horror of the Red Wedding in George R R Martin's A Storm of Swords, *the third novel in the* Game of Thrones *saga.*

The Douglas youngsters attended the Great Hall at Edinburgh Castle that evening at the behest of the infant James's official guardians, Sir William Crichton and Sir Alexander Livingston, two Stuart loyalists who feared and mistrusted the Douglas family as overmighty subjects. Indeed, William Douglas, who, for all his tender years, could call upon thousands of warlike clansmen if he wished, was already displaying a haughty and troublesome attitude when it came to the balance of power in Scotland.

That said, there was no trace of this during the banquet, so it came as a complete surprise to the guests when the meal was concluded with the ceremonial delivery to their table of a black bull's severed head.

Those among the Douglas party who recognised this as an age-old threat of death, did not respond quickly enough. All were promptly overpowered and slain in their seats, while the youthful earl and his brother were taken captive. Despite young King James's repeated protestations, for he had known nothing about this in advance, he was taken outside into the yard, and there made to watch while grinning men-at-arms gave the boy-earl and his younger brother the most ferocious beating and then dragged them screaming and bleeding to the block, where they were beheaded by repeated blows of a heavy axe.

The 'Black Dinnour', as it became known, was an infamous incident, enough you'd have thought to cow any recalcitrant nobility, but though James II of Scotland, as he grew older, would demonstrate political acumen and the ability to win over both friends and enemies alike, he continually struggled to offset the ruthless ambitions of the Douglas family, which left him ill-tempered and suspicious.

In 1452, he summoned the latest earl of Douglas, William the 8th of that name, to a royal feast at Stirling Castle. Given what had happened previously, such an invitation should surely have seemed ominous, especially as Douglas was known to have been forging new alliances with other great lords who were hostile to the House of Stuart. But perhaps through arrogance, or perhaps because he felt that to ignore a royal summons would be tantamount to open rebellion, the defiant earl attended the feast as required.

Amid regal standards of entertainment, music, fine wine and the most succulent delicacies, James repeatedly entreated his guest to desist from his scheming, to abandon his new allies and return himself to royal favour. Earl Douglas continually refused to give any such guarantees, and at length, the king, red-faced with rage, gave a signal to his men, who immediately attacked the Douglas party. The earl, possibly stunned that history was repeating itself, was held fast in his chair, while James drew a dagger and stabbed him 26 times, before dashing out his brains with a pole-axe. The mangled corpse was then flung from a window, castle groundkeepers dragging it off and burying it in an unmarked grave.

But even this wasn't the end of it. According to Walter Scott and other balladeers, the gory apparition of the murdered Douglas would regularly rise from its last resting-place, prophesying that his murderer would shortly die in a welter of his own blood.

Sure enough, in 1460, not yet 30 years old, James II, who had become a keen advocate of heavy artillery after using it to great effect against Douglas armies in the intervening years, was besieging an English garrison at Roxburgh Castle on the border, and personally commanding a heavy cannon called 'the Lion', newly arrived from Flanders, when it misfired and exploded, blowing him to pieces.

ECHOES FROM THE PAST
Graham Smith

Jennifer's eyes fly open when she hears the baby laughing. She doesn't have a baby. Has never had one. She dismisses the noise as a subconscious trick played by a tired mind.

Again the sound comes. Not spooky, or eerie, just the bubbling laughter of a happy baby. The innocent sound breaking and racing her heart in equal measure.

She is alone in the house.

No children.

No grandchildren.

Just her and a judgemental cat.

Yet Jennifer is sure the sound she'd heard didn't come from outside.

Her fingers fumble at the switch on the bedside lamp. Light fills the room chasing away the dark thoughts. Ears strain, reaching out through the house, searching for the unfamiliar, finding nothing out of place. The creaks and whispers of a tree blowing in the wind, the hoot of an owl and a dozen other country sounds she is still growing used to, but there were no more of the burbling giggles.

She would pass it off as a dream had a second outburst not echoed through the house.

No matter which way she examines the situation, there is no way she could have heard a baby laughing.

It is a weird sound to have heard. Nobody she knows would arrive in the night with a baby. Likewise, those intending to steal from or harm her wouldn't bring an infant with them.

One foot finds a slipper, then the other. She stands, pulls on her dressing gown and listens again. The mobile phone lifted from beside the lamp and ready to dial the police fills her hand.

Jennifer had done her usual rounds before going to bed. She mentally retraces her steps. Nothing had been missed. Outside doors were locked, ground floor windows closed and snibbed.

Thirty years of living in London had ingrained household security into her. Now, living in a Scottish Borders farmhouse two miles from the nearest living person and ten from a shop, the lockdown is more habit than necessity.

Her husband was a Borderer through and through. Rugby mad and descended from the reiving clans, he'd always wanted to return to his homelands. He may have an organisational mind and a talent for managing people, but his heart lay in the Borders. He was always at his happiest when fewer than ten miles from Selkirk.

She'd fallen in love with the area many years ago when he'd brought her north to meet his parents. The rolling hills and straight-talking locals both felt welcoming, although it had been years before she'd got her ears fully wrapped around the unique dialect they uttered in thick accents.

Her fingers grip the phone tight as she repeats the lockdown route. Everything is as it should be. Locked, closed, snibbed.

The security light by her car is off, un-triggered by a vehicle or aggressor passing through the only entrance.

'You're a bloody idiot Jennifer Kerr. It's your imagination.' Her attempt at self-chastisement doesn't work. If anything the lack of vocal conviction heightens her unease.

Had the sound been a more dismissible one she would have blamed a slipping roof tile or piece of tin flapping on one of the farm buildings. A baby's laughter though. That is something else. Not just innocent, cruel

For ten years she and David had tried to conceive. She'd had eight miscarriages and no children.

The exhaustive tests they'd undergone had found nothing wrong with either of them. None of the doctors or consultants had been able to give a medical reason why she could never carry a baby to term.

She knew why though. It was a secret burden she'd carried since the age of fifteen. Molested by an uncle, she'd fallen pregnant. Too scared to tell her parents she'd confided in a favourite aunt.

Ivy had been a good woman, despite being the family's black sheep. She'd taken a distraught Jennifer to see a doctor she was friendly with. Four Aspirins, one injection and twenty humiliating and painful minutes later Jennifer was no longer pregnant.

Her tears back then had been of relief. Not one to believe in karmic elements, she'd never quite been able to dismiss the notion her failure to carry a pregnancy to term had its roots in that illegal abortion. After every miscarriage her tears became less sorrowful and more guilt ridden. It was as if her decision to have the tiny unborn foetus removed by the whisky-sodden doctor haunted her, condemning her to a life of barrenness as punishment for ending an unborn life.

Jennifer sits on the bed, tells herself the baby's laughter isn't real. That it is just a figment of an overactive imagination. Perhaps the wind had blown from a different direction and had prompted thirty years of guilt to distort an innocent sound into one of condemnation. Another option is her ears mistaking some animal call for a baby's laugh.

They'd only moved into the house a month ago. While David had country living in his blood, she'd always been a city-girl.

Her feet push their way back under the single thin sheet on the bed. As she lays her phone back onto the bedside table, she reaches for her book.

Her fingers touch the cover but she doesn't pick up the novel. Instead she lets herself fall back onto the bed laughing at her own stupidity. It's no wonder her mind is playing tricks and scaring her, the book she's been reading is the latest Stephen King.

Jennifer's smile is still on her lips as her head touches the pillow.

A scream rings through the air. High, piercing and filled with absolute terror it dispels any doubts she has about her imagination playing tricks.

Again her fingers fumble at the lamp until they find the switch. As soon as she can see her phone she grabs it. Drops it. Draws a breath, forces herself to calm down. Picks up the phone, calls the police.

The voice on the end of the phone is Glaswegian. Calm and reassuring but not at all local. She recalls David telling her about the amalgamation of Scotland's regional police forces into one national body. It makes logical sense that call response centres will also have been conjoined.

'Help, please help. I've just heard someone screaming.'

The woman on the other end of the line takes her name, verifies her mobile number. 'I need to know where you're calling from. Can you give me your address?'

'Beckfoot Farm. Near Selkirk.'

'Do you have the postcode?'

Jennifer's brain went blank. 'It's TD7 … I can't remember the rest.'

'Okay. Is Selkirk the nearest town or is there a village nearby?'

'Yes. Yes there is. It's called Yarrowford.' Village might be an exaggeration for the hamlet that is Yarrowford, but at least it is a name she could give to the woman.

'That's good. I'll send a police car as soon as possible. Please stay on the line while I make the call. I need to get more details from you.'

'Thank you, thank you.'

Jennifer puts her mobile onto loudspeaker, turns the volume up and half pushes, half walks a small chest of drawers until it stands in front of the doorway. It isn't a substantial barricade but it is better than nothing.

Her ears strain for more sounds, the local accent of the woman on the end of the phone, another scream or more baby chuckles.

Nothing comes except the lowing of a cow and the hoot of an owl.

The disembodied voice of the call handler piercing the air makes her jump. A shriek leaps from her mouth.

'Are you okay? What's happening now?'

'Sorry, you startled me.' Jennifer feels her cheeks burn as she switches her mobile back to its normal volume.

'Sorry about that.'

The voice remains calm, reassuring. Jennifer recognises that the woman will have been trained to remain professional and empathetic. She'd like a great deal more urgency in the drawled tones. For the woman to understand she is alone and terrified.

'Can you tell me more about the scream you heard, was it definitely human?'

'Absolutely. It was one of those blood-curdling ones, the type you get in the old horror films. But that's not all I heard.'

'No? What else was there?'

'I heard a baby laughing. But there's no baby here, I'm alone. I heard it just as I was about to go to sleep.'

A pause as the woman evaluated her words. 'Did you drink any alcohol tonight, a glass of wine perhaps?'

Jennifer thought of the bottle of Merlot she'd finished off. It had been a little more than half full. She'd not felt at all tipsy while drinking, but now she feels the prickle of embarrassment. Afraid she's underestimated how much the wine had affected her.

The doubts come rushing back. She now wonders if the wine and the book have conspired to encourage her imagination into overactivity.

She opts to tell a sanitised version of the truth. 'I had a couple of glasses but didn't feel drunk.'

'That's okay. Where are you now?'

'In the bedroom. On the second floor.'

'That's good. I take it the house is securely locked.'

'Of course.' Jennifer tosses a look at the Ikea barricade in front of the bedroom door. Feels a fraction safer. 'Will the police be here soon?'

'Don't worry, they're *en-route*. What can you hear? Can you see anything out the window?'

'Good. I can't hear anything. I mean there's no more screams or laughing babies.'

'What about the sound of someone trying to break in?'

'No. There's nothing like that.' As she says the words her doubts return only to be washed away with a feeling of relief. 'Wait. I can see the flash of a blue light. The police are nearly here.'

'That's good. Stay where you are until they arrive. I'm going to go now.'

Jennifer pulls her slippers and dressing gown back on, returns the chest of drawers back to its usual home. She can feel her heart rate slowing as she descends the stairs to answer the knock on the door.

There are two coppers standing at the door. One a six foot bruiser, an obvious son of the hills. The other young, female, half her own age and three quarters her height. PC Tiny may have all the training in the world, but it is PC Bruiser whose presence gives her the feeling of security she craves.

She relates the basic facts to them. PC Tiny comes in, checks the inside of the house while her colleague takes a walk round the farmhouse and the outbuildings.

With her reconnaissance completed the young copper has gravitated back to the kitchen where Jennifer is boiling the kettle. From outside there are flashes of light as PC Bruiser makes his rounds.

'The noises you heard, did they sound like they were inside or outside the house?'

'Inside. Definitely.'

'You didn't leave a TV or radio on did you?' Her eyes flick to the Merlot bottle protruding from the bin.

'Absolutely not. I'm not stupid. It was the first thing I thought of.' The words may be a lie, but Jennifer doesn't like the way PC Tiny is judging her. Besides, if that had been the case there would have been other sounds. Conversations, adverts or music would have alerted her to her mistake.

She wishes the explanation was that simple. She'd rather it was her own carelessness that was responsible, because the alternative terrifies her.

Jennifer dumps a spoonful of instant coffee into a cup. No way is she going to try and sleep now. 'Do you want a cuppa?'

The offer is borne of an ingrained politeness coupled with a desire to extend the police's stay by any means necessary.

PC Tiny holds up a finger, takes three steps towards the door, answers the crackle of the radio clipped to her stab vest.

She speaks in a low tone which stops Jennifer hearing even one side of the conversation, turns back when the crackles end.

'I'll pass thanks, but PC McLennan never says no. You said you heard the sounds while in your bedroom. If it's all right with you, I'd like to go up and wait a few minutes, see if I hear anything.' A finger points at the torchlight wobbling across the farmyard. 'He takes his coffee black, with three sugars.'

Jennifer duly makes the coffee for PC Bruiser. A large part of her grateful he takes it without the cooling effect of milk or cream. The longer it takes him to drain the mug, the longer he'll be here.

A gentle but firm knock at the door signals PC Bruiser has finished his external search.

'There's nowt there.' His voice is deep, the thick accent filled with the earthiness of all Borderers. His twang reminds her of the way David had spoken when they'd first met until he'd learned to soften his vocabulary to save constant repetition.

She gives him his coffee. Made in the largest mug she possesses. 'Your colleague has gone upstairs to listen for any more noises.'

He nods. His eyes flit round the room. When they stop they are locked onto the bottle protruding from the bin the way PC Tiny's had.

'You're no' frae roond here. Where dae ye come frae?'

'Birmingham.' He says nothing so she keeps talking. 'My husband is originally from Selkirk. We bought this farmhouse from his uncle. He owns the rest of the farm.'

'Aye, a ken the uncle. He's a guid mon. Is your husband no' here?'

'He's down in Birmingham, finalising the handover of his

business to new owners.'

'Aye.' His eyes do another circuit of the room. Again they finish on the bin. 'When's he back?'

'The weekend.' Jennifer finds herself adopting the clipped sentences of PC Bruiser. He may have kind features and a wisdom about him but she can feel him judging her. Knowing he's reached the conclusion she's nothing more than a southerner who's had too much to drink and been spooked by the first unusual noise she's heard.

'Long you been here, a month?'

'That's right.'

While there may not be the twitchy curtains of suburbia in the Borders, there are the ever present gossip-mongers. Everybody is aware of everyone else's business. The little shop she uses to buy cigarettes and essentials like milk and bread always has at least one or two people exchanging tid-bits with the shop keeper.

Jennifer isn't sure she'll ever be able to get used to this but knows she has to accept it as a part of rural life.

PC Bruiser looks at his watch, drains his mug and says a few words into his radio. 'Thanks for the cuppa. We'd best be going.'

'You're leaving me here? Alone?'

Jennifer knows the answers to her questions. The police are too stretched to offer bodyguard services to everyone who hears strange noises. Add the pointed looks at the empty wine bottle and their conclusion became obvious.

Her finger depresses the switch on the kettle. If the police aren't staying, she isn't even going to attempt sleep. She can't even go to a hotel as there is every chance the police will breathalyse her if she gets behind the wheel of her car.

PC Tiny's police issue boots give muted thumps as she returns downstairs. As she enters the room she gives Jennifer a patronising grin. 'I didn't hear anything. You'll be fine now.'

'Are you sure?' Jennifer finds it hard to accept PC Tiny's attempts at reassurance, when she has socks older than the girl.

'Of course.'

'You got onybody tae come bide wi ye?' PC Bruiser makes for the door.

'Nobody I want to bother at this time of night.'

'Well if ye hear onything else, be sure to call ou.' His words are undermined by the resignation in his voice. As if he wants her to know they think she's wasting their time. That he expects to return for a second wild goose chase.

Jennifer locks the door behind them. Calls David. Leaves a voicemail begging he come home as soon as he gets her message.

She doesn't know what to do next. Isn't brave enough to try going to bed again. Wants the comfort of company. Thinks about putting on the TV, but doesn't dare in case it covers the next noise.

Even if she does put the TV on there'd be nothing worth watching at this time of night. None of the DVDs she's unpacked so far will provide a good distraction from her fears. Like her reading taste, she prefers the macabre over the mawkish. She's never seen *Titanic* or *Love Actually* but often re-watches *The Shining* and *Scream*.

She puts her coffee mug on the table beside her chair, lays her mobile next to it and returns to the kitchen. When she comes back to the lounge and sits down, the largest knife she owns is placed beside the mug.

The cynicism shown by the police has dented her already fragile confidence. Made her afraid of more than just the noises she is so sure she'd heard.

If the cops were right and she'd been drunk and had imagined the laughs and the scream, her sanity may be in doubt. She's been drunker in this house. While the book she is reading is a horror story, it is gentle by comparison to others she's enjoyed.

Another factor is the realism of the sounds. If her imagination had conjured those noises, her subconscious is trying to tell her something. Something she probably doesn't want to hear.

Jennifer goes to the kitchen, draws a cookbook from the shelf and carries it back to the lounge. If she can't sleep, watch TV or read her normal kind of thing, she may as well fill her time doing something useful.

David's mother was one of those old school country wives who always had fresh scones and cakes available. It was the one thing about her Jennifer liked. To that end she'd insisted on having an Aga in her new kitchen just like her mother-in-law had. With her and David retiring in their fifties, the plan was to settle into a comfortable domestic routine. No longer will they be ships passing in the night, grabbing shared moments and takeaway meals whenever their respective schedules allowed.

They'd grown to crave a home to live in, rather than lived to finance. She wants to bake and prepare meals from fresh ingredients instead of the microwave and freezer. David has talked of a vegetable garden and meat bought from a local butcher not a supermarket chain.

Now it's all in jeopardy. She can't stay in the house long term if it terrifies her. Can't bear the thought she may be losing her mind, that their dreams will crash to the ground because she's began to hear noises that aren't there.

Or worse, noises that are.

Once upon a time, she'd have loved to live in a haunted house. Not now though. All she wants is for David to be by her side. To verify one way or the other whether the noises are real, or if her mind is slipping.

She wakes in the chair, startled by a shrill noise. The cookbook she's been reading has fallen to the floor. Her mobile rang, its tone identifying the sound which has disrupted her slumber.

'Oh thank God you've called.' Her mouth dries as she speaks. The morning sunshine filtering through thin curtains seems friendly and warming. The doubts about herself which had tortured her dreams temper her words as she tells David of the noises she'd heard.

'Your imagination's running away with you. Did the police come out?'

'Of course they did.'

'And yet you haven't mentioned them finding anything.' The statement hangs like an accusation. He'll never go so far as to be scornful of her, instead he'll use reason and logic to dispel her fears. 'Remember what we talked about last night?'

She did. The memory made her feel stupid. They'd chatted about their respective days and she'd told him of her plans for the evening.

'You probably think I'm being silly and imagining all this?'

'Not at all.' His tone calms the anger she's injected into her voice. 'I think you're being normal.'

'Normal? Normal people don't hear noises they can't possibly hear.'

'They do after half a bottle of wine, a scary movie and a few chapters of a horror novel.' Jennifer doesn't speak. As usual, she's beaten by his logic. 'Add in the fact that last night was probably the first night you've spent alone in the country. And I'd say it's entirely normal for you to imagine things after scaring yourself with movies and books.'

'I feel such a fool, David. I could have sworn those noises were real. I've wasted the police's time and everything.'

'Of course you thought those noises were real, you have a good imagination.' He laughs a low rumbling chuckle. 'You even call me handsome. Being serious though, I'm glad you called the police. It will have reassured you.'

They chat for a while, then David rings off to start his day.

With the curtains opened and friendly sunlight illuminating every part of the room, Jennifer finds herself tutting at her own silliness.

All the same, she plans some changes to her routine. There will be no wine, scary movies or horror novels until David returns.

Jennifer switches the light off, snuggles into the pillow. Her day has passed with her oscillating between surety of what she'd heard, and the cold hard logic of David's assessment. By turn she'd felt silly and defiant.

Even before she closes tired eyes she hears it.

A scream. High, shrill and piercing.

It wasn't outside.

It seemed to come from above.

By the time she has switched on the light and snatched up her phone, the laughing has started. Again it is the cheerful, burbling giggle of a baby.

Twice it rings out.

Silence.

The braying of a sheep drags her eyes to the window.

'*Mum-my ...*'

The single word pulls a scream from the pit of her stomach. It was uttered in a throaty, undead voice. The kind she's so often heard in the scary movies she loves so much. The two syllables drawn apart and separated by a burring growl.

Jennifer freezes with one foot halfway to the floor. The voice had come from underneath her. From below the bed.

'*Jenn-i-fer ...*'

Again the burring growl stretched and drew out the one word it uttered.

Her name being spoken this way is too much for Jennifer. She leaps from the bed and runs for the door. Her bare feet thumping a staccato beat as she hurries downstairs.

There will be no calls to the police or pleas for David return home at once. All she can think about is getting out of the house. Away from whatever demon or creature is calling to her.

The fact it knows her name multiplies her fear many times over. This isn't some random ghoul haunting a property, this is specific.

She grabs a jacket from the newel post at the bottom of the stairs, pulls it on over her pyjamas as she retrieves her handbag from the lounge.

With every morsel of her concentration on getting out of the house as soon as possible, Jennifer pulls on a pair of wellies and makes a clomping dash to her car.

Fifteen minutes later she finds herself sitting outside the Best

Western. The engine of her car ticking itself cool after the thrashing she's just given it.

With the car stationary and the comforting lights of the Best Western's car park illuminating her tear-stained face, she forces long calming breaths into her body. She has no recollection of the journey but doesn't care.

She is out of that damned house.

Safe.

Jennifer wipes her face with the palms of her hands and opens the car door.

The receptionist takes one look at her and gives a pitying shake of her head, the silver bob swaying as she does so. 'Are you okay? What's happened? Did ye catch him with anither woman or did the bastard raise his hands?'

'Huh?'

A deeper concern passes over the receptionist's face as she gestures at Jennifer's red fleece, pink silk pyjamas and green wellies. 'Are you okay? You look as if you've ran out on someone.'

'Yes, yes, I'm fine.'

The way Jennifer stammers makes a liar of her words. The woman has a point with her assumptions but it isn't a man she's just ran out on. It was a … a … She can't finish the thought. Whatever she's escaped, it wasn't a man. She isn't even sure it was human.

'I take it you're efter a room?'

'That's right. A single please.' Jennifer roots in her bag, pulls out her purse and hands over a credit card without even asking for a price.

Jennifer puts her handbag on the bed, pats her pockets. Empty. Her mobile must be in the house somewhere. Or maybe the car. She remembers picking it up but has no idea what she's done with it during her mad dash out of the house.

There's a phone by the bed but as far as she's concerned it's useless. Twenty years ago, she carried an address book in her handbag with all the numbers she needed. Like so many others, David's number is stored in her mobile so she doesn't have to remember or record it.

Jennifer goes outside, checks the car for her mobile. Doesn't find it. Passes by the concerned receptionist without speaking for a second time. Her focus on trying to remember David's mobile number.

She locks the hotel room door, sits on the bed fighting against the sobs which are threatening to overwhelm her.

With no way to contact David, there is nobody else she can turn to. His parents or another relative may take her in for the night but they won't give her story any more credence than the cops who'd turned up last night. At this moment in time she needs reassurance, comforting words and a feeling of security, not questions posed in doubtful tones.

Jennifer reaches for the phone, stops with her hand an inch above it. Calling the police now won't achieve anything. They'll just insist she return to the house with them.

There is no way she can face stepping foot back in that house at night without David by her side. Preferably with some holy water, a stake and a cross.

Tomorrow morning will be soon enough to contact the police. When she can present herself in a rational fashion. Her eyes fall to the wellies beside the bed, the red fleece draped onto a chair. Before she visits the police station she'll need to get some clothes. A pair of jeans and a t-shirt will do. Some underwear too. There is no point turning up dressed like a scarecrow. Above anything else, she needs the police to take her seriously, although she's not sure how much use they will be if the house is haunted.

It will be embarrassing walking into the supermarket in pyjamas and wellies but it is a necessary evil.

Jennifer shudders. Even thinking the word evil affects her. She believes whatever was behind the noises she heard is unworldly.

Worse still is the way the sounds had come last night.

The scream.

The laughter.

The sole word 'Mummy'.

Most damning of all was hearing her name uttered in that foul voice.

Put together, in that sequence, the sounds tell a story. A tale of the death of a child by its mother. Her name being said identifies her as the mother.

Guilt and shame wash over Jennifer as she yet again torments herself over a decision taken many years ago. She falls back onto the bed and lets fear and self-loathing absorb her.

When the gut-wrenching sobs draw to an end, she hauls herself upright with a start. Another thought dominates her mind. One more terrifying than anything she's yet considered.

This is personal, it's about the baby I had aborted. I can't escape it. It will follow me wherever I go.

Jennifer stands in a swift motion as her natural inner-strength returns. She refuses to be afraid any longer. No more will she allow the strange noises to dominate her.

Instead she reaches for the remote control. Switches on the TV and finds a mindless comedy about a rich guy living in Malibu with his brother and nephew.

As she turns up the volume, a realisation strikes her.

Since entering the hotel room, she hasn't heard anything untoward. As the thought calms her, she has another less welcome one.

I only heard them when I was settling down for the night. Lights off and eyes closed. What if it's my imagination? Or is the creature behind the noises watching me?

Jennifer thumbs the remote again, gets off the bed, switches on the tiny kettle and pours instant coffee from the tiny pack into the cup. There will be no sleep for her tonight.

As she returns to the bed, a knock at the door startles her. Hard, insistent and accompanied by a muffled voice.

She can't hear what the voice is saying. Despite herself she turns down the TV and strains to hear.

'Mrs Kerr? Are you in there Mrs Kerr?'

'Who is it?' Even to her own ears, Jennifer's voice is laden with tremble and fear.

'It's Mhairi, from reception. Can you turn your TV doon

please?'

'Of course.'

She realises how loud she's had it. And why she'd held onto the volume controls too long. The racket from the TV isn't just a source of comfort but a barrier against other sounds she doesn't want to hear.

With the volume set at a level more considerate of the hotel's other guests, she sips her coffee and prepares for a long sleepless night.

Jennifer forces herself to get out of the car. As she walks the four steps to join PC Tiny she gives a little stumble, exhaustion making her unsteady on her feet.

PC Tiny points towards the house. 'Did you leave the door open when you left?'

'I ... I don't know. Don't think so.' In the warmth of the mid-morning sun the fear she'd felt in the night seems ridiculous.

Once again she wonders if her imagination is behind things. Her sanity slipping as she approaches the last third of her life expectancy.

'Shall we?'

'Yes. Let's do it.' Jennifer follows PC Tiny into what she'd once thought of as her dream home. Now it's the home of nightmares.

Everything is as she remembers leaving it when going to bed the previous night. She finds her mobile on the worktop beside where her wellies are kept and lifts it. The battery is dead so she makes a mental note to get the charger.

Ahead of her PC Tiny pushes on, impatient. She'd caught the roll of the girl's eyes when the desk sergeant had told her to check out Jennifer's home.

She follows PC Tiny from room to room. They find nothing of note. Nothing is missing. No books have flown off the shelves and there are no bloody pentagrams drawn onto the walls or floor.

PC Tiny's demeanour becomes more scornful and mocking

as each room is checked. There are no open criticisms or spoken words. It is the way she carries herself, the exhaled huffs as each room reveals a complete lack of disturbance.

Jennifer trails the diminutive constable back to the kitchen with mixture of embarrassment and defiance coursing through her. 'I know we didn't find anything, but trust me. I heard those noises. They were real.'

'Of course you did.'

The patronising tone causes something to snap inside Jennifer. It is bad enough she is doubting herself, but for a slip of a girl to treat her as if she is stupid, or worse demented, is too much. 'You can go now. I'm going to pack a bag and stay in a hotel until my husband comes home.' The dismissive words are delivered in a harsh tone but Jennifer is beyond caring. All she wants is to get enough clothes to last until the weekend, her Kindle and get away from the house.

Ten minutes later she is climbing into her car with an overnight night. She'd spent a moment petting the judgemental cat and making sure it had enough kibble and water to last a few days.

Upon her return to the hotel she books the room for an extra three nights, lays on the bed and tries calling David. As usual his phone goes straight to the answering service.

'C'mon, Jen. Let's get home.' David's tone is calm but Jennifer can sense the irritation radiating from him. He'd returned her call, calmed her down and told her to stay at the hotel until he could return.

He'd been his usual pragmatic self and had worked longer hours so he could get back a day sooner. Yet there is a sense of mistrust about him, as if he doesn't quite believe her.

She gets in his car and sits in silence as he drives them home. Bedtime will be when she is proven right. When the lights go out and the house falls silent he'll see she is telling the truth.

There will be confirmation.

Validation.

She doesn't know what the next step will be. David may want to sell the house. Or perhaps he'll laugh it off as harmless and tell her not to worry.

As the scenery flashes past, Jennifer wonders if it's possible to get a house exorcised.

There is another possibility and it's one which scares her as much as the voices using her name.

If she hears the noises and David doesn't, there will be no escaping the fact she is losing her mind.

To lose her sanity will be a terrible thing. For it to be lost in a way that echoes her past will be more cruel than she can bear.

'You never heard the noises at the hotel did you?'

'I've told you I didn't.' Jennifer gives an internal wince at the irritation in her tone. Apologises.

David deserves better. His eyes are bloodshot from driving through the night and he's never uttered one word of complaint about being tired or having to cut short the handover of his business.

'I'm just working through things in my mind.' David pauses. 'If you only heard the noises at the house, then it would suggest they are common to the house rather than you. If you'd heard them at the hotel we'd have an entirely different problem to solve.'

'Thank you.' Jennifer reaches across and squeezes the hand resting on the gearstick. This is typical David. He is approaching this whole situation as if it is a problem which can be solved through logic. His very presence is calming but his words give her a reassurance she isn't sure she merits. By reiterating the point of where she'd heard the noises, he's removed her fears of insanity. 'What are you thinking?'

'I'm planning to have a nice day with my wife in our new home. If the noises come tonight, I'll look into them. Find out where they're coming from. Then I'll stop them.'

'How?'

An expression that's half smile and half grimace stretches David's face. 'I don't know yet. That's something I'll need to work out when I find where they're coming from.'

The certainty in his voice gives Jennifer strength. It is only a temporary panacea as persistent thoughts once again push themselves to the fore.

She's only heard the voices and noises at the house. Which is specific.

Only she has heard them. Specific.

They played on her past, echoing both longing and regret. Specific.

The first two points can be dismissed as only she'd been present to hear them. The third is debateable as it was possible she'd fitted generic facts to her assumption.

They had named her. Specific.

Regardless of what David or anyone else says, Jennifer believes the sounds and voices are aimed at her.

Tonight will be the night she learns whether she is going insane, or has moved into a haunted house which somehow knows her darkest, most deeply-buried secret.

Neither option appeals, although she is beyond desperate for confirmation one way or the other.

David lifts his cup, drains the last of the coffee and reaches for his Kindle. 'C'mon then. It's starting to go dark and I'm shattered.'

'You won't fall asleep will you? You promised you'd stay awake.' Jennifer knows she is being unreasonable but she can't face the idea of David sleeping through any noises.

'Of course not. But remember what you've told me.' He stops talking, gives a loud yawn. 'The noises came within a couple of minutes of you switching off the light.'

'So?'

His voice softens a little. 'You're a creature of habit, Jen. You go to bed after the ten o'clock news. Read for half an hour or so and then it's lights out.'

'There's nothing wrong with having a routine.' Jennifer doesn't like the defensive tone that has crept into her voice.

'Nobody said there was.' He points at the clock on the

mantelpiece. 'It's almost your usual bedtime and I want to fill a flask with coffee before we go upstairs.'

She realises the sub-text behind his words. Instead of doing his usual thing and staying up watching TV until after midnight, he is preparing himself for a vigil.

Jennifer stands in the doorway watching as he readies himself.

'Come on then. Let's go to bed.'

As she follows him up the stairs, Jennifer has to swallow down her nerves. As calm and reassuring as his presence and practicality might be, she doesn't want to hear any of those noises ever again.

David eases himself into his side of the bed and lifts the cup to his mouth. Gives that little grimace he always does at the first taste of black coffee.

'Have you got a weapon? A knife? Or a stick?' Jennifer hears the tremor in her voice. Doesn't like it. Can't help it.

There's a smile in David's voice when he replies. 'I don't need one. You haven't seen anything, nothing has been moved. There have been a few noises that's all. I can't attack a noise or stab a sound. I'm fact finding tonight, that's all.'

She falls silent. Aware of which facts he's trying to find. She wants to protest, to fight her corner but knows better. The only proof of her sanity will be David hearing something when she does.

David switches his lamp off, gestures she do the same. Before she even reaches for him, his fingers grasp hers and give a gentle squeeze. Not hard or insistent, just enough to offer comfort.

They lie in silence. Waiting.

She wants to talk, to hear his voice reassuring her in the darkness. Knows better than to disturb the quiet.

All she can hear is his breathing. It's the slow, measured breaths of someone calm and at peace. She fears he's fallen asleep until he gives another gentle squeeze to her fingers.

She glances at the clock. Ten to eleven. It was right around this time she heard the noises.

A twitching of her right leg betrays the tension she's feeling. Another squeeze from David.

Four minutes pass by at a glacial pace.

Then it happens.

The giggle.

The scream

Jennifer feels David's movement as he sits forward. His fingers releasing hers as he readies himself for movement.

'Mum-my.' Once again the horrible voice sends shivers through her. Although a separate part of her is glad to hear it. There's no doubt in her mind David has also heard the noises which means she's not insane. 'Jenn-i-fer.'

'Wow.' David's voice is soft but there's no mistaking the disbelief. 'No wonder you were scared.

Jennifer releases his grip and turns to switch on her lamp. His hand on her shoulder stops her.

'Don't. I want to see if the noises come again.'

'Why? You've heard them for yourself.'

'Shush. Listen.'

Jennifer wants to argue but there's something in David's tone which halts the words in her throat.

Again the four sounds ring out.

'See, I told you this place is haunted.'

'No it's not.' David switches on his own lamp. 'That giggle is familiar.'

'What?'

'I've heard it before –'

'Where?'

David waves a dismissive hand. 'One of the young girls in the office had it as a ringtone or alert. Remember I told you I had to discipline someone for always being on their phone?'

'Shit. You mean this place isn't haunted, that the noises are someone's ringtones?'

'That's exactly what I'm saying. Some bugger is playing silly games with us.' David swings his legs out of bed. 'The first two noises were above the room. The next two sounded as if they were below the bed.'

'There were words, David. They knew my name.'

'I'm sure it's easy enough to add voice recordings as ringtones.' David pauses. 'The fact they used your name means it's someone who knows us, or you at least.'

Jennifer steps onto the floor and helps David as he pulls the bed away from the wall. Now there is a rational explanation for the noises her fear has been replaced by a cold anger. 'Why would someone do that, what do they have to gain?'

'I don't know and right now I don't give a monkey's.' David pulls the sheets off the bed, tosses them into a corner and grips the mattress. 'When I lift, you look underneath. See if there's a phone anywhere.'

Jennifer does as she's told but finds nothing. She catches David staring at the plug socket before he drops the mattress and strides out of the room.

When he returns he's carrying the aluminium briefcase which holds his tools. He selects a screwdriver and after unplugging the two lamps starts turning the screws holding the faceplate to the socket.

'What are you doing?'

'Looking for the phone or phones. I should have thought of it before, they'll need a power supply.'

When he removes the faceplate he bends it downwards, taking care not to touch any of the wires.

'Look at this, Jen.'

She leans over him and looks at the back of the plug. Sees flat grey wires and one round white one. All of them are connected into the back of the faceplate.

'What am I looking at?'

David uses his screwdriver as a pointer. 'These grey wires run the electricity around the house. The white one has no place being here. It looks like one from a domestic appliance. I bet that if I take this apart, I'll find a short extension lead with a phone charger plugged into it.'

He doesn't need to say anything more. Jennifer can picture a mobile phone left in the gap between the old stone walls and the new studding they'd had fitted.

'What do we do now?'

'We go and have a night in that hotel. This can wait until the morning.'

Jennifer kisses him. 'Thank you.'

Even now she knows the noises are real and man-made, she doesn't want to hear them all night. The sense of malevolence hasn't been lessened by the knowledge a human is behind them. If anything it has increased.

Whoever is behind this act of terrorisation must have an agenda, a reason to want to scare them.

David is tight lipped when he re-enters what should be their dream home as Jennifer follows in silence. Once warm and welcoming, the house now conveys a brooding menace and unspoken threat.

He'd spent the night tossing and turning as his mind worried at the question of who was trying to scare them. None of their discussions had unearthed a likely candidate but until they had proof of his theory, there was nothing they could do to verify the wild guesses they'd made.

Jennifer watches as he throws the switch and cuts the power to the house. He marches upstairs to the bedroom with a few screwdrivers in his hand and sets to work on the plug socket after using his mobile to take a picture of the back of it.

David lays the disconnected faceplate on the carpet and starts to unscrew the plastic box behind it. A moment later he draws the white cable out of the hole with slow gentle movements.

A socket with a mobile charger appears. David picks up his phone, takes some more pictures then lays hold of the charger's lead.

Seconds later a mobile phone appears.

Again he takes pictures before pulling the device free of the hole.

Jennifer reaches for it, intent on smashing it against a wall but David stops her. 'Don't touch it. There may be fingerprints on it.'

She stands motionless. Torn between the desire to exact revenge on the offending object and the realisation it isn't responsible for its master's actions.

David uses the tip of a screwdriver to press the phone's sole button. Its screen lights up and shows missed calls and message alerts. He stands, a triumphant expression on his face. 'You go and call the police. I'm going to look in the attic. I reckon there's another phone up there.'

Jennifer makes the call with a song in her heart. While there's anger towards the perpetrator, the sheer joy of knowing she's not going insane and the house isn't haunted threatens to overwhelm her.

The Detective Sergeant who comes isn't the typical grizzled copper portrayed on the screen. He's a normal guy in a grey M&S suit.

Jennifer leads him upstairs where David shows him the still connected phone.

The DS pulls on a pair of nitrile gloves before bending down and picking up the phone. He fiddles with it for a moment. The baby giggles rings out. He fiddles again. The scream. He pulls out his own mobile and makes a call.

'Run this number for me please.' He reads a number from the screen of the offending phone then hangs up.

David points at the ceiling. 'I found another in the loft.'

The detective hangs his suit jacket over the bannister before following David up the loft ladder.

Having heard the noises coming from the mobile, Jennifer takes a seat as relief floods her body making her legs unsteady. Her sanity is sound and the house isn't haunted.

When they return from the loft the detective has a stern expression and a mobile phone and charger in his gloved hands.

'I've a few calls to make and a couple of leads to follow.' He moves towards the door. 'I'll be in touch as soon as I have something to tell you.'

David spends the day checking every socket in the house while Jennifer gets to work unpacking the last few boxes. He doesn't find anything and she's happy making a house a home.

Jennifer takes a call halfway through the afternoon. Listens, thanks the caller and hangs up.

'Well?' David raises an eyebrow.

Jennifer sinks into a chair as sobs of relief wrack her body. When she recovers her composure she looks at David. 'The police traced the number that had been calling the phone. It belongs to the electrician the builder used when renovating the house. They've arrested him.'

'Why? Why did he do it?'

'Because he missed out to us when the house was sold.'

When their drinks are finished Jennifer rises and takes her husband's hand, leads him towards the stairs. 'C'mon, Mr Kerr. We've got us a new house to christen.'

As they lie in bed, sweaty and sated they both start at the same sound.

A baby's giggle.

Time and again it comes.

From every corner of the room.

THE MURDER DOLLS

In the year 1836, three boys were hunting rabbits on open land to the east of Edinburgh. On Arthur's Seat, the high point of the area now known as Holyrood Park, they were digging in rabbit burrows when they made a remarkable but macabre discovery.

Behind a pile of broken slate, 17 miniature coffins had been concealed. When the boys opened them, each coffin contained a figurine, a male doll, all made from wood, all with intricately carved limbs and faces, all dressed in garb improvised from plain cloth that had been carefully cut and stitched. At first they saw no value in these curiosities, and threw them around, and within a very short time only eight of the dolls and their coffins remained intact. For some reason, the boys brought these back to their homes in the town, but when they were finally seen by adults and an explanation offered as to where they'd been located, there was consternation.

These clearly were not toys that someone had lost. The boys had disturbed what appeared to have been the representation of a mass burial, a sacred site of some sort. As the dolls passed from person to person, each time handled with greater reverence, a variety of theories emerged.

Arthur's Seat overlooked the Firth of Forth at a point from which many tragic shipwrecks had been witnessed; could the miniature effigies have been made in honour of sailors who had drowned?

Alternatively, could they have been used as part of a witchcraft ceremony?

Could it even have been a combination of the two? In the witch-hunting era in Scotland, dark magic was often believed the cause of maritime disasters.

On second or third glance, perhaps less worryingly, the figurines were deemed similar to Napoleonic-era toy soldiers. All wore dark boots and had marks around their heads to indicate that they might once have worn caps or hats. But if that was the case, why had someone gone to the trouble of making coffins for them and replacing their uniforms with *grave clothes?*

Efforts to lighten the mystery were made by referring to the find as the 'Lilliputian Coffins' or the 'Faerie Coffins'. But the air of unease lingered until at last someone, no one is sure who, made the inevitable association between the 17 dolls and the 17 victims of the infamous West Port Murders.

The names Burke and Hare are tossed about with ghoulish glee these days, almost as if they were fictional characters, gaslight-era fiends from some lurid Gothic novel. But unfortunately, they were every bit as real as Jack the Ripper, and their crimes every bit as atrocious.

William Burke and William Hare were a pair of Irishmen who had arrived in Scotland separately in the early/mid 1820s, and who became friends while working together as agricultural labourers. By 1827, Hare had purchased a low-rent rooming house in the West Port district of Edinburgh. Burke was a resident there, but primarily the house was reserved for alcoholics, prostitutes and other street-people; in short, the sort that Edinburgh society didn't even know existed let alone would miss.

When, in the November of that year, one of these unfortunates died on the premises from natural causes, Burke and Hare hit on the idea of concealing the death and secretly delivering the corpse to Dr Thomas Knox, the senior anatomist at Edinburgh University, who was known to be in need of fresh cadavers. Whether Burke and Hare had been 'resurrection men' themselves before this is unknown but it's highly possible. Given that the anatomy schools could only lawfully utilise the corpses of executed felons, they were always short of material. So, it was an easy earner, not just for gangs of villains, but for any enterprising group with access to a couple of shovels, a sack and a two-wheeled cart, to open the graves of the recently buried and deliver corpses by the back door.

Even if Burke and Hare had been involved in this grisly trade already, they were surprised by the money Knox paid them for the deceased lodger: £7 in total, which was a significant sum in 1827. Of course, waiting around for the rooming house's other inmates to depart was a non-starter. So, they hastened the process, picking on those whose absence was least likely to raise concern, and killing them by suffocation when they were drunk (which wasn't always as clean as it sounds; many victims reputedly struggled, and were often left covered in blood, bruises and saliva).

The evil duo's official tally was 17 in October 1828, when fellow lodgers became suspicious, found one of the bodies and ran for the police.

Despite this, there wasn't much evidence connecting Burke and Hare to the crimes, but life was made easier for the investigating authorities when Hare opted to turn king's evidence against his partner in return for immunity from prosecution. Burke was thus tried alone, convicted, hanged in front of 25,000 people, and, in an ironic twist of fate, handed over to the dissectionists; even today his skeleton can be viewed in the Edinburgh Medical School, while a surgical textbook bound with his skin and containing notes written in his blood exists in the Surgeon's Hall Museum. It's impossible to imagine that Dr Knox, a trained surgeon and a veteran of the battle of Waterloo, hadn't soon realised that the corpses he was receiving were the victims of violence. Some of his students had certainly voiced their doubts, but though his reputation as an expert on anatomy saved him from prosecution, a mob attacked his house after the trial and his reputation in the field was ruined.

It is still believed that the Murder Dolls found near Arthur's Seat are a memento of this horrific crimewave. Sceptics have argued that there may only have been 16 West Port murders, not 17, and that while all the dolls recovered depict males, 12 of Burke and Hare's victims were female. While others have asked that, if they are a representation of the West Port unfortunates, who made them and why? Could it have been the murderers themselves in a fit of remorse? That seems unlikely given that Burke and Hare were in the act of another murder when their deeds were uncovered. Even Hare, who escaped the hangman, is an unlikely candidate. It was considered a scandal that he was spared, and he needed a police escort to the English border, after which he disappeared into obscurity. Could it have been Dr Knox? He would have had the tools and the hand-and-eye coordination, but scholars who know the case don't think it fits with his personality.

The mystery of the Murder Dolls is unlikely now to be solved. What remains of them can still be viewed by the public at the National Museum of Scotland. They are regarded as a strange antiquity rather than a grim relic, but whatever their origins, they've become so interwoven with the mythology surrounding Burke and Hare that there will always be an air of the grotesque about them.

HERDERS
William Meikle

No limbs, no limbs, no head, no head, left arm gone, left leg gone, no legs, no head.

The stick figures on the screen frustrated him every bit as much as they had when he'd originally seen them on the newly exposed wall at the dig site. At first he'd been excited, thinking them to be a simple code, ranks of figures that with a bit of work could be easily interpreted as a message from the people who had lived and died here all those years ago.

But if it was a code it proved to be one that was beyond Brian Meadows' ability to crack ... beyond anyone's ability to crack from what he could gather. Not for the first time in the past fortnight he left his trailer in a grump and headed down the winding track that led into Moffat for something he knew he could always rely on.

The Ram's Head was almost empty, which was just fine by him. The first beer went down quickly, the second a bit slower and by the time he got to his third he was getting his equilibrium back; it was a state he'd found increasingly difficult to maintain in the roller-coaster that was their first month on the dig.

It had started with hope. The local farmer's discovery of a previously unknown Roman structure in a copse by the side of a field had made the papers and enabled Brian and his team to rustle up enough cash for an exploratory dig. He'd come down from Glasgow with four post-grad researchers, three trailers and a lot of that aforesaid hope.

Then it had started raining. The first two weeks were spent

in a muddy field in daylight and a rowdy local bar in the evenings. But although the work was slow and heavy going it was becoming clear they were definitely on to something as the remnants of walls, rooms and evidence of long occupation began to emerge from the soil. There was more hope, especially from Brian who began to dream of the big find; a mosaic floor maybe, or a hoard of jewellery or silver. The day it stopped raining was also the day of their breakthrough into what proved to be a large chamber under what they'd thought to be the main floor.

There was no treasure. In fact Brian thought they'd got nothing until he'd washed the walls down and found that all of them, even the floor, were covered in line after line of three-inch high stick figures, most of them missing either limbs or heads or both.

No limbs, no limbs, no head, no head, left arm gone, left leg gone, no legs, no head.

Now, even after a farther two weeks investigation and the closing of the dig site to leave Brian the sole researcher remaining, all he had to show for the work was a couple of thousand stick figures that he'd scanned into his laptop and an ever growing sense of frustration that was leading to nightly drinking in the hope that sleep might bring oblivion.

He was finishing off his third pint when someone spoke behind him.

'You look like a man who needs another pint.'

'And you look like a man ready to buy me one. Caley 80 please.'

Brian watched Dave Smith make his way to the bar. Dave was the local policeman and had become a drinking buddy of Brian's these past few weeks. Dave told him the local gossip and Brian bought him beer. They both seemed happy with the situation, and Dave was probably the only person who knew how much the frustration had been eating away at the archaeologist.

'Still getting nowhere?' Dave said as he returned with two pints.

'It's not even as much fun as banging my head against a brick wall. I've got that talk to give in the Church Hall tomorrow night and I've got bugger all to tell them or show them apart from photos of muddy students and these blasted stick figures I cannae make head nor tail of.'

'I wouldna worry about the meeting,' Dave said laughing. 'There'll be naebody there apart from me and a couple of auld biddies who think it's bingo night.'

Brain had turned to Dave ten days ago in the hope that a fresh pair of eyes might help.

'I'm no Sherlock Holmes,' Dave had said. 'But I like puzzles. Leave it with me.'

But Dave hadn't got anywhere either and neither had the folks back in Glasgow who were also looking at it. The wee figures just kept dancing on the pages as if taunting them.

At the same instant Brian had that thought, Dave sat down and drummed out a beat on the table with the palm of his hands, a habit the cop had that Brian hadn't paid much attention to until now.

Dancing. Drumming. Could it be that simple?

Ten minutes later he was back in his trailer with a bemused Dave in tow.

'Whisky's in the cupboard, pizza in the freezer and you ken where the microwave is. Give me ten minutes with this. I've got an idea.'

It took twenty minutes in the end, by which time Dave had got through most of the pizza and a good part of the whisky; Brian had been too excited for either.

'I think I've got it,' he said when he finally looked up from the laptop.

'Okay,' Dave said, handing him a glass with three fingers of Scotch in it. 'Start at the beginning, remembering that I'm just a country copper.'

Brian smiled. 'Right you are. I've told you already that I think the site was a wee fort, more of a keep really, an outpost on this side of the wall at the time when the Romans were just starting to move further north. Everything we've found suggests that the legionnaires here were Syrian conscripts, mountain people originally. They kept goats and sheep judging by the amount of bone we've found and now, judging by this, I'd say they liked to make music too.'

'What do you mean?' Dave said.

Brian waved a sheaf of printed papers.

'It wasn't a code at all, not any kind of writing. It's a transcript of a rhythm, a drumbeat. It took some trial and error and a wee bit of code in the computer, but I've got it. Once I sussed it must be six beats to a bar and that each figure represented any one of six different beats within the bar all I had to do was find a place to start it then it all just fell into place. Listen.'

He turned on the laptop speakers and set a programme running. The trailer filled with a drumbeat. It wasn't anything you'd fancy dancing to but there was an urgent quality to it, a drive that made Brian think it had a definite purpose. The trailer began to vibrate in time; first the cutlery in the drawer, then the plates by the sink. The light faded and brightened and the whole trailer yawed and pitched as if suddenly launched into the sea. Brian's stomach lurched and he tasted whisky as it threatened to come out faster than it had gone in.

'Turn it off,' Dave said, shouting to be heard over a beat that was now amplified ten-fold and booming in their ears. 'Switch the bloody thing off.'

Brian reached over and stopped the programme. The trailer fell silent save for one last rattle of the cutlery in the drawer.

'Fucking hell,' Brian said.

'My thoughts exactly,' Dave replied. 'Do me a favour, Brian, don't switch that on again.'

'I need to. It's an important discovery…'

'Maybe not so much a discovery as you think,' Dave replied.

'What do you mean by that?'

'I mean I've heard it before.' The policeman held up a hand

as if to block the protest he knew was coming. 'You'll need to trust me on this. There's something I need to tell you and something I need to show you, but it'll have to wait till morning; I'm not going off half-cocked in the dark with a belly of beer and whisky in me. I'm off to bed to have a think. Come down to the station in the morning; I'll stand for a bacon roll and coffee and I'll tell you then. Just promise me you won't play it again until we've talked?'

Brian grudgingly gave his promise. After Dave left he looked over the printed output of the figures again but didn't switch on the programme. Even so he felt the beat grow in his head, an earworm as bad as any catchy pop song that threaded its way in and around the empty spaces inside him and threatened to have him vibrating and rocking again. He tuned it out with the help of a large whisky and managed to sleep fitfully but woke with the rhythm still ringing in his ears.

The beat was still there, a dull throbbing reminiscent of a hangover at the back of his head, when he went down the hill to the small police station. Dave was waiting for him in the hallway and thrust a bacon roll and a plastic cup of coffee at him.

'Don't say I never get you anything. We'll eat on the move. It's just a wee walk then all will be revealed.'

They talked about the quality of both the bacon rolls, excellent, and the coffee, shite, while they strolled. It was obvious Dave didn't want to discuss much of anything else at that point and the thumping in Brian's head was making it hard for him to concentrate on anything but breakfast in any case.

He was surprised when Dave stopped them by a small stone building above a steep riverbank. Brian had passed it many times without paying it much note; it was little more than four rough sandstone walls and a sagging slate roof, typical of the over-wintering farm sheds that dotted the landscape in the area. Dave took a small torch from his inside pocket and waved Brian into the doorway.

It was dry inside, a chamber some sixteen feet long by ten wide, dry straw on the floor and empty.

'So what's the story?' Brian said.

Dave washed an oval of light over the far wall that had been in deep shadow until then. Brian's breath hitched. Depicted there in what looked like black paint were four stick figures, each a foot high; no head, no legs, no left arm, no right leg. Dave moved the beam upwards. Above the stick figures was a huge crudely depicted head of a ram, horns curving up into the darker shadows in the rafters, black eyes seeming to stare directly into Brian's soul. The thumping in his head rose again, the beat pounding, his guts roiling. He barely made it to the doorway before his bacon roll and breakfast made a reappearance in one hot steaming bundle.

'You tried to tell me last night, didn't you?' Brain said once he'd recovered enough to accept a smoke from Dave. They stood away from the doorway, taking in a view over the rolling hills to the south. 'My discovery isn't a discovery at all.'

'I don't know about that,' Dave said. 'I do know that nobody's dug near your site for a wheen of years.'

'So how did somebody know about the stick figures? What's the story?'

'Maybe coincidence. Maybe something else. It's time for the tell part. But for that I'll need a beer. Come on, I'm off duty and The Ram will be open by the time we get there. It's my shout.'

They were the only customers in the large bar. Brian didn't usually start this early but the sight in the barn had shaken him and the thump of the beat was still there behind his eyes, lessening slightly as he made his way down his beer. Dave got half his own pint down before speaking.

'It was ten year ago,' he started. 'I was a young copper wet behind the ears, on the night shift when we got a call about kids causing bother out at yon barn. I thought on the way there that I was going to be breaking up a rowdy 'beer, pot an lassies' party; it's no' as if we don't get our fair share of those in these parts. What I found was something different aw the gither. I heard the drums fae near half a mile away.'

Brain started, nearly spilled his pint.

'Aye,' Dave said. 'That drumming. The same as you've got on your wee laptop. My guts were fair boiling as I went up to the door. I shouted out, as you do, but didn't get an answer apart from the fact that the drumming stopped and everything went quiet. I think I preferred the drums, there in what was now near pitch dark. My haunds were shaking as I got the torch on and went inside. There was naebody there, nae sign there had been a party. What there was was the same drawings on the wall I just showed you. That, and a big dead ram, lying there below the drawings, still warm, its blood looking black in my torchlight where it pooled on the ground.'

Dave downed the rest of his beer in one and without asking went to the bar for two more.

'And that's not all,' he said when he returned. 'I asked around, non too discreetly, and for my sins I got called in to see the boss. There I got yet anither story, and was told to keep my mouth shut if I kent what was good for me. I'm telling you now for your own good. Let it lie, Brian.'

'Let what lie? You'd told me a lot of fuck all so far.'

Dave's answer threw Brian off for a while as it seemed to come from nowhere.

'Towns have got Masons. The country has Herders.'

'What the hell does that mean?'

Dave took another deep slug of beer before replying and when he did his voice was low, even though there was no one else to hear.

'Tradition, that's what I'm talking about. Auld words, auld rituals, handed down over the years while watching over the flocks in the hills. There's been Herders here ever since the land was cleared; since even before your Romans if the stories are right.'

'Rituals? You mean the stick figures and the drumming? It's a folk memory, is that what you're saying?'

'Aye. And it's one folks round hereaways would rather

keep to themselves. They've got a way of doing things, a way of keeping the flock protected. Just let it be; I'm telling you the same way I was telt, for your own good.'

Brain didn't push the matter; he was surprised Dave was so serious about it, but not surprised enough to take his friend's advice; he had a talk to give that night in the Church Hall and had nothing but the stick figures to talk about.

What harm can there be?

Brian went back to the dig sometime later, belly full of beer, head full of drumming. He stood for a while at the edge of the site, looking down into the chamber, but was forced to retreat to the trailer when the beat ramped up and the engraved figures on the wall and floor appeared to dance and jig in time.

He made a pot of coffee, sat at the laptop and tried to compose a coherent presentation for his talk that evening but the beat would not let him be, a constant drumming in his head that he started to tap out with his fingers as he typed. And after he pushed the laptop away and started in on the scotch it got little better; his fingers rapped the rhythm out on the side of his glass or on the table on which he sat. He knocked back nearly a quarter bottle of liquor in short order and took to bed. Sleep came slowly, and when it did his fevered dreams were populated with serried ranks of figures dancing across the screen of his mind.

No limbs, no limbs, no head, no head, left arm gone, left leg gone, no legs, no head.

He woke with a mouth that felt like a badger had shit in it and a head full of tiny drummers. Toothpaste took care of the taste but the drummers were still there as he began to gather his things together for the evening's presentation.

He was going to have to wing it for the most part; his notes were a mess. But he had the slides on his laptop, his wee projector would work just fine and as a university lecturer he was more than experienced enough in talking on the fly and responding to changing circumstances. He was still trying to convince himself of that as he made his way back down the hill to town, his footsteps beating out the rhythm on the road surface.

It was getting dark by the time he reached the town. The gaudy lights in The Ram called him, offering solace in more beer, more scotch but that was another thing he was more than experienced enough in; more booze now was the last thing he needed. He lowered his head and quickly made his way to the small Church Hall.

He turned the door handle and pushed; the door opened, light too bright inside sending his pounding headache up another notch. Somebody had been making preparations; there was a white projector sheet at the far end of the hall in front of four rows of six seats. The smell of fresh-brewed coffee led him to a small kitchenette at the rear, where the coffee pot sat next to polythene-covered trays of neatly cut sandwiches. He helped himself to a coffee and went back through to the hall where his clumsy, drum-addled fingers fought to attach cables, turn on and focus the projector and get the slide show set up on the laptop.

His audience started to gather while he was preparing.

At first he thought Dave was going to be proved right; the front row was filled with little old ladies who looked like they were indeed there for the bingo. Then Dave himself arrived, unsmiling and serious, with two of his fellow police officers in tow. The local minister arrived with two overly made up and manicured middle-aged women and, lastly, the farmer whose ground Brian was digging up came in, a craggy old chap with three equally craggy sons in the same mould. Brian gave it another five minutes to see if there were any stragglers, then had the minister dim the lights as he turned on the slide show.

The first slide showed the dig site as it had been before Brian arrived. He started with the history of how the site had been discovered, went on to a bit about how he'd procured the grant money to get going and was getting into his stride when he made the mistake of looking up. It wasn't that the audience weren't paying attention that was the problem; it was the fact that they were paying too much attention, not to the images on the protected screen but to Brian himself, all of their gazes fixed directly on him with unblinking stares.

He faltered, and this time it was the rhythm in his head that saved him, gave him something to focus on. He flipped quickly, on the beat each time, through the slides of the actual progress on the dig until he got to the first clear shot of the ranks of engraved figures on the walls and floor of the exposed chamber. As soon as the slide came up the beat rose and swelled in his head.

'I believe this is the most important find in archaeology in Scotland in recent years,' he said.

The audience shifted in their seats, all at the same time as if controlled by a puppeteer.

'Dave here will vouch for the fact that the interpretation of what these figures represent has occupied and frustrated me – even drove me to the drink – in the past week or so.'

He didn't get a laugh. They shifted again as one.

'But I believe I've now got to the bottom of the matter. I'd like to play something for you.'

He looked to Dave, expecting to see disapproval in the cop's face, but like the others, Dave's gaze was still fixed on Brian as the beat came through the speakers.

No limbs, no limbs, no head, no head, left arm gone, left leg gone, no legs, no head.

The audience stamped their feet in time. Despite himself Brian clicked back and forth between the slides that showed the ranks of figures. The beat went up a notch, took on an almost choral quality that echoed and rang around the church hall. The audience added clapping to the beat, all gazes still fixed on Brian.

The room swam in his vision, getting darker, dimmer. Guttural voices rose to join the rhythm and from somewhere distant, as if heard in a stiff wind, Brian heard the course braying of a ram join in, in time.

He realised he was stamping his feet too and even as he noted it the control for the projector dropped to the floor unheeded as he brought his hands together in clapping.

No limbs, no limbs, no head, no head, left arm gone, left leg gone, no legs, no head.

It felt like the top of his head was going to lift off as the beat grew and grew, the hall shook and swayed as if caught in a swell and the voices and the drumming and the clapping and the stomping rose to a frenzy.

The darkness swallowed up the light leaving Brian alone in a vast cavern of emptiness where all that mattered was the beat. The flock ran there, all dancing, each of them lost.

Lost to the dance.

Brian came out of it lying on his back, looking up, not at the roof of the church hall but at a carpet of stars dancing across the night sky. He tried to sit and found he was restrained – spreadeagled, with wrists and ankles tied to metal stakes pounded into the ground. He knew immediately where he was; he lay in the bottom of the dig site on the stone floor and, judging by the chill he felt in all extremities, he was completely naked. People stood up on the rim of the site, ranks of them, all silent, visible only as darker shadows against the sky. The pounding of the beat had stopped and the only sound was Brain's own breathing, fast, terror-filled.

'What the fuck's going on here?' he shouted.

He heard a thud, someone jumping down into the dig, and looked up to see Dave bending over him.

'Thank the Lord,' Brian said. 'Get me out of here. The joke has run its course.'

There was no sign of amusement on Dave's face.

'I told you to leave it alone, Brian,' he said. 'If it's any consolation, you'll be added to the flock, have your own wee figure on the wall. You'll always be remembered, you'll always dance.'

Brian heard four more thuds, more people coming down into the site. Up above the Herders began to stamp their feet.

No limbs, no limbs, no head, no head, left arm gone, left leg gone, no legs, no head.

The stars danced overhead as the drums rose up in Brian's head and despite himself his hands and feet twitched with the beat. The Herders above started to clap. The stars swirled in great spirals in time.

No limbs, no limbs, no head, no head, left arm gone, left leg gone, no legs, no head.

The ground beneath Brian bucked and swayed. The figures on the walls glowed, almost silver, dancing in the moonlight. Brian's gaze was taken by a shifting in the sky overhead. The beat got louder and the stars appeared to coalesce and form into an image he thought he should recognise.

Guttural chanting joined the beat, all singing, stomping, clapping, all dancing.

Somewhere a great ram barked and brayed, closer now. Brian was aware of people bent over him, one above each of his outstretched limbs. He saw moonlight glisten off the blades of the heavy shovels they carried, felt the cold steel at his wrist as the blade was applied and a foot put down on it.

No left hand.

Heat left him in a rush but he felt no pain, he was in the grip of the dance, part of the flock. He felt pressure again.

No right hand.

He looked up and saw the ram looming over him in the sky, felt himself sucked into the great black eyes as the beat filled him.

Pressure at his ankles now.

No feet.

He smiled as the ram took him and he joined the flock as Dave's shovel was pressed against his neck, lost in the dance.

The beat rose to a final cacophony and Dave's foot came down hard.

No hands, no arms, no feet, no legs.

No head.

THE VAMPIRE OF
ANNANDALE

The Bruce family are remembered as the great freedom fighters of Scotland, Robert the Bruce (1274-1329) in particular regarded as one of his nation's greatest heroes, a tireless warrior who battled long and hard to secure his country's independence from England. However, like most of the great baronial families of mainland Britain in the 14th century, the Bruces' origins lay among the Norman conquerors who gained their foothold on this island in 1066.

Robert the Bruce's ancestor, Robert de Brus, is first recorded in history as having fought for Henry I of England at the battle of Tinchebrai in 1106, participating in a great victory, and subsequently being rewarded with rich estates around London and Chester. A decade later, his good friend, David FitzMalcolm, Prince of the Cumbrians and later King of Scotland, (who also fought at Tinchebrai) invested him with the Lordship of Annandale, which brought the Brus family into Scotland for the first time. Shortly after these victories, however, things would go badly wrong, a succession of grim events culminating in a vampire-like visitation, the mere memory of which would haunt the family for centuries to come.

Even when Robert the Bruce was King of Scotland, he believed that his family was cursed. His own father was stricken with leprosy, which was quite unusual in Britain even during the Middle Ages, while the Bruce himself, in his early years, suffered several military defeats and spent much time on the run from the English. But this was nothing compared to the misfortunes of his ancestors, who in their early years at Annandale suffered under the aforementioned reign of nocturnal terror.

According to tradition, the origins of this chilling tale lie with the 1st Lord of Annandale, who not long after his arrival in Scotland, and with his castle still a relatively new fixture on the landscape, welcomed a visit by Maolmhaodliog ua Morgair (later known as St Malachy), the Irish Bishop of Armagh. While there, the bishop noted that a gibbet was being prepared. Brus explained that a noted brigand had been captured and was to hang in the morning. The bishop interceded and Brus agreed to imprison the brigand instead. But in the morning, as the bishop left Annandale, he spied a ragged figure swinging from the gibbet. He was so angry to have been lied to that, there and then, he cursed the Brus family.

A momentary loss of temper, you may think. But in the early medieval age, this sort of thing was taken seriously, especially when the harsh words were uttered by a man who shortly afterwards would be canonised. In 1148, Brus's son, also Robert de Brus, sought to lift the curse by adorning the bishop's tomb at Clairvaux with votive lamps, but to no avail. In fact, it was during the tenure of this 2nd Lord of Annandale that things became much, much worse.

Apparently, a Yorkshireman fleeing the Anarchy that was fast engulfing England, was given succour at Annandale Castle, but for reasons that aren't entirely clear, he died shortly afterwards and was buried nearby. The matter was thought to be closed, until reports came in that local people were succumbing to an unknown wasting disease, which struck them down so quickly that they would go to bed in reasonable health but by morning would be dead. Around the same time, rumours were circulating that the deceased Yorkshireman was being seen on local roads late at night, always accompanied by a pack of savage, drooling dogs.

Tales of vampirism were so rare in Scottish folklore, and British folklore generally, that the word was not even used in these islands at that time. Perhaps that is why no one made the immediate obvious association. At first, the mysterious night-walker was regarded simply as an unhappy ghost, and the Brus family responded by hiring clergymen to attempt to pray it into the afterlife. But this didn't work, and more and more village folk were found dead each morning, apparently drained of all life. At last, a connection was made. Had the undead thing been visiting local homes at night? Had it been feeding on the Lord of Annandale's tenants?

From here on, the tale becomes very familiar.

Men-at-arms were despatched to open the dead Yorkshireman's grave, wherein they were shocked to find a corpse that was ruddy and bloated rather than shrivelled. It was an even greater horror to them *that, when they hacked it to pieces, fresh blood poured out. After the remains were taken away and burned on a pyre (the heart burned separately with great religious ritual), the problem appeared to ease. There were no more nightly attacks and even the pack of snarling dogs appeared to have left the district.*

All the usual caveats are applicable to this age-old story. When the grave was opened, the swollen state of the corpse could easily have been the result of an expanded gut due to gases caused by the action of microorganisms, while blood can re-liquify even during decomposition, so the fresh bleeding might also have a scientific explanation. As for the deaths in the Annandale villages, it seems highly possible that the newcomer from Yorkshire had brought some kind of contagious illness with him, which killed him soon after his arrival but continued to infect local people. The presence of snarling, slavering dogs might even imply that this disease was rabies, their eventual disappearance meaning that they too died, possibly while hiding in the woods.

The fact that the dead man was allegedly seen walking is harder to dismiss, but life would be boring if we had blithe explanations for every one of these eerie legends.

BIRDS OF PREY
S J I Holliday

Dallis was impressed with her new NARS concealer. She'd gone for the yellow-tinged version that was supposed to tone down redness. One of the online forums she'd been on said it was the best shade to counteract the myriad colours of a bruise, especially around the eye socket.

Sometimes, at the height of it, she wanted to scream at him – 'not the face!' like something out of a gangster film, but always, at the height of it, she didn't stand a chance.

Boys like Tommy are old school when it comes to violence. They like to make their mark, have their victims wear the resulting damage displayed like a badge of honour. Sure, there was all that awareness now about it – secret hand signals and code names to mention in the pub, so you can alert someone that you're in danger. But who'd do something like that and risk their man finding out?

Not Dallis.

She'd tried, once, to break up with him. But the outcome of that was her being unable to walk without wincing for a week. She probably should've gone to the doctor on that occasion, but the blood in her pee had stopped after a few days so she'd reckoned it had only been a bit of bruising around her kidney.

Daft, really.

When he was off the drink, he was one of the nicest lads in the wee town that she'd called home since she'd legged it from her overfamiliar stepdad and oblivious mother on the other side of Edinburgh, over two years ago. She'd been lucky to get this wee house for herself in Prestonpans. A cute top-floor maisonette near the sea, the view out into the Firth of Forth making her feel like she was part of something bigger, something bold and alive; and the memorial she'd come across in the local park – the shimmering silver woman a beautiful apology to the eighty-one pardoned witches from the county – made her feel strong, and settled, like she'd finally found the place and the person she was meant to be.

She'd started work at the local florist on the High Street, delighted to have found someone to train her and give her a chance, when all she really had in way of experience was an eye for colour. A creative flair was intuitive. Something you were born with, her boss had told her. All Dallis needed then was to find some friends, people her own age to spend time with – but that had proven more elusive. Without kids, she had little in common with most women in the houses in her street, and those around. But she was working on it. She knew that these things could take time. So when she'd met Tommy that night in the Cross Keys, up the road in Tranent, him being so good-looking and attentive, and wanting to move in with her after only a month of a whirlwind romance, she'd felt like her life was really turning a corner.

The first time had been an accident, really. Her own stupid fault. She should've known not to throw out the sports pages of the Sunday papers before he'd had a chance to read them, and to be honest, he'd seemed as shocked as her when the glancing blow to her cheek had knocked her clean off the kitchen chair. It wasn't his fault that she'd fallen all funny, and bumped her head on one of the heavy table legs. The wee dunt above her eyebrow had held together fine with those sticky stitches, and with the dark coloured lino on the floor, the blood had barely left a stain.

Last night's had been avoidable, too. She knew fine that he hated those skinny fries from the Co-op. That he only liked fries from McDonald's, otherwise it was chunky chips all the way. But they were on offer, and she'd fancied a change – and they had less calories per hundred grams and she knew she'd put on a couple of pounds lately. Well, she hadn't noticed it herself and her jeans felt fine, but when Tommy had grabbed the soft skin of her belly, twisting it hard, she'd realised he was right enough. On the plus side, she'd definitely lost weight since he'd said that last week, because now the waistband of her jeans was loose, and the bruise on her belly was faded to nothing but a small yellow crescent beneath her belly button.

Last night though, he'd eaten his meal in silence, and she'd thought she'd got away with the frozen chips not being to his liking, until he threw his empty plate at her like a Frisbee while she was doing the washing up. She'd only caught a glancing blow. A bump, not a cut. He'd gone out after that, and he hadn't come back.

She held her breath, as she pushed her feet into her trainers, checked herself once more in the hallway mirror, then tiptoed outside, closing the door quietly behind her. Outside, she breathed out hard, then smiled to herself, and her own daftness. He wasn't back. He hadn't come back. No need to be so quiet. She wasn't going to disturb him.

She felt light as air as she walked through the estate, down towards the sea.

Maybe he was gone for good. Maybe he'd got fed up of her at last. He hadn't been paying her much attention lately, and while she missed the intimacy and the warmth of his body cuddled in behind her, it meant there hadn't been quite so many *accidents* or *misunderstandings*, either. The plate had come as a bit of a shock, if she was honest.

It was her day off and she was in no real rush. She wandered along the High Street, glancing in the shop windows. Barbers busy at with their clippers, butcher wrapping parcels of meat in waxed paper. She stopped at the bakers and bought herself a jam and cream doughnut, glancing around guiltily as she walked back onto the street. She would go down to the beach to eat it. The sea breeze would be good for her healing skin, and her tortured mind. Dallis knew she was in a bad relationship. Denial would only take you so far. But denial's big brother was fear, and that was the real place she found herself every day. She could leave – but it was her flat; and even under the denial and the fear, there were the last remnants of strength. Or was it indignance? Her mum had always said she was a contrary wee thing. But was just it her way of fighting against the injustices of her life?

She was licking the last remnants of cream off her fingers when the dog came running towards her. Her eyes widened in alarm, hundreds of tiny wings fluttered in her chest as she shuffled back onto the large flat rock she'd been sitting on, a moment of panic as she realised she had nowhere to go. But then the dog had slowed, its tongue lolling out of his mouth, panting as it walked towards her. It nuzzled its head against her ankle, and she felt her heart slow down to its normal pace.

'Agnes ... for fuck's sake, leave her alone.' A woman was running towards her now, crunching over the shale. 'I'm so sorry! I hope you didnae get a fright. She's friendly enough, but I know not everyone wants someone else's mutt slavering all over their trainers.'

The woman looked about Dallis's age. She was wearing a black belted raincoat, and her bright red hair whipped in the wind. She had a sharp, angular face, but she was smiling. Until Dallis looked her in the eye and the smile slid away, just enough. Just enough to know she'd noticed.

So much for the expensive concealer.

The woman's eyes turned steely. Her jaw set.

'Opened a cupboard door on myself, didn't I?' Dallis said, her hand automatically going up to cover her eye. The excuses erupting like lava, free-flowing of their own accord.

The woman held out a business card. The sleeve of her coat had slid upward, revealing a tattoo on her wrist. An eagle, something like that, intricate in black ink. 'Give us a call.'

Dallis took the card, again, without thinking. She was losing herself, piece by piece. Her free-will fading away like the misty morning haar retreating back to the sea. 'Wait,' she said. But the woman was already in the car park, heading away. The dog trailing close behind. A beautiful, shiny black Labrador, it turned to look at her once more, then she and her owner disappeared out of sight.

Dallis turned the card over in her palm. One side was blank. On the other, that same bird – the black tattoo – and a phone number. She slipped the card into her jeans pocket and picked up her balled paper bag, just as a seagull cawed and swooped, sniffing out the remnants of her cake.

Back home, the air was different. She pulled the front door closed quietly and crept inside. She heard the sound of the shower running, over the muffled sound of football commentary leaching out of the portable radio she kept in the bathroom. She hesitated, briefly, in the small, dark hallway. She could turn around, go somewhere else. Anywhere else, she could ...

'Is that you, doll?' A squeak of metal on metal as he turned off the tap, followed by the sound of the shower curtain being flung open.

Dallis swallowed. Waited.

Then he was there in the hall, walking towards her, wet footprints on the carpet. Grinning. 'What's wrong wi' your face?' He grabbed her and kissed her hard on the lips. 'I'm away out with the boys tonight.'

'Where were you last night?' she blurted, instantly regretting it.

His eyes flashed red, his mouth twisted into a grimace. She braced herself, cowering back against the wall. Then his face changed, and he started to laugh.

'Fuck's sake, sort yersel' out.'

He pushed past her, nudging her shoulder with his, knocking her back against the wall. She waited until he'd gone into the bedroom, until she heard the scoosh of his deodorant, then she hurried into the bathroom and locked the door.

She waited until the front door banged closed, then she splashed water on her face, avoiding looking at herself in the mirror. She walked gingerly out into the hall, into the living room, knowing he was gone but still taking tentative steps, just in case. She wouldn't put it past him to have slammed the door but be standing on the inside – waiting for her.

He'd done that before.

But not tonight. Tonight he was gone, and tonight Dallis was going to be strong and brave and she was going to do something about this whole sorry situation that she'd found herself in.

She took the business card from her jeans, and without giving herself time to think any more about it, she dialled the number. It was answered after two rings.

'I was hoping you'd call.'

Dallis sat down hard on the sofa, phone still in hand. 'How did you know it was me?'

'45, Glenbervie Crescent. Come now, while he's away.'

'But how did you ...'

The woman was gone.

Dallis took a deep breath, then grabbed her handbag and hurried out of her flat. The night was dark, but muted with the yellow glow of the streetlights.

The tones of the light reminded her of her bruise, and her concealer – the so-called cover-up had clearly fooled no one. *Idiot.*

Glenbervie Crescent was only a five-minute walk. She found the house, amongst street upon street of similar builds, and wondered how this place was going to save her from her life. At the end of the crescent, a neat green park. One that she'd walked round many times. Right in the centre, the statue that she'd marvelled at before. The glistening silver woman holding a book of names. A book of pardons, for people misunderstood. Distrusted. Mistreated. She took a deep breath and rang the doorbell.

A young girl answered the door. Shining copper hair and a grin full of braces. 'Are you mummy's new friend?'

'Get away up and do your homework, Lauren.'

The girl scampered up the stairs, and the woman from the beach ushered Dallis inside, gesturing towards the living room, where three other women sat, their keen eyes trained on the door. Their faces softened as Dallis walked in to join them. They were all holding books.

Dallis put a hand over her mouth, stifling a giggle. It was a book group. Bloody hell. What had she expected? The woman was just being friendly, that's all. She sensed that Dallis was lonely. She clearly gave off those vibes.

The woman followed her in, then closed the living room door.

'We're not a book group, Dallis.'

The other three threw amused smiles.

She knew she should've been scared, but she was anything but. A strange woman, with strange friends. They could be anyone; they could do anything. But she felt the opposite of scared. When she was at home, waiting for Tommy's next move, trying to assess his mood, she felt dark and heavy, like she was sinking into the floor. Now, in this room, she felt as light as a feather, as if her feet might lift from the ground and a puff of air could glide her across the room.

The woman from the beach smiled. 'I never get this wrong. Please, Dallis. Take a seat.'

Dallis perched on the widest sofa, at the other end from a short, blonde-haired woman in a tie-dyed hoodie. The woman nodded as she sat down.

'I'm Meg,' the woman from the beach said. 'And these ladies are Elspeth, Helen and Isobel.' She gestured around the room. The woman in the hoodie was Isobel. Elspeth was streak thin with black curly hair and a long black cardigan over her skinny jeans and Metallica t-shirt. Helen was older, and she was dressed in a floral pleated skirt with a neat lemon yellow cardigan. Her hair was silver and pulled back in a bun. Meg was in an emerald green velour tracksuit, her red hair striking against the colour. 'We call ourselves the Birds of Prey,' Meg continued. They all rolled up the sleeve of their right arm, showing their matching tattoos, bursting into peals of laughter as Dallis's jaw dropped.

'Bit cheesy, I know,' Meg continued. 'But … well. It's kind of obvious, eh? I assume you've worked out what we're doing here.'

Dallis must've looked confused, then they all turned to her, reaching up to their eyes in unison. Staring at her. She felt her own hand go to her bruised eye-socket. She hadn't re-applied the concealer. Shit. It must look awful now.

'Yes, it does look awful, honey. And that's why you're here. You can tell us about it if you want. You can tell us how it only happens after a drink, or when he's had a bad day, or when he's tired. You can tell us how he doesn't know his own strength, how he doesn't mean it. How he loves you really, truly. And that no, he's not out shagging someone else right now. You can tell us that, or ...'

The woman trailed off as Dallis burst into tears. Then the four women were around her, fussing over her, dabbing at her face, stroking her back, her hair. Whispering soothing words.

'What ... what are you going to do?' Dallis managed. The women backed off, all retreating back to their seats. Someone had placed a cup of something hot and herbal on a side-table next to her. She picked it up, inhaling the scented steam. She noticed, then, a candle in each corner of the room. A sweet, cloying aroma filling the air.

Helen spoke. 'What do you know about witches, Dallis?'

Dallis shifted in her seat. 'Well I know it's not about pointed hats and broomsticks, if that's what you mean. I know that thousands of women—'

'And men,' Isobel cut in.

'Right, and men,' Dallis continued. 'They were persecuted for things that we'd know now were nothing unusual. Herbalism and maybe, I don't know, hormonal disturbances. Petty squabbles. Not anything actually supernatural ...' She let her sentence trail off, aware of the others staring at her. Their looks were not unkind. Far from it. But the intensity was unnerving. Meg gave her a small smile, and she remembered that Meg had known who she was when she called, had known her name, and seemed to know at least once what she was thinking. She felt a trickle of fear edge slowly down her spine. 'It's not ... I mean ...'

Meg came over and wedged herself in between Dallis and Isobel. 'The thing is, Dallis. They may have been pardoned ... you saw the memorial, aye? It's a pretty thing. Does it make up for all the wrongful deaths, though? You know they didn't burn the witches alive in Scotland – they strangled them first. That's after they'd been locked in a dungeon with no food or water, subjected to constant noise to prevent them from sleeping ... had a three-inch needle stuck in to them, all over their bodies – '

'I think she gets the picture, Meg.' Elspeth stood, crossing her arms. 'Let's get on with it, shall we?'

Meg laid a hand on Dallis's leg, squeezing gently. 'The pretty silver lady doesn't make up for the horrible deaths. But you know ... whether they were wrongful or not is a different story. Maybe these so-called witches did cast a few nasty wee spells, eh?' She winked, then stood up next to Elspeth.

Helen and Isobel followed suit, the four of them forming a circle. They held hands and raised their arms up to shoulder height. They looked like they were waiting for the ceilidh music to start so they could kick off a reel.

'You'll need to go in the middle, doll,' Isobel said.

Dallis stood, then ducked her head under Meg and Elspeth's linked hands. She stood in the middle of the circle, her heart hammering in her chest. Her cheeks burned. She had no idea what was happening, but still, it felt right.

'Kneel down, Dallis. Close your eyes tight.'

She did as they said, and after a moment she felt the air shift around her. The smell from the candles grew stronger. The four women started a murmuring chant, a whisper of words that she couldn't make out. She heard their soft footsteps as they moved around her. The chanting grew faster, louder. The candles seemed to be giving off a thick smoke that caught in her lungs, and she tried hard not to cough. She was desperate to open her eyes, but daren't. She felt like she was in the centre of a small tornado, a whistling wind whipping her hair against her face; but the sound of the footsteps was gone, then the chanting became nothing but a buzzing sound in her ears.

She kept her eyes tightly closed, terrified, now, of what she might see if she were to open them. She clenched her fists, tried to keep her breathing steady. Spinning, whirling, flying ...

Then it stopped.

She opened her eyes, and screamed.

She was face to face with the shining wet eyes of a huge black dog. She fell backwards onto the carpet, and was only vaguely aware of the women around her retreating.

'Agnes, come here,' Meg said.

Dallis sighed. Of course. The dog from the beach. Friendly, but a bit fond of licking. She glanced around at the door, still tightly shut.

'How did …?'

'Never mind that.' Isobel was holding out a glass jar filled with a gloopy, golden liquid. 'Take it. You might need to reheat it a bit when you get home, but it should stay soft for a while.'

'It's the wax from the candles,' Helen explained. 'You'll need it for the effigy.'

Dallis spun around, looking at them all. 'What just happened in here?' The room looked the same as before. As did the women. She wished now that she'd opened her eyes to see what they were doing.

'If you'd opened your eyes you'd have broken the spell,' Meg said.

'Are you four …?' Dallis couldn't bring herself to say it.

Isobel nodded. 'Aye, that's us. There are more, of course. We're still finding each other. Meg brought us together.'

'I think we can credit Agnes with that,' Meg said, but she didn't elaborate further. She stepped forward and put a hand on Dallis's shoulder. 'I'm sure it goes without saying that this never happened, okay?'

Dallis nodded.

'It's all pretty simple from here.' Meg gestured towards the jar in Dallis's hand. 'Get yourself home. Then get something of his. Hair works well, or failing that, even some skin flakes. You'll find them in your bed, or in his underwear …'

'That's rank,' Elspeth said, screwing up her face.

'He has a hairbrush …' Dallis said.

'Perfect. A couple of hairs is all you need. Get them in the wax while it's still liquid. Swirl it around. Close your eyes, and just remember how you felt tonight, in the circle. Then stick the jar in the fridge. Once it's solid but still pliable, scrape it out and shape it into a ball. Then you need to toss the ball in the fire. Do you have a real fire?'

Dallis shook her head. 'Not even a fake one. Only radiators.'

'Fine,' Meg said. 'We'll go with the modern take. Put it in an oven dish and shove it in at two-hundred and fifty degrees. Don't use an oven dish you like, mind. You can't use it after.'

'Okay ...'

'And then, when it's nearly melted, nearly gone ... you need to take a spoonful out, drop it in a glass of water, then drink it down in one. Okay?'

Dallis swallowed. Nodded. 'Then what?'

Elspeth stepped forward and flung an arm around her shoulder. 'Then comes the fun part ...'

Dallis listened to the instructions, and felt something flourish and grow in her stomach. It grew bigger as she walked home. It grew arms and legs and tentacles and all other sorts of appendages, until it consumed her whole body, right up to her grinning face. But there was no fear. Not anymore. The thing that flowered inside her was called hope.

When Tommy came home at nearly 4am, Dallis was ready. She'd changed the sheets, had a bath with her favourite scented bath oil. Spritzed herself with perfume, slipped on a tiny satin nightie that she didn't really like but she knew Tommy loved. She heard him crashing about in the bathroom. Held her breath, waiting. Finally, he stumbled into the bedroom. She usually feigned sleep when he came in like this, hoping to protect herself, but tonight was different.

She rolled over to face him, propping herself up on one arm, shaking her hair to make sure it tumbled seductively across her shoulders. 'Hey babe. Good night?' She affected a sleepy, just-woken-up voice.

He pulled off his t-shirt and flopped onto the bed, confusion on his face. 'What you doing awake?' he slurred.

Dallis leant in towards him, stroking his chest. He smelt of beer, and a definite hint of perfume. Not one of hers. Something cheap and nasty, one of those cloying scents that got stuck in your nostrils.

'I missed you.' She ran her hand lower, towards the top of his boxers.

His face changed. Confusion replaced by a sneer. 'What you after, eh?'

He pulled her on top of him, and she felt him growing hard beneath her. She leant forwards, kissing his neck. Trying not to recoil at the stale alcohol fug coming off him. She felt him shift, trying to pull his boxers down, and she lifted herself off to let him. He was more than ready.

But she was ready too.

She let him slide himself inside her, and as he did, she kissed him on the mouth, probing inside with her tongue. She ran the instructions through in her head, barely feeling what he was doing to her now, even as he grabbed her throat, squeezing tight. One of his little games.

Focus, Dallis, focus.

Her head started to swim. He was taking her breath from her, but she kept her mouth on his. He squeezed harder, she breathed harder. Into his mouth. She recited the words she'd been told, in her head, over and over.

What comes to me, will come to you. What ails me, will ail you.
What comes to me, will come to you. What ails me, will ail you.
What comes to me, will come to you. What ails me, will ail you.

And right at the point of no return, his hands loosened on her throat, and she gasped, sucking in air – just as he opened his mouth wide, crying out in ecstasy – and she blew hard into his mouth. The regurgitated ball of wax flew out of her and into him – exactly as she'd been instructed.

His eyes bugged-out for a second, the shock of it, as the pellet shot down his throat. Then he sat up fast, throwing her off.

'What the fuck was that?'

She pushed her hair out of her face. 'What was what? Did you not enjoy it?'

He stared at her, suddenly sober. 'You put something in my mouth.'

'Normally the other way round,' she muttered, her mouth lifting in what she hoped was a sexy half-grin.

'Shut up you stupid cow. Tell me what the fuck you just did.'

She took a breath, tried to shuffle away from him a little. Not keen on where this was going. He leant forward, grabbing the tops of her arms. Squeezing hard.

'Ow. Fuck!' he said, letting go of her quickly, like he'd been burned.

Dallis felt nothing. Usually his squeezes were enough to earn her a bruise, but she'd barely felt his touch at all. Her half-grin turned into a full one.

'Pulled a muscle?' she said, her voice full of innocence.

He scrunched up his face. He was not happy.

'Trying to be smart?' he said. 'You know I don't like you acting smart.'

She sat up, and he shoved her hard in the face with his palm, knocking her back into the pillow.

'Ow,' he said again, wincing. He put a hand to his face. 'Must've been some shit in that coke I had round Kev's. Doing something weird to me.'

Again, Dallis felt nothing. Although her heart had started to beat a little faster, an adrenaline burst building in her veins.

It's working.

Meg's voice came into her head. 'I told you ... now hold your nerve. Keep going.'

She nodded, smiling.

'What d'you think you're smirking at, bitch?'

She lifted her chin, defiant.

He was on her in a second. Hands around her throat. Squeezing. This time she did feel something. It reminded her of being at the dentist, when your whole face is numb, and you can feel the dentist's fingers rooting around in your mouth. An odd sensation, but without pain. By now, in this little game of his, she should be struggling to breathe. She should be feeling the heat in her cheeks. She should be burning, choking, bucking against him. Her hands would on his, nails digging in to his flesh, trying to make him stop. Stop.

STOP.

He stopped, falling away from her onto the bed, hands going to his own throat as he wheezed and choked. Trying to speak but no words were coming out. He rolled over onto his side, away from her. He coughed for a while, then he stopped. She lay there watching him until he fell asleep.

He came through to the kitchen several hours later. He looked horrific. His neck a mess of purple and black.

'I think someone spiked my drink last night,' he said, his voice thin and reedy. Barely a croak. 'Feels like I've swallowed broken glass.'

'I've made scrambled eggs,' Dallis said. She lifted a piece of tinfoil off a plate and slammed it down on the table. 'Made it a few hours ago. It'll be cold. Tea's hot though.' She plonked the mug down, slopping dark brown liquid over the side.

He looked at her. Blinked. The pathetic broken tone of a moment earlier lifted off him. His nostrils flared. He spoke through gritted teeth. 'You expect me to eat that muck? You know I hate scrambled eggs. And stone cold, too? You stupid cow.' He lifted the plate and flung it hard against the wall.

Dallis flinched, but stayed where she was by the kettle, her own mug of tea in her hand.

'I'd like you to clear that up, please. I need to go to work.'

She watched calmly as his face turned red. His shoulders tensed. He balled his hands into fists.

'You need to start doing more around the house,' Dallis continued.

Tommy snatched the mug of tea off the table and threw it at her face.

She took a step back, the liquid spilling down onto her clean top. The mug fell to the floor and smashed.

'Aaaarrghhhhhh!' Tommy screamed, his hands flying to his

face. It was redder now. Burning, in fact. A jagged cut opened up on his forehead, just above his eyebrow.

'That looks nasty,' Dallis said, leaning against the worktop. 'There's a first aid kit in the bathroom.'

He lunged at her, pinning her against the worktop. Then he punched her in the face.

But it was his head, not hers, that snapped back, propelling him across the small kitchen. He landed on his back on the table, the chairs scattering and tipping. Blood was pouring down his face.

Dallis caught a glimpse of herself reflected in the window. She looked fine.

'What's happening to me?' Tommy pulled himself up, stood facing her. The anger was still flashing in his eyes. His face was a mess, matching his ruined throat. 'Are you doing this to me, you bitch?' He took another step towards her.

She put a hand behind her, sliding a knife out of the block. She held it in front of her.

He laughed. Blood was coursing down his face, into his open mouth. 'And what exactly are you planning to do with that, eh?'

Dallis smiled. Held the knife out to him. 'I'm not planning to do anything, you stinking, useless, cowardly waste of fucking oxygen. Do what the hell you want to me because I am long past caring.' She took a sip of her tea, then laid the mug down.

He snatched the knife from her hand. 'Oh, mind-games is it now, doll? You been talking to some snooty fucking therapist or something?' He waved the knife in front of her. 'You think you can mess with me?' He took a step forward, touched her neck with the tip of the blade.

It felt like a fly had landed on her.

He flinched, his free hand going to his neck. Brows knitted in confusion. He held the knife out in front of him, the tip of the blade pointing towards her chest. She watched his Adam's apple as he swallowed. Saw the change in his eyes. It was there. Definitely there. Fear.

Do it, Dallis.

She leant forward, pushing her face close to his.

'You need to start being a bit nicer to me, Tommy.'

Dallis took a step, closing the distance between their bodies. There was a soft sucking sound as the knife plunged into her chest, but just as before, she felt no pain. The sucking came again, as he pulled it back out. Then he staggered backwards, the knife dropping from his hand, bouncing off the floor. No blood. Not on the knife. Not on her.

His hand went to his chest, his mouth dropped open. 'Dallisssss …'

He crumpled to the floor.

Then the blood came, a pool of crimson on the lino.

Dallis watched as the light left his eyes. A dark cloud, like candle-smoke, whirled around him. Then it was gone. He was gone.

It's done.

She picked up one of the upturned chairs and sat down hard, letting out a long, slow breath. She looked at her hands, expecting a tremor, but they were as steady as a surgeon's. She picked up her mug from the side and took a sip. Closed her eyes.

There was a single bark, then a low growl. She heard the *tap tap* of the Labrador's feet on the wooden floor of the living room. Dallis opened her eyes just as Agnes appeared in the kitchen doorway. The dog sniffed at the thing on the floor that used to be Tommy, then padded over to her and licked her hand.

Meg's voice spoke from inside her head again. 'You did well. We'll deal with it now.'

Dallis patted the dog on the head, drained the last dregs of her tea, picked up her keys and her handbag, and headed off to work.

THE SELKIRK UNDEAD

Aficionados of TV ghost stories may have fond memories of BBC2's 1979 adaptation of Sheridan le Fanu's ultra-chilling short story of 1839, 'Strange Event in the Life of Schalken the Painter'. For those not in the know, it tells the tale of a poor art student in 17th century Holland, who falls in love with his tutor's niece but loses her to an arranged marriage with the mysterious Vanderhausen of Rotterdam, a suitor who comes and goes in the blink of an eye and yet who inevitably brings with him an air of darkness and menace.

In the words of Le Fanu, Vanderhausen was:

'... an elderly man: he wore a short cloak, and broad-brimmed hat with a conical crown, and in his hand, which was protected with a heavy, gauntlet-shaped glove, he carried a long ebony walking-stick, surmounted with what appeared, as it glittered dimly in the twilight, to be a massive head of gold ... the face was altogether overshadowed by the heavy flap of the beaver which overhung it, so that not a feature could be discerned. A quantity of dark hair escaped from beneath this sombre hat ... There was an air of gravity and importance about the garb of this person, and something indescribably odd, I might say awful, in the perfect, stone-like movelessness of the figure ...'

In the BBC2 version, in which Vanderhausen was played by the late, great John Justin, he was all that and worse, a sour, stone-faced zombie of a man who appeared to embody the very nature of death.

You may wonder what relevance this has to any kind of true terror tale from the Scottish Lowlands. And in actual terms it doesn't. However, those familiar with 'Schalken the Painter' will surely never deny its similarity to the story of the Selkirk Undead. This is a folk-tale rather than an attested-to factual event, but this too dates from the mid/late 17th century and exudes an air of genuine horror.

It concerns one Rabbie Heckspeckle, the shoemaker (or 'sutor' as they were known in those days) of Selkirk, who, along with his wife, Bridget, was also considered to be the town gossip. No one had a secret that either Rabbie or his wife wouldn't soon discover and hurriedly pass on. For these reasons, the Heckspeckles were not a popular couple. That said, Rabbie's skill was undeniable and his business much sought. This necessitated that he work hard, regularly rising at dawn to meet his orders.

On one such occasion, the sun wasn't yet up and he was hard at work, when he suddenly became aware that a customer had entered his shop without his even noticing.

Immediately, there was an air of darkness about this newcomer.

He wore a heavy black cloak and a broad-brimmed hat, which was pulled down low, concealing most of his face. At the back, long lank hair hung out in rat-tails. Most alarming of all, the figure was utterly motionless, like a statue, when he spoke, requesting a pair of boots in a strange, sonorous voice. When Rabbie got close so that he could note the details and the shoe-size, an odd smell assailed him. Something rank and indefinable. Moreover, the stranger's dark clothing had the air of mouldiness.

Never one to turn down work, Rabbie accepted the commission and the stranger, who had offered no name or address, handed over a purse and said that he would return for his goods at the next cock-crow.

Rabbie prided himself on creating quality merchandise, and was irritated to be given such short notice, but he was cowed by the unnerving presence in his shop, and simply glad when the stranger had departed, which he did before Rabbie had even realised that he'd gone. The sutor set to work quickly, but not after checking inside the purse, which contained more than adequate gold, but also beetles and worms. Rabbie was horrified, but despite this, the payment was generous, so he proceeded.

The task kept him busy all that day until not long after midnight, at which point as fine a pair of boots as the shop had ever produced sat packaged on the workbench. Rabbie had barely fallen asleep when that terrible voice spoke in his ear, asking if the boots were ready. Again, the sutor had not even heard the customer enter his shop, but as was predicted, the nearby cockerel now began crowing.

Almost mesmerised, Rabbie handed over the boots, and before he knew it, the ghastly customer had left.

Knowing that he'd never be able to tell the story if he didn't find out who this person was, Rabbie grabbed his red work-cap and hurried outside. Rather to his own surprise, he spotted the cloaked figure at the end of the street, walking swiftly away. Rabbie followed, turning many corners until at last they entered the kirkyard. With a growing sense of unease, Rabbie briefly lost his target among the tombs, but then spied him again, descending into an aged, moss-covered sepulchre.

Though almost paralysed with fear, Rabbie descended in pursuit, but found the vault below empty except for a single stone sarcophagus.

He dashed back to the town, thankful to still be alive. Of course, in no time the whole of Selkirk knew about his adventure, but fear spread too ... until the authorities decided that action needed to be taken. The sarcophagus was exhumed and opened, and found to contain the skeleton of an unknown man dressed in the rancid, rotted clothing of yesteryear, but wearing the fine new boots that Rabbie had made. Whether the sutor had been telling the truth or this was all part of some macabre joke that he'd been playing on his neighbourhood was unsure, but the decision was taken to return the sarcophagus to its resting place and fill the sepulchre with earth. Before this happened, Rabbie opted to retrieve the boots, saying that the dead had no use for them.

The next morning, he followed his usual procedure, rising very early and heading down into his shop to commence work. At which point, just as the cock crowed, his wife heard him issue a blood-curdling scream. She rushed downstairs, only to find the place wrecked and no sign of her husband.

She took her story to the town watch, who arranged a hue and cry, but no trace of Rabbie was found. At length, the search brought everyone back to the kirkyard, where, with some reluctance, orders were issued to disinter the unknown corpse yet again. With the sepulchre filled in, it was a more complex business this time, but at last the stone coffin was brought to the surface and reopened. There was no sign of Rabbie Heckspeckle, but the skeleton lay as before. Somehow or other, it wore its fine new boots again.

While on its head was the sutor's red work-cap.

THE CLEARANCE
Paul M Feeney

When I was a wee boy, I was terrified of the dark. I suffered near pants-wetting, nightmare-inducing, sleep-depriving terror every time my mother turned the light off. I was convinced all manner of phantoms and spirits were manifesting and 'walking' the earth, restless and uneasy. Coming back to haunt the living; to haunt me. I imagined them spilling forth from my wardrobe or slithering from beneath my bed, arms outstretched, mouths open in silent screams. I was convinced they were coming to get me.

In a way, I was right.

I get off the train at a small stop about three hours north of Glasgow. The sign above the platform says Carrock. It is, typically for Scotland, a chilly, grey day, the ground damp, the trees sodden and dripping with water. What my mother would call *dreich*. Dull clouds above promise further rain. I pop my small rucksack – it has supplies in case I need to stay overnight – down at my feet and pull my light jacket tight around me, zipping it up. Somehow, the thin coat seemed perfectly adequate whilst in the city, but out here, the weather appears to be sharper, more biting. A shiver ripples through me. I always forget how drastically the climate in this country can change, even in places only a few dozen miles apart. Maybe it doesn't feel as bad in the city because the taller buildings act as a break, the heat from structures, vehicles, the populace itself creating a communal haze of warmth. Or maybe it's something else, something unique to Scotland.

One good thing; the air smells different up here, cleaner, and

I take a deep breath through my nose before hoisting my rucksack back up and slinging it over my shoulder.

Besides me, only a couple of other people have disembarked, and they quickly disappear. I'm soon left alone on the concrete platform, the train receding into the distance as it continues on its way. A heavy quiet descends, as if someone has turned the volume down. Even the wind makes no sound.

I look around, wondering where my welcome party is. The station is one of those tiny, two track affairs – a north and southbound – though it does have a small ticket office, a rickety looking wooden building that doesn't appear to have been renovated much since it was built in, I'm guessing, the late 1800s or early 1900s. It puts me in mind of the MR James and Charles Dickens's ghost stories I remember seeing on TV when I was a kid. How depressingly apt.

If it weren't so dreary, the place would be quite picturesque; in the distance, low hills cut sharp, dark shapes against the sky and either side of the trainlines are the edges of wild woods. It's camera fodder for the tourists, which is what this stretch of railway is mainly used for; to ferry visitors slowly up and down what is undoubtedly a beautiful part of the country without really letting them know about its dark, bloody, and violent history. It's all surface veneer, sanitised and safe. A lie.

Just as I decide to go in the office, the door opens, juddering as it pops free from the frame; clearly the old wood of the door has expanded in the cold weather, the person on the other side opening it having to expend some force to move it. A tall figure exits onto the platform.

'James Sinclair? Hello. I'm Randolph Lumley.' He stops for a second and I can almost see his brain do that double take most people do when they first meet me. I can imagine what he's thinking; he's looking at someone who is in their mid-twenties (twenty-five to be precise), and ostensibly a professional worker, yet the tired, dry skin stretched tight on a too thin body and the dark circles under the eyes suggest a much older and burnt-out individual. I've often been mistaken for a junkie and been treated accordingly by, amongst others, neds (the Scottish equivalent of chavs, but worse, believe me).

He recovers quickly and holds out a hand which I take in a quick shake.

'Mr Lumley. Good to meet you. Aye, sir, I'm James.'

Lumley is my client, for want of a better word, and the reason I'm up here in the wilds of Perthshire.

He waves his hand in dismissal. 'Psh. No need for formalities. Call me Randolph.'

How gracious of him. The tone is friendly enough, though the accent – clipped and precise – speaks of either someone who's upper-class English, or whose private education has eradicated any trace of their heritage. I have to supress an instinctive, almost unconscious, dislike and mistrust of Lumley (who probably *is* an actual 'Sir'); I grew up in a staunchly working-class family, and anything bourgeoisie or above was seen as the enemy. It's hard to shake the indoctrination of youth.

I nod, curtly. 'No bother, Ran*dolph* ...' Drawing out his name as if testing how it sounds. 'Are we far from the house, or is it easy enough to walk?'

He blinks, either at my abruptness or because – dear lord, please don't let him be senile; he looks maybe late '50s, early '60s, but that doesn't mean he's in possession of all his marbles – he's forgotten why we're here. Why *I'm* here. 'Oh, of course, of course. My car is parked outside. The house is a couple miles or so outside the village, but the road is rather steep and winding.'

He doesn't move, as if waiting for instruction. I really hope he's not a simpleton. I remind myself it could be worse and as long as I get paid, I don't really give a toss, but already I'm starting to feel this job's going to be a pain in the arse.

Pulling my rucksack tighter on my shoulder, I gesture with my free hand for him to lead the way.

I saw my first ghost when I was eight.

It wasn't at night, thank fuck, and it wasn't especially

dramatic, but it still terrified me.

I was out at East Kilbride shopping centre (a trip a few miles outside Glasgow was considered an event for our family back then, something to be anticipated and savoured) with my mum. I was looking around in wonder at all the different shops, taking in a place that to my young mind was full of marvels and infinite promise. If you've ever been to that place, you'll know how rose-tinted my child's eyes were. Despite being built in the early 2000s, the glass and concrete façade looks as dull and utilitarian as something from the '80s, yet inside was a magical wonderland to me.

We were walking along the upper concourse, my mum continually and impatiently telling me to hurry up as I dawdled to gaze into each new shop, when we happened upon a small group of people gathered around something lying on the floor. I didn't become aware of the crowd till I bumped into the back of my mum's legs when she stopped walking.

Gazing between the cluster of bodies, I could make out what I thought at first was a pile of clothing dumped on the floor. Maybe someone had dropped their shopping; perhaps a bag had split. My mind was already turning away from the tableau, towards more interesting – to me – concerns; maybe today would be the day I'd get a 'new' game for my Nintendo 64 (being that at this time, the N64 was already an out of date console – it was the only one my parents would buy for me, and even that had been a hand-me-down from a neighbour – a new game would still be second-hand, verging on obsolete; like I said, we were working class, and definitely not well-off). It was only when some of the onlookers' legs moved that I saw the large, round, and bald head.

Just for a moment, I thought the head was lying there by itself, and my heart gave a tiny, painful lurch. Then I realised the pile of clothes had a body in them. One of the bystanders knelt beside the man and put his lips to the face of what I'd thought was a severed head. My heart gave a different kind of squeeze and I felt heat rise into my cheeks. But when he put his hands on the man's chest and started pushing up and down, I simply felt confusion. CPR wasn't something that was taught at my school.

As I stared on in bewildered fascination, I became aware of an odd and unfamiliar feeling growing inside me. It began as a low buzz, almost on the edge of hearing. Not entirely unpleasant, it reminded me of the drone of bees in summer. Then, I felt a slight chill leech into me, as though I was being slowly, slowly submerged in cold water. A little shiver flitted up my spine.

And even as I started thinking maybe I was coming down with something, my vision grew ever so slightly hazy, as though I was viewing the world through a film, or as if someone had turned down the colour just a touch.

It was then I spotted the second man and for the third time, my heart did a funny little unpleasant dance.

He was standing just a touch apart from the main crowd, staring down at the body (as I was coming to think of it; I might not have known what CPR was, but I'd watched my fair share of police dramas) with an intense look of sad puzzlement. But it wasn't his expression that had made my heart skip a beat or two. No, that was due to his uncanny resemblance to the man lying unmoving on the shopping-centre floor. He too was rather large and had a big, round, bald head. Not only that, but his clothes were almost identical; they were a similar make, just a more faded colour. The pallor of his face was pretty close to the one lying down, though.

My mouth went dry while I stared, feeling as if I was frozen, as if time was standing still. I might have stayed that way forever – or at least until my mum gave me a slap – except that the man, the one standing, suddenly moved. His brow crinkled and his head titled up, as if hearing something but unable to make out what it was. Then his big face turned, and he stared right at me.

My guts tightened and I felt a sharp, near overwhelming urge to piss. And *then* – oh my word, but my mind was suddenly screaming inside my skull – he started coming towards me, moving almost sedately, smoothly. Some small part of my mind, detached and remote, realised it was because he wasn't walking but floating, gliding just an inch or so above the scuffed tile floor. I wanted to run, wanted to scream, to shout for my mum, but I couldn't move; I was held rigid by traitorous muscles and ligaments, by a treacherous nervous system overloaded by fear. I could do nothing but watch the man, the strange, floating man, hover towards me until he was only a couple feet away, all the while that buzz turning into a deep, resonant hum. Just before he reached me, looking for all the world as if he were going to simply ram into me, a warm, soft white light bled in from the fringes of my vision, the man began to shrink down, and then he *did* reach me and went inside. I can't explain it any other way. His rapidly diminishing form, which also looked bizarrely as if he was moving into a great distance, disappeared as he touched me, except he didn't actually touch me as I felt nothing. He simply vanished – into me, through me, whatever – and was gone, along with the light, the noise, and the weird lensing of my sight.

The world of the shopping centre popped back into reality and my mother finally became aware something was wrong with me as I slowly fell to the floor myself and darkness rushed up to enfold me.

Lumley is right. The road to the house isn't especially long but the winding route snaking this way and that uphill, often barely wide enough for one vehicle, makes the journey more drawn out than it would be if it were straighter. Luckily, we don't meet any other traffic, though the cracked tarmac and occasional potholes are hazard enough. Lumley drives slowly, hunched forward over the steering wheel.

I gaze out at the thick woods bordering either side of our less than perfect road. After an initial burst of mindless chatter on getting into his vehicle – a Bentley, of course, albeit an older model – Lumley has fallen silent. Perhaps he's simply concentrating on the drive, but I wonder if there isn't more to it.

The trees are dense and wild; none of that cultivated,

organised carry on here. Like the weather, it makes me think again about that peculiar duality Scotland seems to have in abundance, an almost schizophrenic quality. On the one hand, it presents itself as a welcoming, tourist-friendly place, all smiles and tartan and shortbread tins. And there *are* genuine examples of that. But there is also a darker side to the country, to its history, to the here and now. Murders, wars, hatred, oppression. Maybe all countries have this; maybe it's an inevitable aspect of the emergence of 'civilisation' from the more violent and aggressive natures of our ancestors. But I feel that dissonance is particularly strong in my homeland.

The big car slows even further, and my train of thought falls apart as Lumley guides it off the tarmac and onto a rough dirt track. It's immediately apparent this backroad hasn't seen much in the way of traffic recently; the tyre ruts are covered in a layer of dead leaves and twigs, and the centre line is thick with grass and weeds. I can hear them swishing against the underside of the Bentley as we make our slow, bumpy way along.

After a fair amount of silence, other than the sounds made by the vehicle, it's almost a rude shock when Lumley speaks again, echoing my observations.

'I've only been up here a handful of times since the house came into my possession. Before that, it lay empty for decades. I hope you'll forgive the state of disrepair.'

I mumble something non-committal as an attempt at reassurance. I couldn't really give a shit if the place is a burned-out shell. He's paying me for my services whether I do anything or not; I'm not here to evaluate his property.

Like many before him, and no doubt many after, when Lumley first contacted me, he had the tone of one who absolutely did not believe I could do what my adverts say I can. I suppose you can't blame him. The online directories are full of charlatans and con-artists, and I gather he'd already had dealings with a couple of those. But I suppose something in my voice gave him pause. I don't put myself across like those others; I don't dress up what I do with theatre or melodrama, I simply explain my ability calmly and quietly. Lumley had come into ownership of the house through some complicated line of inheritance. I wasn't interested in the slightest and tuned out as he relayed that to me over the phone. Then, as he eventually came to why he'd contacted me – early on, I pegged Lumley as a waffler – I did perk up.

He continues speaking as he navigates the rough track. 'It was quite the surprise when the solicitor contacted me, I'm sure you can imagine. I mean, I knew my family had ties to one or two of the more established clans of Scotland; lairds and titles and such, if you will. But to inherit a stately home with such historical significance to the local area, well …'

I grit my teeth and try to ignore the irritation which blooms within. Lord, but he's such a bore. Thankfully, I'm spared more of it when we round a bend and the house looms up in front of us as though it's just materialised. Lumley's inane prattle fades away to nothing.

I say house, but the word is barely adequate to describe the sprawling, towering construction squatting at the other end of a clearing that once must have been a cultivated garden and courtyard. Built from sandstone, it's spared the fate many city properties suffer in that the walls aren't discoloured by soot and fumes. But they are still stained by years of neglect and the reclamation of nature; moss, ivy, and damp.

I'm not prone to foreboding but something in the mansion's profile, the way it seems to draw shadow around it like a cloak, its bulky outline crouching like some huge animal, sends a shiver up my spine. Or maybe it's just the weather getting to me again.

As Lumley brings the car to a halt a few metres from the house, I gaze up at it, musing grimly on the black windows that reflect nothing; they give me the impression of hooded eyes staring back at me.

I've seen a lot of weird shit in my two and a half decades, but this place fills me with a sense of low dread and anxiety.

After I came around to find a young shop assistant wiping my brow with a damp cloth and assuring my mother I was okay – she was a student nurse – I tried to tell mum what I'd seen. She dismissed it as a dream, as something brought on *after* realising the man on the ground was dead or dying. I tried again, though weakly, both embarrassed about fainting and being nannied by the shop girl (who I remember being extremely pretty and looking at me with pity and amusement as if I was one of what my mother called 'God's special children'), until mum gave me that tight-lipped look I knew so well that said further attempts would be met with a slap, or worse.

After a few weeks, I came to believe I'd imagined it, and stopped thinking about it, stopped having the nightmares, until a few months later it happened again.

This time, it *was* at night, and this time I didn't even try to tell anyone after.

Across the road from the council house we lived in was an old fella called Grant McArliss, though most of the local kids called him 'McArseless' and other such witty utterances. My parents always tried to instil a bit of respect in me by referring to him as Mr McArliss, but I could tell my dad especially didn't like the old man; when he, my dad, was drinking, he'd often keep up a growled litany of everything the world had done wrong to him. Once or twice, McArliss had featured in the roster. It could have been more often, but I knew to make myself scarce on those nights lest a fist or thick belt find my hide.

McArliss didn't really help himself. He was one of those miserable old fuckers every street has; any balls that landed in his gardens got burst, any kid that made noise he deemed to loud was subject to screeched proclamations of retribution and hellfire. You know the type.

Anyway, one warm August night, McArliss passed away from a severe stroke (I found this out the next morning at breakfast). I remember lying on my bed with the lights off, watching the silent blue strobes of the ambulance wash across the walls. I didn't get up to gawk out the window like I knew most everyone else would be doing. That was because McArliss was already in my room with me, staring down at me from the bottom of my bed.

I was frozen in place with terror. I think I might even have pissed myself. I don't remember. What I do remember is McArliss looking at me with what I at first thought were accusing eyes, a typically sour expression on his ghostly face.

Yes, even then I think I knew he was dead, and I was being visited by the spirit of our street's most hated figure (and whom I was sure had hated all of us). I only discovered the word 'baleful' years later, but that was exactly how he was looking at me. And other than a slight paleness to his features and the tiniest hint of transparency, he looked much as he had in life.

After a while, he began gesturing. He waved his arms, slowly, languidly, as though he were submerged in thick fluid. I couldn't understand what he was trying to convey, but all of a sudden, I was engulfed in a wave of sadness, a sense of regret. I felt sorrow, and a deep longing for forgiveness. And then it came to me, like a revelation, in snippets and slivers of understanding. The stroke had taken its time to extinguish his life, though it was still relatively quick. McArliss had had time to contemplate – beneath the pain, beneath the confusion – how he had no-one to care for him, no-one to turn to or check on him. He was utterly alone, and it had been all his own doing. And so he wanted to attempt some small measure of contrition to those he felt he'd wronged, and since no-one but me was able to see or sense him, I was the recipient of that penitence.

I felt a lump form in my throat and a tear slip from one eye. As soon as I nodded to him – whether in acceptance of his atonement or simply to say I understood, I cannot say – he began to fade, until it was as though he'd never been, and I was left only with a great feeling of emptiness and fatigue. The fear that had come over me when he'd first appeared had blown away.

In the years following, I had many more encounters, each one as different as the last, souls that had passed on with unfinished business, those that simply feared to move onto the next phase (whatever that may be; that, I'm not party to), and those who seemed to use me as … well, as a conduit. Whatever was in me, drew these wraiths to my presence and allowed them to put their souls to rest.

After I left college, I set myself up in a professional capacity; not as medium or clairvoyant or psychic, but simply as someone who could clear restless spirits. Perhaps a shade arrogant, but I was young. I still am, though I don't look or feel it. For long, I wished I couldn't do what I can, but eventually I came to the realisation it wasn't going to stop, so I might as well profit from it like all those fakers.

When Lumley unlocks the front door and we move over the threshold, my sense of disquiet increases. As I said, I don't claim to be psychic or a prophet; I don't know why I can see ghosts and I gave up wondering a long time ago. But the fact remains I can, and part of that is being able to sense places where the dead linger. As they can clearly sense when I'm near, so too can I, though it's usually faint. Not here, though.

Pausing in the hallway, a grand, wide space with a double-staircase curving upwards, I'm simultaneously assaulted by the stink of rot and mould, and by the soft, psychic battering of the unsettled dead.

There must be more than a few here.

I shouldn't be surprised. The area this house was built in would have seen those living there mostly subjugated and oppressed over the centuries. And even before that, almost endless conflicts between clans shedding lakes of blood on the land. Again, I think of the two Scotlands; the sanitised face presented to visitors, and the other soaked in murder, war, and massacre.

Lumley makes to speak, and I hold out a hand to silence him, taking a few steps further into the mansion. For the first time, I'm presented with more than genial affability from Lumley. His face pinches and I imagine he's channelling all the privilege and status his lineage has enjoyed, looking down on me as some upstart commoner. Fuck him. I'm here to do a job.

Moving away, I speak without looking back. 'You can follow or wait here. I need to walk through the building, see what's what.'

He remains where he is.

I start with the downstairs rooms. Beyond the hallway, off to the left is a waiting room, presumably for visitors. It's grander than anything I've ever lived in. Imagine; one minor room in this mansion is bigger than my entire flat. Nothing comes to me and I move swiftly on.

The next room is some sort of drawing room or parlour, and again I sense nothing here. Nothing more than the background hush I'm already experiencing, anyway.

I move through each chamber of this huge place, wondering where the phantoms are concentrated. I would have expected them by now to have sensed me and to have sought me out. But no-one and nothing comes.

The interior of this house is in an even worse state of repair than its outside.

Bare walls, stripped of ornament and paintings, are streaked with damp and mould, and where there is paint it is flaking, where there is wallpaper it is warped and peeling. The plaster on the ceilings is cracked in numerous places. I see now why the windows reflected nothing. On this side, they are covered in a layer of grime, permitting little light. The house is shrouded in darkness within as well as without. Thankfully, there is little in the way of furniture aside from the occasional forgotten chair or desk. As I traverse the floor, I only have to worry about rotting floorboards and tattered remnants of carpet.

I don't encounter anything until I go upstairs and reach the first bedroom.

Pushing open the door, which creaks ominously in a manner worthy of the cheesiest horror film, I find the first room so far that has light. This is because two of the windows are smashed. It's a weak, watery light, reflecting the cold sky from outside.

I step cautiously, not wishing to plummet through the floor. And I'm not more than five steps in when it manifests.

On the wall to my left, adjoining the next room, is a big stain

I at first assume is just water leakage. Then it shifts subtly, and the dark shadows coalesce into the figure of a faint young woman, barely a few years into teen-hood, dressed in clothes I only know are old-fashioned (perhaps, given my ability, I should be more interested in history, but I'm not). She seems to materialise from the wall itself. Not as though she has drifted through from the next room, but as if she has been inside the wall, invisible, waiting. I can still see the outlines of marks on the surface behind her. I've noticed this only a handful of times because most phantoms I encounter tend to be relatively recent deaths. But on the rare times I see much older ghosts, they are always in various states of transparency. I suspect the longer they've been dead, the less 'substance' they have in the world. This might account for why I'm not constantly overwhelmed with them. Thankfully.

On her face is the most mournful expression I've ever seen, and even though her eyes are barely sketched lines, I can see the pain there. Above all that, though, I can *feel* her torment. Decades old – maybe more than a century – post-life distress and it's lost none of its potency. It hits me in waves, almost like a physical force. I want to cry; bitter tears prick my eyes, and a hard pain blocks my throat as I swallow. I wait to see if she entreats me or simply uses me to pass on. Neither happens. She continues to look at me with those sorrow filled eyes, and I begin to get snippets of her life. Rarely do the dead speak to me; mostly, I glean snapshots of their own memories. I don't know if this is directed by these spirits or if it's something I'm simply able to pick up, but it doesn't really matter; the end result is the same.

If I could look away, I would. Out of sheer instinct, I try and block out what I'm seeing and sensing, but it comes, nonetheless. It's a tale as old and as sad and as grimly mundane as time. A servant girl, subject to the abuses of her masters, treated like property, then cast aside when no longer of use, a broken plaything. And this isn't unique to my home country. Wherever there is inequality, subjugation, imbalances of power, there will be these base injustices. If I were more cynical, I'd say it's wherever humanity is.

I'm almost overwhelmed with the weight of her anguish. After who knows how long, I decide I need to leave the room. If she won't go or communicate her needs, I can't help.

As I close the door softly behind me and walk away, the barest hush of noise makes me glance back. The young woman has followed me, drifting through the door. This is new. I feel a sharp spike of fear I've not had since my earliest encounters. But when I stop, she stops. All I can do is continue.

The rest of the upstairs is devoid of presences but when I go back downstairs and take a narrow staircase to the basement level, to the servants work areas and quarters, the sense of crushing anxiety grows.

Down here, I encounter a number of phantoms. The first is a young boy, only five or six when he died. He too, suffered abuses, though his were only of the hitting and kicking variety (inside my head, I laugh bitterly at my use of 'only'). A child of one of the workers, he was put to labour cleaning the lower areas, crawling up chimneys, and other dogsbody tasks designed to keep him out of view of the upper levels. For when he *did* come to their attention, he was beaten like an unwanted puppy.

This little fellow rises through the blackened-tile floor of what I guess must have once been the kitchen. He actually gives me a start when he appears. Because there is no light down here at all, I'm having to use my mobile's torch function to see and his sudden appearance is startling. When the boy ascends, he is also mostly see-through, but I can see the dark circles under his eyes, stark against very pale skin. Again, I'm battered by sadness, but the boy also exudes confusion and loss. He only wanted to please his family and their employers, and his child's mind cannot understand why they treated him so harshly.

Like the young girl, he simply stands and looks at me, neither requesting nor moving on. Instead, he drifts to stand beside her.

Further on down here, I pick up an older man, one who, after long years of faithful service to one generation of lords and ladies, slipped down the stairs one night and cracked his skull open. He was buried in pauper's grave beyond the house grounds and his family were given no time to mourn. There are others who perhaps did not have too awful a time of it but were still treated shabbily. They linger, but I don't know why. I don't know why any of them are still here, beyond those who have suffered great trauma, struggling to move on.

I'm perplexed and frustrated. I've walked the entire house and need to make my way back to Lumley. Yet I have not been able to do what I've been contracted for. But I have to tell him.

I make my back upstairs and my coterie of ghosts follows.

Lumley is where I left him, looking bored and haughty. Gone is the slightly bumbling, genial persona, the image of an ageing Hugh Grant. Instead, he watches me return as if studying a vaguely unpleasant insect. Snooty bastard. Whilst I know he believes something resides here – he admitted as much when he contacted me – I think he's starting to become suspicious I might be a charlatan. What I'm about to tell him isn't going to make him any friendlier.

I open my mouth but before I can find the words, that background hum indicating the presence of ghosts intensifies, grows louder. It's obvious Lumley can't hear or sense it. He has no idea half a dozen stand behind me like an entourage.

He folds his arms. 'Well? Is it done? Is the place … cleared?'

I don't care for the impatient tone.

Again, I'm about to speak when I'm halted by a rising darkness.

This time, I think Lumley *does* feel something. He frowns and looks about himself.

Not really talking to me, he mumbles: 'Why's it getting dark? It's too early and there wasn't a storm forecast.'

I know there's nothing natural about this … at least, nothing most would consider natural. It is the dead, and not just those that have followed me as I've made my way through this crumbling ruin. As I said before, this place, and others like it, have long suffered from centuries of bloodshed and violence. All the way back to clans fighting over patches of mud to battles against invading armies. Then, there were the aristocracy, either homegrown or south of the border, treating their subjects with disdain and casual cruelty. And all that is merely universal. Scotland went further with tales of cannibal families like the Beans; with body-snatchers and murderers such as Burke and Hare, Bible John, Ian Brady; the Glasgow razor gangs in the Twenties and Thirties, and the later ones in the Sixties; the sectarian violence; and so on.

Scotland loves to hide these things behind a mask of friendliness, much like the older parts of Edinburgh being buried beneath the new. But you can't hide it forever. It has a way of clawing itself from the dirt.

The darkness in the hallway grows, and I see it as a cloud rising up the walls, choking what light comes through the dirty windows and the open front door.

Whilst I know I'm seeing more than Lumley, he's definitely aware we're not alone, now. His grumbling fades away and he begins to look around, almost in panic.

I stop where I am a few feet away from him because I'm waiting with mounting dread.

Soon, they come, drawn by whatever signal it is I give off.

Drifting in through the walls, up from the floor, even down from the ceiling, are dozens and dozens of spectres, some far more faded than others, but all showing the transparency of the long dead. Again, I'm no historical expert but I recognise clothes and uniforms from many different time periods. Yes, uniforms, for many of these individuals were clearly soldiers when they died; or at least, they were in battle when they were cut down.

Peasants, servants, conscripts, and common soldiers. Ordinary people, not even forgotten by history but never known in the first place. Exploited and ruined by their supposed betters, ancestors of Lumley, the privileged and elite.

Accompanying this throng of spirits is a crushing sense of despair, almost too much for me to bear. I feel my legs wobble, the accumulated injustice of the ghosts trying to drive me to my knees. And underneath, a growing wave of anger, of blind rage.

The throng of ghosts fills the hallway, mingling at the edges in a circle. Lumley still cannot see them, but he definitely knows something is wrong. So do I.

'What … what is going on? Sinclair! What's happening?'

I wish I knew.

I can't summon the strength to speak. All my concentration is bent on keeping the energy from overwhelming me completely. But I know it's a losing battle. Finally, the ghosts that have accompanied me *do* come closer, to partake of whatever it is I am able to offer the dead. But instead of dissipating to whatever realms those in the past have gone, these ones seem to be *feeding* on my energy, amplifying and projecting their own emotions. Not only them, but the others that have now joined us. They close in on me and I feel connected to other souls in a way I've never felt before. I am both weakened and strengthened by the contact. I feel their pain, their fury, their sense of abandonment and injustice and it threatens to blow my skull apart.

And yet they also absorb *my* emotions, my deep-seated neuroses. My anger at the world and its many unfair systems, the advantages the 'strong' have over the rest of us. My ingrained mistrust and childhood indoctrination against those apparently above me.

This grows and grows, feeding on itself like some psychic feedback loop until it seems to reach a crescendo. Now I do fall to my knees, barely aware of the pain as I hit the floor. Just when I feel I might expire and join the ranks of the dead, I feel a shift in the power. It focuses on Lumley, seeing him as a legitimate target for its ire. Too late, I realise what's about to happen and I'm powerless to stop it.

The ghosts move through me at last but instead of passing on, they converge on Lumley. I try to scream at him to run, try to beseech the spirits but my efforts are batted aside like a feather in wind. Through a haze of extreme sensation and a light that almost blinds the inside of my head, I see Lumley swat the air around him. Of course, he still cannot see the ghosts but now he can feel them. He swirls, his movements becoming more frantic as their efforts become more agitated. Using my own emotions as fuel, the horde of ghosts attacks over and over, becoming almost one as they converge on my client. I watch helplessly as they force him onto his hands and knees, buffeting and battering him. They must be growing in strength because their efforts become more apparent. Bruises appear on Lumley's skin and blood begins leaking from his eyes, nose, and mouth.

And then the ghosts begin to tear him into pieces. I shut my eyes but still see after-images projected through the ghost-light, still hear the wet cracking and tearing, still experience the awful screaming of the man's terrible death.

Eventually, it's over. The multitude of ghosts, having exacted some sort of rough justice as they saw it, disappear, finally content to move on. I'm in the hallway as daylight returns, flat and normal, left with the red mess that is Lumley.

I lie prostrate on my knees, my head on my arms, crying. Snot drips from my nose.

I know I can't stay there forever but it's a while before I can move and when I do, true darkness is falling. I'd hoped in my feverish thoughts the night might make the remains of Lumley easier to contemplate but the half-seen glistening ruin is somehow worse. I give it a wide berth and exit the building, pausing only long enough to retrieve my bag from the car, and run down the road in the dark.

I waited on the outskirts of the town. When the next day arrived, I got on the first train home and holed up in my flat. I spent a week waiting on the police knocking at my door, as they must surely if Lumley had left any records about contacting me. But it seemed he hadn't. Perhaps he'd been embarrassed to admit he'd sought the services of one such as me.

At any rate, no authorities ever came to ask, and I was left to carry on with my life.

But I find that difficult. If it were only the nightmares, I might have managed. If it were just the guilt, I could have persuaded myself what happened wasn't my fault. But everywhere I go, now, I'm accompanied by Lumley's ghost. He stares at me, accusation and anger written across his eyes. He makes no attempt to move on. I can only guess at what he's waiting for. An opportunity, a time when my defences are at their weakest. Or perhaps for that moment when I die myself and we meet again on equal terms. Lord only knows what will happen then.

Until that day, I live my life in perpetual anxiety, the spectre of Lumley a constant reminder of that horror. And I think I deserve that.

THE OVERTOUN BRIDGE MYSTERY

There are many places on Earth that are renowned as suicide hotspots. It's obviously a sad boast for any location to make, though mostly they are chosen for the sake of convenience. For example, it's a straight, quick fall down a sheer cliff face, such as with Beachy Head in East Sussex. Or it's very public and will ensure that countless others witness the tragic event and share in the suicide's distress, such as with the Golden Gate Bridge in San Francisco. Or it's very quiet and there's unlikely to be anyone there who'll interfere, such as with Aokigahara Forest in Japan.

However, there is one place in the Scottish Lowlands where self-destruction has occurred many, many times, sometimes in public and sometimes in private, but where no convincing explanation has ever been offered.

In short, because the victims are mostly not humans, but dogs.

Overtoun Bridge, near Dumbarton, is already well-known as the place where a considerable number of pet canines have seemingly taken their own lives by suddenly and inexplicably running away from their owners, bounding onto the stone balustrade and then leaping 50 feet down to the rocky riverbed below. The problem is now so well attested-to that the Scottish Society for the Prevention of Cruelty to Animals have held their own enquiry (which drew no useful conclusions), while the local authority has put up warning notices for dog-walkers. And yet, though this has now been going on since the 1960s at least, the mystery has only deepened.

The press, both local and national, have been all over this baffling case for many years, offering continuously different numbers for the casualty totals. Most estimates vary between 300 and 600, though the actual figure is believed to be 50 at the very least. Whatever, the bridge at Overtoun is now known the world-over as 'Dog Suicide Bridge'.

It's perhaps no surprise that supernatural theories abound, though the bridge itself, despite its ornate structure, has no esoteric past and is not even a particularly unpleasant place.

Originally, this was all just farmland, but in 1859 the property was acquired by a lawyer-turned-industrialist, James White, who built Overtoun House. It was his son, also called James White, who in 1895 built Overtoun Bridge to extend the driveway over the Overtoun Burn, which runs through a deep gorge on the approach to the premises. Very soon afterwards, because Overtoun Bridge was somewhat picturesque – it consisted of three large arches, the central one straddling the waterway below – while the gorge itself is thickly wooded along both of its sides, it became popular with walkers. But since then, innumerable reports have come in that dogs have suddenly fought to get free of their masters and immediately jumped to either their deaths or serious injury.

It is a bizarre and distressing phenomenon.

There have even been sightings of dogs coming along the burn itself, scaling the steep slope to the top and then voluntarily jumping back down from the parapet of the bridge. In one account, an out-of-control animal survived its first leap, promptly limping back up to the bridge and jumping a second time.

A range of explanations have been offered by canine behaviouralists, from dogs scenting mink or pine martens in the woods below, to dogs simply being playful and mischievous but, lacking the perspective of their taller, two-legged owners, not realising how far was the drop on the other side of the balustrade until it was too late.

But few of those who've lost their pets in this place are convinced by this. Some have reported strange and uncharacteristic behaviour from their animals the moment they walked onto the bridge, almost as if they had become possessed. Others have said that their pets simply froze, as though hearing or seeing (or both) something that humans could not.

Inevitably, there has been talk of spirits infesting the bridge and even Overtoun House itself. There was a human suicide there in the past, and a murder, while local folk whisper about the White Lady of Overtoun, who may or may not be the late-wife of John White, the original bridge-builder. However, others regard this as silliness, and point out that the matter of the Dog Suicide Bridge is a sad and serious issue for which a remedy needs to be found sooner rather than later.

THE FOURTH PRESENCE
S A Rennie

During that long and racking march …
over the unnamed mountains and glaciers
… it seemed to me often that we were
four, not three.

South
Sir Ernest Shackleton

They buried the dead explorer on a cold day in November.

There is little on this Earth that is more desolate than a cemetery in Scotland in the depths of winter. The pinched-faced mourners muttered their discomfort as they watched the cortege proceed up the drive that wound up the hill like a serpent's coils through the tilting tombstones to the chapel at its summit. They watched the slow plod of the black-plumed horses straining to pull the hearse with its grim cargo. The lady in widow's weeds, tall, stately, stared straight ahead as if determined to deny the morbidly curious the satisfaction of seeing her express the slightest sliver of emotion. A retinue of dour retainers followed in her wake. The wind piped around the gargoyles perched on the gothic chapel's roof as the horses' breath steamed and the coffin was unloaded, shouldered, and carried within. A flock of rooks took off overhead from a nearby copse; the doors slammed shut, and the organ's stertorous wheeze began.

Among the bystanders a young man watched, shivering, his worn overcoat too thin for the biting winds that swept the hillside. As brother of the deceased, he knew his place was within, at the widow's side, and as recognition rippled among the crowd he drew back slightly to stand amongst the gravestones. Hugh Creighton had sworn an oath that he would only return to the place where he was born once his brother was dead; he was here today to honour that promise.

Charles Creighton's renown as an explorer of places cold, distant and desolate had been legendary, his voyages to the frozen south recounted in breathless prose in newspapers and periodicals. His distaste for his fellow man, and especially those who occupied this sleepy corner of East Fife, had become equally well known. He had nothing but disdain for his neighbours, for their simple lives and small ambitions: only those who could be of use to him in ensuring the success of his expeditions, or who pandered to his ruthless ambition and vast self-regard, were deemed worthy of civility. His voyages to the Antarctic continent were littered with recriminations and dead men; those who had once admired him now detested him, and amongst those assembled there was a distinct appreciation for the hand of Providence, that a man of such arrogance and ungodly hubris had met such a fitting end. He had been found dead on the great glacier that led up onto the Antarctic plateau. There had been rumours of discontent among the party, furious disagreements and confrontations that had turned violent; even, it was whispered, of madness in the confines of the hut that served as the expedition's headquarters during the long, dark winter.

The service was short, the hymns few. The barest obsequies having been observed, the chapel's doors reopened and the coffin was carried to a nearby open grave and lowered within.

Hugh waited while members of the local gentry approached the widow, offering their obligatory condolences before hastening, with as much speed as decency allowed, back down the hill to their carriages. The lady's head inclined in bitter amusement as she watched their swift dispersal. As Hugh approached, she turned to face him, lifting her veil with a slender black-gloved hand to reveal a face that was pale and drawn but still finely, aristocratically beautiful.

'The vultures have scattered, but the storm crow remains. I knew that if I ever saw you again, it would be today.'

'Hello, Kathleen.' He took her outstretched hand, clasping her thin fingers, holding them for a few seconds as though to convey what he could not put into words. 'I'm sorry.'

'Are you?'

'Well.'

'Yes.'

'I read about his disappearance, followed the story in *The Times*. There was no love lost between us, but I should have come earlier. For that, I am truly sorry.'

'Will you come to the house?'

He paused before answering. 'I'm staying in St Andrews. I've taken a room there.'

'It was your house once, too.'

'Not for a long time.' Hugh hesitated. 'May I call on you tomorrow?'

'I would like that.'

He escorted her down the drive to her carriage. Sleet, falling from a leaden sky, caught like feathers in her veil. Cold from the frozen ground seeped through the soles of his shoes as he watched the carriage recede down the narrow lane.

Something touched his elbow; he turned to see an old man regarding him with a blaze of burning intensity, a muffler wrapped round the lower part of his face, twitching and shivering like a scarecrow on the point of collapse despite his heavy overcoat.

'You are Hugh Creighton?' the curious figure asked. Hugh nodded. 'I knew your brother. I was once his friend. Please … come and see me.' He thrust his card into Hugh's hand and rasped, urgently, as if sensing the young man's hesitation, 'Please. It's important.'

Hugh watched as the strange figure scuttled through a gate halfway down the lane like an arthritic spider and took off across the fallow fields.

He looked at the card.

Professor John Lorimer, School of Geography, University of St Andrews.

The oddness of the encounter felt strangely appropriate to the occasion. Pondering the man's curious appearance and the urgency of his message, he dismissed the old scarecrow as a harmless crank. As he made to walk to the station for the short journey back to St Andrews, he felt a cold breath at his back, and turned to look at the Leng chapel on its high eminence. The spire was silhouetted against the darkening firmament like the mast of a ship beset in ice. Dear God, that he should find himself back here.

His room at the Gowan Hotel proved adequate: simple, but all he could afford. As he ate his evening meal by lamplight in the small dining room, he was aware of the other guests glancing at him with interest. Word had spread that the black sheep of the Creightons had returned. He could not help that; nor did he care. He would pay his respects to his brother's widow tomorrow, make his farewells, and return to London.

The scrutiny, however, began to wear on him, and, leaving his meal unfinished, he stepped out into the night air. The sky had cleared and the moon was high; the air felt as cold as diamonds with a sharp, hard edge to it that made him pull up his collar. As he set off along the street the harsh metallic clangour of St Salvator's bell struck the hour, spearing through the air like a javelin, making his head ache.

Back in the city of his youth, his thoughts full of the funeral and Kathleen, he felt like a stranger.

He made for the seafront and the cathedral ruins, as if to ground himself with familiar scenes. The desolation of the old grey stone made him feel even colder. The twin spires against the stars; the empty portals and crumbled arches; the tower in which, so they said, had been found the body of a young girl, perfectly preserved, wearing a white dress and white leather gloves; a saint, perhaps, whose remains had been worshipped and then entombed in the tower's base. White ladies, black monks, devil dogs, and phantom carriages: Hugh had devoured these tales as a boy. On leaving the university he had even tried writing his own, pursuing his hopeless dream of authorship through long, dark evenings in an unheated room in a Bayswater boarding-house, subsisting on stewed tea and stale bread, with only a few publications to his name. His days were spent as a lowly insurance clerk, earning barely enough to pay the rent. Nevertheless it was the life he had chosen. He'd endured his father's scorn and his brother's vindictive antagonism for as long as he could, and had known that Forgan House, St Andrews, and Fife could no longer be his home.

And there had been Kathleen. Daughter of a rich family, proud, headstrong, with a will that more than matched his brother's. It had been love, at least on her side, but it had grown quickly obvious that Charles had married her for her money to fund his expeditions, and when he was not away at the ends of the Earth or travelling the world on lecture tours, he could barely stand to be in the same room as her. And when Charles had suspected that the quiet, sympathetic understanding his wife shared with his younger brother was something more, his barely concealed resentment had turned into brutish rage.

A low, mournful keening that shrilled to a whistle like the howling of wind across a snow-swept plain sounded from somewhere in the cathedral's grounds before dying away to nothing.

Hugh gripped the iron railings fiercely, straining to see into the darkness. Everything was silent, as though the world held its breath. The muffled roar of the sea, the soughing of the wind, the soft rustle of the grass verge at his feet; all had gone quiet, as though a bell jar had been lowered on the world.

A violent, bone-deep shiver went through him. The temperature was dropping rapidly; his limbs felt swathed in it, deadened by it. Charles, after his first expedition, had gleefully recounted the stages a body goes through as it freezes to death, the point at which vital organs begin to fail and death is inevitable.

Once you start shivering, it's too late.

He wrenched his frozen hands away from the railing and forced his limbs to move, stumbling down onto the cliff path that led to the castle, desperate to put as much distance between himself and the source of the sound as possible. He heard it again, like the call of an infernal horn blown by a devilish huntsman. During his staggering, desperate flight he glanced, briefly, out to sea; a diseased, greenish glow gathered on the horizon, advancing towards the shore, illuminating the lines of jagged black rocks that extended like talons from the base of the cliffs.

The cry sounded once more, closer now. The need to get back to warmth and humanity became imperative. His eyesight was failing and his legs on the point of collapse as he ducked up a narrow wynd and back onto North Street.

The landlady looked up, startled, as he entered: 'Sir! Is everything all right?'

He reflected wryly that perhaps she thought he was drunk; God knows, during his university years she would have had cause. He barely made it to his room, and spent that night under the blankets fully clothed, dreaming of his brother and an evil thing that walked with him, an agreement, an understanding, a grotesque bargain struck out there on the frozen surface of the coldest place on earth; anger and hatred and many men dead and time and distance traversed as though they were nothing; fear and insanity, and the sense of something coming.

In the morning, when he woke, exhausted and half-feverish, he saw that the inside of his window was covered in an impenetrable sheet of ice.

Kathleen Creighton called immediately for hot tea and whisky as he was shown into the drawing room at Forgan House. The short train journey from St Andrews to Newport had been spent huddled in the corner of a compartment in which every finger of frigid air had seemed to find ingress; the two miles' walk to the old grey stone manor house of his childhood had taken everything he had left in him.

'Blankets, too, William. And send Annie to build up the fire.'

Her brisk command of the situation, the hot strong tea and the flames leaping in the hearth helped warmth return to his frozen flesh. 'Thank you.'

She looked at his face, white and pinched, frowning.

'You didn't walk from the station, surely? You look frozen.'

'It's not far. I'm sorry: I meant to call ahead, but I woke later than I intended. I went for a walk last night, after dinner, down to the cathedral and along the Scores. Maybe it was just a case of my mind playing tricks, being back after so long, the circumstances ...' He shook his head. 'Something spooked me. Nothing, probably. I don't know.'

At this her frown deepened. 'It seems the circumstances have affected both of us, then. My night too, was ... disturbed. Strange, when Charles was away I never minded being alone in this house, but last night in the early hours, I thought I heard something. Of course, living in these lonely places one always hears things.' She laughed self-consciously, but he caught the tremor in her hand as she reached for a cigarette.

He leaned towards her. 'What?'

'I'm not sure. It sounded like the wind, low at first, prying at the house. Then it became ... something else. Like a child, but not ... human. I thought I saw something out in the garden; tall, thin, under the old cedar. The way it stood, unmoving, was odd. As though it was here, and yet not here.' She paused, as if unsure how to express it further, then shrugged. 'Likely a reporter, lurking for some sensationalist titbit so he can write some rubbish for the gutter press about how the grief-stricken widow can't sleep now her lord and master, the great Charles Creighton, is dead. Ha!'

Her laugh was bitter, defiant, but he saw she was shaken. She seemed to gather herself, and once more turned her bright blue eyes on him, smiling. Her hair, red-gold threaded with silver, blazed in the weak afternoon sun. How beautiful she still was, even after all this time.

'And now, tell me: how have London and the literary life been treating you? I read your story, "The Jade Sarcophagus", in the May edition of *Blackwood's*. I thought it very fine.'

'Thank you. Success has been … elusive. The drawers of my desk are overflowing with returned manuscripts. But your kindness and encouragement have always meant the world to me.'

'Nonsense. Some dreams are worth pursuing. Although some dreams can drive men mad.' He was about to answer when she rose and rang the bell. 'William. Take the car, go into St Andrews and fetch Mr Creighton's things from —' she turned to him, 'where is it you are staying?'

'The Gowan. But —'

'And William, please ask Annie to prepare Mr Creighton's old room for him. He will be staying here tonight.'

She would brook no argument. Of course she had, in the space of a few moments' observation, seen how things were with him: his undernourished frame, his shabby clothing, the effect of the walk from the station in bitterly cold weather. He was grateful he did not have to explain further.

At dinner they found themselves slipping into their old, easy companionship, sequestered from the dark and the rising wind that began to buffet the house by blazing candelabra and a roaring fire.

'I forgot to mention: I met a Professor Lorimer yesterday, at the cemetery. Odd old bird. He asked me to go see him. Said he knew Charles.'

Her look became guarded.

'Yes. John Lorimer was something of a mentor to Charles in the early days, and was a member of his first expedition to map the Antarctic coastline. Recently a rift had developed between them; I do not know the cause. Charles convinced him to go on this last expedition despite John's extreme reluctance. He too has just returned from the Antarctic. He led the party that found Charles's body.'

'There was something strange about his appearance … the

way he kept his face covered …'

'Yes. Much of the lower part of his face was eaten away by frostbite. He keeps largely to himself now in his office and rarely emerges.'

'My God. Kathleen, what the hell happened out there? The little I know from reports in *The Times* is that Charles left the main party and struck out on his own, and leading up to that there'd been an almighty row between him and the other members.'

She looked down at her plate before answering. 'You know yourself that Charles was never an easy man to live with. After you left, things got considerably worse. Antarctica had always been his dream; the last unconquered continent. Penetrating into the interior was to him the only true test of a man's courage and endurance. He felt that what was to be found there was reserved for him and him alone; his birthright. It was why he went back again and again. It had become more than just simple obsession. Anyone who stood in his way was to be dealt with ruthlessly, sometimes brutally. Over the course of his expeditions he had also become reckless, and many men died.'

'I read that many died on this expedition, too.'

'Died, or went insane. Men were nothing but dumb instruments to him, a means to an end. This final voyage, given his worsening reputation for ensuring the safety of his men, was a step too far for the institutions and commercial backers who had been eager to sponsor him before. They had already started melting away in any case; perhaps they had sensed the madness in him, that he was willing to go too far for the sake of success. Charles did not care. Of course he had long ago spent all that we had, but this time he managed to find … other sources.'

Her eyes grew shadowed, pained, in the candlelight.

'We had many visitors here in the months leading up to his departure. Men from abroad as well as home, from Europe, the United States, even South America; men of very obscure backgrounds with dark pasts and obscene wealth. Some he had met on his lecture tours; with others, he had conducted a voluminous correspondence. He and his guests would lock themselves in his study till the early hours.

'These men terrified me. There was a miasma of evil that surrounded them, an aura of dark power and absolute malevolence, and they looked at me as though I were lower than the smallest insect. Charles would tell me nothing of these conversations, or of the details of the expedition, but I believe all the money he needed came from these men. In fact he would boast how he was no longer beholden to the likes of the university and the Royal Geographical Society and their limited conception of 'what lay in the hidden places'. He became short-tempered and paranoid when I questioned him too closely; on one occasion, when he judged me too insistent, he used his fists. I felt nothing but relief when he left. God help me but I prayed he would not return.'

'Kathleen.'

He reached for her hand across the table. He regretted leaving the way he had all those years ago: the drinking, the rage, the arguments with his father and his fights with Charles; a promising academic career cut short by anger and alcohol and his expulsion from the university: he had thought his presence could only be making things worse for Kathleen, and leaving had seemed the only option. Now, with her hand in his and seeing the stoic endurance and haughty defiance that masked a deep sadness, he wished more than anything that he had stayed.

She smiled though her eyes glistened with tears. 'We were both targets of his rage. I'm glad one of us escaped.'

'And I'm glad I'm here now.'

'As am I.'

As they rose to take coffee in the drawing room the heavy brocade curtain at the window ballooned in the draught, its edge whispering across the parquet floor. The wind whistled through the crevices. A breath of air, cold as a whispered curse, frolicked around them.

The ormolu clock on the mantel chimed the lateness of the

hour. As the house braced itself against the battering gusts, the window frames rattling and the glass tinkling in the chandeliers, Kathleen reached for the bell. 'I shall have a fire made up in your room. It would seem there is a storm coming.'

He woke in a world of ice.

His old room, strange enough in its rediscovered familiarity when he had turned down the light and lain listening to the wind, waiting for sleep to come, now seemed filled with a spectral green light that had no discernible source.

He sat up, fumbling for his watch, dropping it as the cold metal burned his hand.

The fire had gone out and the logs were dusted with snow. The mirror over the mantle glowed opaquely, like an alabaster vase lit from within; a layer of ice dulled its silver to a dim sheen. He pushed back covers that crackled with crystals; the lamp by his bed would not light, and he fumbled for a candle and a match. His breath plumed.

The wind still boomed and buffeted at the house, but now it had a different note: a fretting moan, rising and diminishing like a sobbing soul. Snow dappled the rug by the bed. He dressed quickly as the candle flame leapt, sank, and then sputtered to nothing. He could barely feel his hands.

The air was moist and heavy; beside his bed, the wallpaper sagged, rotting, to the floor to reveal pine boards instead of lath and plaster. He stepped into the hallway, to find it lined with packing crates piled high against timber walls, *Creighton Antarctic Expedition 1909* stencilled on their sides.

The sound of the wind here was even worse; a maelstrom of pounding and shrieking that made the walls bend and creak. From somewhere outside came a distant cacophony of dogs barking and yowling in almost unhinged frenzy. Faint snatches of music, cracked and tinny, drifted to him from somewhere ahead. The corridor stretched into darkness, unending.

Somewhere, someone screamed: '*Oh God, oh God*'.

He came to a door of rough-grained wood that opened onto a dank, abysmal space divided with partitions and more crates into a primitive living area containing bunks and equipment; the smell of human sweat, of paraffin fuel and rotting meat assailed him, but he forced himself to go on.

It seemed to be the interior of a large wooden hut, built for perhaps a dozen men, but it felt cold and abandoned, with no human presence. Blackened grease covered the iron galley stove on which a pot of stew stood congealing; furs and woollen clothing, grey and limp like cast-off skin, hung from a makeshift line across two bunks. Boots and tools lay scattered on the floor; books were torn, photographic plates smashed, scientific equipment – jars, test tubes, microscope – obliterated. In a corner a windup gramophone shrilled its warped, distorted tune. It was a scene of squalor and defeat, a despairing, failed attempt to construct a rudimentary version of civilisation in a hostile environment that showed no mercy.

The record on the gramophone came to an end, the needle grinding in the silence as the wind dropped. Green light bathed the floorboards. At his feet, a long, dark stain led to a door in front of him. From somewhere, like a distant echo, the sound of dogs yowling and a voice screaming: *'For God's sake, don't go out there, you bloody fool!'*

From across a great distance, came an ululating call that seemed to come closer, rising to a savage shriek that oscillated around the walls of the hut before dying away on a crooning note of sobbing exhortation.

He approached the door; he could do nothing else, and as he pulled it open the wind, quiet before, hit him like a punch, attacking the flimsy hut with renewed frenzy. The world he stood looking into was a white vortex of whirling snow and as the wind pulled the breath from his lungs he saw a tall grey shape emerge from the maelstrom and walk towards him, humanoid but its limbs angular and disjointed, more spirit than flesh but flesh that was very real, its skull craning forward and its mouth opening to reveal long teeth like jagged ice.

He cried out and thrust his hand forward to ward it off, and as the chill travelled up his arm like a cold electric current a woman screamed somewhere behind him. 'Hugh! Hugh!'

He felt Kathleen grab his other hand and pull him back, back through that horrible scene of filth and squalor and blood, back through the weird light and down the corridor and back to his room, and as he slammed and locked the door behind them the green light blinked out, and it was dawn, and all was still, and cold, cold as the frozen earth, cold as death. They clung together as she sobbed.

Annie, blowing into her chapped hands as she came in to begin her day's work, found them huddled together on the settle near the kitchen range as though to extract every last ounce of the previous day's heat from it. Her gasp of surprise woke them, and as they blearily realised where they were, they saw the look of shock on her young face as she stared.

'Mr Hugh, your hand!'

His fingers were black, the skin blistered and suppurating, the nails loose and rotting. The smell of decay rose up to greet him. Regarding it with disbelief he felt the pain hit him, a numb throbbing as though his hand had been hit with a hammer. From somewhere outside himself he heard Kathleen's voice, hoarse with alarm and exhaustion.

'Frostbite. But how ...?'

He looked at her. 'Please tell me you saw what I saw ... Oh God, that night down by the cliffs ...'

'The thing in the garden ...'

He gripped her hand, tightly.

'It's here. Kathleen, you said the men who came to the house, who financed the expedition... you said there was something about them, that they felt wrong. Evil. They have something to do with this – I know it. They – and Charles – are the reason that thing is here. Lorimer. I have to speak to him.'

He staggered to his feet but Kathleen, with Annie's aid, restrained him. 'Wait. Your hand ... You need a doctor.'

'No time. I need to stop this. Annie. Where is William?'

'He'll be here directly, sir. Sir ... please be careful. It's deathly cold out there.'

'Stay here with Mrs Creighton. The three of you lock the doors and windows. Stay in one room. Keep the fire going. I'll be as quick as I can.'

Kathleen swiftly barred his way. 'Not until I bandage that hand. You'll lose it if I don't.'

As she carefully helped him into a heavy overcoat, taking care with his bandaged hand, she cautioned: 'John Lorimer. He's pretty far gone. I doubt you'll get much out of him.'

'I have to try. Everything about this: the weather, the creature, what we saw; it feels like ...'

They held each other's gaze as she completed his thought.

'Vengeance.'

St Andrews when he arrived was deserted, a ghost city of looming forms and freezing fog. The pavements were slippery underfoot: buildings emerged like ancient mausoleums from the mist. It was a Sunday, and there were no students, no pedestrians. He knew the weather alone would have discouraged all but the hardiest from venturing abroad, but nevertheless the utter stillness unnerved him.

The ornately-gabled building that housed the School of Geography echoed with his footsteps as he roamed the corridors searching for Professor Lorimer's office. He found it at the top of a winding staircase leading up to a small corridor on which the Professor's was the only door. He knocked, and the door swung open.

The eccentric figure he had encountered at Charles's funeral was bent over the fireplace, feeding handfuls of paper into the flames. John Lorimer straightened and turned, regarding Hugh wryly, not least his bound hand, weeping through its dressing.

'So. You too have made its acquaintance.'

'I need you to tell me what it is.'

'You left it late. I asked you to come as a matter of urgency.' He unceremoniously cleared a pile of journals and papers from an old armchair and bade Hugh sit. Seen in the grey light, Lorimer's face was a grotesque ruin of scarred and ravaged flesh. He seemed to be in the process of packing; a tea chest and wooden crates were filled to overflowing with books, rock specimens, maps, charts, and meteorological instruments. Twitching with agitation, he darted quickly to the window to look down into the quadrangle.

'You are leaving?' asked Hugh.

'Yes. And so should you.'

'Not before you tell me what that thing is and what it wants. Kathleen told me you found Charles's body.'

'And I wish to God I had not brought it back.' Lorimer ceased his pacing and reached into a crate, pulling out a whisky bottle and two glasses. He thrust a generous measure into Hugh's good hand. 'I'd drink that if I were you. You're going to need it after what I tell you.'

A whispering rustle at the window signalled the start of snow. The light, grey as damp gauze, was rapidly fading.

'I rather think that time is against us, so I will make this quick. Do you know why your brother wanted to go back down there?'

Hugh gingerly flexed his hand; the pain was growing worse by the hour. 'The papers said it was in the name of science; to collect rock samples and take weather readings up on the plateau, perhaps even to attempt to reach the Pole.'

Lorimer laughed; a gurgling snarl of bitter hilarity.

'Yes, that is indeed what Charles told the gullible gentlemen of the press before he left. If only they knew the real reason: what a story they might have had! Charles had absolutely no intention of contributing to our scientific knowledge of the world's most godforsaken hellhole, nor did he nobly intend on striving for the Pole for the glory of the nation. His destination was to be somewhere else entirely.

'I don't suppose you've read the more outlandish theories of Halley, Symmes and others, the hypothesis that says the world is hollow, and that the Poles do not exist but instead there are entrances through which one can access the Inner Earth, a chthonic realm of tunnels and passages leading to a great central cavern in which there shines a black sun? This notion was scientifically disproved decades ago, but there are still many who believe it: men with money and influence, and who are willing to finance expeditions to prove it.'

'And Charles believed this?'

'Oh, my dear sir, he did not just believe it – he thought he had proof of it. He was no willing dupe of fantasists and occultists – he actively sought them out to reinforce what he knew to be true. He also sought their money: for buying a ship, for supplies, equipment, crew; everything he would need for a long voyage. The worst thing of all was that I did not know the full extent of his madness until we were on the ice. Our friendship had become strained over the years as his preoccupation and paranoia deepened; he believed the scientific community was trying to suppress the theory, and he counted me amongst their number. He told me that he could prove the truth of this other world's existence, and I would see it for myself if I came with him.

'I don't know why I agreed to go. A sense of responsibility towards the men who signed on to travel with us and who believed that this was a voyage of scientific discovery? Perhaps I thought I could shield them from Charles's obsessions; perhaps I was nostalgic for an old friendship that had long ago turned sour. Perhaps, too, there was a certain measure of curiosity on my part: who, after all, can say with any certainty what lies beyond our basic understanding of the laws of space and time? We are, after all, but children on this Earth, and while we have conquered most of its surface, there are other realms – and perhaps other dwellers in these hidden spaces – of which we know nothing.

'My noble intentions came to naught once we were snowed in during the long Antarctic winter in a hut barely big enough for fifteen men, and where every fear, neurosis, and terrified imagining was brought to the surface, while the blizzards assaulted the hut for weeks on end and the wind made us mad. Our landing at McMurdo Sound had been without complication; the stores unloaded and the assembly of the hut accomplished quickly and efficiently after a long and sometimes turbulent voyage, during which the largely young and inexperienced members of the expedition acquitted themselves admirably. They were relieved to have reached our destination and were excited to begin work in a terrain which was unfamiliar and awe-inspiring to them. We constructed kennels for the dogs, made exploratory sledging journeys to study rock formations, and set up a weather station to take regular readings. An air of industry and cheerful occupation reigned in those early weeks, but Charles took only desultory interest in these tasks. From the moment he landed he seemed preoccupied and kept himself apart, choosing instead to spend as many hours as the cold would allow gazing into the vast distance of the great ice shelf that stretched towards the mountains, with the plateau beyond them immeasurable and unknown. I saw it as my duty to encourage an easy-going atmosphere and maintain a sense of busy camaraderie, but Charles's distraction was worrying and I feared that the men would notice and remark on it.

'When the dark descended on us and the bay froze over we dug ourselves in for the winter, awaiting the spring when our work could begin in earnest. At first, all was well. We prepared for the coming season and our trek up to the plateau by making repairs and modifications to our equipment. We passed the time with lectures, slide shows, and theatrical skits, and young Barrington even had the idea of setting up a magazine, to which the men contributed enthusiastically.

'It was around two months into our long isolation that things started to unravel. The now constant darkness, extreme cold, and smothering blizzards took their toll; the men, mindful of what they'd left behind, became snappish and quarrelsome with each other. At night, as the candles were extinguished and we lay unsleeping in our bunks, we began to hear things: the cry of something across great distances, an ululating lament, like a child weeping for its mother. All hell would break loose as the dogs would respond as though they were demented.

Each man must have questioned his own sanity, but we all heard it.

'Only Charles remained unaffected. Occupying the bunk next to mine, I could almost sense him smiling in the dark as he leaned over to me one night and murmured, 'Do you hear it, John? It's coming.'

'We found out what that was on Midwinter Day.

'The customary festivities and toasts made in anticipation of the daylight's return were observed with only hollow jollity. Half the polar winter still to endure seemed no cause for rejoicing. The weather, at least, was merciful: after days of blizzards the wind had dropped and the sky was clear. Everyone was on edge except for Charles, who seemed positively ebullient. He drank far more than the rest of us, I remember, and midway through the celebrations he pulled me aside to a quiet corner. His eyes blazing with almost ecstatic elation, he gripped my arm fiercely and told me his plan would soon be coming to fruition: that something was waiting for him out on the ice; that it had already made its presence known and was calling to him and that soon would be the time for his departure. He told me that if he did not return I was to assume command of the expedition and make sure his body was found and returned to Scotland. There was an agreement, he said, that his funeral was to be held at the Leng chapel, and that this was of the utmost importance. He made me swear on all that I held holy.

'Dear God, I had thought his lunatic theories a delusion that had passed, some storm in the brain that had affected him through repeated exposure to these cold wastes, but from the moment we set off until now he had not mentioned it, and I had thought his sanity had returned. I was to learn to my cost, and the cost of many men's lives, that his silence had been merely that of calculated planning and patient waiting, and the moment of its realisation had come.

'That night was a bedlam of horror and darkness. The summons came again, in the early hours, but it was closer this time, fading and returning like it was circling us. Charles was not in his bunk. A putrid green phosphorescence poured through the skylight, flickering across the floor in waves. The dogs gave one last frantic volley of barking, and then were silent. Barrington started screaming. The gramophone began to play, a military march that wobbled and screeched through air thick and gelid. Charles was at the door of the hut, wrestling with Joseph Crealey, our biologist, who was trying to stop him from going outside. I watched with horror as Charles embedded an ice-axe in his shoulder and then pushed Crealey's body away from him. One of the men dashed forward and pulled the stricken man to safety, smearing the floor with his blood.

'I yelled something: a warning, a plea, I don't remember. Charles threw the door wide and stood on its threshold before turning back to look at me. 'It's waiting for me, John. It's waiting to show me the way. Remember your promise.' I should have stopped him, but I did not. He walked out into the darkness as the aurora unfurled its eerie effulgence above us, and as he vanished into the black the cry rose again in the distance and the dogs resumed their racket. The injured man in the hut behind me whimpered softly. Just before Charles vanished I saw a tall, glowing figure like some mythological revenant waiting for him out on the ice.

'We locked and barred the door. Charles did not return that night, or any night thereafter. The blizzards and fierce winds returned but the creature's cry did not. Crealey recovered from his wound, but the mental scars of what had happened that Midwinter Night stayed with us while we waited for the spring and the return of the ship from New Zealand to take us home. I did not tell the men anything of what Charles had told me; it was enough for them – bad enough – that he had gone insane. Only Barrington dared to ask me, hesitantly and as if afraid of the answer, what Charles had meant by asking me to keep my promise, and the knowledge that once the temperatures rose and the days grew longer I would have to take a sledging party and go out and find him tortured me beyond belief.

'We set out, myself and three men, together with a support

party, on a crisp clear day in October. As the bay was still frozen I had convinced the men we should continue with our scientific work before the ice broke up and the ship came. We made good progress across the ice shelf, and at the foot of the glacier that winds up through the mountain range the support party left us, and we pressed on through conditions that tested us to our limits: crevasses and plunging temperatures and great pressure ridges of ice with the mountains looming to either side of us; sometimes, in the twilight haze, they resembled terraces of some strange city that, by its vastness, could not possibly have been built by man. Near the top of the glacier the weather deteriorated dramatically and the ferocious, biting wind that streamed down from the plateau forced us to stay in our tent for two days. We would hear whisperings outside, and on the second night the dogs turned on each other, each driven by fear to attack its teammates; we lost four of them and had to abandon one of the sledges.

'At the top of the glacier, where it began to open out onto the plateau, we found Charles, his frozen limbs twisted in death, his face hard and white like marble. The look on his face was that of a man who had seen both God and the Devil before breathing his last. The men were profoundly affected by the discovery: it brought back everything that happened that winter with full force. As we loaded his body on the sledge the dogs became uncontrollable. As Murray battled to restore order I looked into the distance of that great white desolation and saw, far beyond, twin pillars of gargantuan height like the pylons of some ancient gateway, and, spilling out between them, a host of wraiths, advancing towards us with inexorable intent. I cried out, and the others looked, and saw, and frantic with terror we descended the glacier with as much speed as was humanly possible, stopping only to set up camp when on the point of complete collapse, suffering frostbite and starvation and finally reduced to man-hauling the sledge as the remaining dogs became too crazed and had to be destroyed. We lost Stevenson down a crevasse, and from then on we were three, but something else walked with us as we fought through the whirling snow across the ice shelf and back to the sanctuary of our base.

'All the men we'd left behind at the hut were dead. Two of them had committed suicide. Barrington had cut his own throat. Campbell had ingested formalin. The floor was spattered with congealed blood and vomit. The rest were frozen in their beds. We buried them in the snow and built a cairn over their bodies.

'The voyage home I will never forget. Beset by storms and rough seas, with Charles's body in the hold, and the sound of moaning at night as something stalked the decks, the crew believed their ship cursed.

'Whatever came back with us is with us still. God help me, I indulged the delusions of a madman and now innocent men are dead. Those men were my responsibility. Their blood is on my hands.

Snow flurries beat at the window. The room was dark. Lorimer lit the lamp.

Hugh's voice was hoarse. 'Charles's theory. It's real, then. You saw it up on the plateau.'

Lorimer searched through his papers. 'I don't know what I saw. But it is here now, and it means us harm.'

'I don't understand.'

The professor handed him a page torn from a journal, smudged with grease and soot and bearing words faintly inscribed in pencil.

'We found this on his body. This will tell you what you need to know.'

The words Hugh read, and the hatred of the hand that had written them, chilled him to the core.

'*It has waited for me. It has shown me the way. What things it has shown me – the world within – the black sun that illuminates all – such terrible, wonderful things! We are of a kindred nature, my emissary and I – it feels my rage, my hatred … We have made a compact – my duplicitous brother, my faithless wife, John Lorimer … all the unbelievers … They will know the truth. It will come back with me, and we will show them a new world …*'

'Christ almighty. Oh God, Kathleen …'

Lorimer turned to resume his packing. His words were low but there was no mistaking their urgency. 'If you want to save her, you should hurry.'

Annie's face was a mask of panic as she opened the door to his frantic hammering.

'She's not here, sir – she just took off, up to the chapel, in a terrible state – '

William was at her shoulder. 'She said she was going to talk to Mr Creighton, to reason with him, she said. We tried to stop her.'

Annie began to sob. 'There is something in the house … we are frightened out of our wits here … Sir, please find her.'

'Both of you need to pack some things and get as far away from here as possible. Whatever that thing is, it is not Charles. If we stay here we are all in danger. Drive very far, and very fast, and don't come back. Don't worry. I'll find her.'

He screamed her name as he crossed the fields, every footstep dragging against a wind that bent him double as he battled through the maelstrom.

The cemetery gates stood open: up on its hill the Leng chapel blazed forth an evil phosphorescence that poured from its windows like candlelight through the eyes of a skull. As Hugh climbed the hill he looked up and saw the roof squirming with movement; the gargoyles seemed to stretch and contort, until he realised it was a legion of wraiths thronging the buttresses, drawing themselves up like corpse candles to stare down at him with indifferent curiosity as he cried Kathleen's name and wrenched open the chapel doors.

She was sitting in a pew at the front. Before her, like some infernal prelate delivering an unholy mass, the thing stood before the altar, a wraith as tall as two men, a half spectral, half solid abomination that inclined its head towards the woman cowering before it as if about to bestow some obscene benediction. Its outline quivered in the frigid air, as it moved between one state and another, present and yet unreal, a look of impersonal yet unmistakable malevolence on its gaunt, tight-skinned skull with its hollowed, half-erased features.

Kathleen turned slowly in her seat and saw him. She wore a look of bewilderment and her voice was that of a frightened child.

'Hugh, is it Charles? I've asked it, but it won't answer me.'

He held out his hand to her, approaching slowly.

'It's not Charles. Kathleen, come away, slowly now. Take my hand.'

'Why won't it speak to me? Why is it here?'

The walls of the chapel, cracked and eroded over time, streamed with moisture. Underneath his feet he felt the vibration of distant detonations, fissures opening far below in depths unimagined, another world contorting, flexing, preparing to break through.

'We should go, Kathleen.'

The walls around them began to change: the moisture became ice, the stone became wood, timber, rough planks of cabin walls; the air darkened and became obscured by smoke and grease and somewhere was the sound of a gramophone, and a man screaming and dogs howling in the distance.

As he reached for Kathleen and pulled her to him the floor was slick with ice; he felt her breath against his face as she cried out, and the air became a whirling vortex of snow and shrieking katabatic winds and the walls around them disappeared but for the great window in the west wall, wiped clean now of its symbols and saints and through it they saw a black sun seething in a corroded green twilight, and the creatures on the roof began to howl, wailing as one like a blasphemous choir heralding a new age.

They turned and ran blindly through the tumult, slamming against the doors and bursting out onto a hillside hard and snow-covered as behind them the Leng chapel began its final transformation.

Its buttresses collapsed, the walls folding inward, the

windows shattering, the spire collapsing down through planes that were shifting, reforming and remaking; the spire rose again but now it was the mast of a great ship, its prow crashing up though the frozen ground, cresting a wave of earth and the buried dead and sending tremors surging down after them as Hugh and Kathleen careered through the falling gravestones. A car waited for them at the gates, and they saw it was John Lorimer.

The professor got out of the car; the horror and awe on his face made them turn.

The ship rode as if at anchor on the summit, its spars hung with stalactites of ice and its timbers grey with frost. In the rigging, like St. Elmo's fire, the wraiths hovered, their voyage at an end, their destination reached. Tongues of ice spread down the hill like quicksilver, advancing inexorably in runnels and streams, covering the ground, creeping along the driveway towards where they stood.

'It's the *Agartha*,' Lorimer croaked. 'It's Charles's ship. God forgive me, and may God help us.'

'John, we need to get out of here.' Hugh helped Kathleen into the back seat. She tried to say something but he could not hear her.

It was only as Lorimer had turned the car and they were speeding down the lane that he noticed how cold she was. He wrapped his arms around her.

'It touched me, Hugh,' she whispered. 'It touched me.'

The snow stopped. The sky above them was black, and there were no stars, only a long, green ribbon of light, bunching and unfurling, spreading across the southern sky like the banner of an occupying army.

She leaned against him. Her hands were cold, and her face felt like porcelain.

SOURCES

All of these stories are original to *Terror Tales of the Scottish Lowlands*, with the exception of 'Gie Me Somethin' Ta Eat Afore I Dee' by John Alfred Taylor, which was first published in *Castle Fantastic*, 1996, and 'Proud Lady In A Cage' by Fred Urquhart, which was first published in *Prevailing Spirits*, 1976.

OTHER TELOS TITLES
YOU MAY LIKE

PAUL FINCH
Cape Wrath & The Hellion
Terror Tales of Cornwall
Terror Tales of Northwest England
Terror Tales of the Home Counties

RAVEN DANE
THE MISADVENTURES OF CYRUS DARIAN
Steampunk Adventure Series
1: Cyrus Darian and the Technomicron
2: Cyrus Darian and the Ghastly Horde
3: Cyrus Darian and the Wicked Wraith

Death's Dark Wings
Standalone alternative history novel

Absinthe and Arsenic
13 Horror and Fantasy Short Story Collection

HELEN MCCABE
THE PIPER TRILOGY
1: Piper
2: The Piercing
3: The Codex

GRAHAM MASTERTON
The Djinn
The Wells of Hell
Rules Of Duel (with WILLIAM S BURROUGHS)
The Hell Candidate

TELOS PUBLISHING
www.telos.co.uk